SO LONG AT THE FAIR

Recent Titles by Frances Paige

BLOOD TIES*
BUTTERFLY GIRL
THE CONFETTI BED*
GLASGOW GIRLS
KINDRED SPIRITS
PAINTED LADIES
SHOLTIE FLYER
SO LONG AT THE FAIR*

*available from Severn House

SO LONG
AT THE FAIR

Frances Paige

This first world edition published in Great Britain 1997 by
SEVERN HOUSE PUBLISHERS LTD of
9–15 High Street, Sutton, Surrey SM1 1DF.
This first edition published in the U.S.A. 1997 by
SEVERN HOUSE PUBLISHERS INC of
595 Madison Avenue, New York, NY 10022.

British Library Cataloguing in Publication Data
Paige, Frances
  So long at the fair
  1.English fiction – 20th century
  I.Title
  823.9'14 [F]

  ISBN 0-7278-5109-8

Typeset by Hewer Text Composition Services, Edinburgh.
Printed and bound in Great Britain by
Hartnolls Ltd, Bodmin, Cornwall.

Chapter One

'My three girls', as Joseph Winter fondly called them, were busy in the large brick-floored kitchen when he came through the garden door. He kissed Marie-Hélène, his wife, and went to stand behind his two daughters who were engaged in the decoration of a fine recumbent salmon with capers, tarragon and feathery chervil. "Such an air of excitement," he said. "Are you expecting the Emperor and Empress of France with all this display?"

It had been rumoured in England during the past few months that Napoleon the Third and his beautiful Spanish wife, Eugenie, might be paying the Queen and her Consort a visit. If this was premature, at least the bonds of friendship between France and England were beginning to tighten with the prospect of a military alliance in this year of our Lord, 1853.

The girls laughed and Marie-Hélène tut-tutted. "You'd be the first to complain if the repast wasn't to your liking. Now that you *are* here, let us have your comments, pray."

"Let me see . . ." His bright eyes were scanning the large table whose scrubbed whiteness was almost obscured by dishes of every size and description. "Can that be a lobster in hiding?" He pointed to an oval silver plate which supported a mound of pink crustacean flesh gleaming with golden sauce.

"*Curried* lobster," his wife said. "You've told me often enough that's how the English like it. *Pour moi . . .*" She shrugged. After twenty-two happily-married years

1

in England, she still, on principle, preserved her Gallic shrug.

"Ah, yes. I know you think it's sacrilege but your guests won't." He peered at the entrée dish flanking the lobster. "Trout, isn't it? But no doubt far from plainly prepared."

"There I draw the line. It's too sweet a fish in itself to be spoiled by fiddle-faddle. All I've done is to broil it and sprinkle it with herbs to bring out the flavour."

"You couldn't trust Mrs Gossop to bring out the flavour?"

"You tease. Cook had to visit a sick cousin this afternoon, as you very well know, and Lucy is too young for such an important occasion." Lucy, the maidservant, turned round from the sink where she was washing up, and dipped her mobcap at the master. "Besides, it's good experience for your daughters."

"I've been basting the *fricandeau* of veal, Papa." Hannah, at eighteen, had the same colouring as her father, but the matt rose flush over the high cheekbones was, in Joseph's case beginning to be threaded with veins, as his red-fair hair was already threaded with grey.

Mia, Hannah's elder by two years, had kept quiet too long for someone of her volubility. "Come and see what the mistress of the still room has on show." She led her father to the spacious meat larder, light-footed, two steps to his one, and flung open the door. "*Chaudfroids!*" She curtseyed, her mouth quirking in a smile. "*Soufflés de Homard Glacé, Chaudfroids de Perdreaux, Tomates Farcies, Oeufs de pleuviers en Aspic . . .*"

"It's certainly a change from the study of Harding's Celestial Atlas." Joseph smiled at the lively face looking up at him, the fine brown eyes, the hair which had his red in it, but only as highlights to its dark brown sheen.

"At least it will rest her eyes." Marie-Hélène didn't always approve of the heavy tomes Mia poured over under Joseph's aegis. And yet the same quick-witted mind, she had to

2

admit, controlled deft hands which could produce as good a cold table as any French-born housewife might wish.

"But the study of the natural sciences stretches the mind." He returned to his wife, plump and smiling at her mixing bowl, her lace sleeves pinned back above her elbows. "How many guests do we expect? One thousand or two? My little exhibition tomorrow evening will pale into insignificance beside this cornucopia."

"Papa, you're a tease." Mia had followed him, and she put an arm round his neck to kiss his cheek. "You said no expense was to be spared, that the beauty of the food must rival the beauty of your ware . . ."

"Speaking of that," his wife said, "what brings you here when you should be busy at your potworks? It's only three o'clock of the afternoon and you know dinner isn't served until six."

"I had something to ask you . . ."

She glanced at him. "Something special by the look on your face, otherwise you would have sent Robert with a note."

"Robert has gone to the farriers with my cob this afternoon. Besides, it's a favour, dear one. A thought occurred to me in the middle of overseeing a new set of pots being thrown, and nothing would do but that I should acquaint you of it immediately."

"Well, do so, I beg you."

"Would you be prepared to add two names to your guest list to please me?"

"At this late date! Whose names, may I ask?"

"Miss Sarah and Mr Conway Graham."

"The Grahams!" Hannah looked up, the wire whisk she had been using held in the air. "But nobody calls on them, Papa."

"All the more reason why they should be invited."

"Mia's eyes were wide. "The Grahams . . . such a gloomy place they live in! That horrid new house buried in the old trees of the farm . . . incongruous, somehow. Hannah and

I rode past it last week and we saw Mr Graham, but only from a distance. His head was bent, hands clasped behind him, he was walking slowly . . ."

"Mia said he looked like Lord Byron." Hannah giggled. "What was that poem of his you quoted, Mia?"

"Hush!" Her sister spoke sharply. "It was nothing."

"I remember!" Hannah waved the wire whisk round her head in time to her intoning. "'And musing there an hour alone, I dreamed that Greece . . . I dreamed that Greece . . .'"

"'might still be free.'" Mia finished the lines for her, speaking rapidly as if to detract from the flush on her pale cheeks. "The lines occurred to me, that was all. It was the look of sadness . . ."

"No doubt he has plenty to be sad about," Joseph said, "being left with the care of his sister. Still, you're right, Mia. It's a monstrosity of a house. They'd have done better to remain at Well Farm."

"With that view in front of them!" Marie-Hélène's sharp eyes hadn't missed her daughter's blush. "Who would want to look out on the disused workings of an old coal seam, even though it brought them wealth."

Mia laughed. Her cheeks had reverted to their natural pallor. "Had I been in their shoes I should have wished to make obeisance to the man-made mountain!"

"There was no mountain," her father said. "It was open-cast mining, I'm told."

She pouted at him. "Well, then, gone down on my knees to thank Mammon for the black diamonds!"

"Oh, Mia!" Hannah looked shocked.

"Maria, my love." Joseph invariably gave Mia her baptismal name when he cautioned her. "That remark appears to have a slightly sacrilegious air about it."

"Sacrilegious? What does that grand word mean?" Marie-Hélène kept alive a feigned ignorance of the subtleties of the English language along with the Gallic shrug, perhaps because she wished to uphold the reputation of Parisian

4

elegance with which she was accredited in Hessleton. In any case she didn't wait for an explanation. "We seem to have been deflected by those chattering girls of ours. Why do you want me to invite the Grahams on the eve of our soirée?"

"I'll be frank with you. Mr Conway Graham came today to see me with an unusual request, that I should look at some sketches of his sister's. Apparently she has been ill with a nervous complaint and Dr Compson has recommended some kind of interest to divert her. The sketches, to my surprise, were more than good, especially the ones from nature. There was an especially pretty one of speedwells and trefoils, but stylised, just what I need. As you know, I've recently lost Mr Straub on his retirement; a fine artist and a good botanist."

"But you've always said you wouldn't have women working in the manufactory," Mia said.

"That was founded on a sound premise. Nevertheless, this is a special case . . ."

"But we're talking of a young *lady*, Joseph," his wife interrupted him. "Even with my disregard for Society, isn't it unusual for someone of her class to be employed there? They're County, are they not?"

"Gentry, certainly, but Mr Graham assured me that both he and his sister weren't influenced greatly by such matters. Besides, an artist has his or her own place in society."

"You argue uncommonly well for this young lady."

"I know Papa." Mia turned laughingly to him. "You liked Miss Sarah's sketches uncommonly well, you were touched by Mr Graham's request, and you said to him that if his sister cared to submit designs for some of your pieces you'd consider . . ."

"You see, wife?" He spread his hands. "She reads me like a book. Yes, I confess I liked Mr Graham in spite of his taciturnity. There was concern for his sister behind his poker-back stance and stern eye, and I think it must have cost him a lot . . ." Joseph stopped speaking. He knew his elder daughter's sensitivity and vivid imagination. He wouldn't say that had Conway Graham pleaded, he might have declined regretfully to his request, nor that something in the man's demeanour and in his deep-set eyes had remained with him, had indeed been responsible for his leaving his supervision of the throwers in the middle of the afternoon.

Marie-Hélène was vigorously shaking a sieve above her bowl, making the curls on either side of her head dance along with the plump, floury raisins. "There's no need to plumb the depths of Mr Graham's soul, if he has one, that is. Robert shall bear a note to him when he comes back requesting the pleasure of his company and that of his sister. It will give the County something to talk about. One grows tired of their silly tittle-tattle about the Grahams."

"Quite so." Joseph's eyes twinkled. "But make allowances for our provincial society, pray. Hessleton is not, alas, Paris."

"What tittle-tattle, Mama?" Hannah looked up from the cream she was beating, her cheeks flushed, her bosom heaving under its closely-buttoned bodice with the exertion.

"It's not for young ears, miss. You'll curdle the cream if you punish it like that. *Doucement.*"

She'll badger me later, Mia thought, but what do I know about the Grahams except that there's a strangeness about them? She remembered their name whispered by one stout matron to another at a card party, the lowered glances, the unheard remark behind a fan. She saw, as she bent her head to her task, the bowed head, the bent shoulders of Conway Graham as she had seen him walking in his park, the whole frame indicative of sadness.

The contrast between the two sisters was marked, made more so since they had been allowed by their mother to exercise their own taste in the choice of their dresses. Hannah looked like a flushed and buxom fairy princess in her wide-skirted gown of crystal-spangled tulle over white

6

satin, Mia was perhaps older than her years in brown velvet relieved by bands of fine old rose point laid on pink. But the velvet had a hidden russet glow which matched the glow in her smoothly-dressed hair, and the deep texture of the material enhanced the warm pallor of her skin. Marie-Hélène had thought the gown too decolleté, but then had added like a true Frenchwoman rather than a mother, "*Pourquoi pas?*"

"Papa said we weren't to stand together," Hannah said, touching her curled coiffure. "Isn't it a gorgeous party? Is my dress all right, Mia?"

"Lovely!"

"I thought at first yours was too plain, but now I see I'm wrong. It has more style than mine. I might have known. And as usual you've had more beaux than I."

"Nonsense! What about Harry Compson?"

Hannah brightened. "I'd forgotten about Harry. I've stood up with him for a quadrille and a polka. He's droll." She laughed. "He says 'soirée' is old-fashioned. He prefers 'crush' or 'rout'."

"Don't take Harry too seriously. Two years at Oxford have quite gone to his head." He had teased Mia at eighteen as he was now teasing Hannah. Sometimes she wondered if he was on the way to becoming a confirmed bachelor. "Here he comes." She saw him crossing the wide parquet floor towards them. He looked, she thought, as if he was going to burst out of his black tailcoat and brocaded waistcoat, and his plump, red face was held uncomfortably high, it seemed, above his white stock.

"What a pair of ravishing beauties!" He had reached their side. "Upon my soul it's difficult to know who to take into supper." He looked at Mia, saw the mischievous light in her eye, turned to Hannah. "Yes, I'm afraid it will have to be the baby of the family. I well know that if I spurn her she'll fall into an immediate decline."

"What nonsense, Harry Compson! As if I cared. In fact, I've a mind not to go with you in any case."

7

"But you must, dear Hannah. My name is on your programme, and besides, if you don't, *I* might fall into a decline or its masculine equivalent."

Mia laughed. "It's no good, Harry. You've hopelessly compromised yourself already. A quadrille and a polka, with all Hessleton looking on! Dear, dear! You'll never be allowed to live it down."

"Ah me!" He sighed in an exaggerated manner, rolling his eyes. "The Christmas tree fairy wins, then. She's caught me in her spangles . . ."

"Oh, Harry!" Hannah struggled between confusion and the desire to say something witty. "Mia, *you* tell him! Tell him not to be so rude."

"Nothing is further from my thoughts, dear Hannah. Can you tell me of anything which is more beautiful than the Christmas-tree fairy, and so well-connected?"

"What do you mean?" Her mouth gaped.

"The Consort, dear thing. The Prince imported them for the Royal nursery, don't you know, a Germanic conceit."

"Fairies?" Mia said.

"No, Christmas trees, goose."

"Well, *do* you intend to take me into supper?" Hannah said, showing her practicality if not her understanding. "I'm so very hungry."

"Could you think of a greater appeal to my better nature?" Harry offered his arm to Hannah, and then, speaking over his shoulder to Mia as he turned away, "Perhaps you'll keep me a dance, if I can rid myself of the clutches of this intemperate female."

"I'll try." She smiled, consumed with impatience. Go, she was saying to herself, stop talking, go . . . And then, chiding herself, what's wrong with you? One brief lifted glance from dark eyes before a bow, one brief sight of the top of a man's head, the thick black hair whorled like a shell, and your heart's fluttering like your silly sister's . . .

She stood alone, glad of the respite, praying that the

8

beaux whom Hannah had mentioned, Judas Ashworth, Thomas Hyde or John Wyatt, wouldn't descend upon her. Perhaps her mother had linked them with partners and bidden them to make their way to the conservatory where the buffet had been laid. She liked to pair off lonely girls since she said she always felt like an outsider herself in English society.

How charming the large rooms looked with the dividing doors flung back, the soft silk of the walls patterned in fleur-de-lys, the tall pier glasses reflecting the opaque light of the lamps and the shining mahogany bookcases. The servants had taken out the chairs and bric-a-brac this morning, leaving only a few comfortable ottomans against the walls. Compared with other houses in Hessleton, theirs was sparsely furnished, Joseph saying he liked to be able to reach his books without tripping over little tables, although to have books in a drawing-room at all, was to say the least of it, unusual. Marie-Hélène compromised by telling him he was either behind the times or ahead of them, she wasn't sure which.

Under one of the lamps at the opposite side of the room Mia saw two figures, one seemingly bent protectively over the other. Her heart shook. She stood irresolute for a moment and then crossed the wide parquet, smiling slightly, self-consciously, hearing the soft swish of her velvet dress as it slid along the floor, hearing her heart in her ears.

"Why, Mr Graham and Miss Graham!" she said on reaching them. "Aren't you going in for supper?"

Conway Graham bowed as she spoke, murmuring something non-committal, but Mia noticed there was no smile on Sarah's narrow face and that her oddly brilliant eyes were fixed on her brother.

"We're in no hurry, Miss Winter. I've just been telling Conway I'm not hungry. I don't like parties, to be honest, nor does Conway for that matter, but he said your father had been kind . . ."

"Quite so," Mia said, hearing her father in her words.

"But since you've done us the honour of coming, we can't let you go home without supper, especially as Hannah and I helped to prepare it." She looked from one to the other, smiling as she spoke, and met the man's dark eyes again. The same ache set up in her heart. She grew suddenly angry with herself. Why am I trying to appease this . . . stranger, and his rude sister? Here he stands stiffly and awkwardly before me in a suit which might well be his deceased father's, and I could be dancing or supping with almost any man I chose to. I shall laugh about him with Hannah tonight . . . but she knew she wouldn't because Hannah's eyes, sharpened by her own pubescence, would see too much.

"You're very kind," Conway Graham said. "I should like, even more than supper, to see the examples of your father's ware. He told me about them yesterday when we were discussing my sister's sketches."

"You shouldn't have taken them, Conway," the girl said, ignoring Mia.

"Papa was impressed by them at any rate." Mia wondered why she was being so magnanimous, looking at Miss Graham's sullen face. What a strange pair! I've had enough of them . . . She was aware, thankfully, of a familiar scent of *frangipani*, and turned to see her mother bearing down on them in a voluminous cloud of black sarsenet with a jet-encrusted lace frill holding her black curls in place at the nape of her neck.

"Ah, there you are, Mia! I wondered where you had got to." Thomas Hyde was in tow, fair hair sleeked down round his long patrician face, the narrow nose chiselled as cleanly as if made of wood. "Thomas said you promised him . . ." she peered. "My dear Mr Graham, isn't it, with your charming sister! We met briefly when you arrived. Is my daughter taking care of you? Why aren't you eating?"

"Yes to the first question, madam, the second was under discussion at this moment." To Mia's amazement she saw that Mr Graham was smiling at her mother who was looking archly at him above her black lace fan.

"Really, sir!" Marie-Hélène's black eyes danced. "Well, then, perhaps we could settle the matter by you taking Mia into supper if you will, and you, Thomas, might be good enough to escort Miss Graham. Have you met? You'll find her most informed, artistically speaking."

"We are acquainted, madam." Thomas looked down his nose, a sure sign of his displeasure. Mia had been what Hannah called "leading him on" for the past six months, although she had assured Hannah it was rather a question of fending him off.

"If I may have the pleasure, Miss Winter." Mr Graham was proffering his arm, and she laid her hand on it, noticing with sharp eyes that the black broadcloth covering it was tinged green with age. She would tell Hannah . . . no, she wouldn't. Again there was the ache, like a painful tuck being taken in her heart, and to counteract it she smiled brilliantly at Thomas who had offered his arm to a silent Miss Graham. "You lead the way, Thomas, but you and Miss Graham must be sure to leave some of the cold collation for us."

"Mia!" From behind she felt the playful tap of her mother's fan on her bare shoulders and her voice near her ear. "You'll have to keep this daughter of mine in her place, Mr Graham. Her tongue runs away with her at times."

"I'll endeavour to do so," she heard him say, and could have sworn there was a chuckle in his voice. There seemed to be some kind of rapport between her mother and this man. How typical of Mama to favour an unknown rather than Thomas who was so proud of his connections.

They crossed the empty parquet floor in silence. Usually Mia chattered, a happy gift she had inherited from her mother, but the knack had quite left her. She watched Thomas' dutifully inclined head which seemed to gain no response from his partner, since Sarah Graham, tall and excessively slender in a dark, long-sleeved gown, walked as if she were alone.

In the conservatory, where the people seemed to be awash in a green sea, Conway Graham filled a plate and brought it to her without asking if she had any preferences. Robert, butlering in white gloves, an oiled quiff, and with a tremulous Adam's apple, served them with wine. She found her tongue after a few sips.

"You don't go abroad much, Mr Graham?"

"In a general or a particular sense?" She noticed the thick eyebrows raise.

"Well," she was discomposed, "evening parties, picnics and the like. I . . . I mean, Hannah and I haven't had the pleasure of meeting you and your sister before."

"Sarah isn't sociable and I'm too busy."

"At what, pray?"

"I'm endeavouring to restore the farm which my parents vacated when they built Well House, restocking it, seeing to the land which is in poor heart through disuse. There's plenty to be done."

"But I imagine you can't work when the sun sets." She was aware she was being provocative.

"No, that's true. But there are accounts to be done and books to be read, and then Sarah expects some company. It's lonely for her all day."

"But since she doesn't go out she must prefer it that way?"

"There's a difference between going out in the evenings to mingle with others and spending time with someone with whom you're at ease."

"But . . ." she mustn't pry, and found herself doing so in her next sentence. "You have a large, newish house, Mr Graham. I wonder that you wish to restore the farm?"

"It's quite simple. I like the farm, I dislike the house." His lips drew together. "Now may I ask *you* a question?"

She laughed, took another sip of wine. Her food lay

untouched on her plate. "I must apologise. Papa tells me I'm too curious, and yet it's he who has made me so by his example. What is your question, Mr Graham?" She composed her face, plied her fork busily amongst Mama's curried lobster which lay in strange juxtaposition to a plover's egg and a stuffed tomato. Judas and Thomas, or even more so, John Wyatt, who was considered delightfully wicked, usually began in the same way and then proceeded to make some outrageous remark about her divine dancing ability or the effect her velvet-dark eyes had on their sleep.

"I wondered if I might call upon you tomorrow afternoon? I've to come to Hessleton on business, to see my solicitor, as a matter of fact. Between three and four, I thought. I should be finished by then."

She swallowed. *He thought! After he'd seen his solicitor!* Not a word about her convenience or otherwise . . . "I'm afraid the time you mention is unsuitable, Mr Graham. Tomorrow I go with my mother to pay calls."

"She wouldn't excuse you? No, I see that wouldn't do. Ah, well . . ." he smiled briefly, "if you've finished toying with your food perhaps we might inspect your father's exhibition. It has excited my curiosity."

She rose, rebuffed, putting her plate and glass on a side-table. "Certainly. And then perhaps if you'd excuse me . . . I've many calls on my time, you'll understand."

He nodded, and she saw as he looked at her, how the brilliance of his deep-set eyes resembled his sister's. One side of his mouth was raised. Was he laughing at her? She would tell her father that the Grahams were a well-matched couple in their rudeness.

She saw Hannah as they passed through the conservatory, flushed and laughing, surrounded by young ladies and gentlemen whom she knew. She could at this moment, had Mama not forced this odious man upon her, have been amongst them, enjoying herself, being teased, teasing, flirting, feeling the heady power of male admiration. They

13

all glanced up and she imagined a look of surprise on their faces at her companion. He wasn't attached to any set. "Nobody invites them," Hannah had said. She was beginning to understand why. She caught a glimpse of Thomas with the sullen Miss Graham. His head was twisting on his long neck as if looking for succour. No doubt she was being as unpredictable as her brother.

The scent of chrysanthemums was strong in the conservatory, making her head ache, and then, following close on that as they passed through, there was the musky smell of carnations. The velvet gown with its numerous starched petticoats was suddenly too heavy. Its weight seemed to be pulling it off her shoulders, and she remembered when Conway Graham had looked at her she had imagined his glance sliding downwards from her face. She felt acutely uncomfortable, an ache under her ribs, in her temples, there was too much perfume from the flowers, from the ladies sitting like blown peonies in their voluminous skirts.

"Papa has set up the exhibition in his study," she said as they crossed the parquet floor. The Hessleton Ensemble had taken their places again, were plucking at the strings of their instruments, having been fed and watered (as Papa put it), by Mrs Gossop in the servants' dining-room.

Mr Graham nodded.

"There are only a few examples of his best work done during the last three years," she told him.

"Is he afraid of his ideas being stolen?"

"Not at all, but he's very selective, and his standards are high."

"I beg your pardon." Perhaps he had heard the chiding note in her voice.

They entered the study, more and more books towering to the ceiling, her father's leather-buttoned couch for 'cogitating on', and on a side table the long wooden box which contained his telescope. Robert had been taught its manipulation and could set it up on its tripod in the garden. Arranged carefully round the walls on pedestals were the specimens of ware which Mia had helped her father to display this morning. His potworks weren't large, but Joseph liked to think of them as supplying a specialist market.

"Papa used to send his ware to have the prints transferred from copper plates," she said as they started on their tour round the room, "but he's able to do it in Hessleton now. He has some fine artists, and he's quite good himself."

"Are *you*?" His eyes were on a boat-shaped dish with a delicate pattern of shells and seaweed, and, without waiting for her reply. "A trout would look well on that."

"Yes, he likes the decoration to be appropriate. There are game dishes and fruit dishes also." She pointed. "No, I haven't inherited his skill. Hannah and I both draw, of course, but not nearly well enough to satisfy him. I hear your sister is very gifted."

"No doubt you've other talents." He didn't wish to discuss his sister, it seemed. "And this, pray?" He pointed to a large platter. "It's a lovely shade of blue. The lake I've made in front of my farm is exactly that colour on a still summer's day."

"But I thought it was called *Black* Lake?"

"Not without justice. It was a pit-working originally. It can look sullen at times. Perhaps you know coal was found there in my grandparents' time, much to my parents' misfortune."

"But didn't it make them rich?"

"Since when did happiness and material wealth go hand in hand, Miss Winter?" His eyes were like his own black lake.

"This plate you admire, Mr Graham . . ." She changed the subject, "it's an example of the ware my father specialises in. If you look carefully you'll see the picture is an exact replica of Lord Trent's mansion near here."

He bent forward. "Yes, very fine. I especially like the border of flowers and fern. Very delicately executed. Your father is a man of rare taste."

She was pleased. "Then there are his medallions, sometimes on jugs, look there, sometimes on plates. Byron is well-favoured, you'll see, if you look closely. He's even, poor man, on a gravy tureen!"

"Well, they say gravy is the essence of the meat." His mouth quirked. "The poet must be popular with Mr Winter."

"I'm afraid I influenced him there. Sometimes we read together in the evenings. Hannah is more inclined to sew with Mama, which suits me." She smiled up at him. "On my eighteenth birthday he decided to start those pieces you see grouped here, all bearing the poet's medallion. 'Mia's Collection,' he calls it."

"How happy and united you sound, and what a pretty name they gave you." She turned and met his dark eyes which had to her surprise a liquid softness which had taken away their brilliance in exchange for an inner glow. She was confused and touched.

"Maria's my baptismal name but it was shortened in the nursery. Papa, to tease me, says I was for ever shouting "Me! Me!" She bit her lip, smiling. "As to the other thing, well, I hadn't thought about it." She dragged her eyes away from his, with difficulty, looked along the shelves and saw the pink dish which her father called his *pièce de résistance*. "You must come and see my favourite!" She put her hand on his arm to direct him and withdrew it quickly to hide its trembling in the folds of her dress. "Do you think the figures are a good likeness?"

He looked long and closely, and Mia looked with him, glad to rest her eyes on something which in its beauty helped to calm her surprising agitation. "Very good," he said at last.

"The Emperor of France, Napoleon the Third." She spoke softly, "with his bride, Eugenie, the daughter of a Spanish grandee." Napoleon was adequate, she thought, he was the type of man whose charm must lie in his sophistication, but Eugenie, radiant, the pale

16

oval face framed in the red-brown hair, was exquisite. She had entranced most young girls on the occasion of her marriage at the beginning of the year, not least of all, Hannah and Mia. Her deportment, her sense of dress, was an example for provincial misses over the whole of Europe, and Hannah and Mia had wearied their arms often trying out coiffures *à l'imperatrice*. "I find her beautiful," she said, turning to Conway Graham. "Look at the tilt of her head and the purity of her complexion! Even Papa's beautiful glaze gives you no real idea . . ." She stopped because he was smiling down at her. "What is it?" she said.

"Hasn't anyone told you?"

"Told me what?" Again the silly agitation began in her breast. This evening is being quite ruined by this man. "Told me what?" she repeated sharply. She would make some excuse and leave him here, join Hannah's party where she would feel at home and mistress of herself, where all glances would be frank and admiring without innuendo or obtuseness, where she could be winsome, witty or flirtatious by turns, all that was expected of Mia Winter.

"How like you are to the Empress," she heard him say calmly, "I'm not surprised you admire the plate."

"How ridiculous!" she burst out. "Even if what you say is true, I'm not so vain that I should enjoy staring at the Empress Eugenie simply because I resemble her, if such be the case although I doubt it. No one has said so before. It's strange it should be you . . ."

"Perhaps I look more closely." He stopped speaking and against her will their eyes met and held. She was aware of murmuring around her, of the *frou-frou* of women's skirts, of the deeper voices of men, and then out of the general background emerged a girl's voice, imperious, deep-toned. "Conway, I've been looking all over for you. I'd like to go home now." Mia turned and saw the pale face of his sister.

"Have you deserted your partner, Miss Graham?" she said lightly, but the girl ignored her.

"Conway, you promised. You said if I came for two hours that would be . . ." He cut her short.

"All right, Sarah. We'll go. Have you paid your respects to Mr and Mrs Winter?"

"Don't trouble," Mia said. "I'll convey them to my parents. Are you feeling unwell, Miss Graham?"

"No, it's nothing. It's just that I'm unused . . . but Conway said . . ."

"Don't stammer so," her brother interrupted, "Miss Winter understands you wish to leave and will excuse you, I'm sure." He looked at Mia. "She's been indisposed, you know."

"I'm sorry." She held out her hand. "Thank you for coming, Miss Graham." The girl shook it coldly, her eyes downcast. "And you too, Mr Graham. I do hope you found it worthwhile. Such a tiresome journey from Stonebarrow . . ." All Marie-Hélène's training came to the fore.

He bent low over her hand. "It was worthwhile," he said. "Thank you."

Mia had never been gayer, more sought after than in the last two hours of her parents' soirée. She joined the coterie of young people who were still in the conservatory and from there they went back to the public rooms where the rest of the evening was given over to dancing.

The last but one dance she stood up with her father who commented on the rare colour in her cheeks, and the last dance, a waltz, she took the floor with John Wyatt, which piqued many of the young ladies. "You waltz divinely, Mia. In fact, you do everything divinely. You look ravishing tonight, spirited, like a high-steppin' filly. Never seen you with such colour in your cheeks, except when we go ridin'. Any chance of meeting me tomorrow mornin' for a canter? Say six o'clock?"

She made round eyes at him. "I should never be able to drag Hannah from her bed at that hour."

"Who said anythin' about Hannah? Slip out on your own. No one will be any the wiser."

"Except Robert who'll saddle my mare and then run right away to Papa with the news. Not to mention the potworkers we would meet on our way. Really, John, you're exceedingly naughty to suggest such a thing." But she didn't reprimand him when his arm squeezed her waist more tightly than the occasion demanded.

At the hair-brushing nocturnal conference later with Hannah she kept up her gaiety, mindful of her sister's sharp eyes. "It was a most elegant soirée, Hannah, don't you think, kindly unlace me or I'll swoon. I've felt uncomfortably hot all evening . . . this velvet was wrong. You were much lighter and prettier in your tulle, or so Harry Compson seemed to think."

"Fiddlesticks to Harry Compson! Doctors' sons are dull and they smell of disinfectant. I liked *everyone* tonight. I've no intention of settling down with Harry Compson or any other young man until I've finished enjoying myself. Marriage is so dull! I must say you had a gloomy escort for a time in Mr Graham. I saw you both pass through the conservatory as if you were going to a funeral."

"It was Mama's doing. You know how she looks after lame ducks. I was obliged to partner him for supper."

"Thomas said the sister was exceedingly tiresome and intense. She didn't at all understand banter, just looked at him with her brows drawn. They must be a dull family"

"Not exactly dull . . . well, perhaps you're right." Hannah's blue eyes were on her.

"What did you talk about?"

"This and that. He's refurbishing Well Farm with the intention of taking up residence there."

"Perhaps he is taken."

"What do you mean?"

"Don't bite my head off. I only meant that he may be preparing it for a bride. That's what young men do,

19

although he's not so young when you come to think of it. I should say about thirty."

"But what about his sister?"

"I don't know." Hannah shrugged, bored with the subject. "Perhaps she'll live with him or he'll give her that monstrosity of a house his parents built. I don't care. Did you notice something rather strange about her, Mia?"

"Something particularly so? I thought she was altogether strange."

"It was Thomas who drew my attention to it. She was the only young lady in long sleeves. So ageing! And when he asked her if she would care to take the floor with him she drew her shawl tightly about her and said, 'No, thank you, I never dance, nor do I intend to learn.' Altogether charming, don't you think?"

"Yes . . ."

But when she was in bed the ache started again, a general ache this time, not in any specific part of her body, but rather a dull sense of foreboding that in some way she'd meet again the strange inhabitants of Well House, that her life would become entwined with theirs. I could marry Thomas, she thought, or John, or Judas, and escape . . . but when she finally went to sleep the last thoughts she had were of the dark eyes of Conway Graham.

Chapter Two

The September moon rode high all the following week, and the inhabitants of Hessleton and the surrounding countryside took full advantage of it. Evening soirées, buffet suppers, assemblies and card parties followed one another in close succession. Mia danced at the county houses in the neighbourhood escorted by various beaux, but more often than not by Thomas Hyde, or went to card parties in the houses of friends of her parents where, strangely, her skill at Limited Loo seemed to have deserted her. She chaperoned her sister to private dances and felt like a dowager in the process.

Driving home one night in the Stanhope with her parents and Hannah, the great globe of the harvest moon, the calm fields beneath it, the autumn earth smell, seemed to induce in her a kind of pleasant melancholy in keeping with the season but foreign to her volatile nature. Beauty of this kind hurt, she thought.

They passed through Stonebarrow where the Grahams lived, and when she saw the blue-black belt of trees behind their house, contrasted with the pale gold of the fields, the tall chimneys clear in the moonlight, she gave a quick indrawn sigh. To cover it she spoke into the darkness of the carriage. "I've never known a harvest-time like this. It . . . it makes your heart ache."

Hannah giggled, her chin hidden in her shawl. "Hark at Mia! Is it because you lost at cards at Lady Lumley's?"

"I declare," Marie-Hélène said, "it was most unlike you, Mia. Generally you clear the board, but there you were

21

simply gazing into space when you should have been studying your hand. I don't know what came over you."

"She's in love," Hannah said. "Thomas wants to marry her."

"So do half the county," Mia laughed. "I'm *surrounded* by suitors. Quite tiresome." She pretended to yawn.

"And are you enamoured of any of them?" her mother asked.

"Spare us a catechism at this time of night," Joseph groaned from the corner which he had been forced into because of the billowing skirts of his nearest and dearest.

"I'm not a match-maker, never fear. I leave that for the English Mamas. But don't you remember that I was less than Mia's age when you arrived in Paris and carried me off? Ah, happy days, *chéri!*" She spoke with the assurance of a fisherman using a well-tried bait. "Had you not been sent by your father to the Sèvres factory, and had you not been lodged in the house of my Aunt Thérèse in the Pontoise district, and had I not arrived to spend a few days with my aunt . . ."

"We should never have met," Joseph said, knowing what was expected of him. "It's a peculiar phenomenon that when one is middle-aged and looks back on one's youth it always appears happy, and yet if I search my memory I know I was often miserable. You twisted me round your little finger, dear heart, tortured me almost to death with your wilfulness, I was unable in any case to express myself adequately in your tongue, and worst of all I found your aunt's attic bedroom the coldest place in Christendom . . . and yet, yes, you're right, I knew complete happiness in Paris, in July 1830, surrounded by fierce fighting which sealed the fate of the Bourbons. History was being enacted around me and all I worried about was whether a certain Parisian miss would return my love!"

"I should have been the same," Hannah sighed. "As long as one is happy that's all that matters."

"So you think when you're young, pet, but when one

22

is older the outside world impinges. Should I say it doesn't matter that our fleet has now been sent to Constantinople?"

"You don't think that, do you, Papa?" Mia said.

"No." He paused. "But let's stay in the present. For tonight I'm happy enough bowling along on this beautiful evening, even although I'm being stifled to death by all this *frou-frou* around me!" He laughed. "I think I shall have to invent a carriage with elastic sides if I'm not to die an early death."

"My poor one." Marie-Hélène leant forward and patted his hand affectionately. "You shall be revived with a glass of negus when we reach home."

Mia didn't speak. She was gazing out of the window again, wishing the journey would never end, that she would remain like this with her family for ever, no intruders, no heartaches, only laughter. Papa was right. One knew complete happiness in youth. But then again one couldn't ride for ever in a dream carriage, safe from all harm. It was necessary in the end to step out of it.

The following morning Joseph had a surprise visitor in the potworks. "You came alone?" he asked the girl who sat across the desk from him. He had been more than surprised when his clerk had knocked on the door and said, "A Miss Sarah Graham to see you, sir." Why the indefinite article he thought idly because he questioned everything by habit, but the non-habitual part of his mind was asking, why has she come here?

"Yes, Mr Winter." She looked composed enough in her grey mantle edged with purple braid, a purple bonnet on her smooth black hair. "Our groom drove me in the gig. He's waiting in your yard."

"I'll see he gets some refreshment. There's a nip in the air this morning." He rang the bell, and when Jason Berridge put his head round the door, instructed him to give the groom shelter and something warm to drink.

"Thank you. I've heard you were considerate to your employees. They were not mistaken." He saw the thin mouth part over excellent teeth, and thought how much more charming she would be if she smiled oftener.

"They're human beings like you and me," he said shortly, not sure if there was an edge to her tone or not. "May I offer *you* some refreshment, Miss Graham?"

"No, thank you. I came on an impulse. Conway doesn't know." He saw she placed drawing-boards tied with tape on the desk as she spoke, but made no comment.

"I don't expect he keeps you in prison." And then smiling at her with the intention of putting her at ease, "My wife and I were delighted to see you at our little soirée. We hope you enjoyed it."

"Yes, thank you. I meant to see your exhibits but when I came into your study Conway was there with . . . and I felt it was time to go home." Her voice tailed away, then revived. "I was distressed when he told me he had called to see you with some of my sketches. It was presumptuous of him. He should have consulted me . . ."

"I'm sure he meant well."

"Perhaps. It's true Dr Compson said I had to find a new interest, get out more, but I should have preferred . . ." she stopped speaking and he noticed how pale she was.

"If you've come to apologise on your brother's behalf I can assure you there's no need. He couldn't have come at a more opportune moment as it happened. Mr Straub, who has been with me for many years, has decided to retire and devote himself to the study of natural history. My other artists, Mr Day and Mr Victor, are expert in the execution of medallions, views, figures and such like, but the drawings which your brother showed me were of the same *genre* as those of Mr Straub, and allowing for your youth, almost as good. I need above all things delicacy of line for the decoration of my ware. I saw it in your work."

The girl's eyes were downcast and he sat waiting until she should look up at him. When she did he was struck again by her pallor, which seemed, if anything, to emphasise the strange brilliance of her eyes.

"Thank you," she said at last. "For myself, I have no opinion of my drawings, but since his visit here Conway has urged me to do some more. Well," she said abruptly, placing a hand on the drawing-boards, "there they are. A poor thing but mine own." He noticed the hand was trembling.

"May I see them? A quick look will soon let me judge as to their value."

She shrugged ungraciously and indicated that he should lift the boards, which he did. Holding them unopened between his hands he spoke pleasantly. "Should I like them, would you be willing to enter into some kind of agreement with me?"

"I might . . ." She looked away.

"It would mean you coming to the potworks perhaps twice a week to confer with the other artists, the pot throwers and myself. Any article produced in my manufactory is the result of a combination of talent and goodwill. I always emphasise the goodwill because I think it shows in the finished product. Do you find that fanciful?"

"Perhaps." She wouldn't be drawn. "I daresay Conway would like such an arrangement as you mention. I'm quite happy as I am."

"I only mention it, of course. First to the drawings." He untied the tapes, spread the boards flat on the table and took out one of the sketches. He looked long and hard, then up at her. "Even better than I had hoped, or first thought. I congratulate you. Those white umbellifers . . . a delicate line . . . already I visualise them combined with a green glaze . . . a tea-set, I think, possibly called 'Woodland' . . . I like to name my products before execution . . . you see how my imagination runs away with me, Miss Graham?"

"They're nothing . . . of no account. I find pleasure in the study of wild flowers . . ."

"Evidently." He was examining the next sketch. "Less

25

happy, bluebells, speedwells, pretty, I grant you, but too insipid for my taste. Let me see," he flicked over another sheet, "Ah, now we have drama in the conservatory! Arums, unmistakably, drawn with great force." He looked up and saw that the girl was lying back in the chair, her eyes closed. "Miss Graham!" he jumped up. "Are you feeling unwell? I thought you looked pale." He quickly came round the side of his desk and lifted up one of her limp hands, beginning to chafe it between his own. Marie-Hélène, he thought, would you were here . . .

The girl opened her eyes and smiled thinly. "You see what praise has done for me, Mr Winter."

"It was quite genuine, I assure you, but I should rather have withheld it if it had this effect! Rest where you are for a minute." He left her, strode across his room, opened the door and called, "Jason! Run to the house and bid any of the ladies who are at home to come here immediately. Say it's urgent." When he turned round he saw Miss Graham was on her feet at his side of the desk, gathering her sketches together. He went quickly towards her. "My dear young lady, please don't attempt anything for the moment. I've despatched my clerk for help. Surrounded by women as I am, I'm singularly unable to cope with an emergency such as this. Please sit down, I beg you." He led her back to her seat and stood looking down at her, perplexed and just a little uncomfortable at the turn of events. She drew like a Raphael, but did he want womenfolk who fainted or next door to it, all over the place?

"Conway will be pleased you liked my drawings." He heard the deep voice, rich, so much at variance with the thin smile. This one is altogether too self-composed, he thought. He liked what he called "pretty ways" in women. Marie-Hélène was flirtatious still, Hannah was a giggling but still charming adolescent, and Mia combined some of her mother's mannerisms with his own wryness, which he recognised as a powerful combination.

"I shall make an offer to you in writing, and then it

will be up to you to accept or reject. But my dear Miss Graham, until you feel fitter please don't let us discuss the matter . . ." he attempted to keep a desultory conversation going until he heard with relief a short knock on the door and almost immediately Mia burst in with Hannah close on her heels.

"Jason said you wanted us urgently, Papa. Are you all right? We were dressed to go out and so . . . why, Miss Graham!" There was scarcely a pause. "How pleasant to see you! But you look pale. Is anything wrong?"

"Nothing at all, Miss Winter, but I'm afraid I alarmed your father. I had rather a bad headache when I left home, and for a second I felt faint."

"I despatched Jason for succour." Joseph smiled. "I see now that perhaps I was rather hasty. But I explained to Miss Graham that I'm just a poor man in a welter of women . . ."

"Oh, Papa!" Hannah giggled.

"Have you met my younger daughter?" Joseph brought her forward. "Hannah loves excitement, you know. She'd run a mile to attain it."

"Oh, *Papa*! Yes, I've met Miss Graham. You *do* look pale. We always say Mia has no roses in her cheeks but you're much paler than that. Quite ghastly!"

"You notice how tactful she is." Joseph breathed more easily. How beautiful Mia and Hannah looked in their tiered cloaks with the wide French sleeve, (he remembered Marie-Hélène discussing it at great length with them), and their bonnets tied with satin ribbons under their chins. How normal . . .

"I appear to have caused far too much trouble." Miss Graham rose from her chair, but kept one hand on the leather-padded arm.

"Not at all." Joseph gave her a shrewd look, then spoke to Mia and Hannah. "I wonder, my pets, if you could spare the time to see Miss Graham gets home safely?"

"By all means, Papa." Hannah's eyes were shining. "We

were simply going to do the flowers for the church and call on Mrs Braithwaite for Mama. For myself I'll be glad to be rid of it."

"Mia?"

"Of course, Papa."

"There's really no need." Miss Graham was firmly pulling on her gloves.

"Oh, but we insist, we do insist!" Hannah clapped her hands. "Something *dire* might happen to you on the way home, and besides we've never been to Stonebarrow . . ."

"Hannah!" Mia turned to Sarah Graham. "I saw your gig in the yard. I think Papa would be happier in his mind about you if we escorted you home."

"If you say so," the girl said ungraciously. Joseph, watching her, saw her hand go to her temple and then quickly be retracted, and was glad he had a sensible daughter.

"Good-bye, then." He led her to the door. "I hope it will be a temporary indisposition. Please give my regards to your brother."

When he had assisted the three girls into the gig he went back to his room, sat down at his desk and wiped his brow. She was a girl of rare talent, one in a thousand, but, strange . . . Perhaps he'd make a mistake if he employed her. He saw she had left her sketches, and he flicked slowly through them, admiring the delicacy of the flower drawings, their accuracy, recognising lungworts, restharrows, monkshood, pheasant eye, teasels. He sighed with aesthetic appreciation. So often he had rejected sketches submitted to him which were only faithful copies of the original, but this young woman put her own personality into hers, a combination of delicacy and, yes, he looked at the strong sweeping lines of the teasel stalks, aggression. A unique combination.

He sat back. Tonight he'd ask Marie-Hélène for her opinion. She had the hard-headed practicality of Frenchwomen, which he had recognised even in those happy days she so often talked about. He got up, relieved in his mind. He had wasted enough time this morning. He must get himself into the potworks and superintend the body preparation for that important order from Antwerp. The men would be waiting for him.

Mia's mind was in a turmoil as she sat in the gig which the groom was driving smartly down Hessleton High Street. She saw Cantilever's shop on the corner where only yesterday she had chosen a new dress of green organza to be made for the Christmas balls, and discussed with her mother the yardage and the extent of shoulder to be shown. Hannah had chosen blue and begged for a full crinoline since it would soon be her nineteenth birthday. It was like another world.

When she had come into her father's office and seen the narrow white face of Sarah Graham she had experienced the same feeling of inevitability which she seemed to associate now with this family. She had listened to her father's explanation of his summons, and while she did so her quick mind, and no doubt her mother's good training, had put the necessary platitudes into her mouth, while recognising at the same time that the girl was an instrument for conveying her to Well House . . . and a further meeting with her brother.

She was thankful that Hannah was chattering away in her usual fashion. "Oh, do look, Miss Graham! There are the Booths, Madam and the three Miss Booths. Do you know the Booths, Miss Graham? Their mama always dresses them in the same material, colour and style. How very dull that must be for them! I do like the cut of your gown, if you'll pardon me saying so, *très élégante*, as my Mama would say, but rather sober for my taste . . . do tell me if I'm chattering too much since you've been a little indisposed. Did you *really* swoon? I've always longed to swoon, especially in church when Mr Bawtrey has been boring me with those unutterably dreary sermons of his.

I've tried holding my breath and pressing my lips together, like this, but I only become red in the face and if Mia sees me she gives me a sharp dig in the ribs . . ."

Hannah's voice ran on like the Hessleton brook, Mia thought, but she was glad of its cover for her thoughts. Here they were now on the high road to Stonebarrow, the pony stepping out joyfully as if it knew it were on home ground, Hannah's voice weaving up and down with every new idea which entered her mind.

The fields were like yellow fur with their short stubble. No young lady would ever be permitted to walk through a stubbled field however they beckoned, and there, on the sky-line, were the far-off hills which also beckoned and where the curlews called all day. Once they had gone in the train on a special trip with their parents. It had been the first time she and Hannah had travelled by rail and they had rushed from window to window in their excitement. They had walked on the moors above Matlock, and it had been high enough to make one feel one could reach up and touch the swiftly rolling clouds . . .

And now they were over the breast of the hill and she could see clearly the thick belt of trees which lay behind Well House, and beyond that would be the farm which looked on to the lake which Mr Graham had said could appear as blue as Winter ware on a summer's day . . .

"I can see your house quite plainly now," Hannah was saying. It *does* look large. Isn't it too large for only you and your brother?"

"No, we like it." Miss Graham's deep voice had life in it now, as if she drew strength from the proximity of her home. "Conway and I need room. We each have our own places, but in the evening it's pleasant to meet again. We sit together and read or talk . . . I shouldn't like anyone to—" she stopped speaking abruptly.

"Your brother told me he was refurbishing Well Farm with a view to living there," Mia said.

"Oh, it's a game with him!" Miss Graham laughed

30

lightly. "He sees himself as a farmer, but it isn't his forté He's happier writing or studying. He likes the winter in Well House best of all. The branches creak and groan in the high wind, but inside we are comfortable and quite content . . ."

"You must miss your parents," Hannah said. "Can you imagine, Mia, being without Mama and Papa? They're not at all stern with us, Miss Graham. Papa has quite . . . what kind of views has he, Mia?"

"Liberal, pet." Mia smiled at Sarah Graham but got no response.

"That's it. And he believes in treating his workers well. He was in favour of less time being worked each day by them in our manufactory. He supported Lord . . . what was the name of the lord he supported, Mia?"

"Do you refer to Lord Ashley?"

"I'm sure it was he. Besides, Papa is so droll, Miss Graham, and he and Mama tease each other but in such an amusing way . . . oh, what a long avenue! It's not possible to see your house at first. How enchanting to be kept in suspense," and as they rounded the last sweep, "how very *spacious*!" Mia looked with a more educated eye. It was indeed a monstrosity of a house, as her father had said.

The twin oriels on the left of the door jutted out too far and were crowned with a cupola, grey-slated and bearing aloft a weather-vane. Where the other windows were not crowned they were Gothic-arched and pedimented. The slated roof was deeply pitched and there was an ostentatious flight of steps leading up to a panelled door guarded by a pair of lions of most unwelcome aspect with forked tails.

"It's very imposing," she said pleasantly, because although she thought with her father's mind at times, she spoke with her mother's tongue.

The footman parked his whip, laid the reins on the horse's back and then jumped down to assist them to alight. "You wish me to wait, Miss Sarah?" he said.

"Certainly, Frame. You'll be required to drive the ladies back to Hessleton."

"Very good, Miss Sarah." He was a middle-aged man with a long grey face and a taciturn expression, quite different from the fresh, open countenance of their own Robert.

"We'll assist you to your door and then make our way back," Mia said, casting a reproving look at Hannah whose lips were open to make some remark.

"Mrs Frame will be about the premises at this time, I'm sure. Parker is most unreliable." Miss Graham walked to the foot of the steps and the two girls ranged themselves one on either side of her. They ascended the steps together. Hannah was not to be silenced.

"Your brother is very gallant, Miss Graham. I saw him with Mia at our soirée. If he were to go about more I'm sure all the young ladies would be swooning for love . . ."

The door opened and Conway Graham stood on the threshhold. He was pulling on a blue coat over a checked waistcoat, and his appearance was casual, almost elegant, quite different from the one he had presented at the soirée in his old-fashioned attire. The lines of his body stiffened as he surveyed the three girls, Mia caught the expression of amazement in his eyes as they briefly rested on her, then they swept back to his sister. He sounded angry. "I happened to be passing through the hall when I heard voices. What is this, Sarah?"

"I've had an escapade, Conway, and the two Misses Winter have brought me home."

"So I see." The sweeping glance again, the stiffness of his figure remained but his face relaxed. He looked directly at Mia. "Please forgive my rudeness. I was caught unawares . . . has something happened?"

"You see, Papa—" Hannah began, but Miss Graham interrupted her. Her voice was deep, almost beguiling. "Nothing at all except that I took my sketches to show Mr Winter, that's what you wanted me to do, Conway, you pleaded with me, remember? and I felt a little faint. Perhaps it was because I don't go out much . . . I felt a little faint. He was good enough to despatch me home with his two daughters." Mia, watching her, saw that she smiled and her eyes had the same brilliance that she had noticed before.

"Don't act as if I locked you in the nursery, Sarah. I'm glad you went, sorry you felt faint." He drew himself aside. "I'm forgetting my manners, blocking the door in this fashion." He bowed to Mia and Hannah. "Pray come in and rest for a moment before you return. I'm indebted to you for your kindness."

"Thank you," Hannah said, stepping forward with a smile, and Mia was obliged to follow her.

The room they were shown into was as crowded as their own was sparsely furnished. To Mia's bemused eyes it was a riot of horizontals, verticals, curves, loops as to gilt-fringed pelmets, trellised garlands as to the busy wallpaper. Even when she lowered her eyes the pattern of the Brussels carpet and that of the material covering the back-to-back ottomans, made such a merry-go-round of colour that the waxed fruit under the glass globes seemed quite pale in comparison.

"How very . . ." Hannah stopped in the middle of the room. "What lovely things you have and so *many* of them, don't you think, Mia?" She appealed to her sister, and Mia smiled diplomatically.

"Pray sit, ladies," Mr Graham said, offering them chairs with seats done in Berlin wool work. "What *do* you think, Miss Winter?" he looked at Mia. "Your sister has asked your opinion."

She sat, breathed deeply. "I shall have to look around me. I should think it represents a great deal of . . . searching on the part of someone."

"My mother," he said. "She had execrable taste. And yet she painted. Sarah's the same, she never sees interiors, only woodlands and fields where she finds her subjects. I, however, *do* mind, which is why I want to refurbish Well Farm."

"Conway," Sarah said in the new bright voice, as if his presence injected her with animation, "Mr Winter liked my sketches very much and desires me to make designs for him. Aren't you pleased? I know I said to you I didn't want anything to do with it but I changed my mind."

He nodded curtly. "Well, I'm glad you did." He turned. "May I offer you some refreshment?" He made the mistake of catching Hannah's eye.

"Thank you exceedingly. A cup of tea would be acceptable. We generally have tea at this hour, don't we, Mia?"

"Do we?" Mia laughed merrily. "My sister has an incurable curiosity about other people's houses, Mr Graham. I hope you'll forgive her."

He strode across the room to pull the bell, and with his hand on it he turned, looking across the carpeted width at Mia. "Anything which keeps you here is acceptable to me."

The talk became general until the housekeeper came in with a tray of tea things. She was a gaunt, unfriendly-looking woman, and Mia noticed Miss Graham didn't speak to her with the exception of a brief "thank you" when the woman put down the tray in front of her.

"Will it be to your liking, Miss Sarah?" She looked anxious, and Mia, seeing the profusion of silver and the lace-doilied plates on the galleried tray thought that perhaps morning tea was quite an occasion for her.

"Yes, very nice." Miss Graham scarcely glanced at the tray. "Pour the tea if you please and hand the cups round. I'm unused to such a display."

"Yes, Miss Sarah." The woman looked pleased.

"Is Frame still at the door?" Mr Graham asked.

"Yes, sir. Miss Sarah told him to wait."

"Have him take the gig round to the back of the house and we'll ring when we require him. There's no need for him to cool his heels out there."

"Thank you, sir." The woman served the tea to Mia and Hannah, then offered them an ornately-worked silver cream jug and sugar basin on a silver salver and, that done, one of the lace-doilied plates with some rich slices of cake on it.

"We should have been better off with the Madeira minus the cake," Mr Graham said with a short laugh. "Whose idea was this, Sarah?"

"I'm afraid it was mine." Hannah looked confused. "To tell you the truth I thought perhaps you were in the habit of drinking a dish of tea at this hour. I always try to . . ."

"Fall in with the wishes of others? That's a fatal mistake." And to Mia who had refused the madeira cake, "Do you generally drink tea at this time, Miss Winter?"

"Seldom." She smiled. "Perhaps in the afternoon if we pay calls with Mama."

"Well, then," he said, jumping to his feet, "shall we leave your sister and mine together while I show you the farm?"

His abruptness startled her. She saw that although his stance was easy, his hands were clenched at his sides. She glanced at Hannah whose eyes were wide with amazement and then at his sister who was stirring her tea, her head downbent. "Perhaps Miss Graham . . .?"

"Sarah won't want to go. She hates the farm, and she and your sister will have lots to talk about. Isn't that so, Miss Winter?" He smiled at Hannah, a quick, charming smile which evoked an equally quick response.

"Oh, yes, I'm sure we'll get on famously, although I doubt if we'll have much in common. I'm much younger, I think, but we can talk about clothes. Mama says that's always a safe subject between two ladies."

"Sarah is twenty-five, five years younger than I am, and I give you permission to talk about anything you like and for as long as you like." He held out his hand to Mia. "If you're sure you don't want your tea?" Now the smile was on her, mischievous, altogether charming, and that and the combination of the dark eyes made her legs tremble as she stood up.

"Just a brief inspection, then, Mr Graham. We're expected back at our home for luncheon at twelve-thirty."

"I shall see that you are." He held open the door for her, and when he had closed it behind them he offered her his arm. "I'm afraid I'm not dressed for company, but if you'll put up with me as an escort . . ."

"With pleasure." She would be calm, she told herself. She would make polite remarks about his farm and his demesne, and then excuse herself. She didn't wish to be in the company of a man who confused her, disturbed her, made her feel irate one moment, at ease the next. There was no consistency in him, nor for that matter of it, in his sister.

He chatted easily to her as he led her through the back hall and into the wide courtyard surrounded by the stable block. The gig was standing beside the open maw of a coach-house but there was no sign of its driver.

Her natural gaiety came to the surface. "Perhaps your footman is supping a dish of tea with your housekeeper?" She smiled.

"Since they're man and wife it would be a comfortable thing to do. Besides, isn't it so that the kitchen takes its tone from the drawing-room?" His smile was mischievous again.

"Hannah is at that age of wishing fervently to act with proper decorum."

"A tender age."

"She thinks tea is odious!" Mia burst out laughing.

"She'll find in polite society she'll have to do many things which are hypocritical. That's why I've little truck with it."

"I'm sorry you didn't enjoy our soirée." She looked down to hide the laughter in her eyes.

"Now I've offended you! I'll admit I didn't wish to go but did so for my sister's sake. I was further discomfited when dressing to find I'd outgrown my evening clothes which had lain untouched for five years, and had to have recourse to those of my late father!" His voice was too casual. "Perhaps you noticed?" She kept her eyes downcast. "There's nothing makes a man feel more ill at ease than to be ill-dressed. Especially when the same man finds to his great surprise that he's enjoying himself hugely."

"I'm glad of that." She was surprised to find this touch of unsureness in him. "My mother's reputation is safe, then?"

"In what way?"

"As a good hostess. She prides herself on sending her guests away feeling happy . . . Oh!" She stopped suddenly, looking ahead. "Is that your farm? It's quite near Well House. I hadn't realised . . ."

"We've been walking together for above a quarter-of-an-hour. Either you've been in utter misery or utter bliss as we came through the woods . . ."

"Of *course* I noticed the woods," she said sharply, and indeed she had been vaguely aware of gloom around them and the ground slipping downhill away from her, but his presence had dominated her attention.

"Of *course* you noticed the woods," he repeated, smiling. "Now, tell me what you think of the farm? We stand behind it, as you see."

Even from that aspect it was welcoming, warm-tiled, half-timbered, sitting snugly down on a green clearing. "I like it," she said.

"Come and see it from the front. Its eyes are there."

They walked round the side of the house through a tangle of apple and pear trees and suddenly, through the branches, she could see the gleam of water. "The lake," she said, "I'd forgotten about the lake."

"Yes, it lies at the bottom of the slope. The path through the woods is downhill, but I don't need to tell you that." She heard the chuckle in his voice and bit her tongue on a pert retort.

They emerged at the lake-side, silver-grey this morning

and roughed by the wind which had sprung up. "There's no sign of a coal seam ever having been here!" Mia looked across the broad expanse ringed with trees. "My parents said . . . Oh, yes, I can just see some machinery, is it a crane?"

"Yes, it was for the drag line, and there are the remains of trucks and the railway. I intend to have them completely removed and the lake dredged of old timber and generally cleaned up. And I'll plant water-lilies and sedges and perhaps entice the water-heron back. I remember, years ago, when I was young, I used to watch it fishing . . . but I ramble on. What do you think of the farm's face, pray?"

She turned and saw the house obliquely, its flat casement windows, its long, low length, the dormers above the yellow rose which straggled up the side of the door, and said, "I see why you like it. It's a place to be lived in, much more so than—" she stopped herself abruptly, thankful she didn't blush easily.

"Much more so than Well House, you were going to say."

"Not at all." She laughed and put up her hands to the ends of her bonnet ribbons, pretending in her embarrassment she was about to tighten them.

"You shouldn't make a gesture like that." He was standing in front of her, close to her, his back to the lake, the glimmer from the water seeming to outline his figure in light. His face was in shadow.

"Why?" she said, making herself look up at him, finding herself breathless.

"Because it draws my eyes to your face . . ." his voice dropped, "where beauty lies."

She doubted her ears, stood still, held in his gaze. His hair sprang back from a high brow, the sideburns laid a darker shadow on his cheeks making them seem gaunt and hollow, his eyes burned into her. She heard the harsh laugh somewhere of a woodpecker and the faint noise of the wind on the water, like breathing. Or was it her own breathing?

"Is it . . .?" The husky voice sounded strange in her ears. She cleared her throat. "Is it possible to see inside the farmhouse, Mr Graham?"

"I beg your pardon?" His gaze hadn't left her.

"The farm . . . no, please don't bother. Hannah will be wondering where I've got to."

He shook his head, removed his gaze, and she moved her limbs as if they had been released from a vice. "No, it isn't possible. It's been gutted inside, the staircase taken down. Only the shell remains. There are additions to be made to accommodate the servants. I merely wanted to know if the aspect pleased you, if you should like to live there, otherwise . . ."

She spoke quickly, confused by his words, brushing away the meaning which she might take from them. "I find it all very pleasant. I wish you well with your reparations. Now, I really must get back to Hannah. And Hessleton. My father's a stickler for punctuality."

"Of course." He shrugged. "This way, if you please. I'm prepared to accept the excuse of your father's punctuality. I can believe it. But as for Miss Hannah, I've no doubt she'll be thoroughly immersed in telling Sarah about her adventures at the balls and the parties and how she danced with a most elegant fellow all evening and nearly *swooned* for joy . . ."

She had to laugh. "You mustn't mock my little sister."

"I don't mock her. I find her charming, the way I find all lambs and foals charming. I wish Sarah were more like her. But she's capricious, highly-strung, far too highly-strung, and I'm afraid altogether too devoted to me. She's been far from well, recently, as you know . . ." his voice suddenly faltered, "I think it stems from a . . . an illness she had when she was much younger."

"I'm sorry."

"I promised my mother I'd take care of her." He stiffened, said coldly, "I must be boring you."

"You're not. I'm interested." He didn't reply, and she

39

looked around her. Now she was seeing the wood she had passed through on her way to the farm, dark, seemingly impenetrable, except for the narrow path along which they were forced to walk in single file. She felt the coldness of the air on her arms, dampness seeping through her thin shoes, and then another sensation, his hand on her arm. She turned to face him, alarmed.

"You understand about Sarah, don't you?" His voice was urgent.

"Naturally I understand, Mr Graham. There's a close bond between Hannah and me, between any siblings, I should think, all the more so in your case since your sister has been left in your care . . ."

One moment he had merely touched her arm, the next his hands were on her shoulders and she felt his mouth on hers, as urgent as his voice had been. She struggled out of his grasp but not before a swift response had leapt through her body.

"Mr Graham! You forget yourself!" She had to stop while she steadied her voice, her thoughts. "What gives you the right . . .!"

"God knows I've no right! I must have taken leave of my senses. Mia, forgive me. I've no right even to call you Mia!" His cheekbones had darkened, she could see sweat on his brow.

"If I had realised, when I came here with you . . . Oh!" She was boiling with rage, emotion of some other sort, embarrassment and she put a hand to her bonnet to see if it had been knocked askew, that would be the last straw. Then she whirled round and began running along the narrow path, with difficulty since it was uphill, and she soon developed a stitch in her side. She heard herself making ridiculous, choking noises.

"Forgive me! Mia, I must have been mad . . ." He had caught up with her easily and she heard him close behind her.

"Don't speak, please don't speak to me. All I want . . ."

she had started running again, "is to collect . . . Hannah . . . and get out of this place as fast as I can . . ." She ran on, storming, stumbling, weeping, but when she reached the courtyard she had to take a hold of herself. He must have fallen back, or stopped. She slowed down, wiped her face and walked at a decent pace round to the front of the house where by good fortune she saw Frame, the footman, with the gig. She walked up to him, desperately composing herself into calmness. "I'm ready to go now, Frame. Kindly ask someone to inform my sister I'm waiting."

"Very good, miss." He still looked taciturn but not at all suspicious.

She stood with a stiff back, not allowing herself to think, until Hannah came running down the steps. Neither Mr Graham nor Miss Graham put in an appearance. She pretended to Hannah it was of no account and she'd be obliged if her sister would refrain from chattering on the way back as she had developed an unaccountable headache. Hannah took one look at her and kept quiet.

Chapter Three

Marie-Hélène was sitting on a Georgian sofa in the bedroom she shared with Joseph. Georgian because he declared it was more comfortable than the First Empire style she liked, and more elegant than contemporary English furniture which he maintained was hurtful to the eye. He had permitted her one or two First Empire chairs, although he deplored what he called the Roman Conqueror motif, and she had allowed him one or two Georgian mirrors because they adequately and even amply reflected her image.

She was having a last "warm" as she put it before joining Joseph in the French bed where he had so far given way to comfort as to allow a tester and hangings of heavy brocade. It was the end of November now and the nights were cold with the usual English dampness of that month.

"I've been meaning to speak to you for some time about Mia," she said. "I'm worried about her. She's lost her *élan*. Do you think I should restrict her parties? Certainly the girls are inundated with invitations. They're exceedingly popular."

"No, the reason is not a surfeit of parties." His face was grave as he looked across at her. "How pretty your hair is in the firelight! Come to bed, dearest."

"Presently. I want to talk first. Have you the time? You seem always to be immersed in the potworks or the political situation, and today especially you were quite cross with us all at the luncheon table."

"It would be a good thing, Marie-Hélène, if you gave a

thought to politics as well as the welfare of your daughters. I should have thought a European—"

"'When one has been embroiled in politics since one's cradle, one discusses them less. Here, in England, it's a game, usually played away from home.'"

"Touché." He blew a kiss at her.

"I'm aware that today the Russians have won a convincing victory at Sinope, I'm aware that it spells trouble, but which European country has ever been free of trouble? In France we've lived with it since Charlemagne. But that doesn't prevent me worrying about Mia who was *très gaie*, who had such charm and humour and now goes around with a pale face which spoils her looks."

"She's always pale."

"There is pale and pale. It can be like a camellia or the wax of a candle. Do you think she's in love with Thomas Hyde?"

"No, I think he's in love with her which is quite a different matter, and what's more, I think she's sent him about his business because I understand he's paying court elsewhere."

"An easily-mended heart."

"And therefore the wrong one for Mia. Would it surprise you to know that I have here an answer to your question?" He tapped an outspread letter which he held in his hand.

Marie-Hélène turned sharply round. "I thought you were studying some papers in connection with your pots! You generally bring them to bed with you."

"When has there never been room for you as well? No, this letter is from Mr Conway Graham of Well Farm. He's in love with your daughter."

"Mia!"

"Mia. And he's told her so in more than one letter. It says so in this one."

"She's been secretive with letters recently. I wondered . . . read it to me at once, Joseph." Her lips pressed together and she sat up straight in the settee.

"Certainly, since it concerns us all. I guarantee it will surprise you." He held up the sheet before him and cleared his throat.

"'My Dear Sir, I hesitate to trouble you in this matter, but I have approached your elder daughter by letter on several occasions to no effect. I had wished to call and apologise to her for any hurt I might have caused her, but have received no encouragement—'"

"Hurt?" Marie-Helene burst out. "When did he cause her hurt? I know of only one occasion when they met and that was at our soirée!"

"Two, dear heart. The other one was more than a month ago when Miss Graham called at my office and I had to ask Hannah and Mia to escort her to her house when she felt faint. Hannah told me they'd been given tea."

"Was the brother there?"

"I presume so, but you might ask Hannah."

"I shall. Go on, if you please."

"Now, where was I?" He took up the letter again. "Ah, yes . . ."

"'The fact of the matter, dear sir, is that I've fallen deeply in love with Miss Winter and wish to marry her.'" Joseph looked up at his wife and then down again. "'Nothing will change my mind. My heart is hers for always. I'm aware that compared with her many suitors I may not have an immediate appeal, but as regards wealth I'm 'not without' as they say in these parts.'"

Joseph smiled across at his wife. "He has a sense of humour, this one. Ahem! 'The mention of money in connection with your daughter is distasteful to me, but I would willingly acquaint you with details of my fortune at any time convenient to you. I've already requested one favour from you, dear sir, and there my thanks can never be adequate enough, but this is a far greater one that I now put before you. Would you permit me to call and pay my respects to your daughter? I must tell you that my mind is set irrevocably on winning her hand. Yours, etcetera . . .'"

Joseph laid down the letter. "Well, my dear one," he said, "I imagine it's a good thing you're securely seated on that couch otherwise you might have need of your smelling-salts."

"Since when have I had need of smelling-salts?" She got up. "I'm not completely taken by surprise, you know."

"Womanly intuition?"

"Something of the kind. His eye didn't fall on her lightly at our soirée. And as well as love, or regard, if that's too strong a word, I saw an invincibility of purpose. This is not a Thomas Hyde nor a Judas Ashworth we're dealing with, nor for that matter any lily-livered English youth with a patrician nose and a fine pedigree."

"You knew that as a woman too, no doubt?"

"Exactly. The English youths generally make me feel like a mother. This one didn't."

"Spare me any complications!" Joseph laughed aloud. "I know you're irresistible, but it's enough that he says he's lost his heart to Mia without you inferring you've lost your heart to *him*."

"That's not what I said and well you know it. I've only lost my heart once in my life."

"Come to bed, wife," he said, his voice rough.

She took off her negligée, and laying it across the couch she crossed the room to the bedside. Joseph pulled aside the covers, and when she got in he bent over her and gave her a close, husbandly kiss. There was silence in the room. The firelight flickered on the walls, the furniture lay in the shadows except for the chance gleam of brass.

"Enough . . ." Marie-Hélène let the word out on a sigh after a time and released herself. "Has the talk of someone else's ardour fired your own?" She struggled to a sitting position, propping the pillows behind her head. "Tell me. What are you going to do about Mr Graham and his letter?"

Joseph laid his head beside hers. "I shall send him one saying I don't rule my daughters with a rod of iron, that

45

it has never been my way. And even if it had, I doubt if I should be able to influence them. Hannah perhaps, but certainly not Mia. Nevertheless, I should be glad if he would call at an appropriate time when we could have a discussion as to his suitability. I may be liberal but I'm not a loon!"

"You won't say that, Joseph!"

"Not in so many words, although I'll make my meaning clear. Mia is our first-born and very dear to us. But to sugar the pill, would it be convenient for you to provide supper and perhaps some music?"

"Yes . . ."

"What is it, dear heart? You look concerned."

"There are the rumours . . ."

"I thought we'd come to that. But don't they chiefly concern his parents, that they squandered the money they came into from the coal found on their land? Well, they couldn't have squandered it all, since Mr Graham assures us that he's 'not without'. Then, what was the other fault? That they tended to live apart from the community and find their own solaces? I should have thought in your eyes that was to be commended, considering how you regard us here as being in a parochial backwater."

"'Solaces' may be a pretty euphemism, Joseph, but we'll let that be. Gossip says otherwise. But I was thinking rather of his sister. She's purported to be, if not neurotic, at least *plein de nervosité*. And people talk about the close relationship which exists between them."

"I thought you discounted small town gossip, dear one."

"Generally I do." She turned to look at him and saw no shadow in his eyes. "I've the sophistication of a Parisian, you, with all your learning . . . never mind. Yes, let's ask Miss Graham and Mr Graham to supper, and tomorrow I shall have a talk with Mia. I'll tell her I know about the letters she's been receiving, that I don't wish to pry as to their content, but would like to know if she objects to the

Grahams coming here. If it's quite against her wishes we shan't issue an invitation, but if she agrees, we shall. After all, why hang a man before he's committed a crime?"

"He has a champion in you, it would appear," Joseph said. He put his hand under her neck and turned her face gently towards him.

"What do you think, Hannah?" Mia spun round so that the lace-edged flounces of her gown billowed about her.

"I like the peplum. It makes your waist extremely narrow. And the flounces on the sleeves are very striking . . . let me see, how many are there? One, two, three, four, five . . . why, Mia, the same number as on the skirt!"

"That's the point of it all, pet. Dressmakers' cunning. They have minds which dwell on minutiae, what kind of trimming, what kind of bow, where they should be placed. Do you really like it? I don't resemble a Christmas tree by any chance?"

"Certainly not. It's cream, not green, and you are not hung with baubles, unless you count your amethyst earrings. Why are you so anxious in any case? It's only that dull girl and her brother. But, of course, it's her *brother*! How incredibly stupid of me! You went a walk with him that morning, and you looked quite upset in the gig going home, then you've been pale and odd ever since then, getting up in the middle of the night to look out of the window, locking up notes . . . I thought it was all for Thomas!"

"You *are* incredibly stupid," Mia said calmly. She lifted a bottle of cologne from the toilet table, took out the glass stopper and poured some on her handkerchief. She dabbed her temples, feeling the tiny pulse beating there through her finger-tips. Her head spun for a moment. "I don't agree with you in any case. Miss Graham is far from dull. She's one remove from being insolent which is *tout à fait different*. Are you ready? I think it would be better if we went downstairs together."

"I thought you had no qualms about entering a room? You've told me that often."

"I'm quite without shyness, little sister, but I was thinking of you." She smiled at Hannah who was still prinking at the mirror. On an impulse she bent and kissed her, laughing now, but feeling that it was some kind of good-bye. They swept out of the room hand in hand.

He was there. She saw as he stood up how the old-fashioned suit at the soirée, and the country garb which she had last seen him wearing, had in both cases hidden the strength of the figure. The cutaway coat emphasised the flat hips, broadened the already broad shoulders, the white of his stock contrasted with the rich blackness of his hair. Marie-Hélène was there too, performing the honours gracefully from her seat on the sofa beside Miss Graham, whom Mia noticed was wearing a velvet dress with bishop sleeves down to the wrists. She was obviously chary of exposing too much flesh to the public gaze.

"Here are my daughters at last! I expect they've been prinking at their glass this last half-hour. Now isn't it fortunate that there's no need of introductions since you've all met before!"

Mr Graham bowed over Mia's hand and then over Hannah's. There was no glance from his dark eyes this time. His circumspection was more annoying than his presumption, Mia found herself thinking.

"How do you do?" she said coolly, and then going immediately to the sofa where Miss Graham was holding out a limp hand, and dutifully smiling, it seemed, "How do you do?"

"It's extremely pleasant to see you again, Miss Winter. My brother and I are deeply indebted to your mother for her kind invitation." She repeated the words like a well-learned lesson.

Joseph had come into the room on this last remark. "Take my advice, Miss Graham," he said, "and keep your thanks until after the meal. It's only Parisian food we're having tonight. You might have occasion to change your mind."

"Oh, Papa!" Hannah laughed, her hand to her mouth. And then to Miss Graham. "How do you do? Didn't I tell you how Papa teases Mama all the time? Pay no attention, pray. You'll find Mama has planned a most excellent meal for you. At least, so far we've had no cause for complaint." There was the sound of a gong being struck in the hall.

"With which heartfelt recommendation," Joseph said, "shall we go in to dinner?" He bowed to Miss Graham. "Allow me to escort you." Turning his head towards her brother, he said, "There's no formality in this house, sir. Kindly give your arm to my wife and the girls will follow behind." The arrangement gave Mia the opportunity to see Mr Graham's breadth of shoulders again.

The dinner was not an unqualified success as far as conversation went, although no fault could be found in Marie-Hélène's meal of salmon, quail and ice-pudding, livened with French trimmings. The conversation tended to go in fits and starts, depending on the enthusiasm of the speaker on his or her subject and the skill of the inter-locutor. Miss Graham spoke animatedly about sketching out-of-doors when questioned by Mia, and Mr Graham was fervent about the stupidity of being driven into a war for the sake of propping up the Turk. Occasionally there were pauses, and on these occasions Mia found her eyes being drawn to meet those of Mr Graham who sat across the table from her, and having been thus drawn, found it increasingly difficult to withdraw them.

After dinner Hannah was persuaded to sing, and Mia, who had been accompanying her on the piano, was pressed to remain there and render some *morceaux de salon* which she executed only tolerably well. She had never relished rising early in the morning to practise and had been indulged by her mother on this score. Marie-Hélène was a realist, and in her opinion her daughter had but a small talent. Hannah was talking to Miss Graham at the window, and Mia was aware suddenly that her brother stood behind her, his hand on the music-stand.

"Do you read music, Mr Graham?" she asked lightly.

"Enough to turn the pages for you." His voice was low. "Why didn't you reply to my letters?"

She played an arpeggio, haltingly. "I might well ask why you behaved so abominably . . ."

"Nevertheless you could have given me some answer, saved my misery."

"I had first to try and forget what happened, not an easy matter, before I could—"

His voice cut across hers urgently, still low-pitched. "I've apologised to you in all three times for my behaviour. I admit it was dastardly, but my only excuse is that I love you. I've spoken to your father tonight and he's given me permission . . ."

She played loudly, stridently, to cover the painful beating of her heart.

"Mia!" her father called from the fireside. "I would remind you that you're playing a Nocturne. It sounds to me like the crack of doom!"

"I'm sorry. I don't wish to play any more. My fingers are all thumbs." She got up without looking at Mr Graham and crossed the room to join Hannah and his sister. She could hardly see them in her confusion, and the conventional words she spoke had no meaning for her. She saw, out of the corner of her eye, that Mr Graham was making his way to the fireside to speak to her father. If only Lucy would bring in the tea things, she thought, and I would be free of this agitation. Almost with the thought there was a knock at the door, and her mother entered, followed by a blushing Lucy with a tray. "Well, you all look very happy together," Marie-Hélène said. "Put it there, Lucy and you may go. I shall pour myself."

"Thank you, madam." Lucy smiled widely, keeping her mouth closed, and bobbed her way to the door.

"Just a moment, Lucy," Joseph said. "Is Robert about?"

"Yes, sir." She stopped. "He's in the stables seeing to the bedding-down."

"Ask him if he'll please carry out my telescope to the garden and set it up."

"Yes, sir." Lucy gave a last bob and shut the door behind her.

"How do you like your tea, Miss Graham?" Marie-Hélène asked.

"A little cream and sugar, if you please."

"And you, Mr Graham?" She smiled across the room at him.

"Neither the one nor the other, I thank you."

"Has my husband been extolling to you the beauties of the heavens? He's always looking for someone to convert."

"He's been fascinating me, ma'am, by telling me about Jupiter's satellites, its Galilean moons, if I have it aright. And what's more, has kindly offered to let me look through his telescope. I hadn't known he possessed one."

"Ah, but my husband is a man of many parts." She smiled. "Hannah, pass the cups round for me, if you please, and you, Mia, might be good enough to hand the cake. Isn't it a bad night for it, Joseph?"

"No, the sky is clear for November. I've been telling Mr Graham I've been studying the Ephemeris and there might be something worth seeing."

"Do you wish to eat something?" Mia held out the plate, keeping her eyes averted.

"No, thank you. I had an excellent repast." She could feel his dark glance, heard the smile in his voice. "Are *you* interested in astronomy, Miss Winter?"

"Yes indeed she is." Joseph answered for her. She's my amanuensis and calculates with great skill."

"Then perhaps you'll join us and give me the benefit of your knowledge?"

She was forced to raise her eyes. "Perhaps."

"Don't allow yourself to be talked into this tomfoolery, Miss Graham," Hannah said, sitting down beside her.

"Better by far to stay at the fire with Mama and me. Goodness knows what Mia and Papa get out of standing on the wet grass for hours on end."

"We do wear overshoes, you know." Mia tried to speak lightly.

"If you intend to go, Conway," his sister said coldly, "remember we musn't be late. Mrs Frame objects to being kept out of bed."

"She's paid for it." He put down his cup, his face going dark with anger.

"One must keep on the right side of one's servants," Joseph said diplomatically. "Some say that before long they'll be hard to obtain. Indeed, one sees the trends already . . . come along, Mr Graham, a brief look will suffice. Mia, run to the study and fetch me another eyepiece from the drawer, a low-powered one. You know how they're arranged. Robert will already be in the garden."

"I hadn't intended to . . . very well, Papa." She left the room and made her way to the study where she pulled open one of the drawers in the cabinet in which her father kept his astronomical equipment. She read the neat inscriptions, extracted the requisite eyepiece and walked slowly to the hall where she put on her cloak but decided against wearing over-shoes. They'd only be in the garden for a few minutes. She walked even more slowly along the back hall and let herself out through the garden door.

She was glad of the darkness. It would hide her excessive pallor. She had caught a glimpse of her face in the glass above the hall table and had been startled by its paleness. Mama always said she knew when she was excited because she became paler rather than flushed. She rubbed her hands briskly over her cheeks in an effort to drive some colour into them.

In the moonlight the garden looked formally beautiful. It lay behind the tall house in a precise rectangle except for a conifer-ringed corner where her father kept his telescope. They were a good windbreak, he said, and allowed him to make his sightings in comparative comfort. The background of sky was less densely black than the conifers, pricked by the odd sparkle of a star.

She saw someone coming across the wide expanse of lawn and her heart jumped. As the figure drew nearer she realised it was Robert, walking with a rolling sailor's gait, which was a surprise since he had never seen the sea. "Good evening, Robert," she said, as they drew abreast.

"Good evening, Miss Mia. All set up. The master's showing the gentleman how it works."

"Very good, Robert." She walked on, glad of the small respite, but ahead of her now were the conifers casting their black shadows, and coming from behind them she could hear her father's voice. She entered the small enclave, and as Mr Graham turned towards her, she said lightly, "Papa loves a willing audience, but you musn't hesitate to tell him if he talks too much!"

"Mr Graham is a willing seeker after knowledge," her father said. "Come here, Mia, and have a look at this."

"Don't you want the eyepiece, Papa?"

"Not at the moment. Jupiter is excessively clear tonight."

She applied her eye and saw in the field of the telescope the smoke-grey disk of the planet with the irregular disposition of its satellites around it. Her concentration was complete to the exclusion of Mr Graham who stood silently beside her.

"Wonderful!" She sighed and withdrew her eye. "Did you say you hoped to see an eclipse or a transit, Papa?"

"How learned you sound, Miss Winter!" Mr Graham's voice was teasing.

"Not at all. All I had to do was look."

"But you knew what you were looking at."

"Papa's a good teacher."

"Now you've confused me by your question, Mia," Joseph said. "I studied the Ephemeris last night . . ."

"It is of no matter." Mr Graham was bending down to look again through the telescope. "I'm well content with what I've seen. I can hardly wait to buy myself a few books on astronomy. I thought Copernicus had said it all, now I realise that was just the beginning."

"It's limitless, although, believe it or not, a compatriot of my wife's, one August Compte, said not so long ago that everything about stars had now been learned and further study would be a waste of time . . ." Joseph paused. "Yes, I *will* go and consult the Ephemeris again. It will worry me all night if I don't. I shan't be above five minutes. I shall expect you to keep an eye on things, Mr Graham."

"Don't worry. I'll see that nothing escapes while you're gone, sir."

"Hurry, Papa," Mia said, suddenly afraid, "I'm beginning to feel the cold. I've neglected to wear over-shoes." She would have liked to run after him, but dared not, nor in fact would her feet have obeyed her will. She was left with Mr Graham in the darkness. Far away she heard an owl hooting, and closer at hand there was the restless swish of the conifers as they moved in the wind. She looked up and saw the stars whirling and seeming to scatter a diamond spray in their path. Or was it her senses which were whirling? Everything was movement, she felt part of it, part of the Universe.

"I cannot look any more," Mr Graham said. He drew away from the telescope and came to her side.

She made herself look at him, and as she did so the pain returned so fiercely that she had to restrain herself from clutching her side. This was the pain she had felt at her first sight of him, and later, when his hands had rested on her shoulders and he had kissed her. But it had passed the threshhold of what she had always recognised as pain and become a piercing delight.

She was in his arms. His mouth claimed her mouth, and with its remembered touch all common-sense left her. She pressed herself against him, her arms went round his neck. She was no longer in her father's quiet garden. She was lifted on to a plateau of delight which

54

existed only for the two of them. Touch took the place of words.

Realisation returned like a shock of cold water. The swish of the conifers filled her ears again. It must have been there all the time but the sense of hearing had disappeared with her common-sense. She felt the dampness under her feet, knew suddenly where she was and wrenched herself away from him. She put trembling fingers to her hair, attempted to rearrange her cloak which had slipped from her shoulders, pushed aside by his eager hands.

Her behaviour had seemed as inevitable as the stars, now it filled her with shame. Or was it that her body had spoken the truth? No flirtation, silly or serious, that she had ever indulged in had moved her like this. "What . . ." her voice trembled, "what will you think of me? I was going to be haughty, and cool . . ."

"And make me suffer because of the last time?" He gathered her against him. "It doesn't matter. I know now. I knew you had to feel as I did. Such a strong love, Mia . . . it had to be shared. My body has ached so long for yours . . ."

"Hush!" She drew herself away quickly. There had been the sound of a door shutting. How long had her father been gone? She felt confused, dispossessed, the cool, flirtatious *prudent* Mia Winter was a stranger to her. "Papa will be here in a second or two."

"Then there's only time to ask you one question. Please marry me!" His voice was urgent, implacable, and her eyes became suffused with tears.

"I . . . I . . ."

She heard Joseph's cheerful voice as he strode across the lawn. "It's a transit, Mia, not an eclipse . . . Ganymede. I'm afraid we should have too long to wait for it tonight." He rounded the conifers. "Especially as your sister's anxious to be off home, Mr Graham."

"Yes, of course. My sister . . ." His voice was flat.

Chapter Four

Hannah walked along Blenheim Terrace with a sprightly step. She waved to old Miss Crumpsall sitting like a hooded crow behind closed panes, the balcony surrounding her giving her the appearance of being in a cage. All the houses in the terrace were of the same design, flat-fronted, but with a shell-canopied door which Joseph said was Queen Anne if you wished to split hairs. He had bought their own, number twenty-nine, for Marie-Hélène when they were married, because she had said she didn't wish to be buried in a miserable, rainy countryside.

Her idea of England had been the conventional Parisian's, perpetual fog or rain – wasn't it proven by the fact they always drank their coffee indoors? – but he had been pleased to concur. It meant he was near the potworks, and as long as they had an extensive garden, he said it was just as good as living in the country. Besides, the selling of the small mansion which had been bequeathed to him by his father had put a tidy sum in the Bank, and enabled him to be an indulgent husband and father.

Hannah rounded the end of the Terrace, a plump, engaging figure in her peplumed jacket of dark green merino, collared and cuffed in sable to match the muff on her left arm. Grandmama Winter had left a cape of that fur which Marie-Hélène had declared was *demodée*, and accordingly it had been despatched to Miss Dearden, their devoted dressmaker and confidante of Hannah's and Mia's youthful pecadillos, to be used as trimming when the occasion arose. Some of it was at present with

Mia in Paris encircling a delectable bonnet of sapphire blue velvet.

"Good morning," she said, meeting Colonel Pritchard, an elderly friend of her father's with whom he occasionally played whist. Joseph's interests were so eclectic that his friends came from every walk in life and Colonel Pritchard had a double role. When whist palled he and Joseph discussed the Peninsular War.

"Good morning, m'dear. Have you no escort?" He was of the old school.

"It isn't necessary, Colonel Pritchard. I'm on a commission for Mama and it's very near. I'm going to the potworks to take a note to my sister-in-law, Miss Sarah Graham, you remember?"

The colonel cogitated, leaning on his cane, mouth agape. "Miss Sarah Graham . . . yes, yes." He nodded. "Although the town was a *leetle* disappointed, you know. Expected more of a . . . how d'ye call it, splash."

"My brother-in-law wanted a quiet wedding and, of course, there was no need of a lengthy engagement. Mia was pleased to agree. Conway's rich, you know, and not exactly a young boy . . ." She stopped speaking. Her fatal tongue was running away with her again. "Never discuss domestic affairs with neighbours," Marie-Hélène had often counselled her, and here she was doing just that with an old addle-pate like the colonel. She consoled herself with the knowledge that he was deaf. "Will you excuse me, please? I must hurry to be back home before luncheon."

"Give my regards to your beautiful mother and your sister also, Maria, ain't it?" He lifted his top hat, revealing a surprisingly thick head of grey hair, like a wig.

"Yes, certainly. Good day." Hannah breathed a sigh of relief as she crossed into Tumbrill Street, a far cry in name and amenity from Blenheim Terrace. Here Lucy's parents lived, and various small artisans, in a neat, quiet little thoroughfare which was also the habitation of many of the potworkers employed by her father. She

57

was aware of various portly housewives, arms akimbo, nodding knowingly to each other as she passed, and she kept a bright smile on her face, feeling, she told herself, like the Queen herself, and badly wanting to laugh.

She reached the end of the street and here it petered out into a waste piece of ground. At the far end reared the bottle ovens behind high boarded gates with the inscription on them in bold white-painted letters, "Joseph Winter and Son, Potters." She suddenly saw with one of the gleams of understanding afforded to even young girls, the reason for Mia being encouraged in the study of history, astronomy and other unladylike pursuits which her mother so decried. Papa had wanted a son! Was that why Mia had such a strong will, a determination to get her own way which might have been subdued by more purse-netting and less book-learning? She opened the small door set in the left-hand gate and stepped into the yard.

It was swirling in smoke from the ovens, and putting her handkerchief to her mouth she made her way quickly between the discarded wooden moulds, empty barrels in which the clay had arrived, and small mountains of broken earthenware, to her father's office. There Jason Berridge received her, delighted at the unexpected bonanza of a visit from one of the young misses. He thought Hannah far the better-looking of the two, indeed if he'd given rein to his feelings he would have put his arm round her plump waist, but he quelled his imagination and youthful fervour and addressed her with proper deference.

"Good day, Miss Hannah. Your father's with the dippers. It's the finishing touches to a new design today. 'Galaxy' it's called. He wanted to supervise the glazing."

"You seem to know quite a lot about the business, Jason." Hannah peeped from behind her muff at him, deliberately coquettish. She liked to see the easy blush mount to his cheeks. It was a pity it didn't happen oftener with the young men she was in the habit of meeting who pretended to be full of fashionable *ennui*. Oh, for Mia's coolness, but then she hadn't been cool before her marriage, not sleeping, going off her food, writing endless letters for Robert to deliver to Well House, quite like Shakespeare's Juliet, Hannah had told her.

Jason had been enjoying watching her. "I'm interested, that's why, Miss Hannah. I wish your father would put me back in the potworks, but he discovered I had a head for figures, so here I'll have to stay, I expect."

"Perhaps he's grooming you for an important job, Jason." She tried opening wide her eyes and pouting her lips like a picture she had seen once of Mrs Siddons.

"There's nothing I'd like better. I study at nights, and . . ." he suddenly looked older, different to her. His eyes had a shrewdness in them, and then they cleared. "But you don't want to hear about me. Shall I tell your father you wish to see him?"

"But I don't, Jason!"

"Don't you?" Now his eyes were teasing *her*. Why didn't people stay the same? She it was who had always teased Jason.

"No, I was passing and I looked in."

"So you came to see me?"

"Really! Some people . . ." How she wished for the gift of repartee. "I came to see Miss Graham, my sister-in-law. I understand she's here this morning."

"Yes, she is." Now he was over-solemn. "She's in the Design Room, I believe. The second door on the right along the corridor."

"I know where it is. Thank you, and good day." She spoke haughtily, but there was a pleasant little flutter in her heart as she left the room. He held the door open for her, bowing from the waist, rather too much.

Instead of going directly to see Sarah, Hannah went into the manufactory, picking her way daintily between the benches where the men were working, earning a few admiring looks which she was not unaware of, and stopping once or twice to look at plates in various stages of

59

manufacture. The circles of clay being pushed in rows into the ovens reminded her of nothing so much as Mrs Gossop turning out a batch of her famous apple pies.

She found her father, red-faced from the heat of the ovens, standing with Fred Craythorne, his manager. He had a plate between his hands, and he was examining it closely as he slowly spun it. She had often seen him handling pottery in this way, deftly and yet with infinite care. He boasted to Lucy, who was a cheerful smasher of crockery, that he had never broken a piece in his life.

He looked up and saw her. "Well, Hannah, my dear! Have you come looking for employment with us?"

"No, Papa, I just had the urge to look around. Mama would be furious if she knew. This is one of my new outfits. Good day, Mr Craythorne."

"Good day, Miss Hannah."

"It's not the best of places for a young lady of high fashion," Joseph teased her. "There's some clay dust on your skirt already. But I don't see much harm in it, although don't tell your mother I said so. If you don't look you'll never learn. What do you think of this, since you're here?" He gave her the plate. "Careful, now, if you please. It's not long out of the gloss fire."

She took it. "I know its name. 'Galaxy'. Jason told me."

"Did he now? Yes, there isn't much Jason doesn't know. Do you like it?"

Hannah examined the plate, seeing the drift of colours dragged across the surface, no pattern at all, she thought, but it reminded her of something . . . what was it, mysterious, yet familiar . . . "Why, Papa," she said, inspiration hitting her, "it's like the sky at night, isn't it?"

"Your sister could have told you what Galaxy meant right away."

She pouted, and Mr Craythorne saw fit to cheer her. "Not many lasses would know that, Mr Winter, and Miss Hannah hit the nail on the head all right."

"She did. And besides, our pet has other attributes which I mustn't forget. "Does it by any chance remind you of the Milky Way, Hannah?"

"Oh, yes, Papa. That's it! It's really beautiful, sort of . . . luminous."

Joseph smiled with pleasure. "Now, if you had tried for a hundred years you couldn't have found a better adjective than that. Luminous . . . How do you think it would look for a tea-set, or even a dinner service?"

"I can imagine London people liking it, but it's too outlandish for Hessleton."

Joseph laughed delightedly. "This girl has her mother's perspicacity, Craythorne. Now, come along, Hannah," he took the plate from her and gave it to his manager, "this atmosphere isn't too healthy for you. There I agree with your mother." He put his arm round her shoulders, turning his head. "See you don't leave the oxides lying about, Craythorne."

"I'll see to that. Good day to you, Miss Hannah."

"I haven't asked you why you're here, have I?" Joseph said as they walked through the manufactory together.

"I came to ask Sarah to visit us this evening. Mama said you thought she looked ill, and we wondered, when we were talking at the breakfast table after you'd gone, if she was missing her brother. So Mama wrote a note and asked me to deliver it."

"You have kind hearts. She's a strange girl, Sarah, uncommunicative. I know her no better than when she first started to work for me. She'll never admit to being lonely, of that I'm sure, but equally sure you'd be doing her a good turn to have her for dinner this evening."

"Do you like having her to work for you, Papa?"

"She's by way of being a genius, if that isn't too strong a word. Yes, I'm not surprised you look startled. There was a man at the Sèvres factory when I visited them a year or two ago, and I'm reminded of his work when I look at Sarah's. He was a painter rather than a decorator, and his designs were strange, full of feeling, with a quality of . . . well, I can only call it magic. I think his name was . . . Lessore."

"She ought to be happy with a talent like that," Hannah said. They had come to the door of the offices.

"Yes, she ought to be." Joseph looked thoughtful. "But she isn't. There's something inherent in her personality which prevents happiness, some scar . . . I can see why Conway was worried about her. And yet in him also I find—" he stopped abruptly. "Anyhow, you go on into the Design Room and extend your invitation. We'll try to cheer her up." He kissed her.

Hannah walked along the corridor, thinking how the thought of having Sarah Graham as a guest to dinner did nothing to cheer *her* up.

Marie-Hélène sat on the ottoman watching her guest as she showed some sketches to Joseph. Hannah, seated on a nearby chair was pretending interest but slouching in boredom. She caught her daughter's eye and squared her shoulders as an example, and Hannah parodied her mother, pulling her shoulders up to her ears. Marie-Hélène shook her head reprovingly. Her younger daughter was naughty but engaging, not nearly so complicated as Mia, who from a child had always wanted her own way. True, she had developed into a delightful young woman, coolly elegant, but Joseph had made a mistake attaching her to him, encouraging her to use her mind. Girls ought not to use their minds too much. It only led to trouble. Intuition, perhaps, but that was a different thing altogether. Like the intuition she had about this girl, Sarah, so cat-faced, smooth, and yet one knew with a seething mind behind her quiet eyes. Marie-Hélène had had an Aunt Sophie with the same mouth and eyes, and look where she had landed herself! The local people had called it Salpêtrière but it wasn't really that, simply a private place for the mentally-disturbed.

Joseph looked up and smiled at his wife, his eyes full

of love. How lucky she was with such a husband, a lover at forty-nine! Englishwomen didn't understand their husbands, withholding their love when it suited them, feigning invalidism to escape it, making out that the whole business of loving was a stern duty, an imposition . . .

"These coloured drawings of Sarah's, my dear, you must see them. I thought her wild flowers were charming, but here we have, in delicate wash, intimate glimpses of the countryside. One could make up a dinner set with each piece having a different landscape! Can you imagine the talking point that would make for your guests? Much better than Mrs Gossop's conceits when she brings in the pies."

"I have the best subtleties in Hessleton!"

"Well, so you should, considering you're the wife of their only potter." He got up and laid the sketches on Marie-Hélène's lap. "Look through them, I beg you, my love, you'll be enchanted."

He doesn't guard his praise, she thought, turning the drawings over one by one. She'll imagine she's a rarity, a gift from heaven, but she had to admit, even at a cursory glance that they were striking, delicate but far from insipid, stylistic, Watteauish in concept. The gentry would go mad over them. "Very nice," she said. "Sarah, my dear, I meant to ask you at dinner but it slipped from my memory. How are the reparations progressing at Well Farm?"

"Not at all, ma'am." The girl looked across the room at her, self-composed, eyes, hands, still. "The inclement weather, you know . . ."

"Perhaps they need a man behind them. Workmen pay absolutely no attention to women, I've found. I know Conway and Mia are looking forward so much to a place of their own."

"Conway won't mind." The girl's eyes didn't flicker, but Marie-Hélène could have sworn there was insolence in her glance.

"He's used to Well House. It's a foible, the farm, something to occupy him during the day."

"It may be a foible to him, although I doubt that, but it certainly isn't to Mia. There are all the beautiful wedding gifts they received, and Mia will want to exercise her own taste which she can only do in her own home." She laughed, conspiratorially. "I'll let you into a secret. Mia invariably gets what she wants." The girl looked down at her hands without replying.

"Yes, trust Mia," Hannah said, glad the subject had changed to one of interest. "She's a firebrand, isn't she, Papa? Don't be taken in by her cool exterior, Sarah. Even when she was a little girl she ordered people about. Do you remember Mademoiselle Desirée, Mama?"

"Do I remember Mademoiselle Desirée!" Marie-Hélène sighed dramatically, lifting her hands. Desirée, you know, had come with me from France . . . to buffet me against the first impact of England and the English ways." She smiled at Joseph. "She was the personal maid of my mother. Desirée said, and the words are engraved on my heart, my dear, 'Mademoiselle Marie-Hélène . . .' she always called me that even after I was married . . . 'Mademoiselle Marie-Hélène, if I have to put La Manche between me and your daughter, Maria, it will not be wide enough!' Mia waged war against her from the day she found her turning out a stray kitten from the kitchen."

"She never liked animals, poor Desirée," Joseph said, "and yet she was like a little frog herself with her round eyes and wide mouth."

"She was a treasure, but no matter. That's Mia for you!" Marie-Hélène looked across the room at Sarah in time to meet the girl's eyes. They were cold.

"Perhaps had Mia and my brother waited longer before they married . . ." The words in themselves weren't insolent, the look was. Marie-Hélène felt the guilty blood rise in her cheeks since she and Joseph had felt the same. But Mia had been adamant and had rejected, coolly but firmly, the suggestion that she should wait for a year. Her mother had recognised the fixity of purpose, but also the passion.

Conway had been as implacable, and as Joseph had pointed out, he wasn't a boy. Besides, hadn't they brought up Mia to know her own mind? "*You* brought her up that way," she had snapped back and they had had one of their beautiful flare-ups of anger which she enjoyed so much because he could be so excessively loving afterwards. But what had won her over was in fact the love which was looking out of Mia's eyes, and hadn't she herself known that hunger, still knew it? Besides she liked Conway. I'm like their dumpy Queen, she had thought, who likes dark, sensual men, like the Emperor . . .

She waved her fan to cool her cheeks. This cold English miss should not intimidate her. "Your brother isn't a child, and he assured us that Mia would have a home of her own. However, let's not discuss it any more. Hannah, ring for Robert to bring round the carriage. It's past nine o'clock."

"But you said—" Hannah bit back the words, catching her mother's eye. "Certainly, Mama." She jumped up, crossed to the fireplace and gave a hearty pull to the bell.

"We shall, of course, be glad to see you at any time," Marie-Hélène said to Sarah in her most majestic fashion.

"*Notre maison est à vous.* Please don't hesitate to avail yourself of it or of our hospitality." Tonight, she thought, I'll have another word with Joseph. He really is too idealistic for his age and not at all *du monde*.

Chapter Five

"Are you sorry to be going home, my darling?" Conway said. Mia lay on the *chaise longue* in their suite of rooms near the Église du Dome which the Emperor was in the process of having restored in his drive to change the face of Paris. She was surprised at her languor these days, and then not surprised when she remembered their sleepless nights.

"No, not sorry to leave Paris." She smiled up at him, impishly, ticking off the points on her fingers. "I've enjoyed seeing l'Hôtel des Invalides where Bonaparte lodged his wounded soldiers and where now he himself is lodged, and the meeting hall of the Chamber of Deputies at le Palais-Bourbon, not to mention the Legislative Assembly instigated after the *coup d'etat* a few years ago . . ."

"Desist, I beg you!"

"But I haven't finished yet! Let me see, what else? Ah, yes, le Pont des Arts which is the first metal bridge to be put over the Seine, the Sorbonne, of course, which was interesting because Papa attended it, La Fontaine des Quatre-Saisons, not forgetting number fifty-nine nearby, the house of Alfred de Musset, friend of the notorious George Sand, The Trocadero . . ."

He came and knelt down beside her. "There's a wicked elf inside you who likes to tease. Or is it that you speak lightly because you're ashamed still of your own emotions?"

She didn't answer for a second. "It's good to be light-hearted. I'm not a courtesan, Hannah would have a fit if she saw me lying on a *chaise longue*. Underneath I'm still an inexperienced English girl. Sometimes I can't believe it's the carefully brought up Miss Winter behaving in such an abandoned way."

"You *are* ashamed."

"No, only surprised, and then when you kiss me, not even that."

"You're a woman in love. I chose well. I knew, even to look at you, that there were fires behind that level gaze of yours. I knew by your mouth."

"By my mouth?"

He kissed her slowly. "See how full-lipped it is, how eager, how it clings to mine. We belong together, Mia. Nothing must ever part us."

"Indeed, I can't think what might part us," she said, sitting up and lifting with her hands the long chestnut hair so that it fell behind her shoulders. "Keep away, if you please. I wish to dress since this is our last day. What a pity we can't go on to Italy! I've always longed to see Rome."

"The weather is too inclement and the journey too difficult to arrange. Couriers at this time of the year are hard to find."

"But we talked about taking the train to Rouen and proceeding from there by carriage . . . you were quite enthusiastic until this morning when the letters arrived from home. Was there anything in yours to disturb you?"

"Nothing of any account." He spoke shortly. "Well Farm hasn't been touched, since Sarah has been quite unable to make any arrangements with the workmen. I thought I had it all fixed. One can't blame her, of course. It's a wretched time of the year." He got up and strode about the room, stopping to look out of the window on to the *Place*.

"That was another point in favour of going on to Rome. It would have given the workmen more time."

"If you say any more, my darling," he spoke without looking round, "I shall think you regret ever coming here with me."

She was tired and it was only ten o'clock in the morning,

too tired to mind her tongue. "If you rush me home at this rate, my dearest, I shall think you're worried about leaving Sarah alone too long."

He turned to look at her, and she saw his eyes were dark with anger. "Explain yourself, please!"

Her quick temper rose to meet his. "I'm not one of your little misses who's easily discomfited. Yesterday we were planning to have a leisurely tour through Italy. Today all is changed. The only difference is that we have had letters from England . . . can you blame me if I jump to conclusions?" She rose from the couch, and taking off her negligée, proceeded with her dressing. Her fingers trembled, and the long hair swept into her eyes making them start with moisture. So she told herself.

She was buttoning the tight velvet bodice of her day costume when she felt his hands slide under her breasts and heard his voice in her ear. "We've both quick tempers but they cool as easily. Turn round and kiss me properly, like a wife."

She went on with her task.

"Mia, do you hear me?"

"I will not be ordered."

"I don't order, I implore. Dearest Mia, you know I can't bear to be out of favour with you. Don't you see it's better to go back so that I can spur on the workmen? I can do it much more effectively than Sarah, and with you at my side you can advise me as to where this door should go, and how that floor should be laid . . . just think of it." She felt his mouth on her neck. "We'll plan our home together." She still stood straight, but felt the disappointment drain away. She had wished fervently to see Italy, but there would be other times . . . "Besides," now his voice was without cajolery, "there's also a serious reason for returning. You know as well as I do that rumour says war is inevitable soon. England and France will unite to defend the Ottoman Empire, of that I'm convinced. I think we should be well-advised to be in our own country before it happens."

She whirled round and her arms went up round his neck. "Dearest, dearest Conway, you're right, of course. How glad I am that you won't be called upon to fight!"

"I hate the Army and all it stands for, the poor wretches of soldiers, the proud nincompoops who are officers. No, thank God I'm not a member of any regiment. Should you ever lose me, which God forbid, it won't be by my being shipped off to the Crimea."

A chill went through her heart for a second, and then she chided herself. Why should she want heroics from him? Were there still the remnants of a silly girl in her after a month of marriage? "Papa agrees with you that it's a stupid affair, but yes, my darling, we should go home. Will . . . will Sarah mind not joining us at Well Farm when it's ready?"

"No." His voice was distant. "No, I don't think so."

"You've told her, of course, that it would be better for her to remain at Well House?"

"Of course." His voice was impatient.

"Although I'm sure such a personable young lady with such an attractive fortune will soon be married."

"She'll never marry." His voice was bleak, and then as he looked at her his eyes softened, as did his voice. "How beautiful you are, my darling. You've a radiance which blinds me. Have I told you today that I love you?"

"Yes," she said, "but you may tell me again."

That night, since it was their last night, they went to the Opera. The Emperor and the Empress were in the Royal box, and with the aid of glasses Mia was able to drink her fill of Eugenie, radiant in white and sparkling with diamonds. How lovely the angle of her head was, how beautifully set were her shoulders rising milk-white from the low decolléte, how endearing her slightly diffident air as she acknowledged the homage of the audience. Mia was enchanted. She would be able to tell Mama and Hannah about this fairy-tale vision, and congratulate

69

Papa on the likenesses he had achieved on his pink Commemoration Plate.

She was deeply, happily in love, and driving through the dark Parisian streets to their rooms she held Conway's arm tightly, unable to speak for joy. In bed she said to him. "This has been the happiest evening of my life. And the crowning joy was to see the Empress. How beautiful she was!"

"But not so beautiful as you are. I feel very proud." She could feel his eager body beside hers, but she delayed him for the pleasure of the delay.

"Proud? I don't understand."

"Proud that I share a similar taste in women as the Emperor." His hands searched the secret places of her delight.

Chapter Six

They arrived at Hessleton one murky evening in early February after a miserable three-hour crossing from Calais to Dover when Mia was unromantically sick, and then by a slow, dirty train which deposited them at Liverpool. They had left Paris before they could acquaint anyone at home by letter, and since there was no carriage to meet them they were obliged to travel in a post chaise for the last thirty miles.

"Do let's call first at Papa and Mama's," Mia said, "and let them know of our arrival. Robert could then drive us to Well House, or I'm sure we could stay the night. There will be so much to tell." She was bright-eyed again although weary. She anticipated the welcome she would receive, the excited questionings of Hannah, the envy of her Parisian wardrobe. It would be fun speaking to Mama as one married woman to another.

"Only for a moment, then, sweetheart. You have had a wearisome journey and it will be good to be back in our home to rest." She reflected that Well House would never be her home. For her it had an unwelcoming aspect. She closed her mind against the reason for this.

Mrs Gossop opened the door and stood back in amazement. "Miss Mia! I mean, Mrs Graham! I mean ma'am!" She bobbed in confusion to Conway. "But you weren't expected yet!"

"Well, may we come in all the same?" Mia laughed. "Come along, Conway."

"Yes, ma'am. 'Evening, sir." Mrs Gossop stood aside to

let them enter and almost collided with Hannah who flew into Mia's arms. "I *thought* it was your voice! Mia, what a surprise! Why didn't you acquaint us of your homecoming? You said in your last letter you'd be going on to Italy."

"No, pet, it was too cold." She released herself, laughing because she knew there were tears in her eyes. "Say how-do-you-do to your brother-in-law."

"How-do-you-do, Conway," Hannah said, suddenly shy, "I trust you enjoyed yourself."

"Tolerably, dear Hannah. May I kiss you?"

Hannah proffered a flushed cheek, and drew herself away almost immediately. "Oh, come in, come in! Papa and Mama will be delighted to see you! We've talked about you so much. Only a few days ago we had Sarah here for dinner and we compared letters."

"How was she?" Conway asked.

"I think quite well. She was pale, but then that's her normal colour, isn't it? And she brought some drawings which impressed Papa greatly." All the time she was talking they were going along the narrow hall towards Joseph's study. "I know Papa retired here after dinner." She looked up on hearing the swish of skirts. "Oh, Mama, isn't this a wonderful surprise!" Marie-Hélène had appeared at the top of the curved staircase.

"Mia! Mr Graham!" She put her hands in the air. "*Quel surprise!*" She bustled downstairs, her skirts swaying round her and even overflowing between the carved rails. "My dears!" She kissed Mia warmly, then Conway, then examined her daughter at arm's length, a motherly look. "Are you all right, my dearest? You look pale."

"Perfectly, except that I was sick on the Channel crossing. No, don't look alarmed, dearest Mama. I ate too many shell-fish at Calais, that was all. We decided not to go to Italy, that's why we're home so soon. How do you like my costume?" She whirled around, showing off the pink satin lining of her fine grey wool coat.

"French grey!" Marie-Hélène was ecstatic. "It positively

shrieks Paris. Rue St Honoré, I should think. How elegant you look, my darling. Wasn't I right? Isn't it true there's only one city in the world?"

"We thought so, ma'am." Conway smiled at her.

"You must say 'Mama' now as well, and I shall learn to say Conway. Have you taken care of my little girl? Of course it's not her first visit, but a honeymoon is different."

"Rather she has taken care of me . . ."

"Oh, Papa!" Mia ran to greet Joseph who had appeared at the door of his study.

"I thought there was only one bell-like voice like that in the world, my Mia's." He took her in his arms then held her away to look at her fondly. "But you've returned sooner than we expected! There's nothing wrong . . .?"

"I shall begin to think you're all disappointed I returned at all. I should have liked to see Italy, but Conway had business to attend to."

"Quite so." Joseph released her and held out his hand. "How are you, my boy? Women don't understand business, do they?"

"Not only that, but the political situation, sir."

"Yes, it looms more and more heavily on the horizon every day."

"Come along to the drawing-room," Marie-Hélène said. "Why do we all crowd into this narrow hall? Come, my darling." She put her arm round Mia's shoulders and gave her a feminine look, the merest lift of her eyebrows. Mia nodded and whispered under cover of the voices round them. "Oh, Mama, I'm so happy . . ."

"Have you eaten?" she asked when they had all taken chairs. "I'll ring for Mrs Gossop to bring some refreshments. We allowed Lucy to go to see her parents tonight."

"We had an excellent dinner at Liverpool, Mama," Conway said. "We only wished to pay our respects and to ask if you might do us the honour of being our first guests for dinner in a day or two. Mia wishes to show off her prowess in planning a French menu."

73

"He speaks nicely in order that you'll let us have your carriage, Papa," Mia laughed.

"But won't you stay the night?" Marie-Hélène said. "It's dark and miserable outside."

"Oh, do stay!" Hannah added her persuasions. "You've so much to tell me, Mia, and I can sit on your bed and drink it all in about wicked, delectable Paris."

"Mia is a married lady now, don't forget," Joseph said.

"I would willingly permit Hannah to sit on *our* bed." Conway smiled at her, "but truly, I felt we should rest better if we knew we had completed the last part of our journey."

"I understand." Joseph got up. "You'd like Robert to get the horses ready?"

"If you'd be so kind."

"Very well." He rang the bell and Mrs Gossop appeared. She had a flustered air.

"Tell Robert to bring the carriage to the front door, if you please."

"Very well, sir." She hesitated, looked towards Mia.

"What is it, Mrs Gossop?" Joseph asked.

"Beg pardon, sir, but I gave Miss Mia, I mean, Mrs Graham a poor welcome at the door. It was the surprise, you see . . ."

"You musn't worry about that, dear Mrs Gossop," Mia said. "I quite understand. Would you like to see my new Paris costume since you're here?" She got up and whirled round on tiptoe so that the pink-lined skirt flew around her.

"My, my!" Mrs Gossop shook her head in disbelief. "A vision, a vision of delight! My word, that will set Hesselton by the heels, I daresay!"

"When you've done eulogising, Mrs Gossop, do you think you could find the strength to make your way to the stables and do as I asked? Tell Robert I should like him to drive Mr and Mrs Graham to Well House."

"Certainly, sir, right away, sir." She shook her head at Mia as if it was all too much for her and went out.

"You must excuse an old servant's interest," Joseph said. "'She walks in beauty like the night,' seems to be Mrs Gossop's sentiments."

"Ah, Byron!" Conway smiled at his father-in-law. "He could well have been thinking of Mia."

"You'll make me feel quite silly with all this flattery," Mia said. "Let me tell you, Hannah, that I saw the Empress Eugenie at the Opera. Now, *there* was magnificence!"

"Oh, Mia, tell me every little detail, please, I beg you." Hannah came and sat beside her sister, putting an arm round her.

"Aren't they pretty together?" Marie-Hélène said to Conway. "My little one has missed her sister sorely, but *c'est la vie*. You'll have to take good care of Mia for us."

"I'll try." He didn't smile. His eyes seemed to cloud.

"It's obvious you've made her happy," Joseph said. "She glows with happiness. Now, my boy, while we wait for Robert, a glass of wine and perhaps you could tell me briefly what was the political climate in Paris?"

"He says briefly!" Marie-Hélène raised her eyebrows. "I shall go and sit with my daughters. There will be plenty of time."

The house stood, a dark bulk against the belt of trees, so dark that it was difficult to distinguish its shape except for the grey-slated cupola with the weather-vane which indicated its height. There were no lights in any of the windows.

"What time is it, Conway?" Mia asked. Her voice trembled, and she thought, yes, I'm tired.

He took his watch from his fob pocket, peered at its face. "Ten-thirty. Sarah doesn't go to bed early as a rule."

"Where is her bedroom?"

"Above the front door." Mia looked upwards. It, too, was in darkness.

Robert brought the horses to a halt and jumped to the ground to assist Mia down the steps. "Careful, Miss Mia . . . I mean, ma'am." His round face seen in the lamp which he held aloft was admiring, comely. She remembered Lucy's alacrity in running to the stables if asked. They'd make a nice young couple . . .

"I've only hand luggage, Robert. We've left the bulk of it at Liverpool to be brought by carrier."

"Yes, Miss Mia, I mean, ma'am. Follow me, if you please," and to Conway, "There don't appear to be anyone at home, sir."

"No matter. I've a key. Kindly shine your lamp on that flight of steps, if you will. We don't want madam to trip, do we?"

"No indeed, sir." Robert held the lamp even higher and Mia went up slowly. Yes, she must be tired, else why the weighted limbs?

Conway had found his key and was inserting it in the lock of the massive front door. "That will be all, Robert." He turned and pressed a coin in the boy's hand.

"There's no need, sir." He sounded embarrassed. "It's Miss Mia, you see, I mean, madam . . ."

"Precisely. Good night and thank you." He pushed open the door and the hall stretched in front of them, dark, seemingly endless, with a faint musty smell as if it was unaired.

Mia's heart felt weighted, like her limbs, an unaccountable heaviness of spirit. She laughed to dispel it. "Conway, where are you?"

"Here, my dearest, ahead of you. Don't move. I know exactly where the lamp stands, and I'll have it lit in no time." Almost as he spoke an opaque white moon sprang into being beneath his face, lighting it in a grotesque fashion so that the cheeks looked gaunt, the nostrils huge and the eyes seeming to glitter under the pale brow.

"Conway!"

"What is it?"

"Nothing, it's all right now. For a second you looked . . . odd, before you adjusted the lamp." She made herself walk towards him, put her hand in his. "I don't want to lose you."

"Afraid?"

"No, it's . . . unfamiliar. Where do you think Sarah is?"

He shook his head. "The Frames must be in bed otherwise they'd have heard us. They have their own quarters in the stable block. Perhaps Sarah has gone to bed too. We'll go into the drawing-room."

"We should have remained in Hessleton." Unease made her voice sharp. "Now that I come to think of it, our bed won't be aired and the bedroom cold."

"No it won't." He was opening the drawing-room door as he spoke. "I left instructions for it to be aired and fired every day. I know how to take care of a new wife." He put his arm round her and together they entered the room.

By the glow of the dwindling fire she could see the dim shapes of furniture she remembered, the back-to-back settees, the gilt on the over-elaborate pelmets, the pale gleam of the imprisoned wax fruit, and it incurred in her a miserable kind of response, a combination of aesthetic dislike and alienation which she tried to cover by talking brightly. "Well, it's warm in here at any rate, darling, but don't let's bother to sit down. Quite suddenly I'm most terribly tired, and that cosy bedroom you spoke about sounds like paradise to me . . ."

There was a sound in the room, a rustle, and she jumped nervously, clinging to Conway. "What . . .?"

"It is I, Sarah." The voice was calm, so deep that its overtones seemed to ring in Mia's ears.

"Sarah!" She looked towards the fireplace and saw the hunched figure of the girl slowly straighten up from the chair where she had been resting, and stand in the dull glow. She appeared taller than Mia remembered, more slender, and her head was back as if the weight of the heavy hair dragged at it. "What a start you gave me! Do you often sit in the darkness?"

"Conway knows I do. Did you have a good journey?" She came towards them, and instead of greeting Mia first, put her arms round her brother's shoulders and kissed him.

"Very fair," he said. "But you haven't greeted your sister-in-law."

"No, I haven't." She turned to Mia. "Am I allowed to kiss you?"

"You know you are. We're sisters-in-law, aren't we?"

"Yes, we're sisters-in-law . . ." She felt the girl's cold lips not on her cheek but on her mouth, remain there for a second, and then heard Conway's impatient voice. "For goodness sake! Let's have some light, Sarah. This is a bad habit of yours. We can't go on talking to each other in the dark. And Mia would like something to drink, a tisane, perhaps. She's had a long and tiring journey."

"There's no need." Mia yawned exaggeratedly. "I couldn't keep my eyes open until it came. We're sorry to surprise you like this, but my parents wished us to stay at Blenheim Terrace. Conway would have none of it."

"Conway would have none of it," Sarah repeated. Mia watched her raise her eyes to her brother, head tilted back so that her hair swung at her waist. "You must take your wife to bed, then, Conway, since she's worn out. The room's quite warm, as you requested."

"Come along, Mia." Conway put his arm round her waist. "You're sleeping on your feet with tiredness. And you get to bed too, Sarah. We'll talk about things tomorrow."

"Whatever you say, Conway." As they walked to the door Mia felt the girl's eyes on them, making her feel uncomfortable, unwanted, homesick.

She had discovered on her honeymoon night that she had married a passionate man, but even more to her surprise that she could match his passion with her own. "It's your

French blood," he'd teased her. "No English miss would be as loving as you. Their Mamas give them lessons in decorum."

But in the large bedroom with the oriel windows above the drawing-room, warm with the remains of a huge fire, warmly sheeted, she felt cold. "What is it, love?" he said, getting up on one elbow to look down at her.

"I'm tired. It's been a long day."

"Am I too demanding?"

"No ..." She shook her head and turned her face away.

"Have you, then, fallen out of love with me so soon? In Paris you were amorous."

"I'm still in love with you," her voice was muffled, "but tonight, I told you, I'm tired. Besides ..."

He turned her back in his arms to face him. "Besides, what?"

"I don't like it here." She felt like a petulant child.

"In this room?"

"In this house. I felt like an interloper downstairs."

"Because of Sarah?"

"Yes." She looked at him, seeing the dark eyes which could make her weak with delight.

"Look, my love, I know how you must feel. She's difficult, but try to like her. You could do her so much good with your happy nature. She's unhappy often. You see, she depends on me in so many ways. I've helped her to live when she felt like dying because ... because I owe it to her."

"What do you mean, you *owe* it to her? I love Hannah, but there's no question of debt."

"Hannah's a normal girl, light of heart. Sarah isn't. You'll see, tomorrow she'll be friendly. You're tired tonight. Things always look black when you're tired. I'm despicable, unthoughtful, forcing myself on you. Go to sleep, my dearest wife. I shall hold you in my arms, like this, and lay your head on the pillow. Sleep ... sleep ..."

79

But slowly, insidiously, through the tiredness, the urgency came again, and they quickened and sighed together, sighed and groaned together, and she loved him, loved him, until they lay quiet once more.

Long after he breathed deeply beside her, Mia lay awake with the same unease in her heart now that the fever had died. Sarah hadn't been surprised when they walked into the drawing-room. She could understand the comfort of the bedroom, hadn't Conway said he had left instructions for it to be aired and fired, but not the fact that the warming-pan had obviously been freshly-filled in the large double bed with the tester and curtains of gold brocade. She had almost burned her hand when she had lifted it out.

She sat up suddenly, thinking she heard a creak of boards outside the room, like a footfall. The blood rushed to her cheeks, such an unusual symptom in her that she felt faint for a moment. You're tired, she told herself, your brain is addled with the long journey and the excitement of coming home, and coming here, to Well House.

She lay down, wishing she was a child again with Hannah in the high attic schoolroom amongst the branches of the elms. Her own home was free, open, airy, but this one had dark corridors and staircases as if built for intrigue. Her last waking thought was the memory of Sarah's cold lips on hers.

Chapter Seven

Mia had her mother's French briskness, an ability to tackle what lay nearest to hand and to push doubts and indecisiveness to the back of her mind. The next morning she bathed in the hip bath provided by a young maid whom she hadn't seen before, brushed her hair at the ornate toilet-table until it shone, and donned again her travelling costume of grey since it was the only garment she possessed at that moment.

She crossed the room and bent over Conway, still asleep in the four-poster, his frilled white shirt open, sleeves pushed up above his elbows, thick hair disarranged. She studied his face, the pale wells of the eyelids, the thin contour of the cheeks hollowed beneath the bones, the cleft at the tip of the strong nose, the full mouth. Not a common face.

Her parents, after taking a conventional stand against an early marriage had been complaisant, and she had put it down to their comparative freedom from the restraints of the time. Their love and their desire for her happiness she never questioned. But had there, all the same, been a small pleasure at the thought of her moving up the social scale? Her father made no pretence that he belonged to the new middle-class, as he put it, nor did he hide the fact that his father, as a boy, had lived in Tumbrill Street. Her mother came from tradesman stock.

Not a common face, she thought with love. The lines of breeding were there to see, the long fingers, the slender but strong neck. In a wave of emotion she stooped and kissed the hollow there. He stirred and opened his eyes, caught her with one hand as she drew back and pulled her down to kiss her lips.

"Good morning, my darling lazy-bones," she said, freeing herself. "I'm bathed and dressed. Come along! It looks brisk and clear and there are a million things to be done."

"Such as?" He swept aside the clothes and got out of bed. "Come here." His unbuttoned shirt showed his chest, his legs were bare and strong-looking.

"No, no." She retreated laughing. "I intend to go downstairs and look round the grounds, so kindly join me in fifteen minutes. It's eight o'clock and I'm quite sure breakfast will be served."

"You intend to rule me, Madam?" He gave in, smiling, pulling on a robe.

"No, only gently push you in the direction I wish to go. I thought you might apply yourself today to the problem of the reparations."

"Yes, I must." He turned into his dressing-room. "I gave my valet, Parker, a holiday to coincide with ours, so I must fend for myself."

"Then why isn't he back?" The door shut behind him. He hadn't heard her, or had pretended not to hear her.

But this was a new day, she told herself, not to be started with doubts. She ran downstairs without meeting anyone and into the wide gravelled carriage-space at the front of the house, seeing the smooth semi-circle of park skirted by the wall, the iron gates. How strange, she thought, that here is where I first saw Conway walking when I was with Hannah, and now I'm doing the same. The image was strong in her mind, the green sweep of lawn, the stooped figure, like a picture caught in a frame. Now, she was in the frame, not Conway. There's an unreality here, as if I'm a prisoner, as if freedom lay beyond the gates . . .

She followed the broad drive running round the house until she reached the courtyard at the back. Here she saw Frame sitting in the thin sunshine at the door of the stables, horse brasses spread across his knees, cloth in hand. When she drew nearer she greeted him cheerfully. "Good morning, Frame."

He raised his head, said unsmilingly, "Good morning, miss," and lowered it again, applying himself to his task. Either the mode of address was an oversight or a deliberate refusal to recognise her status. But her optimism was firm. If the Frames were surly, there were still the fresh-faced maid and the valet, Parker, whom she had still to meet.

She returned to the front of the house and entered by the panelled door which stood open, meeting the young maid at the back of the hall bearing a silver tray laden with covered dishes. She smiled over her shoulder at Mia and stood aside.

"You go on," Mia said, "I'll follow you." She had no idea where the dining-room lay. "It's a pleasant morning."

"Yes, it is that, ma'am, for the time of the year."

"What's your name?"

"Ruth, ma'am, Ruth Bastow."

"Do you come from Hessleton?"

"No, ma'am, Corby Mill. I only get home once a month." She stood aside at a door. "After you, ma'am." They had evidently reached the dining-room.

Mia entered. It was panelled and hung with portraits, but the flat windows in rows of three on two sides of the room made it bright, and the table-cloth and silver were immaculate. Sarah was seated at the table.

"Good morning, Mia," she said. Her voice was cool and friendly. "You found your way?"

"Yes. Good morning, Sarah." She hesitated, then went to her sister-in-law and kissed her cheek. "You're early. Is this your usual time for breakfast?"

"Yes, but in any case Frame drives me to Hessleton today to the potworks. Your father is most accommodating. He's made our arrangement quite elastic."

"Papa's like that. Where may I sit?"

"You must please yourself. We don't go in for formality here. Sometimes we breakfast in bed."

"All that must be stopped now that I'm here." She said it playfully, as she unfolded her napkin, but as she looked up she saw Sarah's heavy eyelids lift and drop. "I only joke. I was teasing Conway this morning about being a lazy-bones, but he was tired. We'd had a long day."

Conway came into the room in a cut-away coat of blue cloth with brass buttons. He went straight to his sister and kissed her. "Good morning. Did you sleep well?"

"Yes." She touched his sleeve lightly. "You look well-turned out today, not at all your usual attire." Her voice had deepened.

"It's Mia's choice, a wedding present bought for me in Paris. I wish to make a good impression on the workmen." He smiled. "They've been very slack while I've been gone."

"I told you the weather was inclement."

"Quite." He walked towards the sideboard, saying to Mia as he passed her. "Your cover's empty. Come and help yourself."

She got up and joined him. "I don't think I've much appetite. My stomach still churns a little after the crossing."

"Then you must rest and take it quietly for today." He helped himself to kidneys and crisp bacon.

"Oh, Conway darling! You musn't treat me like a baby." He turned to look at her and their eyes clung as they laughed.

"Dearest . . ." His eyes spoke of last night.

"Perhaps you two would sit down." It was Sarah's voice, deep and cold as a well. "It's disconcerting not to be included in the conversation."

"It was so trivial you wouldn't have wished to be included." Mia took her place again. "But Conway must learn I'm not to be ordered about. Papa always said it was useless to try so I'll save him the trouble by making it quite clear." She spoke lightly, smiling at Conway as he sat down but his head was bent to his plate. "When do you leave for Hessleton, Sarah?"

The girl looked at the grandfather clock near the door. "In half-an-hour."

"And return?"

"In time for lunch."

"I shall join you in the carriage, if I may. I haven't a stitch to wear since we await the carriers with our luggage so I must go to Blenheim Terrace and bring a few dresses back with me until it arrives." She turned to Conway. "How long will you be with your workmen, dearest?"

"All morning, I expect, and hope."

"I'm glad of that." She met Sarah's eyes. "This is purely a temporary residence for us, as you know. It's good of you to allow your routine to be upset."

"It's Conway's house, not mine."

"Nevertheless, I shouldn't like to intrude. There's another matter which we might discuss while we're together."

"What is that?" Sarah's face was calm, expressionless.

"It was a suggestion of Conway's, in fact. Conway . . .?" He looked up at her, fork in hand, dark eyes inscrutable. "Do you remember you said we should invite Mama and Papa and Hannah as our first guests?"

"Did I say that?"

"You know you did. I've been thinking . . . shall we have a little evening, just a few people? I thought my parents and Hannah, Dr Compson and Harry, and then, whom shall we have for you, Sarah?"

She ignored the question, said flatly. "We don't entertain."

"Come, Sarah," Conway smiled at her. "You know Dr Compson well."

"Too well."

"Do you feel it's not *de rigeur* to entertain him?" Mia asked.

Sarah shrugged. "Do as you wish." She seemed to have lost interest.

"Well, I must find a personable young man." Mia smiled at her. "Let me see." She pretended to cogitate. "I know!

We'll invite Judas Ashworth. He's just right, quite genteel. Thomas Hyde, I'm told, is now affianced, and John Wyatt is altogether too shallow for your taste."

"Pray don't make plans for me."

"But we must make the numbers balance, my dear."

Sarah turned to her brother. "Do you agree with this evening, Conway?"

"Apparently it was my suggestion." They both looked past Mia at each other.

"Well, now we shall have to fix the day." Mia heard her own voice, hard and bright. "It must be at least two weeks hence, of course, but no matter, since I have some ravishing gowns in my luggage and it should have arrived by then."

"There's one for you too," Conway said to Sarah.

"His choice, not mine." Mia smiled at the girl. "Not at all decollété, although I'm sure you could wear that style to perfection, and with long, fur-trimmed sleeves. However, it's elegant, I give you that."

There was a pause, then Mia heard Sarah's voice, half-whispered, vehement, but addressed to her brother. "I told you not to buy anything for me."

"It's a *fait accompli*." He was calm, almost insolent as he turned to Mia. "Perhaps you'll consult with Sarah as to the menu nearer the time. Mrs Frame is more used to her."

"But certainly." She waved her hands in a manner reminiscent of Marie-Hélène. "I wouldn't dream of usurping Sarah's place."

The girl shrugged. "Housekeeping wearies me. We'll talk about it later."

"Thank you, Sarah." Mia lifted her coffee-cup. "Have I time to drink this? I'm a woman of leisure. I shouldn't like to detain you."

"You still have five minutes." She spoke shortly, turning to her brother. "You'll have trouble with those men. I don't think they approve of your ideas."

"Well, if they don't they must be replaced. In the

86

afternoon, Mia, you must come with me and see the farm again."

"Yes, I'd like to." She got up, smiling at Sarah who was now standing at her chair. "Suddenly the day seems very full. I'm ready, if you are. I'll just ring for Ruth to fetch my cloak."

The maid's ready smile when she came made Mia wonder if Ruth was her only conquest that morning.

Chapter Eight

Not even Sarah's remoteness in the carriage on the way back could dull the excitement at the success of her first foray to Hessleton as a married woman.

Marie-Hélène and Hannah were at home and were delighted to see her. They sat in the drawing-room chatting about Paris until Marie-Hélène declared herself quite homesick with the thought of it. "Such elegance! There's no place quite like it. The urbanity! When the scales fall from your eyes a little you must return. A honeymoon is the wrong time to visit cities of culture."

"Are you very much in love?" Hannah asked, eager-eyed.

"Don't ask personal questions, pet." Mia smiled conspiratorially at her mother.

Hannah sighed. "I should like above all things to feel this passion. It's like a grown-up book which one is not allowed to read. Harry Compson would be eminently suitable for me, not perhaps in the same class as Conway, but a good match. But I feel *nothing* when he comes near me, whereas, well I've watched you, Mia. You positively tremble."

"Oh, nonsense!" But it was true.

They asked how Sarah was.

"Very well this morning when I breakfasted with her, but I screwed up my courage and told her we should be moving into Well Farm as soon as it was ready." Her mother nodded her approval. "To tell you the truth," she looked at Marie-Hélène, "whether it was Well House or anywhere else, I couldn't live for long in the same house as Sarah."

"Don't you like her?"

"It's not a question of that, Mama, she doesn't like *me*. And, naturally, between a brother and sister who've lived so long together there's a bond. I wouldn't mind that, of course, but Conway changes in some inexplicable way . . ." She suddenly saw with new-found wisdom that she was wrong to discuss her sister-in-law. "Pay no attention to my remarks," she said lightly. "I've not quite recovered from our tedious journey home. Perhaps I imagine it."

"Perhaps." Marie-Hélène's eyes were astute. "I should advise patience. She would be the wrong person to have as an enemy. But prevail upon Conway to provide you with a home of your own as soon as possible."

After that they sallied forth into the town driven by Robert and made a triumphal tour of the shops, to Cantilever and Miss Dearden to see how the Spring costumes were progressing, to the printers to order new notepaper for Mia, to Mr Creasey for some madeira which Marie-Hélène insisted on sending as a housewarming gift to Conway. And they agreed to reserve the date Mia had chosen for her evening.

When the carriage called at Blenheim Terrace with Sarah in it, she felt reluctant to leave home, but the thought of Conway waiting for her at the other end gave her impetus. She had only to think of him for her heart to race. Hadn't Hannah noticed it?

The two girls went into luncheon immediately. There was no sign of him but a note lay at Mia's cover. She tore it open quickly and read it.

'I'm truly sorry, my love, but I've been obliged to ride to Galton where the foreman resides. He didn't appear this morning and the workmen were disgruntled. I think a personal confrontation is the best way to settle the matter. Proceed with luncheon without me, if you please. I shall be back before dark. Your loving and devoted husband, Conway.'

Instant dismay seized her. She would have to spend the

whole afternoon without him. She could feel Sarah's eyes on her, the waiting quality of her silence. "Not bad news, I hope?"

She mustered a smile. "No, no. Simply that Conway has had to ride to Galton to confront the foreman. He may not be back until late this afternoon."

"So you won't be able to visit Well Farm with him?" She smiled, but there was a cold gleam in her heavy-lidded eyes.

"No matter." Mia spoke cheerfully. "I've a hundred things to do. My hair needs washing, and perhaps I could borrow Ruth to help me, also I've invitations to write for the evening we discussed. I've decided on the third of March. I hope that will suit you." And then something made her add. "Our luggage will surely have arrived by that time, and you may wish to wear the new dress Conway chose for you." There was no doubt about Sarah's glance now. It was definitely hostile.

"Do I gather from your tone it would not have been *your* choice?"

"Not at all. It's quite charming. Sapphire blue velvet and expertly cut, but for me, well, if a girl has pretty shoulders and arms, why not show them? So Mama says, but perhaps being a Parisian she has encouraged Hannah and I to take an interest in fashion, not to follow it slavishly, of course, but to enjoy it as one of the many smaller pleasures of life."

"I don't place the same importance on it."

Something in the girl's voice made Mia's heart suddenly fill with pity. Sarah had had no mother to guide her when she needed her, to tell her how pretty she looked. Perhaps if she could swallow her unease in the girl's presence she could take that place, or at least that of a sister, such as she occupied with Hannah . . . "I tell you what, Sarah. Since we've the afternoon to ourselves, I've a scheme which may appeal to you. Shall we try one of my dresses on you which I brought from Blenheim Terrace? There's a sweetly pretty pink taffeta which would go well with your dark hair, rather daring, but with your figure . . ." It had been a mistake. The cold gleam was there again.

"No, thank you. I should consider that a stupid waste of time. I intend to go out this afternoon to do some sketching. You must amuse yourself . . . but not at my expense."

"I didn't mean—"

"No more, if you please."

"Very well." The silence of the room almost stifled her. She sat toying with her fork until Ruth came in, when she helped herself with a poor appetite to the dishes which were handed to her. The rest of the day stretched ahead of her, unending, unhappily. What a pity she couldn't take solace in sewing as Hannah and Mama did on quiet afternoons. She had joined them often, simply because she enjoyed to chatter, and if her mother chided her gently, she might produce a purse which she had been netting for a twelve-month and net a few more rounds.

But as she chewed miserably, again her natural good spirits came to her aid. She'd go into Conway's study and write her invitations in her best hand, then she would browse through his books. Afterwards she'd ask Ruth if she would assist her in washing her hair. That accomplished, there would be the joy of chosing one of her prettiest crinolines for his return.

She looked up. "You won't mind if I use Conway's library, Sarah?"

"It's Conway's house. It isn't necessary to ask my permission before you make every move."

"Thank you. I shall remember that." She bit her lip as she bent to her plate once more. I'm unfortunate, or perhaps fortunate, that I've never known hostility in my life, she thought. That must be why it comes as a shock to me. I've never known families who lived in discord. Perhaps I've been too happy . . . but she reminded herself that at the end of the day she'd see Conway, and she raised her head and chatted on innocuous topics until luncheon should be over. Marie-Hélène had seen to her training there, and her natural friendliness aided her.

She was in their bedroom putting the finishing touches to her toilette when Conway appeared. His face was dark with anger, and she pretended not to notice.

"I'm wearing the jade earrings you bought for me in Paris, dearest. Don't you think they're pretty with my newly-washed hair?" Without replying he took her in his arms so roughly that she protested. "I've spent *hours* arranging it, helped by Ruth! Be careful." His mouth came down on hers so brutally that she was alarmed. She struggled to free herself. "What's wrong? You're dishevelled. Were you thrown?"

"No, I wasn't thrown." He released her and flung himself down on the bed, half-reclining on his elbow. "The foreman has taken another job at Merestead Manor, his wife told me. I've spent all day trying to find a replacement without success."

"But why should he do that when you had engaged him and instructed him to proceed with the work in your absence?"

He smacked his hand angrily against one booted leg. "Why indeed?"

She crossed the room to the bed and stood in front of him. "Conway, why should he do that? You told me he was a most reliable man. That you trusted him implicitly." A dull fear seized her like a hand on her heart, twisting it cruelly. "Did he think he was free of his commitment with you? Did his wife say so?"

He didn't look up at her, but when she suddenly shouted, "Conway! Please answer me. Did he?" he nodded, head bent, and she saw the dark flush on his neck and how the cords stood out. His right hand, which had been smacking his boot, was clenched on the coverlet.

She went away from him and sat down again at the toilet-table, looking in the glass at her face which seemed strange to her, as if some of her youth had gone. "I

92

don't understand," she said after a long time. "I don't understand why . . . Sarah doesn't like me. And yet I feel it's not personally directed towards me, Mia Winter, I mean, Mia Graham. That's it! It would be directed against anyone to whom you gave your name. She doesn't want me here." Her voice rose. "She doesn't want you to leave her!"

He looked at her, face still dark with anger. "You're being hysterical. Kindly lower your voice!" His was far from low. She sat stunned for what seemed an unconscionable time. Outside the branches whispered against each other, she remembered their dense blackness . . . like the blackness in the room between them.

At last he got up, and without speaking came and knelt beside her, putting his head on her lap. It was such an uncharacteristic action for him, who was generally so demanding, that she was touched. Pity drove away her anger, and the memory of his. She said, half-laughing, half-crying, "Oh, get up at once, my darling. We're both overwrought. We'll say no more about it. Papa says a period of adjustment is inevitable in every marriage. This must be it." She thought of her father's words when she had left on her honeymoon. "Remember it won't be roses all the way when you come back. That's why we go on honeymoons, to start off with them."

"I apologise for losing my temper." He kissed her on the cheek and got to his feet. "I'm dishevelled and dirty with riding all that distance. And no doubt weary. I saw Parker when I took the horse to the stables. Thank God he's back. I told him to come up. Now, tell me what you did this afternoon." Don't humour me, she thought.

"I wrote my invitations for our evening, in the library, and I looked at some of your books. I had no idea you were interested in natural history." She strove hard to appear normal, but there was a dull ache in her heart.

"Natural history with an end to it."

"Those I looked at were by Charles Darwin. Papa has talked about him to me."

"Like your father I'm interested in the struggle for existence in which the fittest survive. You and I are strong. But there are those . . ." his voice faltered and when she met his eyes she saw pain in them, "those . . . who, through no fault of their own . . ." There was a knock at the door. "Come in!" he called. And then, "Ah, Parker, it's you. I need your assistance." The young man who entered had the blank expression of the well-trained servant. And yet he looked strong and burly, as if he could well work manually with no ill-effect.

"This is your mistress, Parker," Conway said. The man bowed, face empty except that there was a flicker of interest in his eyes.

"Good-evening," Mia said. And to Conway. "I shall leave you to your valet's ministrations. I've a desire to try out your piano."

"You'll find it in good tone. Sarah plays it often. For myself I've no ability in that direction, but I like to listen to her in the evenings." He smiled at her across the room. "Music soothes the savage breast . . ."

She went downstairs slowly, all pleasure in her evening toilet gone.

The impression which Mia had obtained of Well House on her first evening was substantiated in the weeks that followed. It bore little resemblance to Blenheim Terrace in that it was cluttered, dark and with numerous passages and staircases which seemed to subdivide the house into cells. Sarah had her own suite, reached by a private staircase. The servants' quarters were at the end of a long dark corridor running alongside the courtyard. As well as a library Conway had a study on a half-landing off the main staircase. Either the house had been built for the family, or the family had adapted itself to the house, but certainly it suited them in their desire for privacy.

The intervening time until the date of her 'evening' passed quickly enough, engaged as she was in seeing to

94

her wardrobe, paying calls and leaving cards, mostly on her own friends because Sarah and Conway seemed to have remarkably few. Sarah said that in her opinion card-leaving was one of the dreariest customs of society, and for her part she'd be glad to be rid of it, although she demurred about the wisdom of having Dr Compson and his son as guests. "We've never entertained them," she said shortly.

"But he's of good family, Sarah," Mia protested, "and he and Father have had many splendid discussions."

"You might not be here at all if it weren't for him." Conway spoke as shortly as his sister. When Mia glanced at her she saw that her face was closed and dark-looking, her mouth set in a bitter line.

However, as time went on there seemed to be an easier atmosphere in the household, and Mia began to tell herself she had imagined Sarah's hostility. The latter absented herself a great deal of the time in her own suite of rooms, Conway was busy out of doors and at the farm, and they only came together at meal-times and on Sunday mornings when the three of them were driven by Frame to attend the village church. Mia had been in the habit of teaching at Sunday school in the afternoon, but Conway suggested she might give it up now that she was married. "I think," he said, "we shall all have discharged our social duty if we make one appearance."

She gave into this and in the afternoons generally went out riding with him which was a rare treat for her since Hessleton society would not have countenanced the Misses Winter appearing on horseback on that holy day, even although they had a French mother whom it was difficult to 'place'.

The day for the soiree arrived, and she spent part of the morning consulting with Mrs Frame as to the final details of the meal. Sarah had renounced all interest in connection with it a week previously, saying she was working on some important landscapes for the potworks, and didn't want to be distracted.

In the afternoon Mia read while her maid dressed her hair. Conway had freed Ruth from her ordinary duties and another parlourmaid had been engaged, although on this night Ruth would also assist at the table. Parker, after laying out Conway's evening clothes and preparing his bath, had departed downstairs where he was on duty in the hall to open the door to the guests. It was all heady stuff for a newly-married wife, and as she read and alternately buffed her nails she told herself she was happy.

Certainly there were one or two flies in the amber, in that she had a husband who was passionate by night but reserved during the day, who seemed to exist quite well without her unless they had a pre-arranged meeting, but who seemed to find time to go upstairs to his sister's sanctum to indulge in long conversations. The murmur of their voices could often be heard.

But Mia consoled herself with the thought that they'd soon be in their own home. This house was too large, too segregated, the farm would be comforting and welcoming, a place for married love. Conway had managed to find a new foreman and the work was proceeding well, and Mia, with an intuition which surprised herself, hadn't mentioned again her suspicions about the defection of the first one.

At half-past six she was in the drawing-room in one of her Parisian gowns of pale gold mousseline, cut low, with Chantilly lace on the shoulders and the small puffed sleeves. Her hair was dressed to show her topaz earrings, and she wore gold slippers bought in the Rue de la Paix which emphasised her arched instep.

Conway joined her, having rushed through his dressing, rather impatient now that the evening was upon him, but prepared to humour her. So she gathered by his guarded smile. "You look very beautiful," he said, "but why do you require other people to tell you? Wouldn't I have done?"

"You'd always be enough, but I want people to see us happy together."

The door opened, and Sarah came in, narrow face pale

between the dark loops of her hair. "I wore the dress, Conway." She took no notice of Mia. It fits all right. How does it look?"

"It becomes you."

"It's beautiful, Sarah," Mia said, although she would have preferred more flesh and less blue velvet.

Sarah shrugged. "And now we await the lions to devour us. I'm surprised at you, Conway, allowing yourself to be talked into this kind of charade." She looked coldly at Mia now. "We hardly ever entertained, you know, once or twice a year when it was absolutely necessary, but we had lovely evenings on our own, reading and talking."

"Well, you can talk your fill to the guests," Mia said sharply, "and the reading can be a pleasure deferred."

"Puss, puss," Conway said laughing, as the door opened and Parker announced Joseph and Marie-Hélène, followed by Hannah.

"Oh, come in, come in, darlings!" Mia said, rushing to greet them. "Mama, Papa, it's good of you to come first, and Hannah, dear Hannah," she was almost hysterical with joy. "How wonderful to see you!"

"May I remind you that we all met two days ago when you called on your way to town?" Joseph said. Everyone laughed. "How do you do, Sarah?" He held out his hand. "It's hardly necessary for business associates to greet each other formally. And, Conway, well, this is a great pleasure."

"Dr Compson and Mr Harry Compson," Parker announced. "Mr Judas Ashworth."

"Do come in, all of you!" Mia's greeting was more circumspect this time. "Now my party's complete and we can sit down. But you haven't met my husband, Judas, have you, nor my sister-in-law?"

"No indeed. I look forward to that pleasure." Judas was amiable, a land agent for Lord Trent's estate and very eligible, and since he was always being asked to parties by scheming mamas, he was quite at ease in strange drawing-rooms.

The talk became general. Parker passed round wine and Mia flitted from one to the other of her guests, finally settling beside Dr Compson since Conway was talking to Harry.

"How very nice you could spare the time to come and see us, doctor," she said. "I know you're always so busy."

"But my dear Mia, it's a pleasure to see you, and especially when you look so happy. It would appear marriage suits you."

"Oh, it does. I'm very happy here. Of course you know we hope to move into Well Farm within a month or so? Conway has been working hard on it since we returned from Paris."

"And Miss Sarah stays here?"

"In the meantime. Of course she may marry. She's very personable, don't you think? Or if she feels it too large Conway could perhaps arrange to sell it. He's never liked the place."

"Quite. Since she's a young lady of independent means, and also, I know, designs for your father from time to time, it might be a good idea if she moved to Hessleton."

"It would be an excellent idea." She must have been too fervent for she felt the doctor's eyes on her. Too late she remembered her father's words. "An excellent fellow, the doctor, but perhaps a little too interested in his patients." "Well, Dr Compson," she smiled with conscious charm, "I must pass on and have a word with Judas whom I dote on, although please don't tell him to his face."

"Don't let me detain you. Mia . . ." he hesitated, and she saw the essential kindliness of the man in his eyes, "may I trade on an old friendship, even although it's been established mainly at the bed-side?" He laughed. "Do you remember how each winter you had tonsilitis, and you croaked all your nursery rhymes to me?" His face grew serious. "I should like to say that if at any time you need my . . . advice, I shall be at your service."

"You mean in connection with my health?"

"I mean in connection with the health of anyone in the family."

"Thank you, I'll remember." She was confused, felt happiness slip away from her to be replaced by doubt. "Ah, here comes my husband." She breathed freely again. "He pretends to disdain company and yet there's nothing he likes more than good conversation, isn't that so, Conway?" She smiled at him, and he bowed.

"I must tell you, doctor, that I've married a girl who's clever as well as beautiful, so I've to keep my wits sharp."

"An admirable combination, if I may say so."

"And what does my poor Mia get in return? A rebel whose ideals often reject the conventions of society, who prefers to meet individuals as equals, who prefers to dispense with ritual."

"It sounds to me like an exciting partnership."

The doors opened. Parker appeared between them, properly imbued with the importance of the occasion. "Dinner is served," he announced.

"Did you enjoy my evening, Conway?" Mia asked when they were in bed together. As soon as the last carriage had rolled away Sarah had said a brief good night and gone to her room. "Shall we retire too?" Conway had said immediately, and although she would have preferred an enjoyable hour of post-mortems such as took place at Blenheim Terrace after parties, she had agreed.

"Tolerably well." He was lying on his back, hands clasped behind his head, staring at a fixed spot in the hangings.

"Do you think Sarah enjoyed herself?"

"I expect so."

"Hannah and I used to talk for hours about what people said and what the ladies wore. Oh, what good times we had! How we laughed! Really, it was almost better than the party. Hannah is such a good mimic, and she would strut up and down the room pretending to be holding a lorgnette, well, I shan't tell you who she was aping . . ." she stopped speaking, feeling a kind of melancholy creep over her.

"But now," he said in a low voice, "you find you've put away childish things and you aren't quite sure if you prefer it, if you wouldn't rather be back in the safe cocoon of your happy family with your laughter and your pet jokes and your love . . . is that it?"

"No . . ." She, too, lay on her back, bare feet stretched thankfully under the sheets. The Parisian shoes had pinched a little although she would never admit it. "Didn't *you* have a happy childhood? Haven't you any happy memories? There must have been times in the nursery when you and Sarah played together as Hannah and I did, had secrets, confided in each other, even fought and made it up again. I remember once—"

"Keep quiet!" he said roughly. "I don't wish to hear your reminiscences. You're here with me, married, our life together begins from the day we married, we cut out all that went before, a clean sheet . . ."

"But you can't!" She was half-afraid of his quick change of mood. "Everything that has happened is part of your life. It's you, you can't disown it, good or bad—"

"Stop, stop!" He took her in his arms and the violence of his passion was something she hadn't experienced even on their wedding night. Her silk shift was torn as he wrenched it off her shoulders, his mouth was cruel on her bare breasts. For the first time she took no joy in their love. It left her exhausted and bruised, the usual feeling of peace and fulfilment was missing.

She lay awake when he was quiet beside her, trying to find a word for her distress so that she could understand it. At last it came to her. I've been used, she thought, not loved. It was dawn before she slept.

Chapter Nine

Conway looked up from his newspaper one morning towards the end of March. "Two pieces of news. The bad one first although you may already know it."

"Is it about the war?" Mia asked. "Papa was saying it was imminent the last time I called."

"It's more than imminent. It's happened. Britain and France are preparing to send troops to the Crimea."

"I'm sure it's not for any altruistic reason," Sarah said. One hand was stroking her left temple, a familiar gesture of hers.

"Is it ever? They fear to see Constantinople fall into Russian hands. As for the Anglo-French alliance, Napoleon has been courting us ever since his *coup d'etat*. Although our good Queen was suspicious of anyone bearing such a notorious name."

"How cynical you are, Conway." Mia smiled at him.

"Realistic."

"May we then have the good news to counteract your pessimism?"

"You may." He looked towards Sarah whose head was now bent over the sketch book she invariably brought to the table, then at Mia. "Although far from completed, I've hopes we'll be able to move into Well Farm at the beginning of April."

"Oh, how wonderful! I'm so excited at the prospect! Our own home . . ." She stopped herself enthusing and glanced apprehensively towards Sarah whose head was still bent over her book. "You and I will have a lot to arrange,

Sarah, the disposition of servants, for instance. If you wish to keep one of the parlourmaids I shall be happy, but if possible I should like Ruth to come with me. We suit each other. Parker, of course, will follow Conway, but I'm sure we'll find a cook and a groom. You'll wish the Frames to remain, I know . . ." There was no response and she tried again. "Well Farm will always be open to you, Sarah. I want you to know that. And we're at no great distance. Of course you'll have your own ideas on the matter, and whether in fact you'll stay on at Well House . . ." She watched with sick apprehension as Sarah closed the sketch-book, rose from her chair and left the room, shutting the door firmly behind her. It was an insolent action, and she felt sweat break out on her forehead and in her armpits. I'm not used to this, she thought. She's a neurotic young woman. Anyone who makes me feel like this *must* be. She turned to Conway, holding her temper in check. "Apparently I've said the wrong thing."

"Apparently." His voice was terse.

"Or *you* have."

"What do you mean?" He threw down his newspaper which he was pretending to read.

"The announcement of our intention to leave here is more important to Sarah than the war which has broken out." Perhaps, she thought, but not saying it, she regards it as a declaration of war.

"She's had ample warning of both."

"Conway . . ."

"Yes?" His voice was impatient.

"We *will* go, won't we? It's our life together. She must make her own. Isn't that so?"

"It should be so, to any normal person it would be so, but what if she cannot?"

"Are we to suffer, then? There's no point in three lives being in misery which is what would happen if we remained here."

"You're right, of course." His eyes were troubled. "I'll

102

talk to her. She'll see reason. Don't you worry, my darling."
He got up and kissed her, then left the room also. She saw
that his breakfast was untouched.

He was gone all day, and Sarah left in the carriage for
Hessleton when Mia was in her room. From her window she
saw the tall stick-like figure being helped in by Frame, and
even from there she was struck by the unnatural tenseness
of her attitude, the rigid shoulders, the nervous gestures
of her hands as she spoke to the groom.

She was left with the morning to fill, and on an impulse
she ran downstairs and into the courtyard where she
saw Parker coming from the servants' quarters. It was
opportune.

"Parker!" she called.

"Yes, madam." She saw as he walked towards her the
tilt of the brown curly head, the slight swagger, and thought
that underneath the careful training was a character who
would go his own way when it suited him. He wasn't
servant material.

"Would you saddle my horse, please? Frame has taken
Miss Sarah in the carriage."

"Certainly, ma'am. Be glad to, ma'am."

On an impulse she said. "What do you think of the war,
Parker?"

"Oh, that! We'll soon show the Ruskies a thing or two, us
and the Froggies, begging your pardon, ma'am." Even his
speech seemed to have changed from the careful inflection
he used when waiting on Conway.

"I hope you're right."

"Wouldn't mind taking a crack at them myself!" He
smiled widely at her. "I'll get the horse saddled right away."
She watched him walk towards the stables, noticing again
the swagger and the width of the shoulders. Where had
Conway found him? She must ask him sometime.

She rode through Stonebarrow which was a mere hamlet,
and across the wooden bridge over the stream towards the
piece of country she liked best, field and woodland with a

rolling view towards the south, dotted occasionally with the red roof of a cottage. On the horizon she could see the church spire of Galton where Conway had found his new foreman.

She spurred the horse to a gallop once she was clear of the few houses, feeling her head clear and her depression vanish as the wind tore at the skirt of her long riding-habit. She lifted her face to the thin sunshine. It would be all right, she told herself. Sarah would get used to the idea. Once they were gone she'd settle into her own routine. She was a solitary in any case. She had no need of company.

But does she need her *brother*? she heard a voice say in her head. She shivered, and gathering up the reins she urged the horse to go faster, galloping madly up and down bridle paths and through woods until both were exhausted. Near Galton she came across a wide shallow cup of land, flat at the bottom, the sloping sides making it a natural amphitheatre. Here she rested for a time, letting her horse graze quietly beside her while she lay stretched out on the grass staring at the pale blue lid of the sky.

When she cantered through Stonebarrow again she felt calm but the weight was still there, a recurrence of the sick apprehension she had felt when Sarah rose and left the breakfast table without a word.

She wasn't at the dinner table, although Mia had seen the carriage in the courtyard when she had returned from her ride. When Conway appeared, fresh after his evening bathe, he made no comment until Mia pointed out her absence.

"Have you seen her since you returned?" she asked.

"No. I only got back half-an-hour ago. I've been hiring a stockman as I'll have to go to the cattle market tomorrow. We'll have a dairy herd, and some poultry, more or less for our own use, but most of the land is arable and I shall require a good man to act as overseer. Then there are quite a few cottages on the estate which need repair. One can't live in a refurbished house and have one's workers in hovels. After that there's the lake to see to because we shall have a boat on it and I shall do some fishing, and," he looked at her, his face glowing, eyes tender, "perhaps some day, if we have children, they'll learn to swim."

"It sounds like Utopia." She held out her hand to him across the table. "Shall I make a good farmer's wife, do you think?"

"The best and sweetest." He took her hand and kissed it. "Will you forgive my bad temper? I promise you when we're in our new home you shan't know me." His mouth quirked in a smile. "I'll be a reformed character."

"Don't become too angelic," she said, laughing. "I shouldn't recognise you."

The door opened. Parker entered, accompanied by Emma, the new maid, in order to serve dinner. Mia imagined he smiled at her, at least there was a flicker in his eye as he offered her the various dishes. She had the bizarre idea for a second that he might forget his station and ask her if she had had a good ride.

When he had gone she said. "You never told me how you acquired Parker. At times he puzzles me, almost as if he were a misfit."

"He's a good servant, but I think I know what you mean, as if he'd never be quite tamed, though why we should endeavour to remove all personality from those who wait upon us, God alone knows! His widowed mother lives in Stonebarrow, and her husband died in tragic circumstances, caught under the wheel of a reaper on one of our fields. She was worried about the boy's future, and I felt I owed . . . I felt sorry for her. She was struggling to make ends meet, and at the time I had lost my father's valet who had grown too old in service."

"What's his name, I mean his Christian name?"

"Parker? Jack. Why do you ask?"

"I don't know why, but yes, I do. It's something to do with what you said about him never having been quite tamed. He's a personality in his own right."

"He's certainly that. He'd been rather a problem to Mrs Parker, poaching, girls, the escapades of youth, I hope . . . now don't let's waste time talking about Jack Parker. Let's discuss the furnishings of the farm, and if you're free to go to Hessleton tomorrow to choose curtains, no doubt assisted by Hannah and your Mama." He smiled at her.

"You tease me."

"You know you like it. Besides, I'm very fond of your family. They've been good to me in every way, your father especially. Didn't he give me you?"

This, she thought, is how it will be when we're alone, when we're free from the constant repression which Sarah inflicts on our spirits, but with the thought of her sister-in-law the feeling of unease returned, and she said to Conway. "It's very odd about Sarah not appearing at table. You don't think she's ill by any chance?"

"She was out today, wasn't she?"

"Yes, I saw her go. Did you know I've never been in her private apartments? Indeed she's never invited me."

"You wouldn't be able to find a place to sit down, I assure you. It's strewn all over with sketches."

"Papa says she's working on a dinner service for him, and each piece has a different landscape. What an undertaking!"

"Not for Sarah. She loves it." He stopped speaking abruptly, his brows knitted in thought. She watched him as he went on eating in a desultory fashion, and then, suddenly, his knife fell with a clatter on his plate. "It's no good!" He pushed back his chair and got to his feet. "That wretched girl knows I shall go up and see how she is. I can tell you, Mia, if I find she's sulking, by God I'll bundle you up and take you away to Well Farm even sooner than I had intended!"

"She wouldn't be sulking all this time, would she?" And then, because her prison gates seemed to be opening she said. "Be gentle with her."

"Yes, you're right. I must be gentle with her." He flung down his napkin and strode towards the door.

106

Mia sat at the table when he had gone. Any other husband would have asked me to accompany him, she thought, and then again, but any other sister-in-law would have been glad to see me. I ought not to have any fear of intruding. She listened. How quiet it was! The house was wrapped in silence. Because of the distance between the dining-room and the kitchen, no noises penetrated, and outside in the Spring twilight the trees swayed gently, noiselessly.

She got up and went into the hall. Parker or Mrs Frame had forgotten to light the lamp, and the place was eerie with the shadows of the ugly furniture which crowded it. She stole along the corridor towards Sarah's private staircase and halted at the foot of it, straining her ears to listen. It was deathly quiet. Conway must have shut the door behind him. Never, she thought, standing in the darkness, have I eavesdropped like this at Blenheim Terrace, but there the house reflected the inhabitants, light, airy, there the atmosphere was untainted by fear.

Was she creating the atmosphere by her imaginings? There was so little to go on except a jealous sister's love of her brother and dislike of the girl who had usurped her in his affections. But there ought to be room for both of them . . . she summoned up her courage. She would run up the staircase, calling out some friendly warning about her approach . . .

Suddenly she heard from upstairs the dreadful travesty of Sarah's voice, an uncontrolled kind of wailing thickened by tears. "It's no good, Conway! You promised . . . you said you'd never leave me. Remember how I got you to swear on the Bible. I can't help it if you've changed . . . you *promised* . . ." and then the rest was drowned in a burst of hysterical weeping. She heard the low murmur of Conway's voice, on and on and on. She stood still for a long time, and when at last she heard the door open she didn't move. He ran down lightly, almost colliding with her.

"Mia! What are you doing here?"

"I thought . . . I thought I could be of some help. Is she all right?"

"No, she isn't. She's hysterical. Did you hear her?"

"Yes." They both stood looking at each other. His face was in shadow, she could see the grim line of his mouth. The silence enveloped them, unbroken now by any sound from upstairs. What could she be doing? Had she fainted? Was she lying calmly, pleased that she had upset him, that she would upset her sister-in-law. She heard his voice as if he were speaking to himself.

"I can't get her to stop. Hysterics, then that terrible, soundless weeping . . . just lying there and shuddering . . . it would break your heart."

"She must be ill."

"Do you think so?" His voice changed. "You may well be right. She's fevered. Her brow was burning when I felt it. Yes, that's it. I'll ask Parker to go and fetch Dr Compson. He'll come, I'm sure."

"Conway," she wrung her hands in her distress, "should I go and sit with her? Surely I could be of some comfort to her? We're both . . . sisters . . . of a kind."

He shook his head. "No, it's no good. Please go back to the dining-room and ring for Parker. Tell him I should like him to ride immediately for Dr Compson, Frame's too slow, but you can ask Mrs Frame to go to Sarah. I'll join you when she relieves me."

"If you wish." She half-ran to the dining-room and found Parker there with Emma whom he was helping with the removal of the large serving-dishes on the sideboard. "Leave Emma to that, Parker," she said. "Miss Sarah has been taken ill and the master would like you to ride for the doctor immediately. You know where to go."

"Yes, ma'am. I've been for Dr Compson before this." His glance was knowing.

"And as you go through the kitchen ask Mrs Frame to make haste and sit with Miss Sarah. The master's waiting for her."

"Certainly. Right away, ma'am." His face was impassive but his eyes were moving in his head with interest. He went quickly out of the room.

Mia was in the drawing-room when Conway joined her. He didn't speak immediately but crossed to the window and stood looking out into the dark garden.

"Parker's been gone for some time," she said. "Try not to worry." She felt detached now from the whole episode. Her heart was like ice.

"I'm as distressed for you as I am for Sarah," he said. "I know how you feel."

"I'm fit and well." Her voice was low. "You should keep your sympathy for your sister."

He came over to stand in front of her. "You're grieved with me."

"No . . ." She could hardly speak.

"If I tell you I'm convinced Sarah is ill, that it's not simply a fit of pique, will it help?"

She turned her head away, tears blinding her, and he sat down beside her on the ottoman, taking her hands in his.

"Try to understand, my darling. This poor girl was bereft of two parents when she most needed them. I, too, but then I was older, and for some time I had found little support from them, so I'd grown to be self-sufficient."

"How had . . ." she hesitated, "how had they failed you?"

"Dr Compson would no doubt give my mother's malady a kindlier name if you asked him. The plain fact was that she drank to excess, and unless my father joined her, he was morose and difficult. I realise now he wasn't an alcoholic . . . but I preferred him drunk."

"Conway, I'm sorry!"

"Don't be sorry. It wasn't a pleasant background but I'm robust."

"I never guessed. There were rumours, of course, but my father doesn't like gossip. What an unhappy household it must have been for you."

"And for Sarah, don't forget."

"Yes."

"My mother was hopeless with Sarah, quite apart from her little weakness . . ." he laughed shortly. "They were completely incompatible. She provided governesses and riding lessons and French lessons, but no parties, no one of her own sex to chatter with as you chatter with Hannah. Can you blame her if she clung to me, if she followed me about the house asking to be included in everything I did?"

"No." Her directness overcame her caution. "But even so, her reactions are . . . excessive. There's something you're keeping from me." She looked at him, hoping his eyes would meet hers, "I feel it all the time, I feel it in the seams and crevices of this house which I've grown to hate as much as you have. Is your reason for wishing to leave it because it holds something you wish to forget? Is it, oh, is it?" The tears ran down her face. "For God's sake tell me . . ."

He turned and took her in his arms, rocking her gently. "Don't weep, please don't weep like that, I can't bear it." His voice changed. "Before we were married I had a long talk with your father. He was the most understanding of men . . ."

"Conway, I implore you . . ."

"'Mia', your father said, 'has a good head on her shoulders. Confide in her.' He looked at her. "But I didn't. I couldn't. I loved you so much I was afraid I'd drive you away from me . . ."

"But you've told me about your parents, and see, it *hasn't* driven me away from you." She released herself and smiled up at him, wiping her tears. "Can't you see that I want to share, to help." There was a loud knocking and then the scurrying of feet as someone ran through the hall, voices, footsteps which stopped outside the door. Conway jumped to his feet. "Come in!" he called.

Emma, red-faced with excitement, opened the door and stood aside. "Dr Compson," she announced.

"My dear doctor," Conway went quickly forward, "will you ever forgive me for bringing you out at this time of night? Did you come in your Victoria?"

"No, I rode back with Parker." He advanced into the room, shook hands with Conway, bowed to Mia. "It's Sarah?"

"Yes, sit down for a moment."

"Only for a moment, then." He swept his coat-tails to either side of a chair beside Mia.

"May I offer you some refreshment, doctor?" she asked him.

"Later, if you'd be so kind. What is the trouble?"

Conway spoke before she could reply. "I'm better able to acquaint you with the details. Physically, I'm pretty sure she has a fever of some sort. But . . . well, I must be frank with you, doctor, she became upset at the prospect of our imminent departure, mine and Mia's."

"Are you going abroad?"

"No, we're taking up residence at Well Farm. But in all fairness I do know she's been complaining of a headache for the past few days. Isn't that so, Mia?"

She remembered the girl's attitude at table, her hand to her temple. But then there had been the hysterical outburst she had overheard . . . she looked up at Conway. "It could be. I'm not her confidante." And then turning to the doctor, "But I think she overworks on her drawings. Her sketch-book is always with her."

Dr Compson nodded. "She drives herself too hard, always has. Takes things hard too. Perhaps you'll come up with me to her room."

"My wife's tired," Conway said. "I'll accompany you."

"If you wish." The doctor rose and the two men left the room. This time Mia stayed where she was, lost in thought. Was Conway shielding her from another outburst of Sarah's, or was he concealing something? Was this a repetition of the last illness she had had before she started working at the potworks, or was it caused by the thought of Conway leaving Well House? The questions spun in her brain until she could think no longer.

Dr Compson's verdict was equivocal, but his instructions firm. The next day or two would be critical. She must be kept very quiet, since he feared brain fever. Her room must be kept dimmed, and soothing powders given at regular intervals. Nothing must be said or done which might upset her. He looked meaningly at Mia but didn't elaborate.

He consented to drink a glass of wine with them, explaining, possibly for Mia's benefit, that someone like Sarah suffered a great deal more than ordinary mortals. That although their systems were frail their wills were often indomitable. When he got up he bowed over Mia's hand. "Don't take it too badly," he said. His eyes were kind.

"Is it necessary to have a nurse?"

"Not immediately. Someone strange would only upset her. She seems content with Mrs Frame, who tells me that one of the maids can take over the cooking. But I must prepare you for a fairly long illness. I shall be here tomorrow."

When the doctor had gone Mia asked Conway. "Do *you* think her illness will last a long time?"

"I can't say. Please don't ask me at this stage."

"But I have to know, don't you see? It means we shan't be able to go to Well Farm, it means . . ." she caught sight of his face, "Oh, forgive me, in my disappointment I'm forgetting Sarah . . . but you must admit her illness and our intended departure seem to be linked in some way."

"If they are not it's a coincidence we could have well done without. Go up to bed, my darling. You're worn out."

"Yes, I think I shall."

"I'll follow you shortly."

He came to their room long after she had retired. She lay awake in the darkness, but when she felt him bending over her she turned away her head. It was the first time since their marriage that they had gone to sleep without at least some words of love.

Chapter Ten

One fine afternoon in May, Hannah called to see Mia. Marie-Hélène had said to her, "Ride over to Well House, *ma petite*, and see your sister. She worries me. The last time she was here she was as thin as a rake and all eyes." Hannah, plump as the doves which purled on their stable roof was delighted to do so.

"Alone, Mama?"

"No, Robert will ride with you and return to escort you home in time for dinner, which should make the Hessleton vultures happy. Induce Mia to spend the day out with you. She's too much indoors, especially when Sarah's there all the time."

"She's almost better now, Mia says."

"But not to be upset in any way, I understand. Your father will have to have a talk with Conway. I should only lose my temper."

"I thought you liked him, Mama."

"I do. There's a strength of character there, and perhaps too soft a heart under his stern exterior. At least I *hope* so."

Hannah, not overly susceptible to nuances, had donned her riding-habit and clattered out of the yard on her horse, Robert at her heels. Half-an-hour later she was requesting Parker to fetch his mistress. "And saddle her horse, Parker, if you will."

"Yes, Miss Hannah, right away." She thought he smiled at her the way Jason in the potworks might have done, but when she looked again his face was expressionless.

*   *   *

113

As they set off she said to Mia, "I've told Robert not to come back until just before dinner, so we shall have the whole day together. Isn't that fine?"

Mia rode listlessly for a few moments without speaking. She had had to be cajoled by Hannah to join her. The proposed break in the dull routine was in a way more hurtful than the apathy which surrounded her day after day. "I suppose so, pet. Let's ride through Stonebarrow and see where our fancy takes us."

"How is Sarah?" Hannah asked politely.

"Almost better. Well enough to wait upon Conway, to talk to him, to ingratiate herself with him . . ."

"Don't *you* talk to him?"

"I used to." Her tone was bitter.

They clattered down the hill towards the cluster of houses which was Stonebarrow, in silence. What could Hannah, a young girl, know of the situation, Mia thought, how she and Conway could lie close in the darkness, her blood surging slowly in her veins, sweet, sickly thrills running down her limbs making them as weak as water. How she moaned . . . of the polite distance he kept during the day and her protests in their bedroom at night. "I can't stand this house any longer with your sister in it! You don't need two women. I've had enough. You're doing something to me, draining me, diminishing me, I can't stand it . . ." And then his quiet voice. "Mia, just a little more time, I beg you." Once more being enveloped in his arms and in his love. How often his lips were wet with her tears . . .

She had a fear of her own now. That theirs was a destructive love, kept for the darkness, never shown to Sarah who crept like a pale shadow about the house. And because it was a destructive love there could not be a child. She told herself it killed everything it touched.

She became aware again of Hannah riding beside her, and she made herself brighten as they crossed the wooden bridge out of the hamlet. "I'm glad you forced me to come out with you. One becomes introspective, sitting too much indoors. Conway's busy all the time. He's had to go to Liverpool on several occasions recently, something to do with the rebuilding of the estate cottages, but he's very kind. He brought me a boxful of white gloves, and another time a necklace of sapphires." She didn't say they had never been worn.

"Mia . . ." Hannah said. They were riding along a bridle path enclosed with trees, a private place which might be conducive to confidences. "Are you happy with Conway? Oh, I know I shouldn't be asking, but Mama and I think you're getting thinner."

"Wives aren't supposed to complain."

"But I'm your sister. We've always shared everything. Remember our confidences in the attic, and the elms outside, sometimes thick with snow, sometimes with leaves, all the years we've shared secrets, Mia, spring, summer, autumn, winter. Tell me, is it Sarah? We're all so disappointed you didn't move into Well Farm."

"*You* were disappointed!" Mia smiled bleakly. "We must wait until she's stronger," he says, "just a little more time, Mia," "be patient, Mia." I appreciate she's been very ill, of course, at one stage Dr Compson feared for her life, but, Hannah, don't breathe a word of this, I've grown to hate her with her dark, silent ways. What's more I know she hates me. I can feel it. Conway . . . he's loving, very loving, but he only needs me sometimes. Wait till you're married yourself and you'll understand. Something holds him back in the day time. He's like a man torn in half. You can see the anguish in his eyes. I pity him. He had a hard childhood, not like ours, and he doesn't know the relief which complete frankness gives. His reserve is like a carapace . . ." But as she talked, images, remembered sensations tortured her, Conway gay and loving in Paris, loving but circumspect in her own drawing-room at Blenheim Terrace, adoring, holding a candle aloft in their quiet bedroom, looking down on her naked body, his eyes melting as her bones

115

melted into his, his weight as he sank down on her. She suddenly felt faint and reined in her horse.

"What is it, Mia?" Hannah noticed. "Are you . . .?"

"No, I'm not, Miss Suspicious!" She recovered quickly and rode on feeling happier because she had Hannah to talk to. This is what she had been missing, long rides in the warm sunshine, the wind softly lifting her hair, new scenes. "This is lovely, Hannah," she sang out. "Like old times. Why haven't you called to see me oftener?"

"There was Sarah's illness, although we sent messages and flowers. Besides we've been very busy, as you can imagine, with Mama's French friends to stay and some Dutch business acquaintances of Papa's to entertain. And we've been invited out all round the county! Deadly dull, I do assure you." Mia laughed at the sparkle of delight in Hannah's eyes.

"And what about all your beaux? Have you decided whom you'll honour with your hand?"

"No . . ." she hesitated. "Harry Compson was quite attentive for a time, but now he's left Oxford and because of this idiotic war joined the Eleventh Hussars. He's delighted at the prospect of seeing action, although I can't understand the mentality of men who want to fight."

"Perhaps it's really the attraction of the shortness of the jackets and the tightness of the cherry-coloured pants. They can be very fetching to females, I'm told. Possibly if you see him in uniform you'll fall under his spell."

"No . . ." Hannah said again, hanging her head.

"Raise your head and look at me! I know you through and through. You've lost your heart elsewhere. Is that it?"

"Not exactly lost my heart, Mia." Hannah's cheeks were bright pink. "But I've had occasion to call at the potworks from time to time and Jason and I have had some interesting conversations. He strikes me as a young man of high sensibility."

Mia hid her smile. "Jason Berridge," she said, flicking her boot with her whip, "now, there I think I agree with you.

116

He's vastly intelligent, otherwise Papa wouldn't have shown such an interest in him. And quite remarkably handsome into the bargain."

"Do you think so?"

"Assuredly. Consider, Hannah, if you have to rest your eyes on someone for the rest of your life you require someone whose countenance pleases."

"But I wasn't thinking along those lines, far from it. In any case, Papa and Mama would expect me to do far better."

"I doubt it, although I wish sometimes they had been less lenient with me . . ."

"But Papa and Mama liked Conway. I heard them discussing him often. They thought . . . he deserved some happiness."

"How very magnanimous of them. Don't let's talk about my affairs any more." She looked ahead. "I know a broad shallow valley not far from Galton. I used to ride there. It's pretty and there's a little stream which winds its way along the bottom. We might rest there for a time and refresh ourselves."

"I'd like that." Hannah pushed her top-hat back on her head. "I shall be glad to lie down on the grass where we're positively unseen and perhaps take this silly hat off, even pull up my heavy skirt a trifle. Isn't it too ridiculous to be dressed like this on such a hot day?"

"Ridiculous. But then I begin to think many of our customs are ridiculous. I've been doing a lot of thinking recently. Indeed I've had plenty of time for it. What is it, in our society, that we fear? Why do we need so many props?"

"Now you're becoming like Papa, talking above my head. Let's ride on more quickly and find this delectable spot you've told me about."

In another quarter of an hour they were urging their horses up the last incline which would command a view of the shallow valley and the spire of Galton church beyond.

117

It would be covered with foliage now, Mia thought, and the valley floor would be warmed by the sun. They would lie down in the drowsy heat and she would listen to Hannah's bright chatter and tell herself she was happy . . . she was disturbed by her sister, who had ridden on in front of her, calling out in surprise. "Come and see your quiet valley, Mia! There's a shock in store for you!"

Mia encouraged her horse which was panting in the heat. "Come on, my beauty, not far now . . ." She thought she heard music, but it would be some trick of the wind. When she reached the plateau where Hannah was standing, she put her hand to her mouth as she looked down. "It's the Fair! I remember Conway mentioning it! It comes every year at this time."

"Doesn't it look gay from here? And can't you hear the music from the roundabouts? Look, over there, can't you see them?" Mia followed Hannah's finger and picked out the bright colours of the plaster horses circling round a mirrored pedestal which sparkled in the sunlight.

"Yes, quite plainly. And look, those bright dots must be balloons, and there are the stalls, and the tents, see, striped blue and white, and the black and white dots are people weaving in and out!" She was suddenly excited, like a child.

"Let's sit down and watch for a little," Hannah said. "The horses will be glad to graze. Isn't it bright and gay, Mia? Don't you wish you could have some hot gingerbread men or some lovely sticky toffee, or even a glass of sarsaparilla?"

"Or a ride on the roundabouts?"

"Couldn't we slip down? No one would know us."

"No . . ." she hesitated. "Some of the men might be rather rough. We might get involved."

"But you're a married lady. You could be my chaperon."

"Would *I* do, Hannah?" Both girls started in surprise at the deep voice. The noise from the Fair had drowned the sound of any approaching footsteps.

118

Hannah swivelled round first. "It's you, Harry Compson! I think that's most unfair creeping up on us like that!"

"Allow me to help you to your feet and then you can scold me." He did so. "Now you, Mia."

"You're in uniform, Harry!" she said, as she smoothed her dress.

"There are two of us. Cherrypickers both!" He laughed. "Here he is!" She looked up. Another young man had ridden up and was now dismounting. He was wearing the same Hussar uniform, short blue jacket plentifully laced with gold, tight red trousers. He turned and she had a fleeting impression of fairness, eyes as vividly blue as his tunic before Harry was saying. "Allow me to introduce my friend and fellow officer, Lieutenant Brian Moore. Brian, my boy, meet two of the prettiest girls in the county, Miss Hannah Winter and her sister, Mia."

But he didn't say I was married, Mia thought confusedly as she inclined her head, not before she had seen the lieutenant's mouth curve in a smile, a pretty mouth, a shade too pretty perhaps for the square chin and forceful blue eyes.

"This is indeed a pleasure." He bowed low in return. She glanced towards Harry, still confused, saw that he was in animated conversation with Hannah, turned again to the lieutenant. How should she frame it? "As it happens I'm married"? Instead she said. "You've ridden far?"

"From Hessleton. I'm staying with Harry for a few days. We're due to leave for Kingstown shortly and this is our embarkation leave."

"You're going to the Crimea?"

"Yes, please don't look so sad. We're delighted to be going into action at last. It won't take long for old Cardigan to set things to rights out there." He flashed a smile. "It ought to be a glorious romp!"

"I marvel at your lightheartedness, sir."

"I dearly love a scrap, Miss Mia. It must be my Irish blood." His eyes were frankly admiring. "What luck to

119

meet you! We've many pretty girls in Ireland, but none to equal you."

"I've heard Irishmen are great flatterers." She felt guilty for a moment then her heart glowed. How refreshing to be admired, to flirt with one's eyes, to slip back into the delightful bandying of words, to be free and untramelled, no worries, no shadows, no secrets . . . she heard Hannah speaking.

"But Mia, mayn't we? Harry says he and his friend will escort us to the Fair. We should be quite safe with them, he says." She dimpled and blushed.

"Do come, Mia. It's just what you're needing." Harry's eyes were sending a message to her. "You're far too pale."

"May I add my entreaties?" Lieutenant Moore said. "You can't possibly step out of my life as soon as we've met. For the sake of your Queen and country you must be nice to us!" He smiled gaily.

Mia's left hand was in her habit pocket as he spoke. A surge of sheer high spirits ran through her, all the more strong for having been repressed for so long. She slipped off her wedding ring and pushed it in a corner. "Why not? It's our duty to be patriotic."

"Bravo! That's the spirit!" Lieutenant Moore's eyes were bright with an answering excitement. Here's the type of man I should have married, she thought, who could match my high spirits with his, who has no silences, no reserves. "Let's get nearer," he said. "Harry, you ride on with Miss Hannah. We'll follow you."

"Thank you," she said as he assisted her to mount. Her horse, which was inclined to be restless, was quiet under his hands. Devil mend Sarah, she thought, at the same time dowsing the image of Conway's dark eyes. She'd forget about both of them for an hour or two. She deserved some gaiety after those last miserable weeks. They rode off side by side.

Lieutenant Moore's pleasant Irish voice flowed on

effortlessly. He told her his home was in Howth, near Dublin, that he was a member of a large family. That he bred horses, while his father bred daughters, he added with a laugh. He had six sisters who were all fair with blue eyes and fearless riders into the bargain. There were always men coming courting about the place. A picture of a happy family emerged, who enjoyed life and lived only for the day . . . she'd do the same.

And it was a day to remember, a time to remember, the drowsy heat, the dream-like quality, her wilful deception, all made it special. It was the kind of day, she told herself, that long after, when Brian Moore had gone to the Crimea, she'd take out of her memories like a pretty locket to look at. She was awash in Brian's flow of talk, dazzled by the sparkling blue eyes, she didn't mind when he took her arm protectively after they had tethered their horses, nor was she other than flattered by the curious but admiring glances they drew.

"What luck!" he said once or twice. "To meet someone like you. What prodigious luck." She turned the ring in her pocket over and over . . .

They came to the merry-go-round and Hannah demanded to go on it. Mia demurred at first, remembering her status, and then remembering again that the lieutenant was unaware of it she threw all caution to the winds and allowed herself to be lifted up on a gold-painted horse. She was aware of the wind racing past her face as they whirled round and round, faster and faster, whirl of skirts, of petticoats, great rushes of excitement coursing like hot blood through her veins. I must be mad, she thought . . . the giddiness in her head persisted long after they were walking round the Fair again, along with the lilting sound of the barrel organ in her ears.

An afternoon to remember, of wandering round the stalls, eating hot gingerbread men and sweet, sticky tarts, laughing, laughing, feeling Brian Moore's arm tighten round her waist, suddenly seeing the sun sink, the thinning crowds pinkly tinged, coming to her senses.

"We must go back, Hannah. Come here." Pulling the girl towards her, hearing Brian's teasing voice, "Girls' secrets . . ." Whispering, "Hannah, I must be mad. I haven't told him I'm married . . ." Seeing Hannah's eyes fearful for a moment, and then hearing her answering whisper. "I shan't tell. It's only a jape . . ."

They rode slowly behind Hannah and Harry, and Brian's mood altered with the setting sun. He was as open and free as his smile, once again she thought he'd have fitted into Blenheim Terrace as easily as a cup and saucer, but his eyes were contemplative. "Do you believe in love at first sight, Mia?"

"Sometimes." She kept her head lowered.

"It's the wrong time to discuss it . . . but it's odd about going to fight. Because you realise you may be killed, you suddenly value life. Tell me . . . have you felt some kind of bond between us?"

"It's only been a few hours . . ."

"Time isn't important. I feel sure you're my style." Now they were riding along the bridle path, hidden amongst the trees. Hannah and Harry had disappeared round the bend.

"We're coming near my home now," she said. "I've got . . . something to say to you . . . it won't be easy."

"Let's get down then. It might help." He aided her to dismount, and she stood with her back against the trunk of a great oak until he had tethered the horses. She started to tremble as she watched him coming towards her. She'd made it much more difficult, she should have ridden on. "Why so serious?" He was very near her.

She was tongue-tied, full of confusion. She had landed herself in a pretty pickle, she thought. Reality was hitting hard after the dream-like afternoon. She raised her eyes to his, saw that his were dancing, and yet tender . . . involuntarily she moved towards him and in a moment she was in his arms. Her heart filled with a fresh, uncomplicated regard for him as a soldier first, as a charming young man

122

secondly. She felt his kiss on her mouth before he let her go.

"Dammit, Mia," he said. "You looked so gorgeous. I apologise."

"I'm to blame too. It's been a mad afternoon."

"Let's blame the times we live in. We've hardly got to know each other and now it's good-bye. Will you write to me?"

She shook her head. "That's the point. I can't." And I can't tell him either, she thought. "Brian," she tried to steady her voice. "I've been very foolish. Will you ride on and catch up with Harry? He'll explain. He'll have left Hannah . . . where I live."

"I don't understand. Leave you here?"

"Do as I say. It's Harry's fault, partly. He'll tell you the truth about me . . ."

"Mia, *what* truth?" The blue eyes were on her.

"Oh, for goodness sake! If you're as disobedient in the Hussars as you are with me, well I don't hold out much hope for you." She smiled. "On you go. Afterwards, if you feel you can forgive me, write and tell me so, or don't write . . ."

He took her hand. "I like mysteries. And I'll write, whatever Harry tells me. I shan't say good-bye." He went to his horse and mounted it, she watched him canter round the bend without looking back. Well, she had come out of that badly, she thought, and yet, when she mounted her own horse and rode slowly towards Well House she felt light in her body and light in her head, as if she had suffered some kind of strange illness, but a pleasant one.

In bed that night she lay on her back beside Conway and, for the first time, thought of another man. Her behaviour was still inexplicable to her. Perhaps it was revolt against the miserable weeks she had spent while Sarah was ill. She put her hands to her cheeks in shame when she thought of riding like a servant-girl on the roundabouts, strolling through the fairground with Brian Moore. She thought of his bright smile, of his blue eyes bent on her, of how she had giggled like Hannah in his company. Now she didn't know whether to laugh or weep.

Still, how easy life with someone like him would have been! How Mama would have joked with him, admired his tight trousers and short jacket, his gold lace, his shako. She had a great love of the military figure. Was it my French Mama coming out in me, or was it a defiant gesture against Conway, against Sarah, against this dismal house? She closed her eyes, feeling giddy with thinking, and she heard the sad lilting tune of the barrel organ, and Brian Moore's voice above it, the rapid-talking voice of a voluble man, who was without secrets.

And yet, when Conway turned to her, and she was enveloped in the darkness by his darkness, she thought this is the life I've chosen, the love. She heard as he imprisoned her with his limbs the faint tune of the barrel organ in her ears . . . why were they always sad? And then even that memory was swamped by a heavy blood-dark wave of desire and she was borne along with it.

Chapter Eleven

Joseph looked at the finished figurine of Florence Nightingale which Craythorne had brought to him in his office. "It's very good indeed." He turned it expertly in his hand. "So delicate that one wonders how it ever left the potter's hand and kiln unbroken. She's caught the spiritual look. *And* left out the inevitable tea-tray." He laughed. "It may be *made* of clay but Miss Nightingale is hardly of common clay."

"Indeed no, sir."

"They say in the month she's been at Scutari she's worked wonders at the Barracks Hospital there." He tapped the head of the figurine. "It's in here. If the conceptual capacities are there, everything becomes easy."

"You could say the same about Miss Sarah."

"Truly said. I never thought she could do figure work, but I might have known. Delicacy's her forte. There's something alike in both women." He lifted his head at the sound of a knock on the door. Jason Berridge came into the room with a sheaf of papers. "See this, Jason," Joseph said. "What do you think of it?"

The young man took the figurine, spun it slowly in his hand with the deftness he had learned from his master. He pursed his lips. "You'll make a fortune at Christmas with this, sir."

Joseph laughed. "There speaks the business man." He took it back. "I'm going to the Design Room to show it to Miss Sarah. After all, it's her handiwork. Keep an eye on things while I'm gone, will you?"

"Yes, sir." He laid down on the desk some papers. "These are for signature when you get a minute."

Why is it, Joseph thought, going along the corridor to the Design Room, that I don't like people to be too efficient? Is it because I feel it shows a lack of imagination? And what's more, he's showing a decided interest in Hannah . . . He reached the door, pushed it open and went in. Sarah was sitting alone. Her hands were clasped on her drawing-board, and she was staring into space. It was typical of the girl that she made no pretence of working but turned her head towards him and waited until he should speak.

"I've brought your first-born to show you," he said. He put down the figurine in front of her. "Do you like it?"

She didn't lift it, but her large, heavy-lidded eyes rested on the model for quite three or four seconds. Finally she said, the deep voice surprising him as always, "I like it. You have good potters, Mr Winter."

"I have better designers, Sarah. I congratulate you."

"I don't enjoy creating figures. This one was an exception. I feel I understand her temperament. In some ways it's similar to my own."

"In what way?"

"She has a great singleness of purpose."

"That's certainly true." He added to himself, as well as certain peculiarities of temperament . . . "You go from triumph to triumph. Lord Trent is vastly pleased with his dinner service. He says the landscapes are extremely fine, and what's more have proved a wonderful talking point at his dinner parties."

"I'm pleased." The large eyes rested on him. "Now *there* was an undertaking which was a pleasure."

He sat down on a seat beside her at the drawing-board. "Have Mr Victor and Mr Day departed?"

"Yes."

"Sarah," he was aware of her cool scrutiny, "I've meant to say this for some time. I know you're conscientious beyond any shadow of doubt, but to spare you this winter after such a serious illness, would you consider working at home?"

"Are you trying to get rid of me?"

"Far from it. Haven't I been heaping praises on your head?" She didn't smile, and he thought it was a pity that someone with so much talent should have so little sense of humour. "I'm only concerned about your health. Mia has told me how ill you were." He noticed, although her face remained calm, that a film seemed to fall over her eyes.

"Yes?" She waited.

"I have asked *you* a question."

"The answer's no, Mr Winter. Provided you like my work, and you've assured me you do, I prefer to be able to make free of the potworks if and when I like. I draw inspiration from it. I can watch the throwers or the turners and my mind begins to spin with ideas like the potter's wheel. One must absorb the background of one's work, feel part of it."

"You make a good case for yourself, young lady."

"It's your argument too." She smiled briefly. "Once you told me the ware had to be a corporate effort. But it's not only that. Now that winter is with us Conway is more about the house studying his papers and books . . ." She paused. "With Mia there I feel I intrude."

"That will be remedied once they move into Well Farm." He spoke shortly.

"The prospect seems further away than ever at the moment." Her voice was as smooth as silk. "The hard frost we've had has held up the laying of the pipes and the addition of the servants' quarters. The ice has prevented the lake being cleaned out as Conway would wish . . ." She smiled. "He has some grandiose ideas, and he's lost his best workman who went off with Parker to be soldiers in the Crimea . . ."

"Parker?"

"Conway's valet, you remember. A ne'er-do-well whom he took pity on and trained."

"Ah, yes, I remember him. There seems to be a belated sense of patriotism blowing up in England since the disaster at Balaclava. They say defeat brings out the best in us." He felt his lips stiffen for some reason as he tried to smile. "Mia will be disappointed."

"I doubt it. She seems resigned. Besides she too is vastly interested in the war in the Crimea. She has a regular correspondent there."

Joseph felt a prick of fear which was resolved almost immediately. "It will be Harry Compson. He's unofficially engaged to Hannah, you know, but he and Mia have been friends since childhood."

"He must be an active correspondent in between fighting the Russians."

"Perhaps . . . well, you're quite sure I can't persuade you to work in comfort at home?"

"Quite sure, but thank you for thinking of my welfare. This place has become a second home for me." She bowed her head as if dismissing him. "Will you give my best respects to your wife and to Hannah? I hope we'll see them in the near future."

"Certainly. I expect we'll meet during the Christmas festivities. My wife and daughter are indefatigable about parties, in between knitting comforts for the troops and sending innumerable parcels to this good lady to distribute." He tapped the figurine. "Good day to you."

"Good day."

Joseph shut the door behind him, feeling the same unease which a talk with Sarah always left in him. He analysed it, walking back to his room. I'm fifty years of age, happily married, successful in my chosen work, and yet that young miss can induce in me a feeling of embarrassment, of discomfort, as if I was a callow youth conversing with a duchess. She's not patronising, nor overbearing, nor in any sense rude. She has great talent, she's hard-working and conscientious, pleasant to look at, refined in her dress. But there's something, a lack of warmth, as if icy fingers were all the time slowing my heartbeats . . . You're becoming as fanciful as a woman, he told himself, stepping briskly into his room. "Well, now, Jason, let's get down to those letters."

"Yes, sir." Jason, as always, had his favourite steel pen ready to hand.

Mia sat in her bedroom, her writing desk in front of her, a candle by her side. It was an hour until dinner. Sarah was safely in her room since her return from the potworks, Conway had ridden to Hessleton to see his solicitor, saying to Mia, when she pointed out that it was Sarah's day for using the carriage, that the exercise would do him good. She had thought he looked thinner, his eyes were dark-circled. Nowadays he occasionally slept in his dressing-room saying his wakefulness might disturb her.

She acknowledged to herself the deep and apparently irreconcilable rift between them nowadays. He had broken a promise. He had put his sister's wishes before her own. It was a fact that Sarah had been extremely ill for some time, but it was also a fact that she resented her sister-in-law and made no effort to hide it. Well Farm and a life there with Conway now seemed like an impossible dream. And so, she thought, taking the small key from her pocket and unlocking the desk, I've substituted my own. She took out a bundle of letters and untied the ribbon holding them together. In this dark house it was necessary to have dreams of one's own.

She opened the first letter slowly, prolonging the anticipation, smoothing it out carefully with her hand. She would enter a different country, she would listen to the words of someone who would have put her first . . .

'My Dear Mia. Already it is the end of July. I've thought long and hard before I wrote to you. I did as you bade me that day and spoke to Harry who told me you were married. It had been an omission he said

129

to begin with, and afterwards a prank, which to his surprise you supported. That's what has given me the courage to send this letter, that there may have been some reason for your secrecy, some disappointment in your life. I'll say no more.

'But if it was only high spirits, I hope in spite of being a married lady you'll find it in your heart to write to me. Here in this filth and squalor which surrounds us, that day I spent with you is like a mirage, except that this is no desert, but a quagmire.

'The heat's intolerable, there's sickness everywhere. My batman went down with cholera yesterday. I spend a lot of time with the vet tending the horses who suffer badly because of the heat and lack of fodder. I'm sure they must long for the green grass of Ireland. And the rest of the time I spend with Harry who feels the heat as badly as the horses but doesn't complain much all the same.

'I've reread the above and it sounds so dismal! So I must try to make you laugh or you won't relish my letters much. You laughed so easily that day. Now, let me see . . . I wish I could imitate 'Jim the Bear', as they call Cardigan, as well as Harry does. Now that the Earl's back from his reconnaissance it's spit and polish all the time, and 'widing'. He's got a frightful lisp.

'We're now settled in Yenibazaar, and although it looks like paradise with its blue skies and sunshine, it's more like hell. The fevers and sickness are bad enough, but what's much worse is that no one seems to know what we're here for, and the chaps just sit about and moan or play cards. Harry and I were counting it up the other day. Nearly three months here and not a blow struck against the Russians! Widiculous!

'Now it's time for me to attend stables again, so I'll close for the time being and send this letter winging across the Aegean to you. Please write. It can do no one any harm and me so much good.'

Mia folded the letter, smiling slightly, smoothed it with her closed hand, remained still for a moment because she thought she heard a noise on the stairs. Since Parker had run away to enlist there was no one to announce Conway's coming. She listened again. It was quiet, so quiet. She would surely hear his riding boots. He missed Parker. "Let me help you to get them off," she had said. He would not hear of her being in a menial position . . .

Should she read another one? It was scarcely necessary since she knew them by heart. But it was like a drug, an escape from reality, an edifice of unreality which Conway couldn't penetrate, her own . . . he ought to understand I've to defend myself in some way from the situation here, the reality of the three of us living in discord . . .

'September 24th. How pleased I was to hear from you! Yes, yes, I appreciate everything you say, that married ladies don't correspond with unmarried officers unless related, that your husband would be extremely angry. I'll be good, but I knew when I met you that as well as a kind heart you had the courage of your convictions.

'You say, tell me of your life here . . . well, I fear some of it doesn't make entertaining reading for carefully brought-up young married ladies. However, I'll try. We set off at the beginning of September, Harry and I, jubilant that at last we were going to fight. We were like boys released from school. Our joy, I may say, was short-lived, because in the transports we were cramped, horses and men, like birds in a nest, only birds keep their nests clean. The French were better organised. I've often heard they're a logical race, which isn't the same thing when you come to think about it. I was partly educated there, you know, at a Jesuit College. Another life . . .

'We disembarked at Calamita Bay, well-named! I had been as sick as a dog, unusual for me as I've often sailed in Dublin Bay in rough seas with no ill-effect.

However I forgot about it tending to the men who were in a bad way, not to mention the horses.

'And then the march ... what a travesty! No tents, some of the officers without mounts, the men without knapsacks, the medical men without equipment. Chaos! And on top of that excessive heat which nearly drove us all mad. When we reached the Bulganak stream we fell upon it as one man and drank it dry! I think Harry and I were glad of the odd skirmish here and there to make us forget our misery. Gave quite a good account of ourselves, the Eleventh ...

'That's enough battle talk. Mia, I'd like to say much more than 'Mia', but I have to remember you're married. And I'd like to know more about you, what you were like as a little girl, how you grew up, how you met your husband, if you're happy, if you enjoyed that day together as much as I did. It was like a gift to take with me to this wretched place.

'But I hear you say, 'Amuse me!' You sound sad in your letter I wonder why? So what about the nobs? What are they up to? Precious little, I can tell you. Lucan we call 'Lord Look-out' for obvious reasons, Cardigan 'The Noble Yachtsman' because he eats and sleeps in luxury on the Dryad while we live like rats here. They're always at one another's throats. Alma, which was a decisive Russian defeat, was a terrible day for us. The frustration was unbearable! D'you know, all we were allowed to do was to take a few prisoners! I can tell you, Mia, had the cavalry been allowed to go into action there, Harry and I would have been on our way home instead of standing as we did on a knoll watching the Russians stream away to Sebastopol, guns, standards and all. Talk about too many cooks spoiling the broth!

'Harry says better a frustrated live officer than a dead foolhardy one. Maybe he's right. What do you think, Mia? Sometimes death seems very near . . . write again . . .'

Mia paused to listen. So quiet. It made one behave furtively, have secrets. Everyone had secrets in this house . . . she hurriedly opened another letter, saying to herself, I'll just glance, not enough time, too near dinner . . . her eyes flitted like a moth from line to line.

'Only a day or two since the last one, but had to write a bit to cheer myself up. Did I tell you my batman, Lancing, had cholera? Well, he died, poor chap. Have had to write to his wife tonight. And Harry's slightly wounded in the foot, but all right, thank God. Couldn't do without old Harry. I sat with him all night. We were on a reconnaisance, captured convoy, rich spoil, fur-lined cloaks, dressing-cases, jewels . . . and I thought of you, Mia, and how the jewels would become you because you're so beautiful. And I longed in this filthy place to see you and touch you as I did that day.'

She turned over another page, quickly, only skimming the words with her eyes.

'Weather lovely, countryside beautiful, spirits high . . . my writing becomes disjointed as one begins to smell battle. The horses rear and whinny and I spend a lot of time with them. They're nervous too. Go and see to the horses, Moore, the chaps say. You're good with them . . .

'Spirits down, no attack, siege instead, cold, rain, sickness . . . try to cheer men, tend horses. Find comfort there. All agreed that two greater muffs than the Lords Cardigan and Lucan never existed. Feeling low. New batman from your part of the world, Jack Parker, well-trained but odd. His nostrils flare like a horse . . . I'm a bit fevered tonight. Hope I haven't got cholera.

'Fine this morning. Last breakfast, but special thanks to Parker who seems to have fallen on his feet, hard boiled eggs, rum, cigarettes. Good old Parker! We stand on a high plateau looking down. Green valleys and plains, the shining sea beyond, the bright colours of the uniforms, rows upon rows of them, and do you know what this chap thought of? You'll never credit it. That time when we stood looking down on the Fair. No more now, Mia. You've helped me so much. If I never write again, think of me . . .'

Mia bundled the letters together swiftly, tied the ribbon, put them in her writing desk and locked it. "Shameful self-indulgence," she muttered. She got up hurriedly from her chair. She was laving her face at the basin when Conway came into the room.

Chapter Twelve

"I think, pet, you must be drawing your wool too tightly. The top of that sock's like a purse-mouth."

"Oh, Mama!" Hannah looked up from the knitting-needles she was wielding so awkwardly, "How I wish this old war was over and then I shouldn't have to knit any more comforts!"

"I'm surprised at such a selfish remark. Have you forgotten Harry?"

"I beg your pardon. No, I think of Harry quite a lot and I write diligently once every week."

"That will be more of a comfort perhaps than the socks, although the situation of the troops this winter has been appalling according to reports in the papers. No boots, no greatcoats, no medicines, no shelter. And here we sit toasting our toes in front of this huge fire!"

"And I grumble about knitting comforts. In his last letter Harry said he and his friend had managed to sew waistcoats for themselves out of rabbit skins. Can you imagine?"

"Impossible for us to imagine. Poor souls."

Hannah put down her work. She suddenly looked older, the awkward girl was replaced by a young woman. "Mama . . . he also asked me to marry him when he comes home. He says they all find they need something . . . to look to."

"I'm not surprised. War makes men think of home, and the girls they've left behind become angels. Have you decided on your answer? You know Papa and I would give the match our blessing. One has to be realistic, of course, but I think optimistic."

"Yes, I shouldn't like to . . . hurt Harry. But then I wondered if he only wanted comfort, something to cling to. I'm sure he'll come home, of course. But . . . I don't know whether I want to marry . . . Harry."

"Have you someone else in view, miss?"

"No, that is, no. It's just that . . . well, I don't want to rush into marriage. Look at Mia. She's not very happy. Then sometimes I meet young men whom I like tolerably well, and Harry seems so far away."

"Doing his duty, don't forget." She looked shrewdly at her daughter. Papa tells me you seem to sparkle in Jason Berridge's company. Don't try to hide your blushes in your handkerchief. I've been young too."

"I only see him occasionally, and that in the potworks."

"No matter. Your sister didn't see a great deal of Conway Graham before she wished to marry him. Precipitation may run in the family. But perhaps you'll take some advice from me. In Harry, if God willing he comes home, you'd have a man who would treat you gently. In Jason you're dealing with quite another kettle of fish. Someone who intends to get to the top. That kind can be hard to live with."

"He's not at all calculating, Mama."

"He's told you so?"

"No . . . I don't really know him well, but he's pleasant, and admiring . . ."

". . . and *there*."

"Oh, Mama, what do you think I should do?"

"You begin to realise you know very little about him, do you? Well, my advice is to write to Harry. Don't keep him waiting for letters. They're as important to him as food. Tell him you're considering his proposal. That way you'll leave him with his dreams at least, and if what we read is true, he'll have need of dreams in the Crimea."

"He writes to Mia too, you know."

"Does he? Did she tell you?"

"No, it was Papa."

"Ah, well, you need have no worries there. They've

always been friends. But there's only one man for Mia, and that's Conway."

"Do you really think so? She looks anything but happy."

"Being married to the right man and being happy are two different things."

"Well, you've been happy with Papa. It's Sarah, without a doubt. I could understand Mia and Conway staying on at Well House until she was better, but there's no excuse now. Why don't they move?"

"They seem to be up against the same problems as they had last winter, inclement weather and lack of workmen. This time it's because of the war but last year it was for a more mysterious reason."

"I think Sarah dismissed their foreman when they were on their honeymoon."

"What an idea!" Marie-Hélène put her head on one side, pursed her lips. "But perhaps not such a bad one."

"I'm right, Mama. I mayn't be so clever as Mia, but I'm very close to her, and I guessed that about the foreman by what she *didn't* say. Another thing. You know Sarah resents Mia, you've remarked upon it yourself . . ." She paused, then said triumphantly. "Well, I feel she has a hold on Conway, whatever it is. At times when she speaks his eyes are *so* miserable, as if he was trapped!"

"You excel yourself today, pet. He's a stubborn, highly mettlesome, extremely proud man who has need to be treated the way one would treat a horse of the same temperament . . . gently. His whole being calls out for gentleness. I've never doubted his love for Mia. It's steadfast."

"Oh, he loves her all right, his love fills the room when they're together, but I don't think Mia will be good at treating him gently. She's a queen."

"Perhaps no longer, Hannah." Marie-Hélène sighed. "Papa advised me not to meddle with their affairs, but in France the mother would certainly call and see the son-in-law if she thought there was anything untoward in his conduct. And another thing, there are no children. Mia would make a good mother. She would have plenty of adoring subjects then! Yes, the situation is altogether unsatisfactory. I don't know how your Papa has managed to keep me silent for so long. Now that I think of it . . ." Her voice became agitated, and as if realising it she took her handkerchief from her bodice and fanned herself. "Suddenly I'm so hot! Either it's that fire or my health is a little precarious."

"You're never ill, Mama."

"That's what daughters always say, but wait until you're my age. One's equilibrium becomes upset. Nevertheless, you've made up my mind. I'll call at Well House very soon and have a talk with Conway, in a friendly manner, naturally. Surely it's permissible for a mother-in-law to call and receive a welcome."

"Mia and Conway are always glad to see you . . . was that the knocker? Yes, it is. Who can it be at this hour? It's not your 'At Home' day."

"It certainly isn't, and I don't want visitors. I can't think who it may be. Sit straight, Hannah. You've a tendency to slouch and then your chin sticks out. It might be Mrs Ponsoby who comes shopping occasionally in Hessleton and . . . honours us . . ." she made a face, "with a call." She smoothed her skirts and adjusted her cap as the door opened. Robert stood there, but before he could announce the caller, Dr Compson showed himself and stood silently while Robert shut the door behind him.

Marie-Hélène rose. "I trust no one's been injured at the potworks! Joseph has gone to Liverpool today to see about clay . . ." her voice faltered, then she walked towards the doctor, taking him by the arm. "Come and sit down, my dear doctor, please. Hannah, ring the bell, no, go yourself to the dining-room, take one of my Waterford glasses from the cupboard and put in it some of the Barbados rum, a good measure. Go quickly."

138

"Yes, Mama." Hannah got up with a frightened glance at the doctor and ran to the door.

"Now, my dear man," Marie-Hélène led the doctor to a chair, "Sit down and take your time. What a pity your dear wife's no longer with us." She paused, then said in a low voice. "Is it Harry?"

He nodded, felt in his pocket and handed her a letter. "My wife . . . now my son." He put his head in his hands, his voice came muffled from behind them. "I'm not perhaps the luckiest of men."

Marie-Hélène had opened the letter, her eyes were travelling swiftly over it. She raised her head. "Such a stark note! One would think . . . but there, news like this is better to be told briefly." She bent over the doctor, putting her arm round his shoulders. "My poor friend, you've my deepest sympathy. There's no understanding of it. Why one person should be asked to bear so much . . ."

He withdrew his hands, straightened his shoulders and sat up. "I'm able to bear it, thank you. Don't worry about me. Years of dealing with other people's problems, well, you know how it is. But Harry . . . my Harry . . ." He raised his eyes to her. "And, madam, your young daughter . . . was there an understanding?"

"Of sorts. It's difficult to see into a young girl's mind, but she'll grieve for a friend if not for a lover. We'll have to tell her." She removed her hands from his shoulders, her head tilted, then as the door opened she moved quickly towards it and took the tray from Hannah as she entered.

"What is it, Mama? You look so white! It isn't someone who's been burned at the potworks? There was John Gibson last year, remember, and Papa isn't here . . ." she looked from one to the other, "It isn't anyone at the potworks at all. I'm right?"

"It isn't anyone at the potworks." Marie-Hélène placed the tray on a sidetable, then put her arm round Hannah. "You must be brave. You can see how distressed the doctor is. Can you begin to guess?"

139

"Harry . . .?" Hannah looked at Dr Compson sitting stiffly in his chair, then back to her mother. She went deathly white.

"Yes."

"Was . . . was he killed in battle?"

Marie-Hélène looked hopelessly towards Dr Compson. He answered for her. "No, Hannah. I got a fuller letter as well as the . . . the bare announcement. He had an infected foot from a bayonet wound. There was the lack of medical supplies, and the sickness, and the weather . . . he contracted blood poisoning. Maybe in his suffering it was a relief for him to . . . die. Maybe he couldn't bear any more."

"Oh, doctor!" Hannah ran to him, and kneeling beside him put her head in his lap, weeping bitterly. Marie-Hélène stood where she was, tears running down her own face. She saw the doctor's hand come out hesitantly and rest on Hannah's head. "There, there . . ." she heard him say, "there, there . . ." She opened the door quietly, and as quietly shut it behind her.

Two weeks later Marie-Hélène ordered the carriage and had Robert drive Hannah and herself to Well House. The sad news had prevented their going earlier as she had decided, but now Hannah was showing signs of needing diversion and she herself didn't wish to let any grass grow under her feet in the matter of Mia and Conway. The news of Harry's death had upset Hannah deeply, although Marie-Hélène suspected it hadn't been so much the loss as the fact that it was the first time death had stalked into her young life. Her love for Harry had been of a schoolgirlish, flirtatious type rather than a total involvement, but now having come face to face with tragedy she was reaping and even enjoying the dramatic aftermath.

She chose a Sunday afternoon around four o'clock for her visit, and was gratified to find, when she was shown into the drawing-room that Mia, Sarah and Conway were there, Mia presiding at the tea-table, Sarah bent over a sketch-book, Conway standing at the window, gazing on the park.

Mia jumped up when they were announced. "Dear Mama, and dear little sister! How very nice of you to come and visit us today. Sunday afternoons can be so long . . . look, Conway, Mama and Hannah!" But Conway had already turned from the window and was coming towards them, his face glowing. He kissed his mother-in-law and then Hannah.

"Why don't you do this more often? Am I such an ogre?"

"Far from it," Marie-Hélène said. "But you do live a little out of our way." She turned. "And Sarah too! How do you do, my dear? Still with your drawings, I see. Don't you ever give up working?"

Sarah put down her book and got up slowly. "My ideas don't wait upon my convenience." She held out her cheek. "Have you had tea? Mia was just dispensing it. She likes to play hostess."

"We should dearly enjoy a cup."

"Conway," Sarah said imperiously, "ring the bell, if you will."

He did so, and presently an elderly butler appeared at the door and bowed, looking towards Sarah.

"Replenish the tea, Robson," she said, "and bring some more china for our guests."

"You have a new butler," Marie-Hélène commented when he'd gone. She had been seated on a comfortable chair by Conway.

"Yes, Parker's gone to the Crimea, as you may already know. I suppose every man is needed," Conway said.

Mia looked at him warningly, and then at Hannah. "Are you feeling more resigned to poor Harry's death, pet?"

"Yes, one must," she said, seating herself on a sofa and spreading out her skirts with the air of a tragedy queen. "There's suffering all around us. Sit here, Sarah. I don't

141

think I've disturbed your book. I must say," glancing at her, "long sleeves come into their own on cold Spring days like this." Sarah opened her mouth as if to reply, then sat down beside Hannah and lifted her sketch-book with studied nonchalance.

"Harry was such a faithful correspondent," Marie-Hélène said to the room in general. "We had a letter from the dear boy a day or two after his father acquainted us with the sad news. So upsetting for Hannah."

"How long ago was that?" Sarah asked.

"Let me see." Marie-Hélène considered. "I should say fully ten days ago."

"That's strange." Sarah's eyes rested on Mia who had resumed her place behind the tea-table. "Very strange. You had one from him today, hadn't you, Mia? I saw it lying on the hall-table before Ruth took it up to your room."

The door opened and the butler appeared with a laden tea-tray. "Thank you," Mia said as he put it down. "That will be all." Marie-Hélène, watching her daughter's hands moving deftly among the china, saw the whiteness round her eyes, a paper whiteness compared with the warm pallor of her cheeks. She recognised the sign of tension.

"You haven't replied to my question," Sarah said when the door closed behind Robson.

"You must have made a mistake." She looked at her mother, and Marie-Hélène saw the pain in her eyes. "Sugar or lemon, Mama?"

"You know what I take." She spoke lightly, but a great rush of love nearly blinded her as she looked at her daughter.

"How could I have made a mistake?" Sarah smiled. "I must believe the evidence of my own eyes surely? It was the same as the other letters you've received from the Crimea, with the same handwriting."

"You seem to have been at pains to examine them." Mia's chin was high. "Conway, will you pass this to Mama, if you please?"

He took the cup and saucer from her. "What is this about, Mia?"

"The letters weren't from Harry," she said, and then, her voice rising, "I never had any letters from Harry nor do I feel any need to discuss my correspondence. Besides, it's extremely painful for Hannah. Here is your tea, pet. Come and get it, will you?"

Hannah got up, her eyes round. "Mia, was it . . .?"

Marie-Hélène interrupted. "May I risk a little *bon-mot* and say," she clinked the spoon in her saucer, smiling, "it's all a . . . storm in a tea-cup? Mia has always done a lot of charity visiting in Hessleton and I daresay in the village here. Writing has been her forte. Yours, Sarah," she looked coolly at the girl, "is in a different category." Sarah turned her head away and Marie-Hélène delicately sipped her tea.

"A piece of cake, Mama?" Mia said.

"You know I worry about my *embonpoint*, my dear. No, thank you, this is very refreshing." She looked at Conway provocatively. "I must make no bones about my visit this afternoon. I really came to have a word with my son-in-law."

"I'm flattered, ma'am. I beg your pardon, 'Mama'." He bowed. "Tell me," he spoke playfully, "is it for anyone's ears, this conversation?"

"Far from it. It's quite private." Marie-Hélène laughed, her eyes on him, and then, turning to her daughter, "Will you mind, Mia, if I spirit your husband away for a few minutes?"

"If he doesn't mind, I shan't." She looked at her mother suspiciously.

"I can scarcely wait for this tête-à-tête," Conway said, smiling at his mother-in-law.

"Nor I." Marie-Hélène put down her cup and saucer. "Perhaps you could suggest some place where we might talk alone?"

"Certainly." He sobered. "There's my study, if that will suit."

143

"Perfectly."

"Allow me to precede you."

"You must chatter to little Hannah while I'm gone," Marie-Hélène said to Mia. "She misses you badly. I shan't be long." She swept out of the door which Conway was holding open for her.

In his study he poked the fire to a blaze when she was seated. "Are you comfortable, Mama? That chair is an old friend, but perhaps not quite so elegant as those in the drawing-room."

"It will serve my purpose. Conway, I'm going to be quite frank with you. There's no sense in prevarication, and besides the longer I'm away the more Mia will conjecture. Since I've debarred her she'll guess it's something which concerns her, which it is. Tell me," she looked straight at him, all coquetry gone, "why don't you move into Well Farm now that Sarah is fully recovered? Is there anything that keeps you here?"

He was taken aback, she could see his eyes cloud over, but he rallied quickly. "Well, as you know, there have been various delays, especially with the servants' quarters. At first my plans were for a bachelor establishment, but when Mia and I married, I had to redesign them with a view to keeping more staff. The delays are too tedious to repeat to you, but it seems the way of all workmen to be tardy when you wish them to apply themselves."

She shook her head. "It won't do. The same situation existed a year ago. I like you, Conway, otherwise I shouldn't be taking the trouble to speak to you like this, to risk being thought meddlesome, which is the prerogative of English ladies, but not, thank God, of the French. It's Sarah who prevents you going. I shall say it for you. She resents Mia. None of us is blind. Tell me, why do you allow your sister to rule your life in this way?"

He didn't answer for a moment, and when he did his voice was almost too low for her to catch. "You're right, of course. I've no wish to deny it. Certainly her illness was genuine enough, whatever precipitated it, but you'll smile at this, no doubt, I had hopes our departure from her could be made in some . . . amity. There's been too much bitterness. Each day I've looked for some sign that Sarah and Mia were coming together. I've never concealed from my sister that we must eventually leave her, but I've tried to make her look on it as inevitable, to accept it. I haven't discussed this with Mia beyond asking her, out of the largeness of her heart, to be lenient with her. Then, strangely enough, Mia, who wished as fervently as I did to go to Well Farm, seemed to lose interest in it, to withdraw into some world of her own . . ." He got up and started striding about the room, his right fist clenched against the palm of his left hand. To Marie-Hélène it looked like a gesture of anguish, and certainly his face was drawn, his eyes dark-shadowed.

"I'm not surprised," she said. "Not surprised at all. Conway, nothing you've said convinced me that Sarah doesn't have some kind of hold over you. It costs me a great deal to say this, but I'm a woman of the world. I implore you to be as frank with me."

"She has . . . she has!" She could scarcely hear him. "She extracted from me . . . I put it that way deliberately, she extracted from me many years ago a solemn promise that I'd never leave her. I had to swear it. I'm no fool, Mama. I recognise moral blackmail, but you haven't seen her when she's ill. Those attacks of hers can be . . . frightening."

"Tell me what age you were when she extracted this promise from you?"

"Merely a youth. In my early teens."

Marie-Hélène laughed aloud in surprise and relief. "Am I hearing aright? Do you mean to say you intend to keep a promise made when you were a mere boy?"

"You don't understand. It isn't the promise in itself. It's the fearful consequences of breaking it. I've seen enough of . . . rage, and the harm it can do."

"Conway, my dear," she spoke gently. "You lost your parents when you most needed them. You've become

145

over-sensitive, unworldly, if I may say so. Any responsible adult would have told you that childish promises mean nothing. I tell you that now. And if you know moral blackmail when you see it, then don't give in to it. If you do, you're in grave danger of wrecking your marriage. Mia is a girl of spirit. She may be for some reason in a quiescent mood at the moment, but I know her. It won't last. She has a mercurial temperament which I had hoped would become milder with marriage. We took you on trust for our daughter. Don't let us down."

"I've always put Mia first in my thoughts," he said. "But one has compassion also for a girl who's known illness and tragedy . . . but I take your words to heart because Mia is the dearest thing on earth to me." He came over to Marie-Hélène's chair, and to her surprise bent down and kissed her. "As well as being fortunate in my wife, I'm equally fortunate in my mother-in-law, which they tell me is rare enough." His mouth lifted in a smile. He's attractive, she thought, and complex, but then what interesting man isn't? Handsome, and very much in love. His dark eyes were glowing.

"Thank you," she said, touching his cheek. She'd say no more. The trouble would be mended tonight, she felt sure, and the best place for that would be in bed.

That evening after dinner, when Mia was rising to go to the drawing-room with Sarah, Conway said, "Mia, I should like to have a word with you." She sat down again slowly, glancing at Sarah who had stopped on her way to the door.

"Sarah, you're excused." He spoke shortly. "This doesn't concern you." She resumed walking, her face sullen, leaving the door open. Conway got up and closed it, then sat down facing Mia. She smiled at him and she thought, as she had thought before, that he had a noble face. "It's a beautiful night, my love."

"Yes." She looked towards the window, but the heavy curtains were drawn against the sky.

"You've given up all study of astronomy?"

"Yes." She was puzzled. "Papa was the catalyst, and besides, he had a telescope. Here there is none. Why do you ask? I don't suppose you've risked offending your sister simply to discuss the stars with me."

He ignored her remark. "I, on the other hand, have been fired by your father's enthusiasm. I admit I haven't as yet bought a telescope, but I intend to ask his opinion about this. The times haven't been . . . propitious." He looked at her and she lowered her eyes, feeling her mouth set in a bitter line. "I've been doing some reading. I wondered if tonight we might manage to see the nebula in the Andromeda without an instrument, even though it's more than a million light years away. How good is your eyesight?"

"Not good enough to see that distance." She had to smile.

"But good enough to see the dim patch of light we're promised? Mia," his voice deepened, "won't you come out with me and we'll look at the sky together?"

"It's cold . . . I don't think . . ."

"I ask it as a great favour." His eyes were dark and heavy, and as he spoke he stretched his hand across the table to her. "Please, Mia. As you know, I don't supplicate very well. It's a fault of mine."

She hesitated, then said, "Why not?" She got up. "I'll fetch my shawl. It's as good a way of passing the evening as any other." He followed her into the hall, and when she had draped the shawl round her shoulders he opened the door and they stepped out into the night. The moon made the stone lions on either side of the steps appear bone white, the garden had the dream-like quality of all gardens when moonlight bathes them. He put his hand under her elbow.

"I thought we might walk through the wood towards the lake. It's been dry for some days. I'm sure you'll be well enough shod."

"Very well." They walked without speaking until they

drew near the belt of trees, and here he preceded her, stopping to hold aside a branch when necessary, directing her feet by pointing his stick, once freeing the fringes of her shawl when it caught in a long strand of bramble.

"It was a great pleasure to have your mother and Hannah call upon us this afternoon," he said.

"Yes."

"She's an admirable character, your mother. How fortunate you've been. My own mother was made in quite a different mould. Her own . . . preoccupations precluded her from taking much interest in us, and then of course they both died in our adolescence. One misses one's parents then. It's a trying time."

"Yes, Hannah and I were fortunate. Mama has a great sense of humour. She taught us how to laugh at ourselves."

"I expect you've found, like me, that there are some situations where one's sense of humour isn't much use."

"Yes, I've found that."

"I wonder what a wise parent would advise in those cases?" They were now going downwards towards the lake. She could feel her feet slipping away from her and she leant backwards. His hand went out.

"It's quite all right. I can manage. I should think . . . resignation, perhaps a shifting of interest to something more . . . congenial. But you're more versed in metaphysics than I am."

"Better read, perhaps, but it's peculiar that one can be well-versed but unable to apply the teachings when needed. It's reassuring to read that Descartes, whom I greatly admire, found more uncertainty within himself than certainty."

"I don't know about that. Do you think you set too high a standard?"

"Perhaps. And perhaps I bore you with these wanderings. Here we are." They emerged on to the flat ground around the farm. They both stood looking at it, silently. I won't say anything about it, she thought, nothing hurtful . . . "Let's walk to the edge of the lake where we can get a clear view of the sky." He put his arm round her waist as they took the last few steps.

The Black Lake deserved its name tonight, she thought. Its water was like ink, but the small ripples made by the wind were touched with silver from the moon which hung clear and full in the sky. "I can see the Milky Way," she said. "Can you?"

"Yes, it's plain tonight, but where's our nebula? You ought to have a better idea where to look than I."

She searched the heavens, her head tilted back so that it rested against his shoulder. She felt warmed by his presence, the difficulties and doubts seemed to lessen, her preoccupation with Brian Moore, her fear of Sarah. This was the man whom she had married, who had stirred her the way no other man had done. She looked up at him and saw that his eyes were fixed on her face. "Are you leaving all the work to me?" she said.

"Mia . . ." his voice was rough. "I've made up my mind. Tomorrow I set in motion our departure for the farm. We should be installed within three days."

She could scarcely believe her ears. "But Sarah, what about Sarah? And the work that's still to be done?"

"She must fend for herself and the work must go on while we're there. Oh, my darling, will you come? I bitterly regret my tardiness." She didn't answer, and he turned her gently to face him. "Let me kiss you and then give me your answer . . ." His mouth came down on hers and her head reeled, her arms crept round his neck, and then she was kissing him in return, laughing, weeping, murmuring incoherently, "Conway, I thought you had fallen out of love with me, I thought you preferred Sarah . . . I've been so miserable . . ."

"So have I." His arms grew closer. "Mia, I want you . . . I want you very much . . ." He wrenched off his coat and spread it on the grass. "See, it's dry, Mia, Mia, I'm hungry

149

for you, it's been so long . . ." There was the smell of damp grass, not dry, as he had thought, the dazzle of the moon in her eyes, blinding her, then darkness as Conway blotted it out . . .

She was embarrassed, tremulous, happy beyond belief. "How very . . . ridiculous of us." He was fastening his shirt and his teeth gleamed.

"Very ridiculous, when you consider we've a good bed at home." He helped her to her feet and drew her to him, laughing. "Why is it that ridiculous, unplanned actions are by far and away the most enjoyable?" She shook her head, trembling and laughing.

But when they were walking back along the path towards Well House she said. "And even more ridiculous, Conway . . . we came out to see the Nebula and forgot."

"Shall we go back?" He pretended to turn.

"No, no!" She caught his hand.

Chapter Thirteen

This time there were no histrionics, no hysterical bursts of weeping, no scenes, no illnesses. Whatever Conway had said to Sarah, their impending departure was surrounded by an atmosphere of icy politeness with Sarah absenting herself from most meals as if to make the transition easier. On the actual day of the removal she went to the potworks in the morning, and when she had gone Mia immediately rushed around performing last minute tasks, directing the men who had arrived early as to which pieces of furniture they were to take, which ornaments, china and books. This had been agreed upon earlier in a private discussion between Sarah and Conway.

"It might be a good idea if we left while Sarah's at Hessleton," she said to him. "I did say a tentative good-bye to her this morning," which had been received with the same icy brand of politeness, "but it's bound to be painful to her and a *fait accompli* is often easier."

"There speaks the daughter of wise parents," he said, smiling at her. "I agree. I'll tell the men to hurry. What has still to be done?"

"There are still all my clothes and personal possessions in the bedroom. Ruth's been put in charge of them."

"Leave it to her, then. One mustn't delegate then interfere. I'll have you driven by road to Well Farm so that you'll be there when the men arrive to direct the placing of the furniture. Frame was instructed to return from Hessleton without delay after he'd delivered Sarah at the potworks. Upon my soul, there's as much organisation in a simple house removal as in a battle. We might have asked Lord Raglan to spare us some of his time!" He was in high spirits. "Get your shawl and bonnet."

"They're downstairs already."

"Well, come along, dearest." He glanced out of the window. "I see Frame is outside now with the carriage." He put his arm round her and they went into the hall.

She put on her bonnet and shawl with trembling hands. It's arrived at last, she thought. She looked at her pale face in the glass as she tied the ribbons. Her eyes were shining, her lips parted. And yet, as she took a last look round, an odd feeling of sadness overcame her for a moment, partly because of disappointment in her failure with Sarah, and because that, successful or no, this place had been part of her life for more than a year, and now she was discarding it.

"Do stop admiring yourself!" She saw Conway's face smiling in the glass behind her. "'If it were done when 'tis done, then 'twere well it were done quickly.'" He put his arm round her again and led her through the open door and down the flight of steps. "Robson's already in the carriage. He'll keep in the background but do essential errands for you. I've installed a village woman in the kitchen whom I hope will prove to be a good cook, and Ruth will follow when she's seen that your possessions are safely loaded into the cart."

"You're rushing me away!" she said laughing, as he helped her into the carriage. Now that she was going she felt strangely reluctant. "Oh, good morning, Robson!" She saw the dark figure in the corner.

"Good morning, ma'am." He half-rose and bowed stiffly, more through a twinge of rheumatism, she suspected, than any disinclination.

"Take care of your mistress," Conway said, putting his head into the carriage. And then addressing Frame, "Drive into Hessleton when you've deposited madam at Well Farm. Miss Sarah wishes to be collected from the potworks at midday."

"Yes, sir." Mia heard Frame's surly voice. The Frames were two of a kind, she decided, as she waved gaily to Conway who stood in the drive. She hoped he'd obtained a cheerful woman as cook, and Ruth was a sympathetic soul. As for Robson, well he had no obvious faults and no apparent virtues, she thought, glancing at the figure of the butler sitting erect in the corner, his hands clasped on his knees. He's just an elderly man, she thought, really seeing him clearly for a moment, someone's father, or brother . . . but she was too excited to give attention to him for long.

The sun was shining on the farm when Frame left her there, and when Robson opened the door, she saw that the hall was flooded with sunshine from a tall window on the landing which was uncurtained. "I don't think we'll hang draperies there," she said. "All that light is so cheering."

"Well House *was* rather dark, ma'am."

"Did you think so?" She turned to him, ready to listen, but his face closed up like a sea-urchin.

"Only in a manner of speaking, ma'am. Now, if you'll excuse me I'll go to the kitchen quarters and see how Mrs Allenby's getting along." He walked away, a portly figure lancing forward from his small feet in the way of all butlers.

The rest of the day spun by in happy activity, marred only by the fact that Conway arrived at the farm late for luncheon, his face grim. The expected scene had taken place after all, she thought, but she didn't question him. She was especially gay over the meal and he responded to her light-heartedness, the stern lines of his face slowly relaxing, his eyes smilingly resting on her.

"I haven't seen you like this for months," he said. "Don't tire yourself. Remember, Rome wasn't built in a day."

"But Well Farm will be." She smiled back at him. "I intend to have everything shipshape with the exception of the curtains, and Frame shall drive me to Hessleton tomorrow to Cantilever's."

"I'll find a new coachman, and tomorrow I'll accompany

you so that I may order our own carriage, or even better, perhaps the coach-builders may have one for sale."

"Conway," she said, feeling happiness flooding her, "it's so lovely here. The whole atmosphere's different. This house is built to catch the sun all day, one room after another, and it's clear of the trees." She pointed. "Just look at the view of the lake from here. I'll plant a garden under the window, sweet-smelling flowers, and we'll have a white seat . . ."

"I've a suggestion to make," he said.

"What is that?"

"Many things we want will take some little time; the making of the curtains, the furniture you'll order, the carriage perhaps." He looked at her. "Did you know the Emperor and Empress of France are coming to London in the middle of April?"

"Are they?" She was surprised. "During the war?"

"War! It's been bogged down for months. There was a rumour that the Emperor was going to take personal command of his armies, but I should think Victoria wouldn't care for that!"

"So he's been invited to England as a political gambit?"

"You'll be a diplomat yet. Yes, that's about it. A carrot for the donkey, although he's certainly not that. However, *my* gambit is simpler. While we're waiting I'd like to take you to London for a second honeymoon, *my* carrot being that you'd see your beloved Eugenie at the same time."

She clasped her hands. "I should like that above all things! I don't know why it is that I'm attracted to her. But you explained that to me in Paris . . ." she smiled mischievously. "You're more than kind to me. Suddenly my world seems very bright." She put her hand to her eyes and then quickly withdrew it. "I'm not sentimental by nature so I shan't weep. I'll go and direct the workmen if there are still some about, and you may draw up plans for our second honeymoon, how we'll travel, where we'll stay and so on." She got up from the table, and coming round it she bent over and kissed him on the cheek. "Sometimes it's good to kiss without passion. Thank you . . ."

"Mia—"

"No, I'm busy!" She had gone before he could rise.

After dinner they retired to bed, so weary were they with all that had to be done. Ruth had announced their room to be in order, the bed aired. "Some of your gowns are crushed, ma'am, but I've taken them downstairs to see to their pressing. There'll be enough for you to be going on with, I daresay."

"You can refurbish your wardrobe too," Conway said, "when we go to London. And perhaps you'll find that the *haut monde* is reducing the circumference of its skirts. I devoutly hope so, otherwise it will soon be impossible to enter our bedchamber."

In their room, clad in a loose robe, she checked her wardrobe, her chest of drawers, her toilet table. Everything seemed to be in order. "She's a good, kind girl, Ruth," she said, yawning, her hand to her mouth, "tomorrow I must compliment her on her handling of this part of the removal . . ." her hand stayed where it was.

"What is it?" Conway was on the point of going into his dressing-room.

"My writing-desk! Where's my writing desk? It was on top of the walnut chest. Ring for Ruth at once!"

"Is it so urgent? It's past nine o'clock."

"I must speak to her!" She crossed the room and pulled the bell, standing beside it in her agitation. Soon she heard Ruth's step outside. "Come in!" she called.

"Try to calm yourself," Conway said. She paid no attention to him.

"Ruth," she could hardly wait for the girl to enter, "where's my little writing-desk? I cautioned you most strongly to remember it. I don't see it here."

"Oh, ma'am!" The girl looked all around. "I was sure I'd remembered everything. But at the end it was all rushed, like. The men were urging me to hurry, and the

155

master said they were waiting, and what with one thing and another . . ."

"But don't you remember it?" Her voice rose and Conway reappeared at the door of his room.

"It's been overlooked. It'll be quite safe at Well House until the morning."

"Couldn't Ruth . . .?" She collected herself. "No, of course not. Very well," she said to the girl, "that will be all. I only wondered where it had gone."

The girl looked bewildered. "I can't think, ma'am. I was that careful. But first thing in the morning I'll make my way to Well House and get it for you. The master's right. It'll be safe. Don't you worry." She went out.

Mia sat down at her toilet table trying to calm herself. She dabbed some toilet water on her temples, feeling almost feverish. She mustn't let Conway see her distress, or suspect . . . She thought of Well House dark amongst the trees, Sarah creeping about silently at night, up to their former bedroom . . . no, she was being fanciful. There were servants. She rarely left her own quarters . . .

Conway appeared in his night shirt, hair freshly brushed, smiling. "Come along, Mia, come to bed. You've tired yourself out today. You aren't still distressed about that desk, are you?" He came up behind her, put his hands on her shoulders. She thought there was suspicion in the eyes which met hers in the glass.

"Of course I'm not." She made an effort to appear normal. "You're right, I'm tired, and undressing is an additional chore." She smiled at him, but her heart was beating sluggishly in her body with fear.

"Let me help you." His hands were gentle. She felt the fresh night air on her skin as he loosened her robe and the tiredness and dread began to leave her.

The trip to London was all he had promised and much more than she had expected. It was more than a year since she had known such happiness, and the weather seemed to be in tune with her mood. There were soft Spring airs, mild blue skies, pale gold sunshine. The trees blossomed, the daffodils bloomed in St James' Park where they walked, and the streets everywhere were gaily decorated for the Royal visit. London felt like the hub of the world to Mia, and the initials of the two Royal couples intertwined along the processional routes seemed to be a symbol of the close accord existing between the two countries. Everywhere they walked or drove they seemed to hear the faint strains of *Partant pour la Syrie*, the Second Empire anthem.

"It has a slightly melancholy air," she said to Conway when they were standing at Hyde Park Corner waiting to see the Royal procession.

"He's a melancholy man in some ways. What a dynasty, and who knows his destiny? He may be slain in the Crimea if he goes, he may be slain by an assassin if he stays." But she was no longer listening to him. The Household Cavalry could be seen in the distance, a wave of excitement was running through the crowd. "Vive le Hemperor!" shouted a patriotic Cockney voice near them.

And then the carriages were rolling past, the Queen smiling, staid, plump, regal, with Napoleon the Third beside her, saturnine, mustachioed, hook-nosed, buccaneerish in his mode of acknowledging the acclaim – or was it simply French? – followed by Eugenie, pale, erect, her exotic air of beauty enhanced by the solid Germanic figure of the Prince by her side.

"Oh, wonderful, wonderful!" Mia said. "Her hair shone in the sunlight."

"So does yours." Conway smiled down at her. "Now, dear madam, do you wish to follow the Royal trail to Guildhall and then, I believe, to the French Embassy, or shall we go and amuse ourselves?"

"Where do they go this evening?"

"To Covent Garden to hear Fidelio. But I'm afraid I'm one of the hoi polloi. I tried to get seats for us, but it was out of the question. Mr Conway Graham of Wells Farm means less than nothing in London."

"Never mind, we'll read all about it tomorrow," she said. "After all, we saw her at the Opera in Paris."

The London papers were ecstatic about the Empress's appearance. Mia read their various reports sitting up in bed in their hotel in St James' Street the following morning. "Just imagine," she said to Conway beside her, "her white crinoline was trimmed with marabou feathers, and the writer has never seen such vast skirts. You had hoped I'd reduce mine, but immediately I am home I'll go to Cantilever's to order them to add another yard or two."

"I prefer you like this." He fingered the Indian muslin of her night-dress, "you're so very slender, my darling . . . I wonder sometimes if we'll be lucky enough to have a child. Goodness knows it's not for want of loving you."

"There's plenty of time." She spoke hurriedly. "Now, don't let's waste the whole day lying here. Look, the sun's shining and there are a million things to do." But a tiny cloud had appeared in her happiness. She had expected to be pregnant by this time. She had been prepared for it by a sensible mother, and surely she was healthy enough . . . but she forgot about it immediately they were in the streets again.

They took a coach to Sydenham following in the wake of the Royal party who were visiting the Crystal Palace in the morning. This time, as they stood respectfully amongst the crowds when the Royal couples and their entourage passed through them, she was able to look at Eugenie more closely, and for a moment the blue-green eyes seemed to rest upon her. Striking eyes, she thought, and then she remembered she had read that Eugenie outlined them with black pencil. Deliciously French . . . perhaps in the privacy of her bedroom she'd try the effect for herself. She was left with a vague feeling of rapport, until she remembered that Conway thought they resembled each other. It had been like looking into a mirror.

They found the interior too hot for their taste amongst the milling crowds. She liked best the two tall elms which soared towards the galleries, Conway was intrigued by a model of Liverpool docks in which he said he had a proprietary interest since it was near home. The fountains and waving palms were pretty, she conceded, although personally she would rather have the open air with the wind on her face . . .

For some strange reason, high up on one of the galleries, her mind went back to the day she had stood with Brian Moore looking down on the Fair, the same movement of figures, the same bright colours . . . where was he now? The last letter, the one Sarah had seen on the hall table, had said that cholera had struck again, that the camps were seas of mud, that Parker tended him well but himself even better. If there was anything to be had where even the poor horses were eating the straps of their saddles, Parker would get it.

The letter had told her of Harry's death, and that he had died bravely although his leg had been amputated. "It's as if part of me had died," he said, "we've shared so much together. Life will never be the same without him." Some time she might tell Hannah. It had also relieved her of a dreadful anxiety, the thought that Brian might have perished in the battle at Balaclava.

She must arrange with Ruth to intercept any further letters since they would still be addressed to Well House. But that raised another dread in her mind. Had Sarah by any chance managed to open the writing-desk the night it was left behind, and read Brian's letters? There was a box in the library which contained hundreds of keys . . . she reassured herself. Sarah would never have kept the information to herself. Nothing would have prevented her from telling Conway. She was safe. She felt her heart beating rapidly in agitation, and she made a decision standing there. Should there be any further letters she'd tear them up unopened. They were no longer necessary to her happiness.

Weren't they? a voice seemed to say in her head. She bit her lip and half-closed her eyes. How hot it was in here! The heat rose . . .

"You look pale, my darling," Conway said at her elbow.

"I'm quite all right."

"You're sure?" She nodded. He went on in a lower tone. "I've just overheard a gentleman at my side telling his companion that the Empress was pushed in a bath chair this morning when she grew weary. The Prince presented her with it afterwards. Do you think she's *enceinte?*"

She shrugged. "Let's go and see the Winterhalters, and then perhaps we might have tea in one of the restaurants. I find it rather hot."

"If you wish."

She thought that while second honeymoons were a charming idea she'd be quite content to be back in Well Farm. Conway said to her as they made their way downstairs, "I've a feeling that all this is the end of an era." She nodded. It had a prophetic ring about it.

Chapter Fourteen

Conway had been right about the Emperor. They learned from Mr Russell in The Times that he had decided not to risk his life in the Crimea after all. This might have been because an assailant in the Champs Élysées had tried to deprive him of it in Paris, Conway said. The war seemed to disappear into the background, especially as there were no more letters from Brian to keep it alive. But since according to the news there was apparent stalemate in the Crimea, Mia told herself there was no need for anxiety.

Besides it was such beautiful weather. There was the pleasure of putting Well Farm in order and feeling mistress of a home in her own right, of entertaining her own friends. Sometimes she wished they had a child, but most of the time she was too busy to let her mind dwell on it for long.

She and Conway had entered a new phase of loving. He was still as ardent, but more tender, more considerate. He told her one night that before their marriage he had subscribed to the popular belief that man's role was to subjugate women. "How ridiculous all that seems, now that I find your pleasure is no less important than mine." Their love-making had never been richer or more satisfactory . . . except that it was still barren.

Mia thought of Brian sometimes, but it was in a tender, girlish way, like the Winterhalter pictures they had seen at the Crystal Palace, a romantic ideal divorced from reality. She remembered Conway saying long ago that she must put away childish things.

On a burgeoning morning in the middle of June she had

161

Baxter, their new coachman, drive her to the potworks to see her father. She wished to order a dinner service, and hoped he would advise her as to choice. She found him in his room, Jason sitting at his side. She was struck by the young man's smart appearance, and the new air of confidence he showed as he got up to greet her.

"Mrs Graham! Although I still think of you as Miss Mia . . ." He laughed. "How well you look!"

"I might say the same about you, Jason, and prosperous."

"He's trying to get the business away from me," Joseph smiled wryly.

"That would take a much smarter man than me, sir. I'll get on with what we've been discussing and leave you to have a chat with your daughter." He bowed to Mia and went out of the room.

She lifted an eyebrow at her father. "Jason behaves like a member of the firm."

"He almost is. I'm thinking of taking him in, slackening the reins a little myself. Did you know he was courting Hannah?"

"I had my suspicions. He hasn't let the grass grow under his feet after Harry."

"Hannah was never deeply committed. Between you and me, Harry had virtues Jason will never possess, one of them being humility. But perhaps he's better suited in temperament to Hannah all the same."

"He'll ride rough-shod over her."

"Some women like that."

"You don't really believe so, Papa, do you? Conway and I were discussing this very subject the other night."

"Has it taken him so long to discover you aren't that kind of woman?" He smiled at her. "Don't look bashful. Neither is your mother. But you're both still rare enough in this day and age. Hannah likes a master. She enjoys the role of play-thing for a man's lighter moments, and yet in her own way she's quite shrewd. She'll demand her pound of flesh."

"You make her sound not at all like the Hannah I know."

"Her temperament is beginning to set in its mould." He laughed. "Now, that's a true potter's remark."

"And I've come for a true potter's advice. I should like to purchase a dinner service, Papa."

"There will be no question of purchase. Anything you chose will be a gift."

"Then I shan't have it."

"I insist. All I ask is that you let me choose it for you. As a matter of fact I've one in the showroom at present which is quite beautiful. Come and see it."

He got up and together they walked through the floor of the manufactory, a journey she had often made with her father holding her hand and the men nodding and smiling at 'the little missy'. She recognised a turner at his bench from that time. He touched his forelock.

"Well, Mr Grayson, how nice to see you still working." She watched him as he deftly trimmed the vase on its stand. "Don't you ever grow tired of doing the same thing all the time?"

"No." He smiled and shook his head. "Nothing's ever the same, miss, I mean, ma'am, no two's alike. As long as they're hand-worked they'll all be different. You put a bit of yourself in them, like, but come the day . . ." He shook his head. "Ah, well, reckon I shan't see it."

"Don't you worry, Grayson," Joseph said. "There'll always be a place for you."

"Do you think the need for men like Grayson will disappear?" she asked him as they walked on.

"I think we'll always need men in potting. Some of the skills will be taken over by machinery, but it's a peculiar craft in that as far as I can see at present there's no substitute for a well co-ordinated hand and eye." He stopped at a door at the end of the work floor and unlocked it. "You first, Mia. You've come at the right time." He led her to one of the stocked benches. "This service has appealed to my eye so much that I can't bear to sell it. But the thought of you and Conway using it would give me great pleasure, and," he smiled at her, "keep it in the family."

She looked at the plates and tureens, their subtle green colour, their mouldings of gold and white. "You've forsaken all decoration in this one, Papa?"

"Never gild a lily." He picked up a plate, touching the gold rim. "Well, just a little. And that copper green under the lead glaze . . . exquisite. Don't tell me machines could give you such a finish. A man has to have a feeling for the harmony between the body composition and the glaze, the temperatures of the biscuit and glost ovens . . . no, old Grayson can sleep soundly in his bed for a long time."

"Sarah will have had nothing to do with this?"

"No, she agreed with me it would be better to be left plain. She's becoming interested in techniques outside her own, especially in the lead glazes. Craythorne tells me she's become quite an authority."

"We hear very little from her at Well Farm."

"She's sensibly widening her horizons. You moved away at the right time, I think. Have you found it so?"

"Yes. I wondered what had prompted Conway, or should I say who?" She smiled at him. "You have a scheming wife, you know. Anyhow, we're very happy. It's a house which gives you a feeling of peace. Somehow at Well House there was a turbulence, a looming quality, I can't describe it . . . you've found the same difference at Well Farm when you've visited us, haven't you?"

"Yes, I think we have. It's a charming house. But then any house is charming where there's love. So you'll accept this service from me?"

"It's too much, Papa. As it happens I've velvet curtains the same colour in the dining-room, but it's too much . . ."

He laughed. "You've answered my question. The only payment I demand is to be invited to sup off it when you have a mind to."

"You know you're always welcome." She kissed him. "Thank you."

"You look happy, my darling." He held her away from him.

"Yes, happy . . ." And, feeling confused by his scrutiny, "if only world affairs were rather more happier. Conway, who retails the news to me each morning, tells me there's been an assault on Sebastopol which has been a miserable failure."

"Yes, Harry would have been in that had he lived. Perhaps the men who did fight were half-dead with sickness and hunger. God knows they've had a terrible winter."

Her heart sank. Brian . . . perhaps he had been long ago transported to Scutari . . . perhaps he had been wounded, killed . . . "One puts oneself in their place," she said. "Conway rages against the incompetence of the British. He has strong opinions."

"He's a man of strong feelings as no doubt you've found out. Are you going to see your Mama and sister this morning?"

"No, Papa." They walked to the door together. "I must be back in time for luncheon which I like to have with Conway if possible, and afterwards I'm going to the village to do some sick visiting. I've recently taken it up."

"Is it a substitute for anything else?" She thought he glanced at her keenly.

"No, indeed." She laughed gaily for his benefit. "It's expected of me."

"Quite so." She knew that "quite so" of her father's, she thought, an apparent agreement while his mind worked busily behind its innocuousness.

Baxter set her down at Mrs Parker's cottage in the main street of the village. It was Conway's idea. "I ought to have been making enquiries about Jack Parker. You can combine it with a visit to his mother."

The woman who opened the door bore a resemblance to

Parker, the same broad nose, the large nostrils which gave a *farouche* look to the face. But her smile was welcoming enough. "It's Mrs Graham from the big house, isn't it? I've seen you riding past sometimes."

"I'm living at the farm now. Good afternoon, Mrs Parker. I heard you were poorly. I've brought you some strawberries our gardener picked today and cream from the farm to go with them."

"That's kind of you, I'm sure. Will you step inside, please?" The woman was wiping her hands on her apron. "It's true I've been poorly with bronchitis, a legacy from winter. Thank goodness it's making up for it now, shocking it was." She was opening another door into a living-room with a bright little fire in the grate flanked on each side by a brown and white china dog. "In here, Mrs Graham, and sit yourself down. It's too hot and tiring today to be doing errands of mercy." There seemed a slightly patronising flavour to the remark, Mia thought, typical of Parker who always said the unexpected thing. The little room was suffocatingly hot, and she was glad she had worn her sarsenet dress of pale violet which had a cool feel on her skin. "And how is Mr Graham?" the woman asked.

"Very well, I thank you. He's busy restoring the farm at the moment. He intends to have the most modern buildings and cottages erected. He feels it's only right."

"He's a good man as well as a clever one," Mrs Parker said surprisingly. "Did you know I nursed his mother from time to time? Well, least said soonest mended about that! But I know what he had to put up with. And he was good to my Jack, I can tell you. Helped him out of a scrape once or twice. He knew I had a hard time bringing him up without a father . . . then when Jack got into trouble with poaching, and worse, he takes him on up at the House. There's charity for you, rather than the tittle-tattle I had to put up with here. Then what does the bold lad do! Just when he's nicely trained for a valet he's off for a soldier and never as much as a by-your-leave."

Mia was bewildered by the outburst, and upset. Conway had never said anything about a link with Mrs Parker, beyond telling her about the death of the husband. Why was he so secretive? Her old fears and worries returned, but she tried to quell them by speaking brightly, in the social tone she had learned from her mother. "And have you any news of your son, Mrs Parker?"

"News?" The woman looked as bewildered as Mia felt. "Why bless your soul, he's home again, a bit the worse for wear, but trust Jack, he always pops up."

"Yes, that's right, Ma. I always pops up." Mia looked round and saw Parker standing at the door. He had opened it so quietly that she hadn't heard him.

"Why, Parker!" she said. "What a surprise! So you got home safely?"

"Invalided out, madam. All me limbs intact but something wrong with me kidneys. Still, I reckon with some of me Ma's home cooking I'll soon be as right as rain."

"Would you take a cup of tea, Mrs Graham?" his mother said as if she had been reminded of her reputation. "I've a nice scone just out of the oven."

"Well . . ." Conway had said, "Drink a cup of tea with her if you've time. It will please her." And please him?

"It won't take me above a minute." She had seen the signs of hesitation. "You talk to madam, Jack, and tell her all about your adventures. Although," she said, reaching the door of some kind of scullery and turning round, "I expect he'll tell you of some he never had if I know him."

"That's right, Ma." He seemed quite unperturbed at the thought of being left to entertain Mia. "And how's the master?" he said when his mother had disappeared.

"Very well."

"Still working away at the farm? I'll say that about him. When he puts his mind to something he generally goes ahead. A perfectionist I always found him." He smiled a shade too familiarly. "A hard man to cross, though."

"You're feeling none the worse for your injuries?"

167

"Well, I'm alive, that's the main thing. Not like poor Captain Compson. No anaesthetic to take that leg off." He shook his head. "Screamed something awful. It upset his friend quite a lot, that, you know who I mean?" She turned her head away pointedly and looked out of the window. She felt cold inside in spite of the hot fire. "I know you do, but I don't blame you for not wanting to admit it. But you see, when you're someone's man you get to know a lot because they speak to you a lot. It's funny, that, how gents like Captain Moore and the likes of him will chatter away to you, and yet if they met you in the street they might well pass you by. They do the same with their barbers. Yes, he talked a lot about you, Captain Moore did, when he was fevered like, what he felt about you and all that. Maybe because I knew you. He often asked me if I thought you were happy and how Mr Graham compared with him, like. Well, what would you have done? I told him what he wanted to know, that you and the master didn't always . . . well, they were an odd pair those two at the Big House. You fair upset the applecart, like . . ." Mia's eyes misted over and then they were clear again. She must get away. She half-rose from her chair. "Don't go, ma'am," Parker said. "Ma would be real disappointed if you left without drinking a cup of tea with her. Thinks the world of Mr Graham, she does."

She took a deep breath. "Where . . . where is Captain Moore now, Parker?" She had to know if he were still alive.

"He was in the hospital at Balaclava when I was shipped back. Got on nicely once he was cleaned up and fed, like, although I always did my best for him. 'If there's an egg in the bloody place,' pardon my French, 'Parky'll find it,' he used to say. Spoke good French, the captain did, on account of having been partly educated there, same as all the wealthy Romans. Wore a cross, he did . . ."

"Will he still be in the hospital?"

"Wouldn't know that, ma'am. Don't think he'd be good

enough for going into battle, though, after his tummy trouble. Still, you'd be surprised what they throw in when they gets desperate. Always did give a good account of himself, though, the captain, and a fair marvel with the horses."

Mrs Parker appeared with a laden tray. Mia, disregarding the pleased look on the woman's face, got to her feet. "I'm very sorry, Mrs Parker, but I find I can't wait. The time's flown listening to your son. He's told me . . . so many things."

The woman's smile faded. "Have you been after offending Mrs Graham?" she said fiercely, her nostrils flaring. "Can't trust you for a minute when me back's turned!"

"No, Ma, not me. I was just telling her about my life out there and all that. He smiled disarmingly, switching the smile from his mother to Mia like a small boy asking for praise.

"Sometimes I think there's a devil in you, Jack Parker."

"Don't scold him," Mia said. "We've enjoyed our little talk. I'm so sorry I can't wait. Good afternoon, Mrs Parker."

"Good afternoon . . . I buttered all these here scones . . ." She looked discomfited.

"Some other time, Mrs Parker."

She was helped into the carriage by Baxter who was proving to be a good coachman. He tucked her up warmly in a rug. "You look cold, ma'am," he said, "although it's a warm day. Don't you worry. I'll get you back home in no time."

Robson opened the door after what seemed to her an unconscionable wait. Parker would have been much quicker . . . I must see Conway and tell him about Parker, about his familiarity, no, his insolence, that he must never employ him again. She was taking off her bonnet and mantle in the hall while her mind raced. Conway should have told her that the woman had worked in the house at one time. He and

Sarah had such secretive ways, as if they infected each other . . . in the gloom of the glass she saw Robson's moon face, lugubrious. "What is it, Robson?" she said sharply.

"I wondered if there was anything else, ma'am. Ruth . . ."

"Nothing at all. Except, is your master in, or is he . . .?" she saw the ponderous face and imagined the slow brain beginning to work behind it. "Never mind. I'll go into the drawing-room first." She thought he mumbled something but by this time she had opened the door. Sarah stood at the fireplace facing her.

"Sarah!" She felt her eyes widen, and then, recovering herself. "This is an unexpected pleasure. I'd thought Conway would be here . . ." her anger exploded into words. "I particularly wanted to see him just now. I went, at his request, on an errand of mercy to the Parkers and found myself insulted and made to feel foolish. Really, it's too bad . . ." she stopped herself in time.

The girl's face had remained calm, even disdainful while she spoke. "Was Mrs Parker telling you she used to look after my mother when she was drunk? She was the only person who could handle her. Often Conway had to ride to the village."

Mia gathered her wits together. "Don't think you can shock me, Sarah. I knew of your mother's weakness. It's distressing, but no matter, it's buried in the past as far as I'm concerned. Her son's a different matter. Perhaps he's just spiteful by nature and likes stirring up trouble. In any case I'll tell Conway not to employ him again."

"Did he have a message from Captain Moore?" The words seemed to fall like a stone in a well. Mia's hand went out to clutch the arm of the chair she was standing beside. Instead she sat down. Always take a deep breath, Mama said . . . "What do you know about Captain Moore?" She met the girl's eyes steadily.

"Enough. I felt it my duty to come and tell Conway about him today."

"Why today?"

"Because you'd had a long enough halycon period with him, long enough to allow you to be lulled into a false sense of security."

"Where's Conway?" She couldn't look at the hate in Sarah's eyes. She couldn't sit. She got to her feet and shouted the words this time. "*Where's Conway?*"

"I haven't the slightest idea. He ordered his horse to be saddled and rode away in one of his black rages. You don't know his black rages, do you? They can cause untold harm . . . he'll never forgive you for cheating him, you know. He hates to be cheated."

"You told him about Captain Moore." She spoke the words slowly. "I can only believe, then that you knew of him through his letters, through *my* letters. You're quite right, oh, yes, you're quite right. I've been living in a false sense of security. But do you know, Sarah, I didn't really believe in it. Not at the bottom of my heart. You see, I know you. I knew you'd be malicious enough to read my letters if you got an opportunity, which I was foolish enough to give you. And I knew my happiness here was too good to last, that when it suited you, you'd tell your brother and poison his mind against me. Oh, I know how your mind works! I've seen it from the first day, how you've resented me, always resented me . . ."

"You can talk as long as you like. Your guilt shows in your face, your stupid pretty face that took Conway's fancy. Talking won't help. He'll never forgive you, now that he knows you've betrayed him. You haven't seen his temper in action, have you, little Mia? It's honeyed words for you, isn't it? 'Dearest', 'my sweetheart', '*wife*'!" Her eyes seemed to flame red in her white face as she spoke the last word. "But he never really loved you. Lusted after you, perhaps. It's *me* he loves, always, always, always!" She put an arm along the mantelpiece on either side of her body, hunching it forward between them, her eyes blazing.

Mia looked at her. Her own anger died, there was a cold deadness inside her as if she would never be warm again. "I

171

can't believe . . . I can't believe anyone would be so evil, so deliberately evil. I've tried, God knows I've tried with you. But surely my husband isn't intimidated by a hysterical, malicious girl like you? Unless . . ."

The long sleeves were like batwings, her head seemed to be sunk on her neck in some kind of rigor. "Come, come! Such innocence! A silly provincial miss who has nothing but a pretty face and a willing body! What do you know of love? Well, I'll tell you, you milk-white sop, I'll open those wide, pretty eyes even wider . . . *you*'ve never known a relationship like mine and Conway's, tender, deep, how he took care of me, sat with me, read to me, talked to me . . . would you like to hear how our passion grew? How he came to my room at nights, comforted me? *You*'ve never known real passion such as existed between us, such as exists, you with your puny, flirtatious ways, 'Yes, my darling,' 'No, my dearest' . . ." The deep voice grew softer, her head fell to one side. "There we were, so happy in Well House, hidden in the dark trees, no one to disturb us, and *you*, pretending to be grown-up, in your pretty gowns and with your pretty manners copied from that blowsy mother of yours, hoped to take him away from me! I could tell you so much. Listen—"

"Stop! Stop!" Mia put her hands to her ears. "I don't want to . . . you must leave my house at once . . . I can't bear it!" She was weeping now. "I'll ring to have you shown out if you won't go . . ."

"Don't bother to ring," Sarah said. Her arms came down at her sides, the batwings folded and only the white frill of the undersleeve showed. Her face was wiped clean of expression. "I'm going. But you'll find out. It's me Conway will come to when he gets over his sick rage at you, he's always come to me . . ." She walked past Mia, and presently she heard the door shut.

She would be walking back through the woods to Well House, *their* path, where Conway had first kissed her, down which he had led her that night to the lake, made love to her on the damp grass . . . the pain in Mia's heart was unbearable. She ran into the hall and went up the staircase to her bedroom where she threw herself on the bed and burst into uncontrollable weeping.

She didn't know how long she lay there. When she opened her eyes the sun was still shining. In those long, clear June days it would be light until ten o'clock. It had been the longest day of her life. She got up and saw the lake sunlit, the trees freshly green grouped around it, saw underneath her window the white seat round the elm which Conway had made for her, saw the gardener working in the garden bordering the lake which she and Conway had designed. They would have a boat, he said, and he would teach her to fish, and perhaps later there would be a child . . .

All that was finished, she thought, all over. Somewhere he was riding blindly along, thinking of the wrong she had done him in corresponding with Brian Moore, encouraging him, and then when his rage cooled he'd make his way to Well House. Sarah had said so. The bond was deep, close, as secretive as the house where it had grown.

But what about the wrong he has done me? She turned swiftly from the window because the pain was too intense to bear. She must get away. That was it. She must get away before he came back . . . if he came back. It was over now. How could she take back a husband who'd been to his sister far more, far more . . .

She took her valise from a cupboard and threw some toilet things into it, her brush, comb, handkerchiefs, took a night-dress from a drawer and her robe from the end of the bed where Ruth had spread it out for the night. Soon she would be bringing up the water for her bath, helping her to dress for dinner.

She went to the mirror and looked at her face, curiously. When you were young, did anguish show? The tears had dried and she was pale with bruised eyes, but some powder would cover that. Her hair was dishevelled where she had pulled at it when she had lain on the bed. She found a chiffon

173

kerchief in her drawer and tied it over her head. Her hands trembled. She crossed the room and rang the bell, then sat with her back to the door at the toilet-table.

In a few moments she saw Ruth's round cheerful face in the glass. A long, long time ago, in the hall, she had seen Robson's. Her head ached. "Do you want your bath, madam? I was on the point of bringing it. Oh, did you intend to take a walk in the new garden? The kerchief? You're quite right, there's a little breeze springing up with the evening."

"Ruth," she said, not turning, "I want you to tell Baxter to bring round the carriage again. I'm going to stay with my parents at Blenheim Terrace."

"Oh, ma'am, has something happened? They looked so well when they were last here."

"They're quite well, but it's become . . . necessary for me to go home. I'll send for my luggage. Meanwhile, if you'd carry down the valise and see Baxter, I'll follow when I've gathered together a few things in my reticule."

When Ruth had left the room she looked around. There was the writing desk. Should she take the letters? But what was the purpose of that now? She could imagine Sarah's version, related to Conway, and yet, for the most part, they'd been unexceptional in tone. Suddenly her face burned. Hadn't there been one time, when Brian had been low-spirited, and he'd talked about a convoy they had captured, furs, and jewels? She didn't have to get up to find the letter. The phrase came to her mind easily, making her moan and then wipe her lips. '. . . *and I longed in this filthy place, to see you and touch you as I did that day . . .*'

She put her head in her hands, her mind reeling. But how did it compare with what Sarah had told *her*? Wasn't that far worse? There was no need to ask Conway for his forgiveness. Rather should she write a note at this moment telling him she had to leave this house because Sarah had told her . . . had told her . . .

174

She jumped to her feet. It was impossible to think any more, to imagine . . . she snatched up her reticule and ran out of the room.

The hall was deserted, but through the window she could see that Baxter was already at the door. Ruth was putting her valise into the carriage. Presently she came in. "Everything is ready, ma'am." She helped Mia on with her mantle. "What shall I say to the master when he returns?"

"I'll write . . . no, say that Miss Sarah was good enough to remain behind when he left and tell me the purpose of her visit. He'll understand."

"Very well, ma'am . . . there's nothing I can do?" The girl's face was distressed.

"Nothing, Ruth, except to tell cook to serve dinner at the usual time." Their eyes met and Mia turned away. She musn't weep. She walked out of the door and down the steps to the carriage. "I'm sorry to call you out again, Baxter," she said, accepting his help in getting in. "Fortunately it's a fine night."

"Nothing's a trouble where you're concerned, ma'am," he said. Only when they were bowling along towards Hessleton did she weep again, soft, sad, self-pitying tears which did no one any good.

But they came back again when she burst into the dining-room where her parents and Hannah were eating their evening meal. They all rose. "Good gracious, Mia!" Joseph said. "What has happened?" Marie-Hélène was already at her side, her arm around her. "Don't bother to speak. Come along and sit down. Look there's your usual chair, just waiting for you." Lucy came in, bearing a steaming tureen. "Lucy, set another place for Miss Mia. Tell Robert to help you."

"To be sure, ma'am." Emily looked at Mia and bit her lip, her eyes saucer-like.

When the door closed behind her Mia said, wiping her eyes. "She'll go into the kitchen and tell Robert and cook

I've arrived weeping with a chiffon kerchief over my head. In a state. Yes, that's what she'll say, a state! Even the servants can see it." She tore the chiffon from her head and burst afresh into tears. "Something terrible has happened . . . Sarah has . . . and Conway went into a rage and went off. I couldn't bear to listen to her terrible words and . . . my heart's broken." She laid her head down on the table and wept.

She heard her mother's soft "tut-tut", Hannah's, "Oh, Mia," and then her father's voice, tender but firm. "Weep away, but I can tell you, yours won't break so easily."

Chapter Fifteen

It was like being back in Blenheim Terrace as an unmarried woman. She did the same things; talked with Marie-Hélène and Hannah, went for drives, paid calls, rode with Hannah, shopped in Hessleton and knitted comforts for the troops instead of netted purses.

And yet it wasn't the same because she did all those things in a kind of half-world of misery, or rather as a dual personality. One Mia was a dutiful daughter who made the right responses, the other felt at times such agony of mind that she could hardly wait to get into bed to be alone. Nor was it the same as regards Hannah, because Jason Berridge was a frequent caller at the house and he had changed her sister in some significant way so that she seemed frivolous and shallow, or perhaps it was she, Mia, who had lost her sense of humour.

"Are you in love with Jason?" she asked Hannah one evening when they were brushing their hair together. Often her whole body screamed for solitude, but the dutiful Mia, the Mia that was, went meekly through this nightly ceremony.

Hannah blushed. "Yes. If feeling myself tremble when he comes into the room and wanting to please him and be admired by him means anything, I'm in love with him."

"What do you talk about when you're alone?"

"I tell him about my latest dresses and bonnets. He's interested in fashion. For instance, he admired vastly my new small bonnet of Italian straw, the one with bands of white tulle. They were quite the rage at Longchamps this year, you know."

"I didn't. And what does *he* talk about?"

"Mostly of the potworks, I confess. How he would change it and enlarge it, and what kind of house he'd like to live in with me and how many servants we'd have and what is *comme il faut* in the best houses."

"You enjoy this, Hannah?"

"Exceedingly. I should like a grander establishment than Blenheim Terrace. Mama and Papa have never cared for 'frummery' as Papa calls it, and even you, Mia, haven't set yourself up in great style in Well Farm in spite of Conway's money . . ." she put her hand to her mouth. "Perhaps I shouldn't mention his name when you're so unhappy. Why don't you talk about it? I do admit Sarah can be tiresome, but if I had been you I should have given lots of soirées and perhaps a little Ball and got her married off."

"Perhaps I made a mistake."

"You looked just like Papa when you said that. Oh, I know you think I'm stupid and frivolous at times, but I could have handled Sarah!"

"What a pity *you* didn't marry Conway."

"Don't be so odious. He's not at all my style. Indeed, he rather frightens me at times. He's quite charming, of course, but he seems to look through me . . . what's wrong, Mia, have you a headache? You look quite ill."

"I do have a little headache and you've been tugging at my hair in your enthusiasm for your Italian straw bonnet. Run along to your bed now, pet. I must lie down."

Hannah got up. "You're not such fun as you used to be. Good night." She pecked Mia on the cheek.

"Good night. I'm sorry . . ." Mia lay sleepless until dawn.

Marie-Hélène was logical and direct. "You can't go on refusing to see Conway, Mia. You know he calls every day. I've told him how Sarah has upset you and he only asks to be allowed to explain matters."

"Sarah has already done that."

"Can't you tell me what she said? It's bad for you to bottle up your emotions like this."

"Please don't speak of it!" She put her hands to her cheeks to cover the rare blush which was making her feel faint. "Perhaps you can't bear with me here . . ."

"My dear girl, I can bear with you for as long as you want to remain with us. But once a married woman always a married woman. Isn't that so? I can see only too well how Hannah's chatter wearies you, how difficult it is for you to fill the role now of a daughter of the house."

"It's true. Either Hannah has changed or I have."

"Both. My advice to you, then, is to do nothing. Eat a little more, let the time pass and then one day you'll find you can entertain the idea of writing to Conway and asking him to call. You must hear his side."

"There's no doubt, Mama, I must believe her. Please, please don't discuss it any more."

She was comfortable only with her father. Once, after midnight when she couldn't sleep she joined him in the garden where he was working with his telescope. He showed no surprise at her appearance behind the screen of conifers. "Come and see the mountains of the moon, Mia. They're very clear." She obediently put her eye to the eyepiece. The vastness and the sublimity of the sight calmed her, took her mind away from her own problems. "That's Copernicus you're looking at. I find it very relaxing to look upwards when I've been looking downwards all day. I wonder if man will ever walk up there? Or do you think that too fanciful?"

"I suppose nothing's fanciful if you can transport yourself into the future." And then because she felt she should appear normal, "Conway was interested in Charles Darwin's writings. He's followed all his scientific expeditions. He says he'll astonish the world one of these days."

"He has a scientific bent, your husband." Joseph was changing the eyepiece. "The last time we spoke together he told me he was reading and enjoying Humbold's Cosmos."

"Did he?" She couldn't understand her pleasure in talking about him. "He has . . . ideas which astonish one at first, and then when you think of them they begin to make sense. For instance . . ." she had a vivid mental image of sitting talking with him at the fire late into the night, and an even stronger remembrance of her happiness . . . "one evening when we were talking together – we talked a lot, Papa – he said . . . now what was the phrase, I must get it right . . . ah yes, he said that 'the stifling fanaticism of our religious outlook had to disappear in time.' At first I was surprised. It sounded like sacrilege."

"Or sense." And then, bending to look through the telescope again. "But you don't intend to see him when he calls?"

"No, Papa."

"Never?"

"I can't think as far as that. At the moment it's impossible for me to contemplate."

"Quite so. I've no intention of forcing your confidence. You're a married woman, but I'm a little involved in so far as Sarah still comes to the potworks. She has commissions for the next six months or so. You do see I must treat her as I've always treated her, with politeness."

"If she wishes to continue with her work for you, that's your affair."

"You realise my position?"

"Yes."

"You're too hurt at the moment for me to read you a sermon about forgiveness, except to say that no new step is possible without it. I can only make a suggestion."

"What is that, Papa?"

"I'm going to Paris in a few weeks' time to the Sèvres

180

factory. Your mother thinks, and I do too, that it would be good for you to accompany me."

"I couldn't make the effort. Please don't ask me!"

"Nonsense. Anyone can make the effort when they try. Our visit will coincide with that of the Queen and Prince Albert. Aren't you in the habit of following them about Europe?" She knew he smiled in the darkness. "Will you come to please me?"

She thought of Paris and her honeymoon there with Conway, and the passion . . . but Sarah had said theirs was far stronger . . . "No, I can't, Papa."

"Come and see this," he said, standing aside. "The craters are perfectly visible now. I believe I can see the Peak of Teneriffe and its environs." She bent down again to please him. "Quite perfect, isn't it? Don't hurry, take a long look."

She did. Her anguish seemed to lessen, she was able to think of Paris divorced from Conway, a place in its own right, of its gaiety, its bridges, outdoor cafés, its ambience. She said, still looking, "I never saw La Sainte Chapelle when we were there. I was sorry about that."

"I wouldn't mind seeing it either, the richness of the glass. I know we can't produce the same translucence in clay, but it's good to aim high."

She withdrew her eye. "It's so *uncaring*, the sky."

"That can be a good thing."

"I'll come," she said, "I'll come to Paris."

"I'm glad. Let's hope the French cooking fills you out a little."

"You can take me to dinner every night." She kissed his cheek.

The next few weeks passed, Conway still called, still left brief letters imploring her to let him talk to her, Mia grew thinner but more adamant than ever that she didn't want to see him. The outrage, she told herself, was too deep. If Sarah wanted him, then let her have him.

She missed Well Farm. From the first time she'd seen it she'd realised she could be at home there, and now, strangely enough, she wasn't at home in her parents' house. She missed the status of being a married woman, she wouldn't admit that she missed Conway. She envied Sarah in that she had an outlet in the potworks for her talent. Unless one was married with a home of one's own she began to realise how narrowing it was to be confined to a house as she now was with no responsibilities, with nothing to do but indulge herself in a meaningless social round. What she missed most about Conway was talking to him. But then she remembered Sarah had said *they* talked together, read together, sat together . . . hatred would well up in her heart and she would vow never to go back.

As for Brian there was no further news. How could there be since she had changed her address twice since his last letter? He would have decided long ago she didn't wish to write. Perhaps he had forgotten all about her. She scanned the newspapers for news of the Eleventh Hussars, and came across a paragraph saying that the remnants of the Cavalry under Brigadier Scarlett had helped the French to beat off a Russian attack on the Allied rear and there had been severe losses.

Brian had liked her, perhaps even more, she told herself. Parker had said he talked about her when he was fevered. When he was low he longed to touch her . . . it was good to know there was still wholesome, normal love. When she got to this stage in her thinking she would cover her face with her hands wishing she could pray, but even that was denied her.

A few days before Joseph and she were due to leave for Paris, Dr Compson came to dinner. Hannah was at an 'evening' with Jason in the home of his aunt, Marie-Hélène having confided in Mia that she was quite relieved.

"As you can see, Jason calls here frequently, and it would be the height of tactlessness to have him obviously paying court to Hannah while the doctor was dining."

"I should think he's tolerant enough not to mind."

"I'm sure he is, but why rub salt in a wound?"

"Do you think Jason is a good *parti*, Mama?"

Marie-Hélène shrugged. "I doubt if I know what *is* a good *parti* nowadays. All I know is that I don't want her left on my hands. I could never support it. But I can tell you one thing. They'll never be involved in each other enough to quarrel deeply. Yes, they're well-suited. Their aims are the same."

Robert appeared at the door. "Dr Compson," he announced. The doctor entered smiling and bowing, although Mia noticed he looked older and more fatigued since she had last seen him.

"Well, Mia! Your father told me you were off to Paris with him in a few days' time." He made no comment on her presence.

"Yes, doctor. It's a great treat for me. Papa is exceedingly kind."

"He worries about you, my dear. He thinks you need fattening up."

"I'm well. As you should know, parents are too solicitous."

"I should like to be in a position to fuss . . . that was tactless, and even worse, self-pitying. I don't regret Harry's death now. It had to be, and so many more people have lost their sons in this senseless war. I ask myself what is the purpose of their valour, their sacrifices. I read in the newspaper the other day . . . you won't believe this, ma'am," he turned to include Marie-Hélène, "I read, as I was saying, an extract from a soldier's letter from Balaclava, and the words so imprinted themselves on my heart that I'm able to quote them to you now. These are they. 'The blood from my head wound was running into my mouth, and in my burning excitement I drank it as if it were wine.' What do you think of that? I make no apology for perhaps offending your tender susceptibilities. I think we all ought to see wars for what they are – Grand Delusions working on young men's feelings in the name of patriotism. And where have they got us, I ask you? Look at Napoleon's campaign! At the end of all the bloodshed the French were back where they started."

"So you're a pacifist?" Marie-Hélène said.

"Any doctor is a pacifist, ma'am." He laughed shortly. "But I mustn't air my views in this rude manner as soon as I enter your drawing-room."

"I prefer you to be frank. Please sit down beside me. You must be tired."

"Thank you."

"Joseph has been detained in the potworks, I regret, but if you can put up with two ladies we'll do our best to entertain you until he comes."

"I'm in no hurry when I'm in such delectable company, except that I've a favour to ask him tonight."

"Perhaps Mia and I can help you."

"Mia might be able to, since she may well be her father's amanuensis on their trip. It is this. Harry had a friend in the Hussars, Captain Brian Moore."

"Yes . . ." She prayed her mother's eyes wouldn't rest on her with their French shrewdness. "He stayed with you, didn't he? I think Hannah and I had the pleasure of meeting him for a short time. When we were out riding."

"Did you tell me of this, Mia?" Marie-Hélène asked.

"I think so, Mama. I can't remember. It's so long ago."

"I'm very glad if this is the case," Dr Compson said. "They were close friends, and apparently Harry gave this captain some of his possessions before he . . . before he died, his watch, his diary, one or two personal mementoes. Captain Moore writes to me from Paris where he is at present asking what should be done with them."

"Is he ill?" Mia gripped the side of her chair.

"No, he didn't say so, although I gather he's been invalided home and accepted the invitation of a French officer to stop off in Paris before returning to Ireland, someone who served beside him under General Canrobet. Perhaps he's done his part, I mean Captain Moore."

"And they'd no further use for him."

"That seems a hard remark, Mia." Her mother looked at her reprovingly.

"It's true, Mama. They squeeze them dry and then throw them aside."

"I hope in his case you'll be proved wrong," the doctor said, "and you'll find him in good health. Which brings me to my point. I was going to ask your father if you and he would kindly call on the captain and bring me back those souvenirs. I should dearly like to have them."

"Why, of course they shall," Marie-Hélène said. "And perhaps my husband can do something for the captain, take him out to dinner, invite him here . . ."

"Anything you do would be appreciated, I'm sure . . . why," he looked up, "here's the man of the house!" Joseph had opened the door.

"Good evening, doctor." He came forward and shook hands. "I do beg your pardon. I had trouble with the muffle kilns at the last moment, but I know any excuse I may make is going to be deafened by the gong. Robert was poised for action as I passed." A dull booming reverberated through the house. "There, what did I tell you? Come along, doctor. You precede me with my wife, and I'll bring in this beautiful young woman who's honoured us with her presence." He held out his arm to Mia.

"She's promised to execute an errand for me," the doctor said over his shoulder as he escorted Marie-Hélène out of the room.

Chapter Sixteen

Joseph had decided to patronise Thomas Cook, the new travel people, to arrange his and Mia's trip to Paris. The Channel was like a millpond when they crossed, Queen's weather, he called it. It had been a perfect week in April when Napoleon and Eugenie visited England, the return visit seemed to be following the same tradition of cloudless blue skies.

The train journey on the French side from Boulogne was hot and dusty, but there was an air of excitement pervading everywhere, and at Abbeville, Beauvais and other stations, the decorations for *La Reine D'Angleterre* drew cries of admiration from the French passengers. At the lavishly-decorated Gare de Strasbourg, Joseph said he felt quite royal himself.

Mr Cook had arranged rooms for them in a quiet little hotel near the Tuilleries, although Joseph said he quite missed the fun of going to Galignani's for addresses and to buy the English newspapers. "I always run into someone I know there," he told Mia, "the world's a small place." He was beaming, nothing was going to spoil his little jaunt. She would have been indeed churlish, she decided, if she hadn't tried to reciprocate by at least smiling in response.

They were both worn out when they arrived, and Joseph suggested a quiet dinner, early to bed, and then they would wake refreshed for their sight-seeing in the morning. There was a letter from his friend at the Sèvres factory inviting him to go to see him as soon as he was settled in, failing that, for dinner on Monday evening, the 20th August, and of course he would be enchanted to welcome his daughter whom Joseph had said was accompanying him.

"I shan't go with you, Papa," Mia said, "I'd much rather have another early night. The heat has tired me unaccountably." And then, seeing his disappointed face, "Well, let's see what happens tomorrow."

She went to sleep immediately her head touched the pillow. She had thought her mind would dwell on Conway, and from him go to Brian who now was in the same city, but apart from a strange kind of certainty that a meeting would be arranged for her, her mind refused to concentrate. The feeling of lethargy was overpowering, and she was suddenly in a heavy, dreamless sleep.

But the next morning the clear light of Paris, the soft summer air, seemed to inject her with a rare feeling of lightheartedness. They breakfasted *au trottoir*, and after they had finished, Joseph insisted on hiring a carriage in which they drove through the tree-lined boulevards and under triumphal arches, admiring the forest of flags and the general opulence of the decorations. The French did this kind of thing with their special brand of taste, she thought, elaborately-decorated mock-marble columns, statues, full-size portraits of the Queen and Prince Albert above every *carrefour*. Huge Napoleon eagles glittered in the sun, linked coats of arms proclaimed the entwined affections of the sovereigns of the two countries.

"Baron Haussman deserves a special accolade," Joseph said. "There's a grandeur about Paris now which few cities could emulate."

She agreed that one couldn't find such noble boulevards elsewhere. Her spirits rose with the gaiety of the crowds, the hot sunshine, the freedom from the claustrophobic atmosphere of Hessleton where every place where she walked or rode reminded her of Conway and Sarah.

Now her thoughts turned wholly on Brian. How truly exciting it would be to see him, to talk to him. Vague memories of his beguiling Irish voice came back to her.

Would he see any difference in her? She was older, of course, but she thought sometimes her mirror showed a subtle change. Could it be the beginnings of something more than mere prettiness?

They dismissed the carriage for the pleasure of strolling in the Bois de Boulogne, where they lunched in one of the open-air restaurants. Joseph confirmed her thoughts as she sat across from him, smiling. "Fathers are notoriously prejudiced, but I've never seen you look more beautiful. I remember saying to your dear mother that Paris does something to a woman, brings out her true nature, brings out the best in her. The pulse quickens here. Don't you feel it?"

"Yes, I do. I feel alive for the first time . . . since I left. I want to live again. I'd forgotten I was still young, still capable of happiness." She laughed, biting her lip. "I thought my youth had gone."

"You see, I was right in persuading you to come. Now, kindly look at the menu if you will, and choose for us a delectable luncheon which I warn you must be committed to memory because your Mama will want it to be retailed word for word. Then we'll plan how the afternoon's to be spent."

They decided to go to La Sainte Chapelle. The Royal party were to be there at three o'clock, and they might therefore kill two birds with one stone. They could admire the windows, and if they were lucky admire the Empress, although she might not be there, Joseph reminded her. Did Mia know she was *enceinte*?

The remark was made casually as he sipped his coffee, and yet for some reason Mia felt her heart twist painfully with envy. This beautiful woman with whom she had identified for so long had fulfilled herself, she hadn't. The bitterness was like bile in her mouth.

"Are you all right, Mia?" Joseph's eyes were keen.

"Yes, quite all right." She smiled brilliantly, falsely, finished her coffee. "Come along. I don't want to waste a minute." She raised her parasol for protection from his eyes as well as the sun.

They both stood in silence in the upper chapel. The richness of the light filtering through the coloured glass, the multiplicity of the scenes depicted left them without words. Her spirits calmed, she felt radiant, as if the light pouring on them penetrated to her heart. She had the feeling, deeply, surely, that something was going to happen to change her whole life, not necessarily happy, but momentous. She was still quiet as she walked behind her father in the arcade which ran round the wall.

"We shan't do the tour of the *Conciergerie*," he said, "unless you're interested in seeing where Marie-Antoinette was kept prisoner."

"No, thank you. 'It would only spoil what we've seen already."

"Quite so. We'll go out now, and if we're lucky we may see the Royal party." He was looking at her as he spoke. "You're different somehow, Mia."

"Am I? I feel different . . . transfigured." She laughed. "No, that's too extreme, but if I were to see nothing else in Paris this would have been enough to make our visit worth-while. Thank you, Papa." She saw the pleasure on his face.

The crowds were too dense. They gave up the idea of waiting to see the Royal party arrive, and made their way slowly along the *Quai de l'Horloge*, enjoying the sunshine. "There'll be other times," he said.

"Yes, besides she might not have been there since she's *enceinte*." Again she felt the dagger thrust. "What an attractive river the Seine is! Quite a different colour from the Thames, silver-grey like the buildings . . ." Coming along the *Quai* towards them was the figure of a soldier, limping slightly, but smart in his blue jacket and red trousers, crimson and white plumed hat. His *pelisse* swayed on his shoulder. He drew nearer, and Mia studied him, at first only with curiosity, and then as recognition flooded her, with trepidation quickly changing into heart-stopping delight. The face was heavily bearded, but the gait was memorable despite the limp, as was the fair hair showing beneath the tall busby. She put her hand on Joseph's arm.

"What is it?" He glanced at her face and then towards the officer, perplexed. "Do you know this gentleman?"

She stopped. Joseph had to stop. The officer hesitated, seemed to draw himself up, to straighten himself, and then she saw the wide, charming smile lighting up his features. It made recognition complete. "It's Captain Moore, Papa, Harry's friend!"

"Captain Moore!" Her father was at a loss.

There was now only a few yards between them. The officer swept off his plumed hat and put it under his arm. He stopped, waiting.

"Captain . . . Moore?" she stammered.

"Mia . . . yes, it is, Mia . . . Mia! I couldn't believe it at first!" And then he had taken the last few steps and was kissing the hand which she held out.

She tried to control her voice. "Papa . . . may I present Harry's friend, Captain Brian Moore? You remember the doctor telling us . . ."

"Upon my soul!" Joseph extended a hand. "Well met, sir, well met! Isn't this the strangest coincidence since we've a commission to execute in regard to you? What did I tell you, Mia? Didn't I say the world was a small place?"

"I'm amazed," Brian said, "absolutely amazed! It's true I'd written to Dr Compson, but I had no idea that *you* would be coming. Harry spoke of you sometimes, sir. We told each other of our homes, our friends . . . to bring them nearer."

"And you're out of the fighting for good?"

"Yes, I imagine so. They released me from the General Hospital at Balaclava where I'd been treated for cholera, but then—"

"Stop a moment!" Joseph held up his hand. "We've so much to talk about that I think we could find ourselves a more comfortable place. Will you join us in a glass of wine? There must be a café nearby. Paris is full of them."

"I passed one only a hundred yards away, sir, the Trocadero. Half the cafés in Paris are called the Trocadero." Again the wide, charming smile.

"Well, let's find a table there. What do you say, Mia? You're very quiet."

"Yes, Papa." It was a relief to let him do the talking.

They found the café, and a table out-of-doors, Joseph talking busily, obviously delighted with the unexpected encounter. "Garçon, three glasses of Sauterne. Is that to your liking, Captain? Ladies prefer a sweet white wine. Now, please continue. I rudely interrupted you earlier. You were saying you were in the General Hospital at Balaclava?"

Mia had raised her parasol. She hoped its shade would hide her face a little. Even summoning all her calmness she felt her eyes would betray her. She found them constantly straying to Brian, examining him, the brown cheek, the fair beard, the piercing blue eye, the same merry expression which had first captured her.

"Yes, for about two months, worse luck. Though we were royally treated, arrowroot, port wine and all kinds of delicacies. We relished them, I can tell you, after the miserable fare we had had during the winter. While I was there Miss Nightingale paid us a visit . . ."

"Miss Nightingale!" Mia said. "Do tell me how she appeared to you."

"Slender to the point of emaciation, but then she shared the soldiers' rations. We heard she reprimanded our cook for feeding us with the best at the expense of the men, which we were bound to agree with." He laughed. "Anyhow, the arrowroot and port wine must have agreed with me because I was discharged to take part in an assault on Sebastopol in June where I got some grape in my thigh. I think they thought I was of no more use to them so I was invalided home, and that's enough about me!" He sipped his wine, his eyes dancing.

"I'm sure you've left out a great deal," Joseph said, "but we don't want to revive painful memories for you so we shan't press you. You remain in Paris, then?"

"Meantime. I've a friend in the French Cavalry, Leon Fontenelle. He's taking part in the celebrations. Napoleon wants to astonish Queen Victoria and Prince Albert with his magnificence, I think. I'm sharing Leon's apartment with him in the Place de Vosges, next door to where Victor Hugo used to live, if you please."

"I should have thought you'd be anxious to return to Dublin," Mia said.

"I am and I'm not." He smiled the swift, charming smile. "There's an Irish remark for you. Paris is a kind of hiatus between the Crimea and Ireland. It's always been a second home to me and I've many friends here."

"I can understand what you say," Joseph said. "Your mind has to recover as well as your body."

"I admit it's in a convalescent state, sir, but Paris is the best doctor!" Mia, watching him with the aid of her parasol, saw the signs of strain and fatigue round his eyes despite his gaiety. He must have been aware of her scrutiny for he turned towards her. "And how has the war treated you, Mia?" She was stupidly glad she was wearing a bonnet of violet tulle which Hannah had insisted she took with her. She had thought the violets on it too frivolous. His eyes still on her he said, "Have you been breaking the hearts of dashing young officers home on leave?"

"I . . . I . . ."

"Mia's a married lady now," Joseph said. "Perhaps you didn't know. I don't think in England we permit married ladies to break the hearts of dashing young officers, or if they do we pretend not to know about it. We're adept at that." He smiled at Mia.

"I was married when I met Captain Moore," she said.

Her eyes sought his under the shade of her parasol. The letters, she thought, he musn't mention the letters . . .

For once he didn't smile. "May I wish you continuing happiness? Perhaps I've been too familiar in my address to you?"

"Not at all. As a family we dislike formality. Isn't that so, Papa?"

"Unnecessary formality." He changed the subject abruptly. "I said when we met, Captain, that we had to execute a commission in regard to you. You'll realise what it is, to bring back Harry's belongings to his father."

"Yes. Harry and I were close friends . . ." He looked away. "He died in my arms." No one spoke. Mia prayed he wouldn't ask about Hannah.

"If there's anything we can do . . .?" Joseph's voice was kind.

"The souvenirs!" Brian seemed to recover himself. "That would be a great help. Let me call a carriage and you can come with me right away and get them. It won't take long."

"Yes, let's do that, Papa." Mia's heart started to beat heavily again under the pale violet bodice, a febrile kind of anticipation she couldn't understand.

"You forget we've an engagement at Pontoise for six o'clock." Joseph pulled out his watch. "I'm afraid there isn't enough time."

"You're accompanying your father?" Brian said. His blue eyes made her dizzy. Perhaps it was the refracted light from the water.

"No, I've no wish to listen to long dissertations about the relative merits of clay." She saw her father's eyebrows pull together. "I'm sure I should only be in the way. I did warn you, Papa."

"I believe you did." He smiled. "And married ladies are quite out of my control."

"May I make a suggestion?" Brian said. He looked directly at her. "Leon would enjoy very much meeting

193

you. I could give you the mementoes at the same time and then escort you back to your hotel. Would that fill in an hour for you if you're not too weary?"

"That's quite a good idea." Her heart was beating in her throat now. "What do you think, Papa?"

"Since you say our talk would bore you, and I don't really blame you since two smart young officers are infinitely more attractive . . ." She thought his smile was wary and she touched his hand.

"No, I'll come with you."

"I'm only teasing. Do as Captain Moore suggests. It'll be interesting for you and you can practise your French on his friend."

"Good!" Brian got to his feet, helped Mia to hers. She closed her parasol, feeling the hot sun beat through the thin muslin of her dress. "How fortunate! Here comes a carriage. We'll ask him to drop us off at the Place de Vosges, and then, sir, your hotel or Pontoise?"

"I'll proceed directly to Pontoise, if you will. Monsieur Caen and I will fill any amount of time with talking."

The carriage stopped, Mia was helped in by Brian who gave the driver his instructions. When they were all seated, and the carriage was bowling along, their former flow of talk seemed to lessen, as if events had moved too quickly for them. They contented themselves with admiring the streets, Brian pointing out anything of particular interest. Soon they were in the old seventeenth century Place, and Mia kissed her father before she got out. "Enjoy your talk and your meal, Papa. I'll wait up for you."

"No, child. Take all the rest you can." And to Brian, "My regards to your friend."

"But you'll convey them yourself, sir. Tomorrow, I insist, you and your daughter must be our guests for dinner. I'll arrange the rendezvous with her. Au revoir." He saluted smartly and got out of the carriage first, in order to assist Mia. His hand was warm as it closed round hers.

*　　*　　*

194

The drawing-room of the apartment was large, circular, looking down on the quiet gardens of the Place. Mia crossed to the windows draped in gleaming satin. She could see two old women sitting gossiping on a seat in the dusty square of grass. One clutched a basket. Beside the other sat a patient-looking poodle. Brian was silent. She was embarrassed, and made a show of following what went on at street level with acute interest.

"What are you looking at?"

"The people. And a very patient looking dog. They look French, and strange . . ."

"It was strange meeting you." She didn't turn her head. "I'm not yet used to it. And you look different, more beautiful but different."

"I'm older." She half-closed her eyes, seeing the gleaming grey folds of the curtain blur. It was the colour of the Seine . . .

He was behind her, close behind her, his voice was in her ear, his Irish beguiling voice. "How do I look to *you*?"

"Tired, in spite of your cheerfulness. And then your beard . . ."

"It's a fashion. All the men at home will soon be covered with whiskers. Is your husband bearded?"

She turned and she was almost in his arms. "He didn't fight. I don't think he sees much sense in fighting. No, that's a stupid remark to make. What I mean is that he thinks it's uncivilised."

"People who ain't soldiers always say that. But I won't quarrel with you about your husband's opinions. Indeed, I didn't ask for them. Come and sit down." He smiled at her, held out his hand.

She allowed him to lead her to a grey velvet sofa against the wall. She sat down, relieved, leant back. "How pleasant . . . and such a charming room . . ."

"You're very pale. Take off your bonnet, Mia."

"Indeed I won't." She sat up straight. "What if your friend appeared? Is he in his study?"

195

"Possibly. I'll let him know presently you're here. Please let's have a few words together. It was such a surprise meeting you, such a pleasant surprise."

She clasped her hands in her lap. "All right, but, Brian, I'd like to apologise for my absurd behaviour that day we spent together. I tried to explain in my letters if they ever reached you."

"One or two did, and then they stopped."

"So did yours. But about that day . . . you see, at the time Conway and I weren't on good terms, and what I did was in a fit of bravado, as was the writing . . . but afterwards, it became a kind of . . . refuge for me."

"I'm glad. Parker told me a lot about you, and your husband."

"I don't trust Parker, somehow. I hope you didn't believe everything he told you."

"Oh, I suppose I took it with a pinch of salt. I've met blokes like him before. They're not malicious, only mischievous, like . . . like hobgoblins. I think they like to give the pot a stir. But he did tell me you weren't on too good a wicket in your marriage."

"It was because of his sister. She came between us."

"Yes, Parky told me about her too. A jealous spinster, I should think. Anyhow, it's all patched up now?"

"No. In fact I . . ."

"You what?" The blue eyes bent on her.

"I . . . left him. I'm living with my parents. That's why I'm here with my father."

"Because of the sister?"

"Yes. I don't think . . . I'll ever go back to him."

"Is he such an ogre?"

"No, no, he's not an ogre! He has many good points. He isn't gay and light-hearted like you, he's rather stern and reserved, but I believe he'd have truly loved me had it not been for Sarah."

"So *she's* the ogre."

"Please, Brian, I don't wish to discuss it." She rubbed

at her eyes with her handkerchief. She'd done enough weeping.

"Poor little Mia. So you've been having a thin time of it?"

"Well, no, it hasn't been so bad. I've been busy with this and that . . . I must go. Please give me the keepsakes for Harry's father. I shouldn't have come in the first place. Sometimes, these days, I don't understand myself."

"You wanted to come, didn't you?" His voice was soft. Outside she heard the roll of carriage wheels, and then there was a deep silence broken once by the sharp evening call of a bird.

"I don't know . . . it's of no matter." The eyes he bent on her were dancing, and she grew angry, more at herself in her vacillation than at him. "Perhaps because you had to order your men about in the Crimea you seem to have got into the way of *badgering*. You've *fired* questions at me. Kindly fetch your friend if you will so that I can at least tell Papa I've met him. I know it's nothing in Paris, but in Hessleton ladies aren't expected to be alone with men in a strange drawing-room."

"Even married ladies? Even married ladies from a family which doesn't care for formality?" Now his eyes were laughing at her. "And I should think beautiful married ladies like you need care even less about being compromised. But don't worry. I'll ask Leon to come in. It wouldn't be fair to deprive him of such a treat."

He got up, and as he walked past the mantelpiece he stopped abruptly and took up a piece of paper which lay on it. He whistled. "This is a note from Leon . . ." she could hardly hear him. He read it swiftly, then looked across the room at her, his face grave, his eyes dancing. "Now you *are* compromised. Leon's left for Versailles. He's on duty there for the Royal party and doesn't expect to return till tomorrow."

"You knew this!" She had to prevent herself from wringing her hands. "The letter's been opened!"

"Upon my soul, Mia! You ought to come to Paris more often. You're much too suspicious for your own comfort."

"I'm sorry. Am I so naive, then?"

"I don't think you are. You've had a bad time. It's bowled you over. And you've lost your bloom, you're thinner, and your eyes are too large in that pale face."

"I'm sorry if my appearance isn't to your liking!"

"Your spirit's coming back in any case. I like to see that." His smile had the sweetness she remembered and she was disarmed.

"Where are your servants? It's so quiet here." She looked around.

"Leon has only a man servant, and he gave him the day off for the festivities. We eat out. There's an excellent little restaurant in the Place. We even have breakfast there. Oh, bachelors gay are we!" He smiled at her again. "Now I'll get Harry's mementoes and then take you home." He went out of the room.

She relaxed, her head back against the sofa. How provincially she had behaved! Here was a situation, an interesting situation which should have presented no anxieties for any married woman. She really dwelt far too much of herself and her problems, too boring. She'd talk amiably for a few minutes when he returned and then she'd take her leave gracefully. She half-closed her eyes, remembering Mama's injunction. It did nothing to stop her heart fluttering like a trapped bird against her ribs.

Brian came back with a silver tray. On it was a small cardboard box and two tall-stemmed glasses of wine and a decanter. He put the tray on the table in front of the sofa and sat down beside her. "You need some refreshment before you go. Harry's things are here." He smiled at her like a brother. I used to sing him Irish songs to make him forget his pain. 'Sing to me about your mist and your mountains," he'd say. You know, Mia, there's something about the love between two men which is rather special. Sometime I must pay a visit to the doctor and tell him all about Harry, his kindness, his good-humour, his fortitude."

"He'd like that. He's such an uncomplaining man and I think it would mean a great deal to him." Treacherous tears filled her eyes.

He looked at her. "You're a sympathetic girl. Is it because your own heart is sad that you can feel for others?"

She searched in her reticule for a handkerchief. "Perhaps that's the only advantage to be gained." She daren't look at him.

"Poor Mia." The beguiling tones, like someone stroking her brow with soft fingers. "I think he's broken your heart, this husband of yours."

"Yes . . ." She craved comfort. "Yes! *You* understand, Brian. You know how you felt when Harry died. Conway is dead for me, that's what it amounts to." She began to sob, broken, choking sobs which she tried to stifle.

"Hush, Mia. No one should do that to you. Life isn't meant to be unhappy like that, no one should destroy you. If I hadn't believed in happiness, I shouldn't have survived, isn't that so?" His voice was infinitely caressing, and like a kind elder brother he took her in his arms. "Do you remember that day long ago at the Fair? And how young we both were . . . so happy. You were pretty, and lissom," the Irish inflection increased, she imagined, "but now you're beautiful. Didn't he ever tell you? You need someone to tell you. I loved you that day . . . I still love you. It was the thought of you that sustained me, your gaiety, your abandonment. Frenchwomen have this quality, seldom Englishwomen. They're full of rectitude. Don't let your spirits die, Mia."

It was so comforting. "I'm not in the habit of weeping like this, but it was such a shock, you see . . . I never thought Conway . . . Sarah . . ."

"Wipe your eyes and take some wine." He took one arm away, handed her a full glass, took one for himself. His other arm remained behind her shoulders. "Try not to think."

She sipped slowly, feeling the warmth of the wine steal down her veins like a kindly thief. It was much more full-bodied than the Ladies' Sauterne her father had ordered. It swelled into a rosy cloud in her head so that she was able to speak freely to him.

"How strange life is, Brian, meeting you like this, a surprise and not a surprise . . . in everyone's life, I think, there are people who sustain them, as you've done me. When I was miserable because of Sarah, *so* miserable, I'd read your letters and find some kind of peace from them. In a lesser degree, Eugenie, the Empress, you know, has been important to me. Isn't that even stranger? I shouldn't have been here at all had Papa not thought I should like to see her. And Conway thought the same once . . . Oh, he was kind in himself! We had a second honeymoon in London when Eugenie was there. He was so kind and loving, and we'd moved into our own home, away from Sarah. Only not far enough . . . But I was talking about life. It's like a stage, that's Shakespeare, of course, but so true. There are the chief players, first of all oneself, because let's admit it, one is most important to oneself, and then one's husband comes next, and one's children . . . but I haven't any. And lots of other players who contribute something to one's life, sometimes beauty, sometimes fun, like you, sometimes dread . . . am I talking nonsense?"

"Delightful nonsense."

"I'll drink some more wine and it'll clear my head. There's a rosy cloud already there, flooding into every part of it. Tell me about *your* life, Brian, your stage."

"Mine's a picture, rather. You needed a picture in the Crimea, I can tell you. *You* were in it, Mia, the way you were that day, laughing, your thin waist, and there were horses, not the poor hacks I was looking after but proud Irish horses in the Curragh, and the wind blowing the sea into curled waves in Dublin Bay, and my sisters riding, their hair stretched in the wind, the horses' tails stretched in the wind, country balls sometimes, a blind fiddler . . ."

"But being married I ought not to be in your picture."

"You are you, married or not. If you were so miserable surely there was no harm in me trying to make you happier by writing to you?" His voice dropped. "Surely there's no harm now . . ."

"You've a lovely voice, Brian, so beguiling, so full of charm. You should have been an actor and strutted on the stage."

"I have been." He laughed. "I used to recite poems in the drawing-rooms of Dublin. I liked the importance of it, knowing I could sway people."

"Could you say one to me now? I'm happy enough, but I feel I could be even happier." She drank from the wine glass, deeply.

"I will too. Rest your head against my arm and I'll give you a rendition, as we used to say in Ireland. Do you want a happy one to make you sad, or a sad one to make you happy?"

"I'm searching for happiness."

"You shall have it then. Let me see . . ." It was like a spell. She closed her eyes, thinking that if his letters had been a drug, his voice was even more potent.

> "The dragons of the rock are sleeping,
> Sleep that wakes not for our weeping
> Dig the grave and make it ready,
> Lay me on my true-love's body . . ."

"It's too sad, Brian."

"It'll make you happy. Lie still and dream."

There was a mist about her, the grey sitting-room melted and blurred. She dreamt of being a child again with Hannah, of the high attic and the elm trees, and then the scene swirled away and out of the mist came Conway's dark eyes, meeting hers, stirring her so that she felt herself rising, going to him . . . but as she drew nearer they lightened, became cold, they were no longer Conway's eyes, but Sarah's . . .

"Dig the grave both wide and deep
Sick I am and fain would sleep . . ."

Sleep, sleep, the mist was here again, soft, warm,
enveloping her in its grey folds. She made no struggle
as the voice fell away. She welcomed the strength of his
arms, the fire which his mouth started in her body so that
it burned up furiously, spreading to the tips of her fingers.
This was passion such as she had known with Conway,
but untainted by the thought of Sarah. And there was an
element of defiance in it which was new because it was
illicit. She wasn't going to be deprived of happiness, no
one could live without it, she needed all the things which
happiness could give her. Something vexed her, the memory
of Eugenie's eyes on her at Sydenham, like a warning . . .
she moved restlessly.

"Don't," he said, "please don't . . ." the voice was
different. His mouth was on hers again.

She tried to struggle upright. "I must . . ."

"Your father will be at Pontoise until late." With one
hand he released her bonnet, and as it fell back he said,
"Let down your hair."

"I can't. Brian . . ."

"There, I'll help you. There it is, that lovely hair I've
never seen properly, silken hair . . ." she felt his hand
pass over it and she could feel its silkiness through him.
"Put your arms round my neck, Mia, slowly, slowly. I've
thought of it often, how it would feel . . ."

Her arms went slowly, slowly round his neck, like two
soldiers, she thought obeying an order, and she struggled
feebly to free herself to tell him how vastly amusing
it was to think of her arms like two soldiers obeying
orders . . .

She felt his hands on her clothes, practised, and as
the warm air of the room lay on her bare shoulders all
common-sense left her. She was in Paris where no one
knew her, in a circular room above the Place de Vosges

with Brian who said he loved her, in the circular room of his friend Leon . . . Leon . . . her head spun.

She shut her eyes, and behind them was all the glory of the Paris streets, the golden eagles, the oriflammes, the fountains, the coloured lights. And emerging from the crowd, coming straight towards her was an officer dressed in blue and red, fair, bearded, blue eyes like needles which pierced her soul.

Chapter Seventeen

Mia was in bed in her room when Joseph returned and he didn't disturb her. The next morning he commented on the signs of fatigue in her appearance but she said she had found the heat tiring yesterday which he seemed to accept, going on to tell her of the wonders of the Sèvres factory, the charm of their ware and the information he had exchanged with his friend, Monsieur Caen.

"He's arranging for me to visit the new manufactories at Limoges the next time I come to France. Can you imagine, Mia, Monsieur Caen remembers me coming here twenty-three years ago! He married about the same time as I did, and even more amazing, he has two daughters, Hortense and Leonie. He says if you've any time they would dearly like to meet you."

"That's very kind of them. We'll see. There are so many things to do in Paris, and we've only two more days."

"Quite so. What did you think to Captain Moore's friend? I don't recollect his name."

"Leon Fontenelle." She hurried on. "They look forward to meeting you this evening at the Hotel Meurice."

"That's very friendly of Captain Moore. Did you accept for me?"

"Yes. They said eight o'clock. Apparently one dines later and later in Paris."

"Ah, well, when in Rome . . . now, what would you like to do? I'm entirely at your disposal." The excitement and the glamour of the Royal visit had died for Mia. All she wanted was to get home, to lie in her bed where no one could question her or expect her to appear normal.

"Let's read *Le Figaro* and see what the Royal programme is for today. But if the crowds are as dense as yesterday, we might go to Versailles, Papa. I've always wanted to see Versailles."

"Didn't Conway take you?" She shook her head. "Then we'll go to Versailles and you'll admire yourself in the mirrors of the *Galerie des Glaces*. There's to be a grand ball there, I remember reading, so you'll see it in all its splendour."

All through the day she made the correct responses to her father, admiring the architecture of Mansart, the landscaping of Le Nôtre. Behind her polite remarks her mind seethed, her temples throbbed so much that at times she winced with the pain. Words came back to her, snatches of conversation. *'We must meet again, Mia.' 'No, no, it's impossible! My father is astute . . .' 'I'll take him out to dinner as I said, bring Leon . . .' 'But you can't, because Leon will say he hasn't met me.' 'Don't worry. Leon will say what I tell him to. I've done the same for him . . .'* Was the charming smile for a moment raffish above the golden beard? She hadn't wept in the carriage taking her back to her hotel. She had sat straight and silent until Brian reproached her. "It's no good being haughty, Mia. You wanted it as much as I did . . ."

"Are you feeling the heat, Mia?" It was Joseph's kindly voice in her ear. "I seldom see you flushed. I do hope you haven't caught some infection."

She grasped at the excuse. "To tell you the truth, Papa, I begin to wonder myself. But don't worry. We'll sit in the gardens for a time. It should be cool beside the fountains, and if I don't feel too well in the evening I'll allow you to go and meet the two captains on your own." She even managed to be playful. "After all, I'd only restrict the telling of after-dinner stories."

Later it was easy to insist on Joseph keeping the

appointment alone, and she sat in her room trying to come to terms with her burning sense of guilt. What had come over her? Could she be honest and admit to herself, in spite of her training in reticence, that her body had been starved of love? That she was the type of woman who having once tasted its joys couldn't do without it? She walked up and down the room, tearless now, no time for weeping as she struggled with her conscience.

If, then, her surrender had been actuated by hunger, was it love or infatuation she felt for him? And if it were love, what was it she felt for Conway, who could stir her in the same way? The difference must lie in the attitude of the man to *her*. Whatever Brian's had been at the time, it could be nothing less than scorn now. She'd broken her marriage vows, she'd behaved like a loose woman. He could only think of her in those terms.

There's no solution, she thought. I'm trapped in my century. Abnegation would mean confessing her sin to Conway who was still her husband although she had left him. And should their marriage be at an end, surrender to Brian was impossible unless the first move came from him. And that was a further anxiety. There had been nothing. He could have called on some pretext. He could have sent a note by a messenger. I'm trapped also by my sex, she thought despairingly, by the convention that a woman must wait. But there was still hope. Perhaps tonight he'd give to her father some message, apparently innocent, which she could construe in a different way.

She went to bed finally, beaten, hopeless, lying sleepless through the night, knowing she'd have to live with her conscience and that was her greatest punishment. Or could there be still further retribution in store for her?

In the morning Joseph spoke of the pleasant evening he had spent with the two officers. They both sent their regrets that she had not been present. One was as genial as the other, he said.

"You told them how sorry I was to miss dinner with them?"

"Yes, but you were wrong about the conversation, Mia. There were no barrack-room stories, simply amiable talk larded occasionally with the succint comments of men who've seen much heavy fighting but never question their duty to their Queen and country . . . perhaps their viewpoint is the only sensible one and armchair philosophers like me are of no account—" he stopped abruptly, looking at her. "You're not at all well, Mia, not at all well."

"No, I have to confess it. I spent a wretched night."

"What do you think is wrong? Tell me truthfully. Is it a matter of the heart or the body?"

"The heart, Papa . . ." She faltered, stopped.

"Are you fretting for him? Don't start like that! Your nerves must be in a bad state. I don't intend to discuss Conway, but would you rather we returned today instead of waiting until tomorrow?"

"Papa . . ." She nearly broke down and confessed, and then thought that to shift her burden to a father whom she loved would be senseless and cruel. "Would you greatly mind if we went home today? It may be the heat. It may be that I've eaten something which has disagreed with me." She smiled feebly. "Mama won't hear of that happening in her beloved Paris!"

"I *don't* mind and we'll go home today by all means. We've done what we wanted to do and I've seen Monsieur Caen which, after all, was the purpose of my visit. Perhaps familiar surroundings will help you more than physic." He leant forward, took her hand which lay on the table. "I've a strong back, Mia, if you wish to talk to me."

She shook her head. "No, Papa. It'll all come right in the end. You used to say that to me when I was a little girl and came to you with some sorry tale."

"It's true. Or if it doesn't come right it ceases to be important. Shall we go and pack?"

The manager intercepted them, distressed to hear they

207

were leaving so soon. "And in the midst of such excitement with your Queen here!" He bowed to Mia. "A bouquet of roses has just arrived for you, madame."

"For me!"

"Yes, madame."

"Was there a letter?"

"No, madame. A card, I believe. They were delivered from a nearby *floriste*. Will you take them with you?"

"No, thank you, monsieur. Will you please accept them for the hotel with my compliments?"

"Shouldn't you at least see who sent them?" Joseph said. "It will be written on the card."

"No, it doesn't matter now, it doesn't matter . . ."

Marie-Hélène and Hannah welcomed them with excited surprise. "You've returned earlier than we thought. Did you enjoy yourselves? Don't tell me my beloved Paris couldn't hold you for more than three days? Was the Empress very beautiful? Did the Queen carry her wool-worked reticule? *Mon Dieu!* Were the decorations *magnifique?*"

"One question at a time," Joseph said. "We enjoyed ourselves hugely. We saw all we wanted to see. I had a most rewarding dinner with Monsieur Caen and now we've come home."

"I must be honest, Mama. The heat upset me rather, and so we shortened our visit."

"You're not a girl who gets easily 'upset' as you call it," Marie-Hélène said, and then she must have caught a warning glance from Joseph. "Well, of course, I read in the Times that the heat was excessive and because of it Eugenie didn't make many appearances."

"She's *enceinte*," Mia said.

"How very direct of you." Hannah looked surprised but then her face burst into a broad smile. "I simply can't wait to tell you my news. Guess what? I'm engaged to Jason! He said you gave him permission to speak, Papa."

"I did. And after due consideration you accepted his offer?"

"You're a tease! Of course I did. Jason thinks we're in every way suited to each other."

"Why didn't you tell me, Papa?" Mia rounded on him. "Oh, Hannah," she embraced her sister, "are you very happy?"

"Very happy. We've all our plans made already and Mama has conceded that we may have a short engagement since I pointed out how short yours had been. We've so much to talk about now, Jason and I, when we sit together in the drawing-room. Never a dull moment. Where we shall live, the number of bedrooms . . ." while she chattered on Mia thought that perhaps her father had kept his secret lest the thought of Hannah's happiness might distress her when her own future seemed so bleak. Suddenly tears streamed down her face and she had to turn away, but not before Marie-Hélène had seen them.

"Now, what's this? Tears, Mia? You're not usually so emotional. *Now* I see why your Papa brought you home."

"I'm simply tired by the journey."

"Those are strange words to hear from you. First 'upset', now 'tired.' You who would never admit to a tired bone in your body. You'll drink a cup of tea with us and then I insist on you going up to bed and having dinner there. I don't want invalids in my house."

"Do you want me at all, Mama?" she said through her tears.

"Now, now, are we to add 'touchiness' to the list as well? That's not my Mia. Tomorrow you'll take a walk to Dr Compson's surgery and ask him for some physic."

"There's no need for that!"

"Well, if you feel embarrassed take poor Harry's mementoes with you which I presume you managed to obtain. You won't have to say anything. One look at your wan face will convince the doctor you need some professional advice."

"I should do that," Joseph said. "You may have picked up some infection in Paris. One can't be too careful in those foreign cities."

"Joseph Winter!" Marie-Hélène shrieked in pretended indignation, "if you've come back only to insult me . . ." She smiled at him and he sat down beside her, taking her hand.

"Nothing could keep me away from you for long, you know that. Indeed, that's why Mia put on this play-acting so that I should have an excuse for rushing home to you."

"You're incorrigible! Tell me about Harry's friend."

"Captain Moore was a charming young man. Mia had met him before, of course."

"I've already told Mama of our previous meeting, Hannah," Mia said, emerging from her handkerchief.

"Yes you have." Marie-Hélène looked dubious. "Although I can't bring it to mind. And the French officer, Joseph, the friend of Captain Moore? He was even more charming, I've no doubt."

"Quite ravishing. Unfortunately Mia was unable to join us so the three gentlemen had an enjoyable dinner together which made me realise how henpecked I am with you three ladies at my heels all day."

"Pay no attention, girls." Marie-Hélène seated herself at the table and began to pour tea. "He'll be desolate when you're gone and he has no one but me to talk to. Take this cup to your sister, Hannah."

"Thank you," Mia said. She was grateful to her parents for their banter which she suspected was to draw attention away from her. She put away her handkerchief and smiled as brightly as she could at Hannah. "Sit down beside me, pet, and tell me of all your plans. I long to hear about everything. Have you decided on the style of your dress? I saw some beautiful confections in the Paris shops."

"Did you?" Hannah launched forth, delighted with her captive audience while Mia let the chatter flow over her as she sought to compose herself and make her plans. She'd go to bed as her mother suggested because that way she could avoid further questioning, and tomorrow she'd please her by calling on Dr Compson, not about her health but to take Harry's keepsakes to him.

There was a small pause in Hannah's quotations from Jason's pronouncements on every subject under the sun from wedding dresses to the poor quality of Sèvres porcelain. Mia seized it. "Hannah," she said quietly, as her mother was listening avidly to Joseph's descriptions of the decorated Paris streets, "has Conway called again?"

"No." She shook her head decidedly. "Not since you left, but then perhaps he knew you weren't at home. What are you going to do, Mia?"

"I have to think, and while I remember, there's no need to talk about that day we spent with Harry and Captain Moore. It's a thing of the past now, you understand, especially as Harry is dead."

"I wondered . . . but, all right, whatever you say. You liked him when you saw him again?"

"Tolerably. He was extremely smart like all the Hussars, and bearded now. Apparently it's the latest mode."

"Oh, I shouldn't like Jason to grow a beard! I much prefer him as he is. Can you imagine being . . ." she put her hand over her mouth, ". . . *kissed* by a bearded man! Don't look so stuffy, Mia, you're married after all. We had a talk last night about what it would be like when we're married. It's necessary, of course, to observe a due decorum in front of the servants, but Jason was saying," she giggled, "yes, I'll tell you, you're my sister after all and we've always said what we wanted to each other . . ." She was in full flood again. She would forget about Brian as she had almost forgotten about Harry with the advent of Jason.

Dr Compson was delighted to see her. She was the last of his patients and he insisted on her taking off her shawl and sitting down to drink tea with him. He looked tired. His pale blue eyes had a basket-work of lines round them.

"I've brought Harry's keepsakes, doctor. I hope they're in good condition." She gave him the small cardboard box and he took it from her eagerly.

"I do thank you, Mia, and your father. Do you mind if I remove the lid immediately?"

"Do, please. I can understand your impatience."

"Anything of Harry's, you understand . . ." He took out a gold watch and examined it, then looked at Mia. "I gave this to my son on his twenty-first birthday. See, I had it engraved on the back."

She took it, read aloud the inscription. 'Henry Charteris Compson, on the Occasion of his Coming-of-Age, 3rd March, 1849.' "It's a beautiful watch, doctor. 1849. He was five years older than me. Dear Harry! It's hard to think of him gone . . ." She saw his face. "Papa gave Hannah and me a pendant each," she said hurriedly. "I always wear mine." She touched the gold locket at her throat.

"Very fine," he cleared his throat, "very fine, I'm sure. I never had a daughter . . ." He lowered his head to the box, turned over the contents slowly. "Letters, my handwriting . . . just fancy, my handwriting . . . a wallet, a small book, ah, it's his diary, badges, buttons . . ." He looked up again. "I mustn't impose on you, Mia."

"There's no imposition, I assure you. Wouldn't it be easier for you if I left? I understand how you must feel."

"Do you?" He looked at her closely. "Do you? I tend to think the young who've been sheltered at home can't know of sorrow, but that's foolish. How could I possibly know what goes on in their minds, what difficulties . . . besides some people are better at concealing their anxieties than others." He brightened. "And you mustn't go on any account. I have too few visitors. See, I'll put this to one side and browse later. Will you try some of this seed cake?" He lifted a plate from the tray on his desk. "My housekeeper assures me it's quite excellent. She always praises her own baking excessively."

"Perhaps in an attempt to get you to do the same." She smiled at him and took a piece.

"And the trip to Paris was a great success?"

"Yes indeed, except that I spoiled it rather for Papa by not feeling too well. Mama thinks I need a tonic of some sort and I know if I don't mention it to you she'll come to see you herself."

"Do *you* think you need a tonic? You look healthy enough to me, but if I may say so, your sparkle has gone. *You* were the tonic generally to those around you. I must be frank, Mia, since I'm a medical man and you're a married woman . . . there might be a reason for that. Do you wish me to examine you later?"

"Oh, no, not at all!" She was flustered. "There's absolutely no need. I'm sorry I mentioned it at all but Mama can be very persistent."

"All mothers are persistent where their daughter's welfare is concerned."

She nodded. "I feel like an interloper at times at Blenheim Terrace. It's difficult to fit in . . ." and then the words came rushing out. "You see, I don't know what to do . . ."

"Long ago at Well House I offered you my advice. The offer still stands."

She shook her head. "No one can help me. No one . . ."

He looked at her, his face grim. "May I presume on an old friendship, Mia?"

"Yes." She drew in her breath. What would he say?

"I see by your expression you'd rather I didn't." He bent forward and took her hand. "But I'm at the age and stage in life when I speak rather than hold my tongue. People who are unduly reticent often pile up trouble for themselves and others. Do you agree?"

She sat up straight, released her hand. "It's such a general statement, doctor, that I can see no argument."

"And far too ambiguous for frankness. I'm talking about

213

you and Conway. And Sarah. Will you give me permission to continue?"

"There's no point in it." She became agitated, moved in her chair. "No point at all. Sarah told me everything . . ."

"But that *is* the point. She told you everything but the truth. Sarah, like many highly talented people, sometimes bends truth to her own ends. I've seen her do that, I've known her, in fact, when she was quite deranged. Don't look so startled. It's an illness like any others, and I've dealt with it as best I could. She's nervous, highly-strung, prone to malaise of the spirit as well as the body. One can alleviate, but the cast of temperament can't be changed. In Sarah's there's something, a bitter seed, which seems to have been planted at birth. Why it's in her temperament and not in her brother's, who had the same distressing environment to contend with, the same parents, I don't know. It would take a cleverer man than I, and perhaps the state of our knowledge isn't far enough advanced. What is certain is that Conway has always borne manfully his disadvantages and he's always tried to support and sustain his sister whom he felt hadn't the stamina to withstand the imprint of their unhappy childhood . . ."

"Doctor, this is most distressing to me . . ." She made to rise but he put out his hand.

"I've nearly finished and I assure you I shan't betray any confidences, but I implore you to go to your husband and ask him to unburden himself to you. It's not what you think . . . oh yes, I can read your mind. Mia, when Conway met you and fell in love with you, I was happy for him. You came from a normal, affectionate family, and I thought you could do him nothing but good. He deserved some happiness. I told your parents, when they asked my advice, that I thought he'd make a splendid husband for you. I knew you both. I thought your qualities would complement each other's. However Sarah has poisoned your mind against him, I assure you she lies. She has an obsessional love for him, that I can't deny, but his is only a normal protective love for a younger sister. Go to him. Tell him that I advise him, no implore him, to tell you what happened, and that if he doesn't I'll be forced to forget my ethics. Upon my soul, I find clever men the most stupid at times, and their sensitivity far too fine for the common herd!"

Her heart was bursting with love, with relief, with guilt, with despair, with such an admixture of feeling that she couldn't meet his eyes. She buried her head in her hands, whispering, "Are you telling me that . . . that there's nothing . . .?"

"Perverted? I'll say the word for you. Nothing on his side. I know him too well. You must make him confide in you, and believe me, that will be better physic than anything I can put in a bottle. You have compassion and love. I know you. Give it to him." He got up and came to her side, bending over to put his hand on her shoulder. "I'm left with not much chance of direct happiness except what I get from serving others. Will you do this to please me?"

She stood up and gathered her shawl and reticule together. Her hands were trembling so much that he took the shawl from her and draped it round her shoulders. She could scarcely speak. "Forgive me for leaving so hurriedly. I appreciate everything you've said to me and I . . . I think I believe it. But you see . . ." she couldn't meet his eyes. "It's too late!" She went swiftly towards the door and let herself out before she should shame herself and weep in his arms.

But she did in fact go to Well Farm in spite of what she had said that afternoon in the doctor's surgery. One morning, at the beginning of September, having gone to bed the previous morning sick at heart, she awoke in the autumn sunshine with her mind made up. She would be destroyed if she went on torturing herself about her conduct in Paris. The longed-for letter from Brian hadn't come, and might never come. Dr Compson had assured her that Conway was blameless as far as his relationship with Sarah was concerned, and if she couldn't trust him whom could she trust?

At breakfast she said, when Robert came in with hot muffins, "Would you please saddle my horse, Robert? I intend to go out this morning."

"Very well, Miss Mia . . . sorry, ma'am." His Adam's apple worked furiously.

"Where are you going?" her mother asked when he had left the room.

"To Well Farm, Mama. I've decided to go and see Conway."

"Good." Joseph looked up from his paper which he studied every morning for news of the war. "You're being very wise. Surely two sensible people can sort out things for themselves."

"We can try."

"I told you, didn't I?" Marie-Hélène said, "that you'd come round to it."

"Yes, Mama." She felt light-hearted, like a child. How simple it all was when you made up your mind.

"I'll ride along with you," Hannah said. "I'm not doing anything particular except checking the still room shelves."

"No, thank you, pet. I prefer to be alone." And to her father, "Will Sarah be at the potworks today?"

He put down his newspaper, looking worried. "I shouldn't like to say. Her attendance has been irregular recently. To tell you the truth Craythorne spoke to me about her. It seems she had been concerning herself too much with affairs which weren't quite hers, frit for the glazes and so on. Well, each to his own, as Craythorne said. She draws like an angel, but the dippers know their own business best. Apparently he said something like this to her, and she took umbrage. That's the way of the talented, I suppose. They've more than a normal sensitivity."

"Dr Compson told me when I called on him that she'd been ill quite a few times. She came to you originally

216

because of that, didn't she?" She paused. "Do you remember when she had brain fever when I first moved into Well House?"

"Yes." She could see out of the corner of her eye that her mother was listening.

"Once I went into her room when she was supposed to be sleeping . . ." She included her mother in her glance. "I've never told you this. She was muttering to herself, strange things . . . she didn't seem to know me. Dr Compson said something like your remark, Papa, about her having more than a normal sensitivity. In fact he said he had known her when she was quite . . . deranged."

There was dead silence in the room. Joseph was the first to break it. "A medical term, I should imagine. A fever makes one behave strangely."

"Yes. I only wondered . . ."

"You might as well know, Mia," Marie-Hélène said briskly, "that it gave us concern at the time of your marriage, Sarah's oddness and the general . . . background. But Dr Compson spoke highly of Conway's qualities, and we felt he ought to know. And, my girl, don't forget your eagerness to be married!" Her voice softened. "Your happiness was our chief concern."

"You're the best of parents." Mia smiled tremulously and then bent her head over her plate. "Imagine becoming emotional at the breakfast-table!" She was on the point of weeping.

"And why not?" her mother said. "You stiff-lipped English people! You shouldn't bottle things up, Mia. It would be better if you ranted and raved occasionally."

"We leave the show of temperament to you, my dear." Joseph smiled at her. "It lends colour to our otherwise dreary lives." She shook her head at him and heaved a theatrical sigh.

There was a tinge of autumn to the landscape as Mia rode along, a golden haze on the distant hills, a drift of golden leaves under the horse's hooves, and a silence in the thickets instead of the noisy spring clamour of the birds. It was fecund, she thought, the pale gold of the wheatfields on either side of her, fruitful . . . her heart seemed to stop beating for a moment at the word, and then she consoled herself. It couldn't be, it couldn't be . . . she was going to see her husband, all would be explained, all would be forgotten, they'd begin their lives again together with the storms and anxieties behind them, with Brian behind them . . .

She took the direct route to Well Farm and so avoided the park and Well House. If Sarah had been a normal sister-in-law, she told herself, she would have called to see her first and they might have chattered together as she and Hannah did, but instead she followed the carriage road which brought her along by the lake and the front of the farm.

It had never looked more beautiful. Nature had taken over again, aided by clever planning by Conway, there was no sign of defacement. The trees were green and gold, the lake surface milk-blue, the lawn in front of the farm was freshly cut and surrounded by the flower border which she and Conway had planted. Asters, chrysanthemums and dahlias tangled in their autumn colours. The white seat round the elm had a spatter of golden leaves on it.

I'm like a visitor, she thought, dismounting, but remaining where she was. I don't know how to approach my own home, what to say to my own husband. Her hand holding the reins was trembling, and the horse moved restlessly. There was the sound of footsteps and she turned. It was a gardener whose name she didn't know. He had a wooden rake in his hand, perhaps to gather up the leaves. She summoned her courage. "Kindly tell Robson to open the door, that your mistress is here."

He looked at her, a gnarled elderly man bent with arthritis. "The mistress? You be the mistress, then?" He must have taken the place of the young boy who doubtless had enlisted.

218

"Yes, I am."

"I's'll do that right away, right away, ma'am." He went off mumbling, and in a few minutes she saw Robson, ponderous as ever, at the door, and at the same time Baxter appeared to lead her horse away.

"Good morning, ma'am," he said. "I'm glad you're back." His face was devoid of curiosity, his smile had warmth in it. She felt cheered.

"Thank you, Baxter." She went towards the door, wilting slightly at the sight of the butler's impervious facade. "Good morning, Robson. I'm going into the drawing-room." She was in the hall now. How bright and cheerful it looked. "Is the master there?"

"No, ma'am. He isn't . . . not at all . . . he . . ." his mind seemed to be working round some insuperable obstacle which was preventing coherent speech.

"I'll go in all the same. Send Ruth to me if you will."

The drawing-room was flooded with light as if part of the lake had come inside. It was charming to her eyes with great bowls of finely-arranged flowers, but strangely untenanted. The fire was set between the dogs but unlit. There were no papers or books lying about, and she had discovered when living with Conway that there was always a trail of papers and books marking his passage. She stood at the window trying to subdue the dread in her mind while she waited. There was a knock at the door. "Come in," she said, turning round. It was Ruth. "Well, Ruth," she smiled at the girl, feeling unaccountably shy. "It's good to see you again."

"Oh, ma'am!" The girl's face was red with pleasure. "I've wearied for word of you. I took courage one day and asked Miss Sarah when she was arranging the flowers when you'd be back but she said she knew nothing about you. And then the master was that strange . . ."

"What do you mean . . . strange?"

"He walked and rode miles, ma'am. Baxter said the horse was in a fair lather at times. And the rest of the time he just sat in his study. Would hardly come to meals. Miss Sarah called often asking him to go to dinner at the big house but he wouldn't hear of it."

"There was no need for that, surely. Mrs Allenby is perfectly capable, isn't she?"

"That's just the trouble, ma'am. She had to leave. Her old mother was took ill in the village and there was no one else to look after her. I've been doing as best as I can since she's gone."

"How long ago was that?"

"Two weeks ago, ma'am."

"Well, the master isn't too hard to please, Ruth, and I know you can pass yourself off fairly well in the kitchen. I remember Mrs Allenby saying you were good at the cold table."

"That's right, ma'am. When I gets time to prepare things I can make a fair showing, but having a dinner on the table in time, the meat and the veg, and what goes before and what comes after is a bit of a trial to me. Still, as it happens, it didn't matter so much."

"Why was that?" She was thinking how much she liked this girl, her honesty and loyalty, and how pleasant it would be to be back in her own house, planning the menus, going into the kitchen in the morning to have a chat with Cook, inspecting the larder and the still rooms, sitting in the library in the quiet afternoons to read some of Conway's books . . . "Why was that, Ruth?" she repeated.

The girl's mouth was round with surprise. "Oh, didn't you know, ma'am? I thought Robson or Baxter had told you. The master left last week."

"Left last week?" She felt stunned. "Where for?"

"A tour, ma'am, a Continental tour, moving on from place to place, like. 'No forwarding address,' he said to Robson. He got Baxter to drive him to Liverpool Station, last Thursday, I think it was. Miss Sarah wasn't well-pleased, I can tell you. Robson overheard her in here. He makes up in his ears what he lacks in his tongue . . . beg pardon, ma'am, I shouldn't have said that."

Normally she would have spoken sharply to the girl for gossiping, but it didn't matter now. Nothing mattered now. "Have you any idea how long he's gone away for?"

"Oh, yes, ma'am. Three months, he said, three months at the least . . . I felt sure he'd have let you know."

"I've been in Paris. The letter will be at home, or he'll write during the journey . . ." she scarcely knew what she muttered.

"Shall I get you a cup of tea, ma'am, after your journey, and then you might like to go up to your room? I've kept it nice while you were away."

"No, Ruth, no, I don't think so. I don't know whether I'll be staying or not. Certainly not at the moment. I haven't brought any clothes." She had had some insane idea, it seemed now, when she left Blenheim Terrace, that Conway would persuade her to remain and they could have been sent for. "I'll have to think . . ."

"Have a cup of tea at least, ma'am. You look fair worn out."

"No, no. I merely rode over since it was such a fine morning, to see how everything was. Tell Baxter to bring round my horse as you go out."

"Very well, ma'am." The girl retreated to the door, fumbled with the handle and then before she went out, gave Mia a mournful look. "I missed you, ma'am, doing your hair and that. It's lonely, like, here."

"It's kind of you to say so, Ruth. Very kind . . . tell Baxter . . ."

She rode back slowly, feeling dead inside. Three months, she kept repeating to herself, three months . . . it was too long.

221

Chapter Eighteen

She didn't know why she remained at Blenheim Terrace when there was a house lying empty beside the lake, except that, although she hadn't confided in her parents, she craved the comfort of her family around her. Both of them, she knew, would have been shocked and horrified had they known the truth about her Paris visit, but she was their child. In the ultimate resort she knew they'd take care of her, and she had an overwhelming need to be taken care of.

She pretended to be persuaded by Marie-Hélène. "Stay with us until Conway returns, although I must say it's very odd behaviour on his part. It would be lonely for you there, and you can help me with Hannah's trousseau. Her demands are never two days alike."

Hannah was delighted. "You're good at making up my mind for me, Mia, and you can cheer me up too. Occasionally I have a little sigh to myself about leaving home. Because however much you love your husband-to-be, there's still the tiniest dread about giving up your girlhood, and . . . you know what I mean, don't you?"

"Yes, pet, I do know what you mean but don't worry. I'm sure Jason will be good to you and you'll be very happy and get all your heart's desire."

Her father liked her there because he said there was nothing but talk of mixing and matching and she at least was an intelligent listener. The war was slowly dragging to a close. The final attack on Sebastopol had been made on the 8th of September after three days of terrific bombardment, the French under General Pelissier showing all their usual dash and constancy, and by their capture of the Malakoff Redoubt making Redan untenable.

All the bloodshed, deaths and suffering had proved absolutely nothing, it was a mad enterprise from start to finish. Only three persons had come out of it well, he said, the German Todleben who was responsible for the fortifications, Russell who had pulled the wool from the British public's eyes, and Florence Nightingale who had made the same public realise that the British soldier was a man and not something on a par with the horses, except that the horses received better attention. Palmerston, he added tersely, should realise we'd had enough.

"I wish Conway was at home so that I could discuss it all with him. You haven't heard from him yet?"

"No, Papa."

"Why don't you ride over with Hannah today and call on Sarah? You could kill two birds with one stone. Find out if she's all right, and ask her if she's heard from her brother. We haven't seen her at the potworks for a week or so."

"I couldn't. I don't wish to see her again. She's been the cause of too much trouble in my life."

"Nevertheless I think you should let her see you're still mistress of Well Farm instead of making Blenheim Terrace your Sebastopol. I know the fortifications of your own family are comforting, but sooner or later you'll have to show yourself." His eyes were shrewd.

"You're right as usual. I'll think about it. I'll see what Hannah says."

Hannah was delighted with the idea of a jaunt. She was growing tired of fittings, fittings, fittings, she said, and she'd had so many pins stuck in every part of her anatomy that she'd been given enough good luck to last her for a century. She discussed her wedding dress most of the way to Well House.

"Do you think white fur round the hem and round the

sleeves is too much, Mia? Your eye is better than mine. I don't want to look frumpish like the Queen, all those ends and bits. But how do you think fur would look with flowers and a veil, and what do you think to the idea of a going-away mantle and bonnet in olive green, the bonnet to be trimmed with ospreys above my chignon? I want to look like a married lady, not just a girl, and olive green seems to me to be the right colour for that although Mama prefers blue. Will you have a word with her, Mia? She respects your opinion. And then tomorrow I thought we might go together and try on my new boots Mr Cantilever's been making for me. I long to be more direct with him. He pinches my toes here and there through them and says 'Quaite parfect, miss,' in that mincing voice of his, and I always end up with a size bigger than I need which is a pity since there's no chance then of one's foot being admired for its neatness. Jason has said on many occasions that I've an exceptionally neat foot, that it was one of the things he noticed first about me but then that was when I was wearing shoes . . .''

The chatter went on all the way to Well House with the horses' hooves ringing on the frosty road in accompaniment. The trees had lost most of their leaves now. It had been a stormy autumn and winter seemed to be approaching too quickly. If she could only halt time . . .

They sent in their cards with Frame who gave them a surly "Good morning," and in a few moments he came back. Miss Sarah was in her sitting-room. If they'd wait in the drawing-room she'd be with them in a few moments.

"What a clutter of a room," Hannah said when Frame had left them. "How did you put up with it, Mia? I must say I don't blame you for going to Well Farm. It's quite charming. Much too small for my taste, of course, even with the additions. I prefer the Palladian type of architecture, but charming all the same."

"I never regarded this place as my home as long as Sarah was here, and I must tell you, Hannah, that I don't expect a cordial reception. I've merely come to please Papa."

"I've sent her an invitation to the wedding. He said I must, but so far she hasn't replied. I gather she dislikes dressing up. I can't understand why. I adore it. Tell me, Mia, what time did you start getting into your wedding gown? Can you remember how long it took you? I should so hate to be rushed, but on the other hand it must be very disconcerting to be ready too early and then to become flustered and unbecomingly hot. Can you imagine if I walked down the aisle with a red nose! My nose always gets red first. You're lucky. You always look so cool. Even now, although I know you're simply *hating* this, you're *surprisingly* cool . . ."

The door opened and Sarah came in. Mia was immediately struck by her ravaged appearance. Her hair wasn't well-brushed, and some strands had escaped from her chignon at one side giving her an unkempt air. Her dress was of some dark stuff down to her wrists, up to her throat, unrelieved by collar, cuffs or jewellery, and her face seemed to be a muddy white, with dark circles under her eyes.

"Good morning," she said. "What can I do for you?" Her mouth pulled sideways in a tic as she spoke.

Hannah rushed into speech. "Oh, it was Papa's idea, Sarah. We're going on to Well Farm and he said we must pay our respects to you. He said you hadn't been at the potworks for a week or two and he wondered if you were quite well."

"I'm quite well, thank you. I've been working at home." She turned to Mia. "I'm surprised to see you here."

"No more surprised than I am at myself for coming." The words came to her easily. "But I make allowances for you, Sarah. I realise now you're not always in good health despite what you say."

"Who says that? Has that old woman of a doctor been talking again?"

"If you refer to Dr Compson, I haven't seen him for

225

some time." Her own coolness surprised her, and with the surprise came the realisation that Sarah could never frighten her again. Her consuming worry put this girl's antipathy towards her in its proper perspective. She had a sick mind.

Sarah remained standing, although they were seated. "Have you heard from my brother?"

"I was going to ask *you* that question."

"No, I haven't. It's most unlike Conway not to keep in touch with me. He's always been concerned about my welfare ever since we were children. Long ago in the nursery . . ." Mia saw the slight tic pull her mouth sideways again.

"Letters get delayed when one is travelling," Hannah said, "and in any case one can look forward to all the wonderful tales when the person concerned returns. When Mia went to Paris with Papa she had so much to tell us about the streets, and the decorations, and the . . ." Hannah's memory or her invention failed her. "Do you intend to come to my wedding, Sarah? It's not far off now, the 11th November."

There was a pause. Sarah's eyes were on the view of the park from the window. "I don't go to weddings . . ." it was as if she had forgotten their presence.

The girls exchanged glances. Mia got to her feet and Hannah followed suit. "We must leave now," Mia said. "I've some matters to discuss with the staff at Well Farm. I shall be taking up residence soon and I must make arrangements."

Sarah turned her head. Her face glowed, her smile was full and soft, she looked almost pretty, it was a complete metamorphosis. "Forgive me, Mia for being so abrupt, but it's quite true, I haven't been well. Please tell your father I'll work on the new designs at home for the time being, and . . ." she hesitated, "if there's anything I can do at Well Farm to help you I'll be only too delighted. I regret many things in the past. It's difficult

226

for me to say more." Her head bent on its thin neck. She looked pitiful.

"That's . . . generous of you." Mia was puzzled, and yet surely the smile and the demeanour were genuine enough? Had she been in fact ill when she had made those terrible statements to her at Well Farm? Had it been a complete aberration, something which could well be buried in the past?

Sarah raised her head. "I believe Mrs Allenby is likely to be away for some time. They say in the village her mother is dying slowly. Please don't hesitate to ask for Mrs Frame's help until you replace her. I know Ruth is attempting the cooking but she isn't well-skilled."

"Thank you, but I'll have no difficulty in finding someone. Now if you'll excuse us we'll bid you good morning. Hannah has many things to attend to in the afternoon so we must make a speedy return."

"I'll ring for Frame. And thank you for coming." She turned to Hannah. "Thank you for the invitation, Hannah. If I don't come, you must realise it's because of an excruciating shyness which prevents me mingling with others, but be assured I wish you every happiness."

"Thank you, Sarah. Thank you very much." Hannah looked gratified. Frame appeared, and they followed him to the door.

"Well," Hannah said when they had mounted their horses, "what do you think of that? I must say I often thought you tended to exaggerate Sarah's foibles. I'm sure she's quite right, it comes from not mixing with people. Now if you'd done what I suggested and given some soirées or even a little ball, you might have had her married off by this time. As it is, she'll only degenerate into a harmless spinster. However, she may come in useful to you at a later date for looking after . . . you know what I mean." Mia kept her eyes ahead. "As for Jason and myself, we think a family of five would be quite in order. Jason likes a large family. He says it gives one a sense of one's place in the world. I can never understand why Mama and Papa had only you and me. It'll be a trial and a bore to have them, but I'm quite resigned to it, and Jason says he'll see we have a properly equipped nursery and staff to take care of the brats."

"Jason thinks of everything." Mia, turning her head, met her sister's eyes. Hannah must have seen the laughter in hers. Her face changed slowly from the sententiousness it generally assumed when she was airing Jason's likes and dislikes, to the smiling mischievousness which Mia knew and loved. Ripples of laughter creased it, were echoed by Mia, and then they were both helpless, bent over their mounts. They both sat up, choking, trying to wipe their eyes, at the same time.

"Oh, that was good!" Hannah said. "Your face, Mia, that smirk of yours, so like Papa's . . . come on, I'll race you to the farm." She was the old Hannah again. But she would never be the same Mia . . . tears blinded her as she spurred on her horse.

Ruth was delighted to see them. They had been shown into the drawing-room by Robson, who this time, having more of his wits about him, got down on a creaking knee, set a light to a well-stacked fire and had it blazing in no time. Ruth arrived shortly afterwards bearing a tray.

"I took the liberty, ma'am, of bringing in some refreshment with me since it's a frosty morning and you and Miss Hannah could do with a warm, I'm sure. It's hot chocolate, just newly made."

"How kind of you. The house looks very fresh and well-aired. Is everything in order?"

"Oh, yes, ma'am. I try to keep it nice. And you've a rare treasure in Baxter, he keeps the stables and the horses in apple-pie order. Robson, well, he does what's necessary. But Mrs Allenby isn't back yet, nor any sign of her."

"Don't worry, Ruth. When I come back I'll see to finding

a temporary cook. What's that on the tray?" She had seen a letter lying beside the silver jug.

"Mercy me, I meant to give it to you right away! I was going to get Baxter to take it to you today. It's like fate come to think of it, you riding up." She handed the letter to Mia. "I took the liberty of looking at the envelope, ma'am. It's got a foreign postmark on it."

"Is it from Conway?" Hannah said.

"I expect so." Mia opened her reticule and made to put it in.

"That will do, Ruth," Hannah said, and when the girl had gone she turned excitedly to Mia. "Don't stand on ceremony with me! You're a tease, just like Papa. Open it at once and let's hear where he is and when he's coming back."

"Very well." She opened the envelope clumsily and took out the letter. She had only to glance at the top right-hand corner before she knew. She stared at the sloping hand-writing for what seemed an unconscionable time, longing to close her eyes, to faint, to be spirited away to a quiet room where she could devour it, far from Hannah's curious gaze.

"He'll be back soon," she said, thrusting it into the envelope, putting it in her reticule. "So now we know. I'll read it at my leisure when we get home. Look at that lovely steaming jug of chocolate! It makes me quite thirsty just to smell it." But in fact it made her sick.

"You're so secretive! Very well, I'll pour you some. But I do think you're odious all the same. Jason has an excellent hand. There you are. Do mind the saucer, Mia. It's not like you to be clumsy."

"Has he, Jason, an excellent hand?"

"Yes. Of course he's done a great deal of clerical work for Papa which has given him a good training in calligraphy. Only last evening he was saying to me . . ."

Mia nodded and smiled appropriately, praying that her outward façade revealed nothing of the torment inside her.

*   *   *

She was in her room at last. Hannah had gone with Marie-Hélène for yet another fitting, Joseph had returned to the potworks. She opened the letter slowly and then sat upright for a moment before she let her eyes rest on it. No more, she said to herself, please, I can stand no more . . .

'Dearest Mia, or if this is not the proper mode of address to a married woman, 'Dear Mia' . . . you *are* very dear to me, and will always be even although we're unlikely to meet again . . .'

Her heart started to beat painfully and she put down the letter to wipe her forehead with her handkerchief. He didn't expect, then . . . There was going to be no release, no way in which Brian could help her, she had known it, she had always known it . . . When she was calmer she took up the letter again.

'I should have written sooner. Indeed I have written, three times in all, and each time I've torn up the letter because it didn't say what I wanted to say or said it badly. Perhaps the roses spoke for me?

'That afternoon we spent together . . . what can I say about it? Oh, I hope you haven't reproached yourself too much, castigated yourself too much! Conventionally it was wrong but how right it felt! Don't feel shame, be like me and console yourself by saying it was meant to happen.

'From the first day we met, through the long horror of the war, I had the strong presentiment we should meet again, that we were meant to meet again, and so I wasn't too surprised when I saw that slim figure in the pale violet dress coming towards me, recognised the dark eyes under the pale violet bonnet. You've a light step, Mia, it's an embodiment of you, your approach to life, your courage and gaiety. I'll always remember that afternoon and the joy you brought me with your loving heart. It's a dream which will never fade . . .'

Her eyes misted at the last words, and she knew terror, stark terror which had been sleeping in her heart but now tore at her with wicked claws. She moaned, the letter to her mouth.

'But it must remain a dream, I know you're saying, and sadly I have to agree. You're married, and although there may be temporary difficulties with your husband I'm sure all will be well. He couldn't fail to love you.

'I envy him. I'm not built for matrimony, and I know I'll miss much happiness because of this. I loved Harry in a particular way, and although I knew joy with you, I know it wouldn't be a continuing joy, or with any woman. I must be frank. Then, I'm fickle. I like to move about the world. I've an insatiable curiosity about other countries. And strangely enough, although being a soldier may put an end to this pleasure, and sharply at that, yet I want to remain one, to taste again the horror but also the elation, and the comradeship of men. There's something in me that asks to be tried.

'You too, dear Mia. You like to dare. There's nothing small or petty in your temperament, you're a woman who'll know great happiness and possibly as great sorrow. But they'll be on a grand scale. You'll go down into the depths but you'll also touch the stars. Do you remember the roundabout at the Fair? And the gilt horses, and how we slid down, down, and then up till we were soaring above the crowd? And how you laughed and flung your head back? I'll think of that girl at the Fair, and I'll think of the woman in Paris. Two Mias. Both beautiful but not for me. Forgive me and think of me sometimes. Brian.'

Mia folded the letter. She put it in its envelope and then she lit her candle. This time there would be no letter to find, no lock to break, no evidence. She held one corner to the flame and watched it shrivel, watched the blue line of the flame spread in an ever-growing circle until the envelope with its contents were shrivelled black. She crumpled the ashes in the saucer, and only then got up and lay down on her bed.

231

She was lying there when Hannah came running upstairs to tell her that dinner was ready. She got up, washed her face and hands, combed her hair and went down to join the others.

Chapter Nineteen

She descended into the dark loneliness of despair, and yet strangely enough she was able to go about calmly, help her mother and sister with the preparations for the wedding, even sit and talk with her father in the evening when Marie-Hélène and Hannah were busy sewing.

"We'll have to leave it to the politicians now," he said. "They'll spend months justifying our part in the holocaust, inventing imaginary aims, seeing results where there are none, and then we'll have a great treaty with everyone shaking hands and congratulating each other."

"You're a cynic, Papa."

"Every potter is a cynic. Isn't everything we make broken eventually? Nevertheless, since I'm an optimistic cynic, which I'm sure is a paradox, I'm going to start working on a dinner service embellished with the Napoleonic eagle, although since the Emperor shows every sign of being the most sensible one in the negotiations he might well change his emblem to a dove. And I shouldn't be surprised, astute man that he is, if he doesn't manage to coincide the Peace Treaty with the birth of his heir."

"Yes, Papa . . ."

He looked at her. "You've changed, Mia. I don't know what it is but you've changed. Hannah said there was a letter from Conway. You expect him back soon?"

"Quite soon." It was easy not to lie, easy not to tell the truth.

The day of the wedding dawned, miserably cold and damp as befitted the month. Hannah went from one extreme

233

to the other, despair that her fur trimmings would look like dead cats, delight that since it was cold they'd be most appropriate and the fur muff the last word in style.

Mia had agreed to attend her. She agreed to anything and everything nowadays, and her dress was of gold velvet trimmed with brown squirrel, also with muff. Joseph said she looked beautiful, Marie-Hélène nodded agreement. She was quieter than usual these days, but she had a lot on her mind and losing her younger daughter was bound to make her sad. Besides she had undertaken to provide the wedding breakfast at Blenheim Terrace with the help of three women from the town and the invaluable Mrs Gossop, and this occupied most of her attention. Mia had specifically wished only a few friends at her wedding, this was to be a much bigger affair, the bigger the better being Hannah and Jason's credo.

Should she have three *plats chauds* and six *plats froids*, or vice versa? What did Hannah and Mia think of *Bavoroise au Chocolate*, *Crème aux Amandes* and *Compôte de Poires à la Chantilly* for the entremets? Or could she also include *Charlotte Russe* without offending any politically-biased guests? It was all settled in the end, as Mia knew it would be, by Joseph sitting down one evening with his wife and firmly writing out the menu, contriving a judicious blend of French *bonne cuisine* and British good eating.

And so the sight which met their eyes when they returned from church was a work of art. The linen on the tables was snowy, the napkins were folded into water-lily shapes and placed on Joseph's best ware delicately painted with the same flower and with a glaze as smooth and soft as satin. The cake was a *chateau de rêves* of spun sugar icing concealing who knew what delights inside, and the dessert centrepiece of white velvet threaded with silver ribbon had an arrangement of camellias and stephanotis in a silver lustre bowl by Mr Wedgwood. Robert headed a row of hired waiters, his Adam's apple aquiver with excitement, and Mrs Gossop waited in the hall with Lucy to receive the women's wraps.

Hannah and Jason took up their places at the large windows of the drawing-room, ready, even eager to be congratulated. They looked, thought Mia, like two people who got married every day of the week. Jason was affable, expansive, given to talking in a loud, confident voice, Hannah was girlish, gushing and delighted to be like the dessert centrepiece, the focus of attention.

"You look lovely," Mia said, kissing her, "and not at all nervous."

"That's the strange thing. I wasn't at all nervous, even in the church. I feel it's so *right*, Jason and me." She cast an adoring look at her husband who smiled down his nose at her.

The wedding breakfast was long, interminably long it seemed to Mia. The procession of different courses, the serving and clearing away of them seemed endless, the speeches were tiresome, long and mostly irrelevant with the exception of Joseph's, the wine made her head ache. She looked at the gaily-dressed people around the buffet with their insatiable appetites for food, wine and chatter, she looked at her father resplendent and urbane in his frock-coat, her mother regal and plumply beautiful in her bronze taffetas with always the simple cornelians in her ears which Joseph had given her when a student. Once or twice her eyes met Marie-Hélène's, and they seemed to be resting on her. She had to turn away her head.

And then there was the clearing away and the shepherding of ladies and small children to the appropriate places for reparations and relief, and then more conversation, a buzzing saw-like noise which went on endlessly until Jason with great aplomb drew out his new gold watch, a wedding present from Hannah, and said, "Well, my dearest, I think it's time we left."

Hannah looked engaging in her olive green and still girlish in spite of the osprey feathers and the low chignon.

"Oh, Mia," she said, clinging to her sister for a moment, "it's sad, isn't it, but so exciting! I feel I'm living, I'm on tiptoe, I'm madly happy! We've such plans!"

The parting glass of champagne had been drunk, the last rose petal had fluttered down, the guests had retired once more to the drawing-room to discuss at length the bridal pair now that they'd gone. Mia stood in the empty hall, quite still, glad of the comparative quietness, feeling the throbbing in her head and the tiredness in her bones. Just a moment, she told herself, just a moment before I face them all again. I've got through it, they'll soon be going, and then I'll have Mama and Papa to myself, then I'll be able to tell them . . .

There was a loud knock at the door making her start. Surely Jason with his well-ordered efficiency hadn't forgotten anything? The valises had been counted when they'd been stowed away in the carriage, Hannah had checked a dozen times that she had her new olive green hand-luggage inside. Robert appeared, face flushed, jaws working, from the kitchen, and seeing Mia he quickly put his hand over his mouth. She distinctly saw his Adam's apple moving as some choice piece from the remains of the wedding breakfast was despatched. She seemed to be seeing and hearing everything acutely, the light sparseness of the hall, the glass panels above the rounded door in the shape of a peacock's tail, the echo of the knocking . . .

Robert opened the door. She heard him say, "Good afternoon, sir," and the emphasis in his voice, the surprise, made her turn round instead of retreating out of sight. It was Conway. He was in a dark cloak and his face was thinner and browner, the eyes sunk deep.

"Is Mrs . . .?" He caught sight of her. "Mia!" He started towards her and then hesitated until Robert had disappeared behind the baize door. She had a clear impression of the boy's excited eyes, the eagerness in his body to get back to the kitchen to tell the news. "Mia!" He was close beside her now. She had to force herself to look up at him, concentrate on him, tell herself that it was real, the situation was real, Conway was standing in front of her. "I went to Well Farm first in the hope you might be there, but Ruth told me you were at Blenheim Terrace. I came right away."

"Oh, yes . . . yes, I've been here for some time. But I've kept an eye on the Farm and seen to the staff and . . . you've just missed the wedding!" She wanted to weep. She wanted to know if he would kiss her.

"You look different," he said, "different somehow."

"This is my wedding dress for Hannah."

"No, it isn't that. Different . . ."

"So do you. Thinner." Why doesn't he kiss me? He must make the first move. *He* went away after all . . . she didn't think she moved, but somehow she was in his arms and still he didn't kiss her but folded her warmly inside the cloak so that immediately she felt cared for. That was what she needed, someone to take care of her, someone to take over from her parents because they had done their caring, they wanted to be left in peace now that their two daughters were married. Her body ached for comfort.

He said in her ear, his voice rough. "Will you come home with me? There's so much, so much . . ."

"Yes," she said. "I'll come home with you."

Marie-Hélène and Joseph had to greet him, of course. He had to drink a glass of wedding champagne and was pressed to sample one of the pâtés with a piece of toast. He refused to eat more, was charming to the guests then began to look impatient as if his social manners were wearing thin.

"Mama," Mia said. "Would it appear rude if I go back to the farm with Conway this evening? He'd like me to accompany him."

"I should think it would be even more rude to show a preference for your parents! Besides, your Papa and I won't be fit for anything when this," her eyes rolled melodramatically towards the ceiling, "is over."

237

"Then I'll go upstairs and pack, but I'll be back, probably tomorrow to . . . to thank you properly. Oh, Mama!"

"There's no need, child. We love you." She kissed Mia. "*Bonne chance*! Now you have need of your husband."

They talked long into the night at the log fire with the curtains undrawn so that they could see the black moving surface of the lake.

"I should have told you I was going away," he said, "but when I called at Blenheim Terrace day after day and you refused to see me I thought what Sarah had told me must be true, that you loved someone else."

"I ought to have seen you, I realise it now. But I was bitterly hurt. To have one's letters read is an assault on one's privacy, and then I was guilty . . ." the pain in her heart made her close her eyes for a second. How small the guilt had been when she compared it with what she felt now.

"What was it that made you feel so bitter?"

"Didn't Sarah tell you?"

"No, not what she had said to you."

"It seems a long time ago. She told me you preferred her to me, that I didn't know the meaning of love, of passion, only you and she . . ."

"Oh, God! She believes it, you know."

"And didn't I? Can you blame me for shutting myself off from you, for loathing the very thought of you together, for feeling *glad* about the letters?"

"How could I? But it's been hard for me too. I've had to face the fact that you preferred someone else. I ran away from it . . . but I've come back. I had to come back. Would you like to tell me about the letters, about the man who wrote them? We have to be frank now with one another."

"The letters . . . they're unimportant now." She felt weary at the thought of them. What were a few scraps of paper compared with a fact which was irremediable? "They

238

supported Brian when he was fighting, they supported me in my unhappiness at Well House which you caused as much as Sarah."

"You thought that?"

"Often. But now I begin to see more clearly, as if I'd lost my girlhood in the last few months . . . you were anxious about her, you wanted her to be happy, for us all to be happy together, I can almost put down her outburst to hysteria . . . almost." She looked directly at him. "You said we had to be frank with one another. I have to tell you that I went to see Dr Compson one day, not about you, but . . ."

His voice was calm. "He felt it incumbent upon him to tell you about the . . . past?"

"No, he's loyal to you. He said I was to ask you to explain, that it was incumbent on *you*, that our happiness was in jeopardy until you did. You see how it is, Conway!" Her voice rose. "I try, but always there's this secrecy . . ."

There was a knock at the door and Ruth came in with a tray. "Excuse me, ma'am, excuse me, sir. I thought as how you might like some refreshment so I've brought a tray. Whisky and hot chocolate and some nice beef sandwiches that I've made fresh. And the fire's burning brightly in your room and the bed's well-aired. So if you'll excuse me I'll take the liberty of wishing you a very good night." Her face was beaming with pleasure and Mia felt the tears start in her eyes.

"You're very good to us, Ruth. We appreciate it."

"I'm that happy things are like what they were, so to speak, ma'am. I like to look after a house that's being used."

"We do thank you sincerely," Conway said gravely. "Perhaps you'll tell the rest of the servants to retire, if you will." His smile made her blush and bob a further good night before she left the room.

"We're blessed with Ruth," Mia said. They looked at each other without speaking. I can understand so well your

239

agony of mind, she thought, how the first word sticks in your throat, how you say words, sentences, phrases in your mind in a hundred different ways without finding the right one. And how much harder it is if you've been reserved all your life, shut off from normal contacts.

"One afternoon Sarah and I were in the old nursery." She realised he was speaking, in a monotonous tone like something rehearsed over a long period. "We were no longer children, of course, since we were both in our teens, but we tended to spend a lot of our time there. It was comfortable. We had our books, we sat round the fire in the winter and talked a lot because we were starved of talk with other people. You see, no one visited us since my mother was rarely out of bed before the afternoon, and the year she died, hardly at all . . .

"I was reading some book or other, well, why should I say 'some book or other?' I shall never forget it. Its title is written in letters of fire on my brain . . ." He gave a short laugh. "*Sartor Resartus*." Do you know it? I was greatly intrigued by Professor Teufelsdröckh . . . but there, I digress because I am fearful . . . She kept teasing me and interrupting me, saying she wanted to talk, and eventually since I would pay no attention to her she seized the book and flung it into the fire. It was a violent action. It brought home to me like a flash of lightning what an abnormal life we led together since she'd do such a thing. I sprang up, resentment and fury boiling inside me, seized her by the shoulders and shook her as violently as her action had been. I was in an adolescent rage, maniacal almost, and I think . . . I think . . . I'll never be sure . . . that I flung her from me. She stumbled and fell heavily sideways, and her right arm with all the weight of her body behind it went into the fire. It was a hot fire. She had amused herself earlier by stoking it up till it was like a furnace, to distract me. It was as if it too had stoked up my rage."

"Conway . . ." she put out her hand.

"Don't touch me," he said, in the same monotonous

240

voice. "She was badly burned. Her right arm. She screamed and screamed, I shall never forget that screaming cutting through me like knives, and Mrs Frame came rushing up to find me trying to beat the flames out. Her very flesh seemed to be on fire . . ." He wiped his brow. "I should have told you that Sarah's governess and my tutor had left together the previous day. They had been carrying on an illicit affair under our noses which Sarah knew about but I didn't. She used to taunt me about it, say that I went around with my eyes shut.

"Dr Compson took a long time to come. He was out at a child-bed, and when he finally arrived Sarah was unconscious. The nursery smelled of burning flesh. I couldn't go into it for months afterwards . . ."

"Where is it?" She cleared her throat. "The nursery?"

"Didn't you know? It's Sarah's sitting-room now." She closed her eyes, sickness enveloping her for a second.

"She was ill for a year. Putrefaction had set in, and a lot of the tissue was burned, charred. It took a year to heal, and in that time it wasted. She used to hold them out together, both arms, for comparison, and say, "See what you did to me, Conway?" She would roll up her sleeve on the bad arm once the bandages were off so that I could see the scarring. It was livid, ugly. Once, early on, when I thought she was going to die, I spent a whole night on my knees. I was only sixteen, remember." He smiled at her. "Perhaps that cured me of religion."

"Didn't you talk about it to your father? He was alive, wasn't he?"

"Yes, but he was rarely at home, and when he was, he stayed in his study. He'd been away on the day of the accident and he said to Dr Compson when he told him about it. 'What else could one expect?' I was there at the time."

"Conway . . . what kind of man was he?" She spoke angrily.

"A man without hope."

241

She looked at her hands, clasped in her lap. What could she say. "Dr Compson . . . what about Dr Compson? Couldn't he help?"

"He tried, but I wouldn't discuss the incident with him. I couldn't. I was shocked, I couldn't speak. When I lay in my bed for the first few nights all I heard in my ears were those terrible knife-like screams of Sarah's. He was kind, very kind, but no one could help me."

"Except your father!" Her anger flared again.

He shrugged. "It's of no matter. I came to terms with it a long time ago. He had a kind of sickness of the soul, who knows whether my mother was to blame for that. And too much money is no cure. But it was useful as far as I was concerned. Dr Compson spoke to him about me and persuaded him to send me to Grenoble University instead of engaging another tutor. I had two years of happiness with young men of my own age . . . and then it all began again." He stopped speaking abruptly.

She sat quietly, her mind full of his suffering to the exclusion of her own. And yet she dared not touch him. It was his Gethsemane. She heard him breathe deeply, his voice began again, steady, colourless.

"When I left Grenoble and came back to Well House I expected changes. That my father had died I knew. His sickness of soul had become a sickness of the body, a cancerous growth which took him quickly in the end. But in the interval also Sarah had become a young woman who had her hair up and who wore long-sleeved gowns to cover her scarred arm, a young woman whom I soon found out had developed an obsessional love for me combined with resentment at the injury I'd caused her. She preyed on my guilt. My peace of mind fell away from me.

One night she called me into her room, the old nursery, as I told you. There was a huge fire burning, as if to remind me of that other time, but no lamp, and in front of the fire there was a small table with a Bible on it." His voice dropped so that she could hardly hear it. "She made me swear on the Bible that I'd never leave her." The words fell into the silence.

"But why . . . why did you do it?"

"It wasn't that I was afraid of her, don't think that. I was afraid *for* her. She was so tense at times, so strange. I felt responsible for her. I was fully aware of the moral blackmail behind her demand, and yet I gave in to it. As I did on other occasions. If I didn't she became ill. Once or twice I went abroad with university friends on walking tours, once or twice I had them to stay, but the results were always the same. You saw it when we said we were moving to Well Farm." He looked at Mia, his face grey with fatigue. "All she wanted was me."

"Leave it, Conway. You've talked long enough."

"Once long ago," he paid no attention, "you may remember your mother and Hannah came to see us, and your mother spoke to me privately. She's astute. She said if Sarah had any hold on me, that I should tell you. It was good advice, but I couldn't take it."

"Because of the vow you'd made?"

"I told myself that was the reason, but it wasn't the whole reason, and this was where, my dear Mia, I had to go down to the pit of hell and wrestle with myself, in hotels and rooming houses in Dieppe, in Paris, in Florence and in Rome. I had to face the truth about myself. I had to face the truth that Sarah and I were linked together in a close bond, not because of happiness but because of unhappiness, which is far stronger. I had to face up to the attachment I had for my sister which was a mixture of filial affection, pity and fear, but which in her case was obsessional, possessive and abnormal. I have to admit to you, my wife, that as a young man I've permitted her caresses, returned them often. Don't turn away from me. You know I've a loving heart and there was no vice in me, never has been."

He looked up at her, his face ravaged, and yet smiling. "When you wrestle you become either the victor or the vanquished. I'm free of her now, free of the guilt she implanted in me. If you want me with all my faults and imperfections I'm yours. But will you want me now?" He stopped speaking, sat quietly beside her, and yet she felt his agony of mind as if it were her own.

Was she shocked or horrified, she asked herself? How could she be when she believed him, believed *in* him? Did she then hate Sarah? She could find no hate in herself. Should she rather try to understand this strange girl, make her welcome, let her see and feel the love which lay between Conway and herself, not a selfish love but one which could include her in their happiness?

And then, like a dagger piercing her, she thought of Brian and the fact that she was pregnant by him. For weeks now she hadn't concealed it from herself, only from others. She was healthy, she had had no sickness, but the tell-tale signs were there. In a few weeks it might well be obvious to others and certainly to Conway who would share her bed. A man could seduce outside marriage, a woman could not be seduced. His voice startled her. "I can see it's difficult for you, Mia. I don't blame you."

"I must talk to you," she said hurriedly, nervously, "about how it started with Brian, first the letters—"

"I don't *care* about the letters. I've forgotten about the damned things long ago."

"But Conway, that was only the beginning . . ."

"You look ill, my darling. Don't distress yourself. Only tell me you forgive me, that we can begin again."

"I want to, oh, I want to!" She found herself wringing her hands, brought them down and clenched them at her sides. "You see, when Papa and I went to Paris, Dr Compson had asked us to call on Captain Moore, the writer of the letters . . ."

"Why?" The word was barked out.

"Because he had keepsakes of Harry's, they were in the Crimea together, only Brian had been invalided out, and so I saw him again at the Place de Vosges, in his friend's house."

"But that's not a crime, my dearest! God knows I've seen the danger of obsessional love, I'm scarcely likely to repeat the mistake. You've said you want to begin again. Let's put what is past behind us, where it should be, begin a new life here . . ."

"I can do that with all my heart, but first, Brian . . . you see, I'm . . ."

He rose from his chair, pulled her up to him, and this time he kissed her, a kiss which made her moan so that he held her more closely in his arms. "I've worn you out with talk. Are you all right?"

"Yes, I'm all right." She had to bite her lip in case she moaned again. "Conway, you've been so brave. Let me be brave also. Let me—"

"All I want is for you to love me." He put his arm round her waist and led her slowly out of the room, across the dim hall and upstairs to their room, ruddy in the fire's glow. He helped her to undress. "Your body's rounder, Mia," he said, smiling at her as he slipped her nightdress over her head. "Is it your Mama's French cooking, do you think?"

"I don't think so. Conway, I'll die if . . ." but he mistook her cry of despair for a cry of love.

Chapter Twenty

She had a week of joy in Well Farm with Conway when she shut her mind to everything but their love. The black dog of despair was kept at bay while they walked by the lake, always talking, as if each day they discovered something new about each other. Only at night after he was asleep did it appear again, jaws slavering, to taunt her with the impermanency of her happiness, the inevitability of its end.

She said to Conway one afternoon when the winter sun was warm in the hollow where the farm lay, "Shall we walk through the woods to Well House? Sarah must have heard from the servants that you're back, and yet she hasn't come to see you."

"I'd realised that. Don't tell me," it was the wry smile which she loved, "you're magnanimous in your victory?"

"I am." She had a desire to tie up all loose ends, to set everything in order before . . . she didn't quite know what, but the conviction was strong in her that somehow, soon, she had to end her agony of mind.

Sarah received them in her own sitting-room which was the first surprise. Mia felt her eyes drawn to the fireplace, she imagined she felt the aura of past violence, even a smell of burning . . . Her sister-in-law was shy but pleasant, seemingly changed. "I knew you were back, Conway, and that Mia was with you. I didn't want to intrude. I waited until you came to me."

"Well, here I am," he said. He kissed her on the cheek. "Safe and sound. How have you been?"

"Not so well, but contrite." Her eyes were full and soft. "I begin to see how wicked I've been." She turned to Mia. "Can you find it in your heart to forgive me?"

She was touched. "I think I can." And then with honesty. "It won't be easy." She looked at the girl, at her thinness, the eyes enormous in the wan face, and she hesitated, feeling shy. "Conway and I would like you to come to Well Farm whenever you wish." She laughed to hide her emotion. "I'd like to try and become a sister to you."

"Oh, Mia!" Sarah came forward and kissed her on the cheek. Her lips were like ice. "Perhaps if we both tried . . ." She was almost gay now. "Please sit down. This is my first attempt at conciliation, having you up here in my room. Do you like it?"

"It's charming." Mia thought it a dark room and overcrowded with books and drawings. And there was the aura . . .

"I know I have my father's temperament. He became a recluse before he died, you know, and I must try to overcome that. But luckily I have my mother's talent, she painted too, although," she laughed, "not her addiction. There, you see, I can discuss my parents! Perhaps if you both help me I'll become a reformed character."

"Don't become too good or I shan't know you," Conway said.

She laughed again. "Now, tell me all about your trip. I long to hear about it. I begin to think that's something I might do, get away from here. I could make the excuse of studying ceramics. Now that I come to think of it I should like to go to Dresden to see the Meissen factory." She smiled at Mia. "That would please your father. He has a great admiration for Meissen."

"Perhaps you could steal some of their ideas," Conway said.

"The penalty is death." Mia laughed. "Or was. I remember Papa telling me that."

"I shouldn't care. I'm quite unscrupulous about getting

my own way. Isn't that so, Conway? Now, I must remember my duties as hostess and offer you some refreshment. I've everything to hand here which saves me bothering the servants. Since it was the nursery wing there's a small kitchen off this room." She pointed to a half-open door. "What would you like? I can offer you tea, chocolate, coffee or some home-brewed wine."

"No, I beg you!" Conway waved his hand. "Not home-brewed wine at this hour! Mia and I should go stumbling home. Chocolate would suit me. You used to make it rather well. How about you, Mia?"

"Yes, chocolate would suit me admirably."

"Make it strong, Sarah. I like to taste it rather than the milk."

"Don't worry, dear brother, I haven't lost my cunning. Excuse me." She got up and went into the kitchen, shutting the door behind her.

Mia and Conway exchanged glances. He got up from his chair, came over to her side and kissed her. When her face remained tilted he kissed her again lightly and then sat down. "The spirit moved me," he said, smiling.

"I'm glad it did." They spoke in whispers. "Because of . . .?" She raised her eyebrows and turned her head slightly towards the closed door.

He nodded, said, still softly, "Would it be too much to hope our troubles are over?"

After a time Sarah came back bearing a tray and set it down on a table against the wall. She came forward to Mia and handed her a steaming glass set on a saucer. "I've sweetened it, Mia, but you must say if there's not enough sugar. Conway likes his bitter."

She sipped. There was the strong dark taste of chocolate behind the sweetness. "It's just right, thank you, and most acceptable."

Sarah went back to the tray and brought another glass to Conway. "Here you are, just as you like it. Now as a reward you must tell me about all the exciting places you saw."

"It was scarcely a pleasure trip." His face was grim for a moment.

"Nevertheless, I know you well enough to be sure your eyes would be busy. Did you see Florence?"

"Yes, I saw Florence."

"And the statue of David? I'm studying the classical figure now, but giving it my own interpretation." She smiled, but more to herself it seemed, and Mia thought for a moment she saw the tic beside her mouth. She turned to Mia, the smile still there, her eyes limpid. "Your father sometimes talks about the return of the Etruscan motif, you know."

"Does he? I'm surprised. Far better to reflect one's own times. But then Papa always says I've my own opinions." She laughed, wondering about the smile.

The talk went on pleasantly for an hour before they took their departure. They walked through the wood, hand in hand, hardly speaking. She could see by Conway's face that he was happy. She thought, despair enfolding her again, that it was the cruellest irony of fate to be unable to share this happiness.

In the evening she was so miserable in spirit that she only made a pretence of eating. She excused herself and went to bed and wouldn't hear of Conway following her. "Enjoy your books, my darling, and come up when you're ready. I've some kind of malaise. Perhaps too much happiness is as upsetting as too much sorrow."

But when she was in bed she lay straight and watchful examining the symptoms which had made her come upstairs. A strange kind of sickness which lay like a weight on her stomach, a slight fever. She had a moment of blind rage against everything, against life, against whoever reigned above that she should have been well all the time she was at Blenheim Terrace and now should have been taken ill. It's cruel, she thought, cruel, it gives me no time . . .

Conway came quietly to bed so as not to disturb her but she turned to him. "I want to tell you. I have to tell you—"

Suddenly, like a knife cleaving her, a pain shot the length of her body. Her mouth was full of vomit. She struggled out of bed, stumbled to the basin and retched violently again and again. At last she turned a ravaged face to him, wiping her brow. "Forgive me . . . forgive me . . ."

"There's nothing to forgive. You're ill. Let me help you back to your bed. Poor Mia." He put his arm round her, murmuring consoling words. "Tell me what to do for you. I'll do anything."

"Some water please, and then I'll rest for a moment." She lay back on the pillows, too weak to say more.

"You'd like Ruth?" He supported her head while she drank, his anxious eyes meeting hers, and then covered her up gently. She could only nod and close her eyes.

Ruth came. "Good, kind Ruth," Mia said, looking up at her with grateful eyes as she was made sweet and clean again. Afterwards Conway sat quietly beside her holding her hand until she fell asleep.

In the morning she felt well except for a headache which seemed to grind sickeningly in her temples making her feel giddy, but she made herself get up and join Conway who was already at breakfast. He rose and came towards her when she appeared.

"Mia! Come and sit down. I left you quietly in order not to disturb you. Why did you rise? I've already told Ruth to start preparing your breakfast."

"Ruth has enough to do. I must go to the village and try to find a substitute for Mrs Allenby. Sarah offered Mrs Frame's services, but I'd rather be independent." She closed her eyes as a wave of sickness passed over her.

"Mia, darling!" He bent forward to take her hand. "Please let me take you back to bed. I'll ask Baxter to ride to Hessleton right away for Dr Compson."

"You'll do nothing of the kind. Once I walk beside our pretty lake I'll feel quite like my old self. Look, the sun's shining on it. I intend to look for the heron today."

He released her hand reluctantly. "You promise, then,

to take things easily? I've an appointment with Fisher, the stockman, this morning at ten . . ."

"Off you go, then." She managed to smile.

He got up, folded his napkin and came to her side, bent down and kissed her. "Don't be ill, my darling."

"I shan't be ill. Don't worry." She kept her head averted.

She put on a warm cloak and forced herself to walk round the lake, although she craved her bed, and gradually the keen winter air revived her so that she was able to go back to the house and see Ruth in the kitchen.

"Oh, ma'am," Ruth was putting a posy of flowers on Mia's breakfast-tray. "You shouldn't be up. You was that sick last night."

"I apologise, Ruth. I was so sorry to disturb you."

"Think nothing to it, ma'am. You've had a lot of worries on your shoulders I'll be bound. My mother used to say the body catches up on you when the mind's troubled. You take it easy for today."

"I was going to ask Baxter to get the carriage out and take me to the village. I must try and find a cook."

"There'd be nobody in the village, ma'am that'd do except that Mrs Parker. Now her son's gone she might oblige. They tell me she worked at Well House, before my time, though."

"No, I think we'd be better with a new broom. Where has Jack Parker gone, do you know?" She didn't usually gossip with the servants.

"Gone for a soldier again, they say. He's a rum one, that Jack." The thought suddenly occurred to Mia that it might have been Parker who had told Sarah about Brian, and so made her suspicious enough to open the letters. She wondered if she should ask Ruth if they got on well together, but she felt a great weariness and a lack of interest in the matter now. It was finished. If it were only the letters she had to worry about . . .

"Very well, Ruth. I'll leave it for today. Perhaps tomorrow I'll go to Hessleton."

But the following day she was too ill to go, no sickness this time, but a general malaise, a trembling of her hands and weakness in her legs so that she could hardly walk. Conway was distracted with anxiety. "I shan't wait another minute," he said, sitting beside her on the sofa. She had refused to be in bed. "Dr Compson must be sent for."

"No, Conway, please, no . . ." The thought of his knowledgeable hands examining her body made her shudder. She put her head in her hands.

"Why not? Look at you! You're unlike yourself. There must be something wrong. Had we been . . . together . . . for the past few months I might have begun to hope, but even my poor arithmetic tells me that would be foolish."

She raised her head, terror-stricken, knowing she would never be able to tell him. "I'm suffering from reaction, that's all. Today I haven't been sick. Ask Ruth and she'll tell you that is so. It takes a day or two to recover from a sickness such as I had. Tomorrow, you'll see, I'll be as right as rain."

And she was. She awoke knowing one load had been lifted from her heart. Her head was clear, her nausea gone, and she had no pain except an ache in the lower part of her abdomen which she assured herself was caused by retching.

"We'll go visiting," she called gaily. "Get on your best frock-coat. I must know if Mama has received word from Hannah and Jason yet."

"I'd enjoy a jaunt." He came to the door of his dressing-room. "I'll tell Baxter immediately and when we're in Hessleton I'd like you to order some new dresses. Even in my wretched state I managed to buy some silk for you when I was abroad, a golden-bronze colour which I thought might match your hair and eyes."

"You make me sound very strange," she said, "piebald eyes and hair?" She was full of laughter. Her body had never been at any time a trial to her. To be relieved of

252

thinking about it made her shut her mind to the other anxiety which had lived with her for three months now. She'd pretend, just for a day, that all was well.

Joseph and Marie-Hélène were delighted to see them and insisted they should join them for luncheon.

"We've a long letter from Hannah," Marie-Hélène told them, "from Devon. The weather is poor, and the seas rage, but Jason walks beside the tumbling waves with her, and . . ."

". . . commands them to stop," Conway said.

She laughed delightedly. "You're very naughty if not sacrilegious, but yes, I like the picture of Jason holding up his hand. And in the evening, she says, they sit cosily round a log fire and talk, the pet."

"And make even more plans," Mia said. "Was there ever such a couple for making plans! One should never make plans . . . oh, Mama! Do you happen to know of a cook for me in Hessleton? Ruth's a treasure but rather heavy-handed with the rolling-pin, and Mrs Allenby has still not returned."

"Usually women are fixed up at this time of the year, but I'll make enquiries."

"Thank you. It's not urgent."

"So all is well with you?" Joseph said, looking from one to the other.

"All is very well." Conway smiled at his father-in-law. "We had a stormy start but I think we've sailed into calmer waters."

"Because we live beside a lake there's no need to become nautical," Mia teased him.

"See how she treats me!" Conway appealed to Marie-Hélène and Joseph. "Had this virago not been ill for the past few days I should not let her off with it."

"What was wrong, Mia?" Marie-Hélène's tone was sharp.

"Nothing. An attack of sickness which quickly cleared up."

"I wanted to ask Dr Compson to call but she wouldn't hear of it."

"I refuse to be coddled. Now, Mama, if you'll excuse us we've a lot of purchases to make in Hessleton together. Conway's going to assist me in the choosing of a splendid new lamp for his study which I want to give him."

"And she turned down my offer of some new gowns although I bought some delightful silk in Florence for them. "Very well, my darling." He got up. "How pleasant it is to have luncheon here! Life has quite taken on a new complexion for me." He looked at Joseph. "Even my worries about Sarah are over."

"She's stopped coming into the potworks altogether now," Joseph said. He had been quieter than usual during the meal.

"As long as she executes her commissions for you."

"Yes . . . yes . . . some of them are rather . . . bizarre. She's taken to the rendering of the undraped figure." He shrugged and smiled. "The first sign of old age, my boy, is when one loses touch with what is current in the contemporary scene."

She had talked about the David at Florence, Mia thought. "We must go, Papa. I never knew I had a chatter-box for a husband."

"Why do you drag him away? We haven't discussed Palmerston's latest, nor what attitude of mind towards our country he found on his travels."

"Then you must come and have dinner with us very soon." They took their adieus.

"I'm very fond of your parents," Conway said later. They were being driven back by Baxter in the short winter afternoon.

Mia snuggled into her furs. She could feel the darkness descending on her mind, as if in sympathy with the gloom outside. "Yes, I've been lucky," she said. But she no longer believed that.

*   *   *

It was a week before she was ill again. Conway had gone off for the day and she didn't ring for Ruth. Instead she wrestled alone with the severe sickness which seemed to go on for ever. When at last she crawled into bed she was shivering with terror. She wiped her damp forehead. What was wrong? Had something happened to the child inside her? She put her hand on her abdomen. There was the slight swelling, still not apparent to others, but no pain. She cupped her hands round her breasts. They were full and sore, but that was to be expected, wasn't it? If only it were Conway's baby I could seek my mother's advice, she thought. She wept bitterly.

After a time she got up and bathed, but there was still the trembling in her legs, and even worse, a trembling in her hands which made her drop her brush as she tried to tidy her hair. It's caused by fear, she told herself, you're sick with fear, and as your mind, so your body. Hadn't Ruth said something like that? She was bathed, dressed and smiling when Conway returned.

He was in good spirits. He'd had a rewarding day at Galton with other farmers, he had made some important contacts. "And on the way I stopped at Well House and asked Sarah to come for dinner. I felt so happy, my dearest. I hope you approve."

"Yes, of course. That was what we agreed." Her heart sank as he kissed her.

The evening went off pleasantly enough. Sarah was still the new Sarah, shy, pleased to be there, admiring the changes they'd made to the house, exclaiming over the view. "And you look beautiful, Mia. Blooming."

"Yes, I'm well, thank you."

"Have you been successful in replacing Mrs Allenby yet?"

"No, but Ruth is managing wonderfully well."

"As long as you aren't burdened."

"Poor Mia was sick one day last week," Conway said.

"Were you?" Sarah's expression was sympathetic. "Let's

hope you don't have any recurrence. You don't want anything to spoil your happiness now."

"No, indeed." She looked away, rested her eyes on the lake between the curtains, black and silver. How lovely it was.

A few days later her parents came for dinner, Marie-Hélène telling her during the course of the meal that she had not heard of a cook.

"I don't think it's imperative, Mama. It was rather a question of sparing Ruth. She's been going to so much trouble for me recently . . ." she stopped herself in time. Her mother would only fuss if she heard that Ruth was preparing special dishes for her, delicate fish with lemon, milk jellies, a chicken custard, or she might grow suspicious. She'd felt Marie-Hélène's shrewd eyes resting on her more than once.

She set herself to amuse her parents, she excelled herself in her gaiety and quick-wittedness, she took them on a tour of the house and they confessed themselves charmed with the interior. "And such a delightful view," Marie-Hélène said, seemingly relaxed, looking out of the window at the lake.

"Mia dotes on it," Conway said fondly. "She won't allow the curtains to be drawn, and sometimes she disappears outside for quite a time. I tell her she has an assignation with the heron."

They all laughed. Marie-Hélène said. "It does me good to see you two so happy."

That night Mia was very sick, and the following morning, wan and hopeless after a sleepless night she gave in and said that Conway might fetch Dr Compson.

Chapter Twenty-One

She lay trembling under the kindly gaze of Dr Compson who had ridden to Well Farm as soon as he was summoned.

"Well, Mia, this is unlike you to be prostrated. Your husband tells me you've been sick several times."

"Yes, it's nothing. Such a fuss." She turned her head away.

"I've never known you to make a fuss about illness yet. You were a brave little girl always. And healthy. Come now, that's better. Let me see you smile. I'd like to examine you, if you don't mind."

"Is there any need?" He must hear the loud beating of her heart. It was filling the room. "I feel quite fit this morning. Conway pressed me to see you."

"He's worried, naturally. I'll ring for your maid if I may." He pulled the bell, and while he waited, crossed the room to look out of the window. "How forbidding the lake looks this morning, but I'm sure it will be charming in good weather. All is well with you and your husband now? You spoke to him as I advised you?"

"Yes. He told me everything about Sarah, doctor, the arm . . . I never guessed, and Sarah still hasn't mentioned it to me. He didn't escape unscathed either."

"How could he? But it's nothing you won't be able to heal. He suffered agony for years, but then so has Sarah, in a different way. What are your relations like with her now?"

"She's different, changed for the better. It's as if she had accepted me now. The resentment's gone."

"I hope so . . ." There was a knock at the door and Ruth appeared.

"Yes, ma'am?"

"Ruth, Dr Compson wishes to examine me. Will you kindly remain for a few moments?" It was the calmness of despair. Her voice didn't tremble.

The doctor had been washing his hands at the basin and now he advanced towards the bed. "Now, please don't worry, Mia. I shan't hurt you." She felt the hands under the sheet touching her abdomen gently, surely. They stopped, he looked at her and then they moved on again. "Tell me if it hurts . . ." She lay still, breathing shallowly, contracting her muscles. "Relax . . ." Only when his fingers pressed into the lower part of her abdomen did she wince, but she thought she concealed it. He straightened. "That'll do. You may go now, Ruth."

"Yes, sir. Is madam going to be all right?"

"I think so."

"Ruth looks after me very well," Mia said with false brightness. "She cooks little concoctions for me, especially designed to tempt my appetite. I couldn't be in better hands." To her surprise the girl turned scarlet, seemingly overcome by the praise.

"I do my best," she mumbled, bobbed and went out hurriedly.

"I must have embarrassed her." She had to go on talking, to delay him. "I'm fortunate with Ruth, don't you think?"

"We should praise our servants more often. Well, my dear," he sat down on the bed and looked at her.

"Yes?" Her voice was harsh in her ears.

"There's no growth, nothing that I can see, at least, although there was an area of tenderness. But I want to get a few facts straight. Tell me first of all, what date were you in Paris?"

"Paris . . . Paris . . .?" She held her breath. "I can't remember . . ."

"Take it easily. Try to tie it up with something else."

It was no good. He knew already. "Let me see . . . yes, our visit coincided with that of the Queen and Prince Albert. Papa would tell you, if you remember . . ."

"Perhaps he did mention it. Well, then, I think I can place it for you. I'm good on dates. The Royal Party, as I remember, set sail in the Victoria and Albert on Saturday . . . it was the middle . . . yes, Saturday, the 18th August. Does that help?"

It was no use. He was playing with her, as a cat plays with a mouse. "Yes, it does. In that case Papa and I were in Paris from the twentieth to the twenty-third."

"And this is the first of December, which makes it just over three months ago. No, no, that won't do . . ."

"What won't do?"

"I wondered if you were incubating some infection you had picked up there, but it's too long a period. Cholera or typhoid would have manifested themselves long before this."

"There you are," it was the bravery of someone reprieved from the gallows, "what did I tell you? I'm sure it's nothing but a stomach upset. And then I've had a lot of worry as you know."

"Yes, I appreciate that." He looked at her so long that the courage drained out of her again and she had to turn her head away.

"Mia," he said gently, "frankly, I'm puzzled. Normally I should have said that . . . well, leave it for now. Would you tell me if you had anything on your mind I didn't know about? I don't want details, but on the face of it you *ought* to be happy, and what's more I know you have an unusually unhappy nature."

"I used to have." She felt weak tears gathering in her eyes. "But I'm quite young, really, and I seem to have been tried beyond my endurance. I blame myself bitterly. Sometimes . . . sometimes I feel the only thing to do is to end it all."

"End it all!" He put his hand on her arm, his face alarmed. "Now that's neurotic talk if you like and unworthy of you. Your nervous system must be badly strained."

"You don't know," the tears slid down her cheeks, "you don't know . . ." I'm crying for help, she thought. If he asks me now I'll tell him everything. The words will rush gladly from my lips for the relief of it . . .

"Now I want you to dry those tears and together we'll try to get at the root of the trouble. You're thoroughly run down. There's a fresh handkerchief my housekeeper gave me this morning, and to tell you the truth she's better at laundering than baking. Would that her cakes were as soft! There now, that's better, isn't it? Nothing can be as bad as that, surely?"

"No . . ." she said, accepting the handkerchief, beginning to mop her face. She could never tell him. His son's friend! Nor could she ever break Conway's heart. It was clear to her now what she should do. There was only one way out. "I'm better now." She smiled at him. Her eyes were burning, her voice rasped in her throat.

"Well, let's dismiss one possibility right away, tempting though it is a solution. You can't be pregnant. You've been here with your husband only a few weeks, isn't that so?"

"Yes . . ."

"And it must have been during the summer that he went abroad?"

"Around the middle of June." She kept her eyes clear. "I remember the day distinctly." Suddenly her tongue ran away with her. "I was happy that day. It was hot and sunny and I decided to go and see Papa and order a new dinner service. He insisted on giving me one. He's so kind . . . oh, I was happy. And then I visited Mrs Parker at Stonebarrow . . ."

"A very efficient woman. She looked after Conway's mother from time to time. Excellent nurse and cook. He relied on her."

"I seem to have maligned Mrs Parker." She spoke almost

to herself. "Anyhow, it's over now, everything's over . . . and after calling on the Parkers I went home and Sarah was there, and Conway had gone." She raised her eyes to him and met his, kind, understanding. "More than five months ago."

"Poor child. You've suffered too much. Anyhow, there would be definite signs by this time. Then Conway tells me your sickness generally takes place at night. Isn't that so?" She nodded. She couldn't remember. How long had they been talking together? She was so tired. "Are you sure, Mia," his voice was gentle, "there's nothing you can tell me, no way I can help you? There's something disturbing me, something I can't put my finger on . . ."

"No, there's nothing to tell, nothing you can do." She felt calm. If only he would go.

He let out a sigh. "Then I'm forced to the conclusion you've eaten something which has upset your stomach. The diagnosis doesn't please me at all but there it is. I thought you had no foibles like that, but as you say you've been under great strain. That may be the key . . ." He looked away, then said suddenly. "Who's your cook?"

"We've no one at the moment. Mrs Allenby from the village had to leave because of illness. Ruth has been coping."

"And according to you coping very well."

"Yes, that's so. She tries to tempt me with all kinds of delicacies of her own making."

"Which you eat?"

"I do my best to please her." She smiled wanly at him. "When someone has gone to so much trouble one feels it incumbent on one. She's been a tower of strength."

"She's devoted to you?"

"I think so. Right from the days at Well House. Servants see more than we give them credit for, and I think she realised the difficulties . . ."

He was on his feet, shutting his bag. "In any case we must get to the bottom of your illness and make you well for your husband. You both deserve it. I'll ride over every week to see you, and when I get back I'll make up a bottle for you if you'll send your groom for it." He straightened, turned a professional gaze on her. "By the way, I ought to have asked you. Do you have any other symptoms?"

"No, I don't think so. Only a general weakness in the limbs." She wouldn't mention the pain. "Sickness would cause that, I imagine."

"Possibly. Well, my dear, I must get on with my rounds. Promise to despatch a messenger for me if you've any further trouble, but I'm hopeful your indisposition will be of a temporary nature. Sometimes the decision to call out the doctor is the best remedy. I'll say good morning to you." He bowed.

"Good morning, doctor, and thank you."

"Try not to worry. It may well be a kind of backlash from all you've had to put up with. Anyhow, I'm sure you'll get over it."

But she didn't. The sickness came and went with varying degrees of severity. Sometimes she was able to hide it from Conway, sometimes not, and when he was there at the time he called in Dr Compson who would change her medicine or perhaps simply stand at her bedside and look gravely down on her. Strangely enough, when he felt the lower part of her abdomen the pressure of his fingers relieved the pain a little, and sometimes in bed, when it became too hard to bear she'd do the same.

She became pale, not a healthy pallor but a greyness, and sometimes when she looked at her face in the mirror she could understand Conway's anxiety, and even understand the cheerful demeanour he showed to her which was belied by his worried eyes. But gripping the toilet-table to lean forward would weary her, as if all strength had gone out of her wrists, and she would go back, defeated, to bed.

Her temper became uncertain, her eyes troubled her, and sometimes she'd shout at Ruth when she brought her some little titbit. "Take it away! I don't want it! I'm tired, tired, tired . . . don't you understand?" But most of the time she'd eat or drink what was brought to her. "You're going to far too much trouble, Ruth. I'm just a nuisance to you." She was developing the invalid's carping self-pity. Once, "What's this today?"

"Carageen blancmange, ma'am. It's made with . . . with Irish sea moss, and . . ."

Mia tried it with a spoon. "There's vanilla in it."

"That's right, ma'am. Vanilla. And . . . and milk."

"Where did you get Irish sea moss? It must be difficult to find in these parts."

"Oh, there are places you can buy it." She seemed flustered. "Now you try to get some of this down you and I warrant you'll feel better in no time."

'A week after Dr Compson had last called she had a new symptom, such an excruciating pain in her eyes that she moaned and moved her head on the pillow in agony. Conway was there at the time. "Do you feel worse again, Mia?"

"It's all right. Only my eyes." Another spasm of pain shot through them. "Oh, God, my eyes!"

His face was frightened. "This is too much altogether! Too much. What can that man be doing!" He rang the bell and in a moment Ruth appeared. "Ruth, tell Baxter to saddle up immediately and ride with all speed for the doctor."

"Yes, sir. Is madam worse?"

"I'm all right, Ruth. Bring me some of my medicine, if you will."

"Do as you're bid first!" Conway shouted. "Tell Baxter. I'll attend to the medicine." Ruth went hurriedly out of the room, and grim-faced, Conway filled a spoon from the bottle of white liquid and brought it to Mia. "This stuff isn't doing you any good at all."

"Oh, Conway, you're such a non-believer!" She was weak with relief now that the pain had gone. "Poor Dr Compson. Am I such a trial to you?"

"You'll never be that." He bent over her and put one arm behind her shoulders to lift her.

"Such a trial . . . such a trial . . ." The intensity of the pain had induced a languor, but also a certainty. Something had happened to the child within her which was poisoning her system. There was no escape from the consequences. The illness would be prolonged, her condition would be discovered with the passing of time, even worse, it now seemed as if she would give birth to a dead child. And hadn't she heard that such births were often premature? It might happen at any time now. She should have told Conway, told Dr Compson. It was too late . . . when she was well enough to get up, she would finish it. She could stand no more.

She dozed until the doctor came, aware of Conway's gentle hand caressing her brow. This, then, was the end. She thought of Brian and the day at the Fair, thought of his handsome gold-bearded face at the Place de Vosges. It didn't seem wicked any more. Their meeting at Paris had been inevitable, hadn't Brian said it had to happen? You couldn't change the pattern of your life . . . I've known love, she thought, two kinds, but the love of my life is this dark anxious man sitting beside me with pity in his finger-tips.

Dr Compson didn't say much when he came. He didn't ask to examine her. He appeared reluctant to disturb her, and indeed she could hardly open her eyes to look at him. To have one's mind made up, she thought, the welcome relief of it! She felt light, light-headed, the pain had almost gone. Under cover of the bedclothes her fingers went to the seat of the pain and pressed gently.

She knew that the doctor and Conway had left the room together, and that Ruth came in, sponged her and gave her something to sip. "One of your concoctions, Ruth? Beef tea? Nice . . ." All she wanted to do was to sleep.

How easy it would be if she died in her bed, if she didn't have to do it for herself. She shuddered. It would

264

be cold outside. The worst part of the year, dark before four o'clock. She would have to wait until then. Between tea and dinner was a good time. The servants would be relaxing downstairs, Conway would be in his study reading some of his pamphlets. His latest interest was ecology, he'd said, but she'd been in too much pain at the time to ask him what it meant.

When she opened her eyes he was sitting beside her. "Did you have pleasant dreams?" he said, smiling at her.

"Yes, so pleasant. I dreamt I was young again . . ."

"My dearest, you're still a girl. You'll always be a girl to me."

"I'm glad. Once, long ago, Hannah and I went to Galton and we met Harry and his friend, the man who wrote me the letters."

"Yes?"

"We had such a pleasant day. We laughed in the sunshine. We were innocent, then. You don't begrudge me that, Conway?"

"I don't begrudge you anything."

"Anything? Do you mean that?"

"I don't expect to be the only person in your life. That would be selfish."

"But *anything*, you said. Supposing I . . . betrayed you? What would that do to you?"

"I . . . I expect it would break my heart."

"There, you see . . . I thought so . . . but I had to ask." She spoke as brightly as she could. "You and Dr Compson were a long time together. What were you whispering about?"

"It's no secret. He asked me to tell you. He's determined to get to the root of your sickness. Your symptoms ring a chord in his memory," her finger-tips pressed the site of the pain, low down, "well, to put it briefly I've been to Stonebarrow to engage Mrs Parker as cook, and indeed I brought her back with me."

"Oh!" She sat up on her elbow. "You shouldn't have

done that. Ruth will be upset. She's been trying so hard and she cooks beautifully for me."

"But it isn't doing you any good, is it? Don't worry. She'll still be here, but the cooking will be in Mrs Parker's hands. She's a good woman and she's doing this for us, Mia. She was happy to be asked."

"All right. I don't really mind." What did it matter, she thought.

Ruth looked tearful when she came in to prepare Mia for the evening. "I'm going to get up, Ruth. I must try to walk."

"Oh, should you, ma'am?"

"Yes, I only grow weak lying here, and there's a lot to be done . . . help me if you will." When she was seated in her chair she looked at the girl. "I'm sorry about the cooking, Ruth. Has Mrs Parker taken over?"

"She's doing the evening meal, ma'am." Ruth sniffed.

"Don't feel distressed. Doctors are meddlesome creatures with fly-by-night theories, and I loved the little dishes you brought up to me. Perhaps you'll still be allowed to do them."

"No, the master says I've to attend to you and nothing else."

"Well, that will be nice for us both. You had too much to do."

"Yes, ma'am." Ruth covered her face with her hand. "Excuse me . . ." She ran out of the room.

Conway helped her downstairs, and to please him she had a little of the excellent dinner Mrs Parker had prepared, so good, in fact, that Conway asked Robson to send her in at the end of the meal. Presently the woman appeared, dark, strong-nosed, but her eyes, Mia noticed, were kind.

"Well, ma'am," she said, "you're not looking like yourself at all, not at all." It was typical of her that she didn't wait until Conway spoke.

"If you continue to cook as you did this evening," he

didn't look at all upset, "we'll soon have her on her feet. I just wanted to congratulate you."

"I've always liked cooking. Got a flair for it, I suppose. Anything I can do, sir, anything at all. I owe you a lot."

"No, no. You've good news of Jack, I hope?"

"If no news is good news it's excellent. Well, I'll get on, if you'll excuse me. Poor Ruth's in a state, weeping all over the kitchen stove. I'm afraid I've put her eye out."

"She'll get over it. Be kind to her. She's devoted to madam."

"I'm sure everyone is, or should be." The woman gave Mia a searching look, turned on her heels and went out.

"She's a strong character," Mia said. "When you're ill you become peculiarly receptive. I could feel the strength of her in the room."

"Yes, she's an intelligent woman. We'll be all right with Mrs Parker. I don't know why I didn't think of her sooner."

It was as if Mrs Parker's positiveness was felt throughout the house. Mia began to feel a little better. The pain was still there, the lassitude in her limbs, but the sickness decreased. Ruth thought it might be the change in her medicine which was causing the improvement, although you couldn't trust doctors much these days, she said.

Hannah came with her mother to see her, radiant, very much married, and wearing the London style, she told Mia, a tiny brimmed hat with a feather curling on her cheek and a much-waisted and importantly-cuffed jacket over her full skirts. She talked incessantly, but even that didn't disturb Mia. Her mother was quieter, she thought, although that might have been in comparison with Hannah, and for the first time she showed signs of age, her jaw had lost its firm line, her eyelids seemed puffy.

When she was going she embraced Mia, and feeling the warm arms round her took her back to her childhood. "Oh, Mama," she said, "I'm so miserable . . ."

"My darling girl." She kissed Mia's cheek. "Don't

despair. You'll get better, I'm sure of it. At the first I had an unwarranted suspicion," she passed her hand over her brow, "what am I saying . . . I mean, I had an unwarranted suspicion the doctor wouldn't be able to make you well, but I'm sure of it now. You'll be my brave, bright Mia, won't you?"

"I want your forgiveness, Mama. I've been—"

"Mia!" Hannah said. "What's come over you? It's not like you to talk like that." Her fair face was fearful. "You're the cheerful one, the sensible one. Don't distress Mama . . ." her lip trembled.

"I'm being silly." Mia wiped her eyes and came out of her mother's embrace. "And hypochondriacal. It's being confined to four walls for so long, but truly, I'm getting better. I haven't been sick for over three days now. I don't know whether any change is a good one but Mrs Parker has come as our cook and she's excellent."

"Perhaps it was simply that Ruth was using all the wrong receipts," Marie-Hélène said, adjusting her bonnet.

"That'll be it." Hannah was gay again. "For my part I've engaged an excellent cook too. Jason said if we are to be known in the district as a house to visit we must see to our table first of all. Jason likes a good table."

"I'm so glad," Mia said. She met her mother's eye and they smiled at each other. "Must you go? I wish Papa had come with you. I should have so liked to see him."

"He's rather tired these days. Things in the potworks upset him . . . has Sarah visited you, by the way?"

"Not very much because Conway tells me she has an aversion to illness. I'm not surprised since she's had so much herself. But she's been kind. She's sent loving messages and she leaves little gifts. Her talents seem endless. She makes pretty pictures from a few flowers and leaves, she covers notebooks and pill-boxes with brocade and braiding, and she's done colour-wash sketches for me. She left one of the lake the other day."

"I'm glad you're on good terms. Well, we must be going."

"Give my dearest love to Papa. Tell him . . . tell him I love him . . ."

The following day she felt better and she got up after breakfast and dressed with the aid of Ruth. Conway was so reassured that he said if she didn't mind he'd make some business calls in Galton. There was to be a meeting in the evening as well and one of the farmers had said he must sup with them, but he had refused.

"Then you must accept. Are you seeing him during the day?"

"Yes. He's selling me some heifers."

"You must tell him you've changed your mind. You've had a poor time hanging about a sick wife, but you can see for yourself I'm truly better this morning."

"You may be but I shouldn't dream of it. If I did I shouldn't be back until after ten."

"I ask you to change your mind, Conway. It would give me great pleasure to know you were enjoying yourself for once."

"I only know enjoyment when I'm with you."

"That isn't so. Didn't we agree that ours should be a wide encompassing love . . ." There was a knock at the door. "Come in," she said. It was Ruth.

"Please, ma'am, the doctor's just rode over from Hessleton. He'd like to see you."

"But he was here yesterday and confessed himself pleased with my progress!" She looked at Conway in surprise, but he nodded curtly. "Very well, Ruth, show him in."

Dr Compson entered hurriedly, head down, then stopped short when he saw Mia up and dressed. "Well, this is a surprise!"

"I felt so much better and I don't want to waste away lying in bed." She smiled at him.

"You're a brave girl. I had a moment and I was

269

passing . . ." He paused, looked at her directly. "Would you sit on that chair, please? I'd like to examine your teeth."

"My teeth!" She was surprised, but obeyed, sitting on a straight-backed chair at a small table. She noticed her hands were trembling as she rested them in front of her. "Do you think now that I may have abcesses, doctor? I assure you at least my teeth don't give me any trouble."

"Nevertheless . . ." He bent forward, and when Mia opened her mouth he looked into it, taking his time, pulling down her front lip. "Thank you," he said.

"Don't you like my teeth, doctor?" She smiled, but couldn't stop the trembling which possessed her hands. She took them off the table.

"They're excellent . . ." he spoke abstractedly, then turned to Conway who had crossed to the window. "I hope to get the samples back any day now. They've had to go to Liverpool."

"They won't keep you waiting long?"

"I hope not."

"I don't like to be discussed as if I didn't exist," Mia said.

Conway laughed. "Doesn't that prove she's getting better, eh, doctor?"

He nodded, still with the abstracted air, his eyes on Mia. "Well, I must get along. Good day to you both." He bowed and went out.

"Dr Compson's becoming mysterious. Do you know why, Conway?"

"Just a matter of leaving no stone unturned." He came over and kissed her. "I'll go now. The sooner I go, the sooner I'll be back."

"Need you go?" She clung to him.

"My dear, I only want to please you. Shall I stay?"

"Yes, please stay . . . no, what am I saying? I told you I was becoming too dependent. I want you to go right away, to have your meeting and then your supper and forget all about me."

"I could never forget you."

"Then kiss me, only kiss me . . ." She clung to him for a long time, and then, dry-eyed, stood at the window and waved until he was out of sight.

The house had an afternoon stillness. Ruth, Betsy, the kitchen-maid and Mrs Parker would be sitting at the kitchen range gossiping over a cup of tea. Robson, no doubt, would be in the coach house with Baxter who had made a cosy den out of the married quarters above the stables. Both men were without wives, Baxter a widower, Robson having never known connubial bliss which perhaps accounted for his stiff demeanour. They would have something in common at least.

She went upstairs and opened the cupboard door where her dresses were kept. Would it be cold? What a silly question to ask! She had seen the lake when she was waving good-bye to Conway and thought how forbidding it looked with hardly a ripple on its grey, steely surface, and that in its depths there would be a bone-penetrating coldness.

She took out the pale violet dress she had worn in Paris. Would it still go on? It would be fitting to wear it. After all, Brian was at the root of her decision. He'd seduced her in that grey drawing-room in the Places de Vosges, in an afternoon quietness like this. But you must be honest, she told herself, especially when there's so little time. You wanted to be seduced, out of hunger, out of defiance. Your body craved love that day, a healthy body, not broken as it is now . . .

She took off her warm woollen gown and slipped into the pale violet one. It was a little tight at the waist, but not too much. It could still be fastened. She held out the skirts and looked at herself in the mirror, a pale violet ghost. Perhaps her hair should be down. She pulled out the pins and it fell about the pale face, over her shoulders, richly chestnut beside the paleness. She saw the resemblance now to the Empress.

Should she leave a note? She shrank from that. Since she had kept her secret to spare him, what was the point in revealing it now? But what about her parents? Poor Papa, whom she loved so much. Poor Mama, but she was stronger, she would take care of him. She thought of the night in the garden at Blenheim Terrace when Conway had first told her he loved her. Had Papa left them alone deliberately? He'd always liked Conway. Perhaps they could console each other, have those long, learned discussions which they liked, talking of great men, of great doings, a century to be alive in, Papa had once said. A century to be dead in . . .

You musn't weep, she told herself, putting on her warm cloak, lifting her hair with the backs of her hands, letting it fall down her back. It was so heavy. How tired her wrists were! So weak . . . if you weep you'll resurrect old memories, and you won't want to go. You have to go. This child in you, alive or dead, must break its way into the world soon. It's as inevitable as the course the planets take round the sun.

She walked slowly to the door, stopped, went back, wrote a few words on a piece of paper, left it lying on her desk. "I've gone to seek the heron . . ." Then she went slowly downstairs, opened the heavy front door and went into the dusk of the winter afternoon.

Chapter Twenty-Two

Conway had spent a lot of money clearing out the lake of silt and rank weeds. Occasionally as she walked she came across clumps of couch grass which seemed tipped with black, and she thought it might be coal dust, and then again that it was her imagination playing tricks. The short afternoon was over now, the dusk was becoming heavy, grey-black, it had that looming quality when objects lose their edges and foreground and background have no division.

It was a good day to choose, quiet, as dark as her thoughts. There was very little wind, and once or twice she thought she heard the cry of the heron, a deep, harsh croak. It would have been good to see it before she died. Other things would have been good, such as having Conway's child, since Brian hadn't wanted a symbol of their love. Love to him was an evanescence. It vanished as he vanished.

She had a sensation of lightness, of being a ghost, that she drifted rather than walked by the lakeside, a pale violet ghost swaying to avoid the low branches, coming to rest beside the bole of an elm when her legs trembled too much to bear her. It grew darker and darker, the grotesque shapes of the pollarded willows became indistinct, on the far side of the lake she thought she saw the vague shape of the crane drag line . . .

Had it all then been an illusion, this paradise, this farm beside the lake, would the water be thick with coal dust when she entered it, would it get into her lungs and choke her, fill her mouth with its filth? She bent down at the edge

273

and put her finger-tips in the water. When she looked at them they appeared to be stained black.

He had tricked her, she thought with sudden fury, that was it. He had said all the signs of the coal-seam had been removed but they were there, that the lake was clean when it was thick with filth, just as he had tricked her when he had said there was nothing wrong between him and Sarah '. . . *I have to admit to you, my wife, that as a young man I have permitted her caresses, returned them often . . .*' And what was it Sarah with the huge eyes, the coal black eyes in the white face had said? '*You've never known real passion such as existed, such as exists . . .*'

Sarah and Conway had tricked her, Brian had tricked her, life had tricked her. It was unfair. She'd been happy, light-hearted, light of step '. . . *You've a light step, Mia, it's an embodiment of you, your approach to life . . .*'

In front of her she saw the landing stage Conway had made, a long black arm sticking out into the water. Or had it been made long ago? She would walk along it and pretend it was the *Quai de l'Horloge*, that she was going light-footed to meet Brian, to meet the trickery . . . She stepped on to it, and holding her cloak about her she walked slowly to the end, seeing the gleam of the water between the boards, hearing the eerie slap of the water against them.

At the end there was a tall post with a boat tied to it. '*I'll take you fishing,*' he had said . . . was it Conway or Brian? She couldn't remember now. '*And perhaps some day if we've children they'll learn to swim . . .*' but how could they teach a dead child, a dead child which lay heavy within her at this moment, a small dead body which had poisoned hers? She clung to the post and put her head down on it, trying to weep, but the coldness had frozen her tears. There was only the nagging pain. She pressed the place with her fingers under her cloak.

Life was trickery, trickery, trickery . . . she didn't consciously go into the water, she clung to the post for a long time, and gradually the bone coldness crept into every part of her body, her wrists grew numb, her hands trembled and the fingers slowly released their hold. The water received her like a lover.

She came to the surface fully awake, fully aware, and began to thrash feebly with her limbs. Her head went under again, and the water rushed into her eyes and nose, she could feel the black silt choking her, clogging every channel between her mouth, nose and ears so that she retched and struggled in a blind effort to survive.

And then quite suddenly she gave up. There was nothing to struggle for. Conway was Sarah's, had always been, Brian was on some far-off shore with Harry or another Harry, Hannah had Jason, Papa had Mama, she had no one. Papa would miss her all the same. He it was who had walked with her along the *Quai de l'Horloge*, gently leading her into . . . trickery. "Papa!" she shrieked once, and with the wild lifting of her arms she was engulfed, hearing the roar of water in her ears and above it and through it a hoarse loud call – could it be Conway? – "Mia! Mia!"

But no, it would be the heron, the lonely heron. What a pity she had never seen it.

She lay in a coma for a long time, coming out of it at intervals to thrash about the bed as if it were the lake, and to implore whoever was there to clean out her nose and mouth. "The dust," she said to someone who was bending over her. "The coal black dust. It's in my throat, my mouth, my nose, everywhere! I can't breathe for it . . ."

It was a strange face, with a white mobcap and a navy-blue gown high up to the chin and down to the wrists like the kind Sarah wore. But she didn't have a withered arm because this woman sometimes rolled up her sleeves and put gathered white cuffs over the rolled-up parts and proceeded to do humiliating things to her body so that it seemed to turn into water and flow away from her.

Then after that there were two faces, one she knew well, Ruth, and the other with a strong hooked nose but kindly

275

eyes. They talked in low voices at the same time as they rolled her about like a fish on a slab, cleaning, wiping, laving, enveloping her in soft, warm cloths.

"Found dead in bed. Terrible, isn't it. Master went there last night when Frame came running through the wood. He was gone for a long long time. Think she did herself in, Mrs Parker?"

"I don't think, Ruth, it's better not to. Watch her arm, there. It's caught under her hip. Poor lamb. Poor Mr Conway. He's tried that hard all the time."

"He was good to his sister, Mrs Parker?"

"Good at all times, although she was hard to do by."

"He'll miss her."

"Aye, but she's better away that one. And he's got a bonny lass here . . . if she lives."

Daily they attended her, the woman with the mobcap was always there during the night. She never spoke but they talked incessantly, or Ruth talked with Mrs Parker curbing her, it seemed, in flat, good-natured tones.

"Did Miss Sarah ever bring *you* invalid dishes for her?"

"Only once, Ruth. My first day. An arrowroot soufflé."

"Did you *give* it to madam? I know you didn't need her help, but did you?"

"No, I'd made her a nice custard." "You'd send her about her business, Mrs Parker, if I know you! But I couldn't bring myself to tell madam her sister-in-law was bringing them delicacies, like. She was that pleased with them, and I wanted to please her, and I was rushed like, with Mrs Allenby being with her old mother. Besides, you see, she came into the kitchen one day, Miss Sarah, that is, sympathetic like, said she wanted to help me. 'Let us have a little pact, Ruth,' says she. 'Your mistress don't want to accept Mrs Frame's help and I know you want to stand well in the poor dear's eyes, so shall we keep it a secret and then no one will be hurt?' Maybe I shouldn't

276

have, Mrs Parker, but then I hadn't got what you've got for cooking, what's it called, Mrs Parker?"

"A flair. Never mind, Ruth, you weren't to know you were being used."

"They say Miss Sarah had a funny arm, all withered-like?"

"Do they? Never mind what they say, just don't you gabble, and hand me over that piece of soft muslin till I wipe this poor one's face."

Sometimes so that they should know she was alive she would beg them to stop talking and let her go to sleep but they didn't seem to hear her.

And always Dr Compson would appear at her bedside. She knew him because she remembered his watch, a large silver one which ticked loudly in the quiet room. She wanted to ask him if it said on the back that it had been given to him on the occasion of his twenty-first birthday, like Harry's, but always the nurse was there, now she had realised the strange woman was a nurse, severe and speechless in her white mobcap and blue gown.

He would lift her limp wrist, the watch held in his right hand. He would gaze across the room as if he was looking at the lake. Or perhaps he was thinking of Harry. Then he'd look at the watch, look at the nurse and say, "Slow, still slow . . ." Once she managed to stretch open her eyes at him and he immediately bent over her. "Mia, Mia, my girl. Can you hear me?" Her eyelids dropped with their own weight. "Open your mouth, Mia." She remembered, and touched her teeth with her finger, trying to smile. "Clever girl," he said, as he examined her mouth. Then he nodded at the silent nurse. "It's going, the blue line round the gum's going."

She began to *feel* more each day, to be aware that the pain in her abdomen was still with her after all, that it was spreading out, growing in intensity, blotting out everything else. But it was no ordinary pain now, nor could it be controlled by pressing it with her fingers. It was the seat, the centre of an all-consuming, all-pervading pain which made her shriek in agony. "I want to drown . . .!" The nurse was there, sleeves rolled up and the gathered cuffs over the rolled-up parts, and the doctor, and there was sticky blood between her legs, she knew it was blood because the nurse's white gathered cuffs were spattered with it. But no one was allowed in, not Ruth, not Mrs Parker, not Conway. And she knew the dead child had been taken away from her.

There came a restful period when she lay watching the window with the branches tossing outside, and because of the lake there was a purling light on the walls. She would think of the lake as beautiful, not the coal black filth it had been that night. But other times she would ask someone to draw the curtains against the view and she would lie in the glow of the lamp, shivering and feeling empty but not unhappy. She told herself the nothingness she felt might be the beginning of something.

Conway began to appear, but to begin with she hid her face behind her hands like a naughty child. When she pulled them away she saw that his face seemed older, the eyes sunken, his clothes hung on him. He'd sit beside her for a long time, then kiss her hand gently and go away. Once she felt his warm tears fall on it.

Dr Compson's face now assumed neck, arms, torso, legs and a voice, an authoritative voice. "Nurse, potassium iodide ten grams daily. Ammonium chloride the same. As much milk as she'll take. *Supplemented.*" Soon the delicate concoctions began to appear again, brought up by Ruth, a smiling Ruth who told her Mrs Parker had shown her how to make milk jellies. And this was strange because Dr Compson had forbidden Ruth to cook them before. But she found when she thought about anything for long her head hurt.

And it was even more puzzling when after a few days of feeling well the retching started again, the feeling of being choked. At first she told herself it was the coal dust, but

278

she dismissed this as she grew stronger and her head didn't hurt so much to think.

"Doctor, I'm sick again. Does that mean I'm not getting better?"

"No, Mia. It just takes time."

"And . . . does it matter *who* cooks for me?"

"Not now."

"But you objected to Ruth doing it before."

"It wasn't Ruth. It was Sarah who brought the dishes and gave them to her, and Ruth kept it a secret because she valued your goodwill."

"And Sarah is now . . ."

"Dead."

"Did she . . . did she . . .?" she started to shiver violently. "I think I heard them talking . . . did she kill herself?"

"Yes, the same way as she tried to kill you. Do you want to know how?"

"No, no! Go away! I've heard enough."

"I'll go. A little at a time. That's the best way. Try to calm yourself. Try to rest."

She lay puzzling, puzzling . . . Sarah had killed herself because she had brought invalid dishes and given them to Ruth to give to *her*. She repeated it again and again but it didn't make sense. And Sarah had stopped when Mrs Parker appeared, when Dr Compson asked Conway to get Mrs Parker. Had he thought at first that Ruth . . . she'd wait until she was a little stronger and then she'd speak to him again. She became cunning in her approach.

"Doctor, I'm being given too much milk. It's always milk. Can't you stop it for a time? I'm sure that's what makes me sick."

"No, Mia, it's the residue in your stomach."

"The residue of what, doctor? But she saw the fear in his eyes and knew he was calculating how strong she was, if she could stand the truth . . .

"Try to keep it down, Mia, for your husband's sake. You're nearly out of the wood."

"My husband . . . doctor, you took away the baby?"

"Yes."

"He knows?"

"I had to tell him. You're his wife. But the rest is up to you. I don't have to know whose it was."

"I want you to know!" She shouted at him because she suddenly hated his tolerance. "It was Brian Moore's, Harry's friend! We knew each other . . . long ago. We met again in Paris. I was so unhappy. Can you understand? Do you think Conway will understand?"

"Try, Mia. You've both suffered, but it's behind you."

"Is it ever? I can't face him."

"He loves you. He saved your life, you know. He didn't remain at Galton that day. He was worried about you, came home early and found your note."

"Did he?" It didn't move her, nor make her feel grateful. He hadn't known when he saved her life that there was someone else's dead baby inside her.

"He has a large heart." But it didn't move her. The doctor went away.

There came a day when she was propped up on pillows and her mother and father came to see her. Her father seemed thinner and older, her mother looked the same. She would live longer.

"Papa, you look older."

"I *am* older. You've been three months in bed."

"No! You mean three weeks!"

"Quite so." He laid a bunch of daffodils on her knees. She put them up to her face and smelled the spring smell. "The Peace of Paris has been signed."

She looked up at him, scarcely comprehending. "So much has happened . . . how are the potworks, Papa?"

"We're doing well. I'll have to be thinking out new designs soon." But he looked tired.

"And the astronomy?"

"Your father's felt the cold more this winter," Marie-Hélène said.

"I'm sorry. Papa, what does it mean if you have a blue line round your gums?"

Marie-Hélène looked away. "What a pretty view it is from this window, Mia. I don't wonder you choose to stay in bed."

"It's a sign of lead poisoning."

"Joseph!" Marie-Hélène's hand was on his arm. "Can she . . .?"

"I can stand it, Mama. Did you say lead-poisoning, Papa?"

"Yes, the dippers used to get it, but we got round the danger by direct mixing of the white-lead pulp with the oil. Before that it was dried out first."

"Must you be so technical, Joseph, on such a nice spring morning!" Marie-Hélène patted her chignon elegantly, but her eyes were pitiful under the bonnet.

"I've got to know, Mama."

"She has to know."

"But you still keep lead in the manufactory?" He nodded.

"Mia, you tire yourself with those questions. You're not well enough. Let things be."

She ignored her mother. "Why did you always say you wouldn't have women working, Papa?"

"It's an old rule. They're more susceptible to . . . lead poisoning."

She was glad she was propped up with pillows. The room swam away from her, there was only the purling light on the walls. After a long time she said. "But you had Sarah."

"That was different. She wasn't concerned with the glazing. At least, she shouldn't have concerned herself with the glazing." His eyes met Mia's. They were anguished. "Yes, I had Sarah." He bowed his head.

"No one is to blame, Joseph, least of all you!" Marie-Hélène turned to Mia. "*She* went and you didn't, that's the main thing. And by her own hand. By what she'd stolen, what she'd given to you in those concoctions. Oh, the cunning of it! I never approved of her being in the potworks. I told your Papa again and again, but oh, no, he knew best! You'll find that of the kindest of men, Mia. They always know best." She burst into tears.

"Take her away, Papa," she said. "I've had enough for today."

She had a relapse when nothing mattered and she wanted to die. Only her family were allowed to visit her. She craved to see Hannah because she belonged to her girlhood. She came with Jason, triumphantly *enceinte*, and talked incessantly about the plans they'd made for the nursery and the nursemaids but her eyes were frightened because Mia lay without speaking.

"Are we tiring you, Mia?" Jason said, and when she looked at him she saw the pride in his eyes at the thought of his unborn child and she was ashamed.

"I'm tired all the time," she said. "I want to die."

"It'll pass." He had the confidence of a man secure in his own convictions, the pressure of his fingers was youthful, sure. He was the type who didn't have to go through the fires to be sure. "If you can get out, Mia, I promise you that you'll feel better. It's springtime. You'll feel it in the earth under your feet." He kissed her, straightened, and said to his for once silent wife. "Come along, Hannah, we've to be back at six to dress for dinner."

"Thank you, Jason," Mia said. "Take care, Hannah." She had under-estimated him.

She was sitting on the white seat round the elm when Conway joined her. "May I sit down?"

"Please do." She moved her skirts.

"How are you today, my dear?"

"I'm very well in myself." She looked towards the lake. It was the colour of the Seine today, slate-blue, a happy colour. A seagull wheeled above it then dived, folding back its strong wings to enter the water smoothly, for a moment there was the outline of a white arrow beneath the surface.

"You like the lake, Mia? Still?"

"I've always liked it." She didn't look at him. "And now I've made it peculiarly my own."

"It won't worry you, the memory, the fact that I lifted you like a drowned rat out of it?"

"I have to thank you for that." She didn't feel grateful.

"I've been to my sister's inquest today. Do you want to know the verdict?"

"Yes." It didn't matter now about the verdict.

"Suicide while the balance of her mind was disturbed. You were kept out of it. There was no purpose in it."

"Yes, it's finished." A small wind blew up and wrinkled the silk surface of the lake. She shivered. It was finished for her because he knew about the child and she had no excuse, as poor Sarah had. Adultery while of sound mind . . . it was finished for her because she had broken her father's heart. Already he felt he'd indirectly caused one death by negligence, nearly caused her own. "I've broken my father's heart," she said. "I didn't have the courage to tell him . . . everything."

His voice was calm. "I'm sure he knows, and hearts are tougher than you imagine." She tried to think what her father had said to her. He'd laid the daffodils on her knees, and then . . . she remembered the spring smell of the flowers, but not his words. Her head ached. "I want your opinion, Mia." Conway's voice was business-like, and she turned to him.

"My opinion?"

"Yes. Shall we move away somewhere else, or shall we stay here?"

But it was finished. "Move away . . . stay here . . .?"

"Do you wish me to repeat it?" There was a touch of asperity which she recognised.

"Do you mean together?" Her breath seemed to be caught in her throat. "Do you mean . . ."

"I mean together."

"But have you taken into account . . ." she breathed in through her mouth, "Brian's baby?"

"I had to when Dr Compson and the nurse were struggling for your life." There was also the wry smile which she recognised. "I did my accounts. It's you who matters, you I need. Can you bring yourself to forgive my sister for the wrong she did *you*?"

She looked at the daffodils bent in the wind, the early green of the grass, felt the Spring in the earth under her feet as Jason had promised. Daffodils . . . the smell came to her, then the words. She turned to him, smiling. "I've remembered what Papa said."

"What was that?"

"'The Peace of Paris has been signed.'"

The world was full of forgiving.